"Nay, warrior. I won't allow you to die."

Soft lips brushed over his brow, lingering at his temple. He turned his face, wanting her mouth on his own. He thought he *might* die if she didn't kiss him again.

There was hesitation, what felt to him like an eternity, before finally, her mouth touched his. Just a simple, innocent gesture that a child might bestow.

He growled low in his throat. Damn if he wanted a simple peck.

"Kiss me, angel."

He felt more than heard her sound of exasperation, but then her breathing hitched and it blew warm over his mouth. He could smell her. He could feel her vibrating against him. The tiny puff of air signaled that she was close. So very close.

It took all his strength, but he lifted his arm and delved his hand into her hair, gripping her nape to hold her in place. He raised his head and their lips met in a breathless, heated kiss.

Lord, but she was sweet. Her taste filled his mouth, slid over his tongue like smooth honey. He pushed impatiently at her lips, demanding her to open to him. With a sigh she gave him what he wanted. Her lips parted and he delved inside, probing and tasting every part of her mouth.

Aye, 'twas heaven. Because, if this was hell, there wasn't a man in the whole of Scotland who'd ever tread the path of righteousness.

His strength gone, he slumped back, his head hitting the pillow with a thud.

"You've overtaxed yourself, warrior," she reprimanded in a husky voice.

"'Twas worth it," he whispered.

BY MAYA BANKS

In Bed with a Highlander
Seduction of a Highland Lass
Never Love a Highlander
Never Seduce a Scot

Seduction
of a
Highland Lass

MAYA BANKS

BALLANTINE BOOKS • NEW YORK

A Ballantine Books Mass Market Original

Copyright © 2011 by Maya Banks
Excerpt from *Never Love a Highlander* copyright © 2011 by Maya Banks

Published in the United States by Ballantine Books, an imprint of The Random House Publishing Group, a division of Random House, Inc., New York.

BALLANTINE and colophon are trademarks of Random House, Inc.

This book contains an excerpt from the forthcoming book *Never Love a Highlander* by Maya Banks. This excerpt has been set for this edition only and may not reflect the final content of the forthcoming edition.

ISBN 978-0-345-51949-8
eBook ISBN 978-0-345-51950-4

Cover design: Lynn Andreozzi
Cover illustration: Alan Ayers

Printed in the United States of America

www.ballantinebooks.com

9 8 7

Ballantine Books mass market edition: October 2011

For TJ

CHAPTER 1

Alaric McCabe looked out over the expanse of McCabe land and grappled with the indecision plaguing him. He breathed in the chilly air and looked skyward. It wouldn't snow this day. But soon. Autumn had settled over the highlands. Colder air and shorter days had pushed in.

After so many years of struggling to eke out an existence, to rebuild their clan, his brother Ewan had made great strides in restoring the McCabes to their former glory. This winter, their clan wouldn't go hungry. Their children wouldn't go without proper clothing.

Now it was time for Alaric to do his part for his clan. In a short time, he would travel to the McDonald holding where he would formally ask for Rionna McDonald's hand in marriage.

It was pure ceremony. The agreement had been struck weeks earlier. Now the aging laird wanted Alaric to spend time among the McDonalds, a clan that would one day become Alaric's when he married McDonald's daughter and only heir.

Even now the courtyard was alive with activity as a contingent of McCabe soldiers readied to make the journey with Alaric.

Ewan, Alaric's older brother and laird of the McCabe

clan, had wanted to send his most trusted men to accompany Alaric on his journey, but Alaric refused. There was still danger to Ewan's wife, Mairin, who was heavily pregnant with Ewan's child.

As long as Duncan Cameron was alive, he posed a threat to the McCabes. He coveted what was Ewan's— Ewan's wife and Ewan's eventual control of Neamh Álainn, a legacy brought through his marriage to Mairin, the daughter of the former king of Scotland.

And now because of the tenuous peace in the highlands and the threat Duncan Cameron posed not only to the neighboring clans, but to King David's throne, Alaric agreed to the marriage that would cement an alliance between the McCabes and the only clan whose lands rested between Neamh Álainn and McCabe land.

It was a good match. Rionna McDonald was fair to look upon, even if she was an odd lass who preferred the dress and duties of a man over those of a woman. And Alaric would have what he'd never have if he remained under Ewan: his own clan to lead. His own lands. His heir inheriting the mantle of leadership.

So why wasn't he more eager to mount his horse and ride toward his destiny?

He turned when he heard a sound to his left. Mairin McCabe was hurrying up the hillside, or at least attempting to hurry, and Cormac, her assigned guard for the day looked exasperated as he followed in her wake. Her shawl was wrapped tightly around her, and her lips trembled with the cold.

Alaric held out his hand, and she gripped it, leaning toward him as she sought to catch her breath.

"You shouldn't be up here, lass," Alaric reproached. "You're going to freeze to death."

"Nay, she shouldn't," Cormac agreed. "If our laird finds out, he'll be angry."

Mairin rolled her eyes and then looked anxiously up

at Alaric. "Do you have everything you require for your journey?"

Alaric smiled. "Aye, I do. Gertie has packed enough food for a journey twice as long."

She alternated squeezing and patting Alaric's hand, her eyes troubled as she rubbed her burgeoning belly with her other hand. He pulled her closer so she'd have the warmth of his body.

"Should you perchance wait another day? It's near to noon already. Maybe you should wait and leave early on the morrow."

Alaric stifled his grin. Mairin wasn't happy with his leaving. She was quite used to having her clan right where she wanted them. On McCabe land. And now that Alaric was set to leave, she'd become increasingly more vocal in her worry and her dissatisfaction.

"I won't be gone overlong, Mairin," he said gently. "A few weeks at most. Then I'll return for a time before the marriage takes place and I reside permanently at McDonald keep."

Her lips turned down into an unhappy frown at the reminder that Alaric would leave the McCabes and, for all practical purposes, become a McDonald.

"Stop frowning, lass. It isn't good for the babe. Neither is you being out here in the cold."

She sighed and threw her arms around him. He took a step back and exchanged amused glances with Cormac over her head. The lass was even more emotional now that she was swollen with child, and the members of her clan were becoming increasingly more familiar with her spontaneous bursts of affection.

"I shall miss you, Alaric. I know Ewan will as well. He says nothing, but he's quieter now."

"I'll miss you, too," Alaric said solemnly. "Rest assured, I'll be here when you deliver the newest McCabe."

At that, her face lit up and she took a step back and reached up to pat him on the cheek.

"Be good to Rionna, Alaric. I know you and Ewan feel she needs a firmer hand, but in truth, I think what she most needs is love and acceptance."

Alaric fidgeted, appalled that she'd want to discuss matters of love with him. For God's sake.

She laughed. "All right. I can see I've made you uncomfortable. But heed my words."

"My lady, the laird has spotted you and he doesn't look pleased," Cormac said.

Alaric turned to see Ewan standing in the courtyard, arms crossed over his chest and a scowl etched onto his face.

"Come along, Mairin," Alaric said as he tucked her hand underneath his arm. "I better return you to my brother before he comes after you."

Mairin grumbled under her breath, but she allowed Alaric to escort her down the hillside.

When they reached the courtyard, Ewan leveled a glare at his wife but turned his attention to Alaric. "Do you have all you need?"

Alaric nodded.

Caelen, the youngest McCabe brother, came to stand at Ewan's side. "Are you sure you don't want me to accompany you?"

"You're needed here," Alaric said. "More so as Mairin's time draws nigh. Winter snows will be upon us soon. It would be just like Duncan to mount an attack when he thinks we least expect it."

Mairin shivered at Alaric's side again, and he turned to her. "Give me a hug, sister, and then go back into the keep before you catch your death of cold. My men are ready, and I won't have you crying all over us as we try to leave."

As expected, Mairin scowled but once again threw her arms around Alaric and squeezed tight.

"God be with you," she whispered.

Alaric rubbed an affectionate hand over her hair and then pushed her in the direction of the keep. Ewan reinforced Alaric's dictate with a ferocious scowl of his own.

Mairin stuck her tongue out and then turned away, Cormac following her toward the steps of the keep.

"If you have need of me, send word," Ewan said. "I'll come immediately."

Alaric gripped Ewan's arm and the two brothers stared at each other for a long moment before Alaric released him. Caelen pounded Alaric on the back as Alaric went to mount his horse.

"This is a good thing for you," Caelen said sincerely once Alaric was astride his horse.

Alaric stared down at his brother and felt the first stirring of satisfaction. "Aye, it is."

He took a deep breath as his hands tightened on the reins. His lands. His clan. He'd be laird. Aye, this was a good thing.

Alaric and a dozen of the McCabe soldiers rode at a steady pace throughout the day. Since they'd gained a late start, what would normally be a day's ride would now require them to arrive on McDonald's land the next morning.

Knowing this, Alaric didn't press, and actually halted his men to make camp just after dusk. They built only one fire and kept the blaze low so it didn't illuminate a wide area.

After they'd eaten the food that Gertie had prepared for the journey, Alaric divided his men into two groups and told the first of the six men to take the first watch.

They stationed themselves around the encampment,

providing protection for the remaining six to bed down for a few hours' rest.

Though Alaric was scheduled for the second watch, he couldn't sleep. He lay awake on the hard ground, staring up at the star-filled sky. It was a clear night and cold. The winds were picking up from the north, heralding a coming change in the weather.

Married. To Rionna McDonald. He tried hard but could barely conjure an image of the lass. All he could remember was her vibrant golden hair. She was quiet, which he supposed was a good trait for a woman to have, although Mairin was hardly a quiet or particularly obedient wife. And yet he found her endearing, and he knew that Ewan wouldn't change a single thing about her.

But then Mairin was all a woman should be. Soft and sweet, and Rionna was mannish in both dress and manner. She wasn't an unattractive lass, which made it puzzling that she would indulge in activities completely unsuitable for a lady.

It was something he'd have to address immediately.

A slight disturbance of the air was the only warning he had before he lunged to the side. A sword caught his side, slicing through clothing and flesh.

Pain seared through his body, but he pushed it aside as he grabbed his sword and bolted to his feet. His men came alive and the night air swelled with the sounds of battle.

Alaric fought two men, the clang of swords blistering his ears. His hands vibrated from the repeated blows as he parried and thrust.

He was backed toward the perimeter set by his men and nearly tripped over one of the men he'd posted as guard. An arrow protruded from his chest, a testimony to how stealthily the ambush had been set.

They were sorely outnumbered, and although Alaric

would pit the McCabe soldiers against anyone, anytime, and be assured of the outcome, his only choice was to call a retreat lest they all be slaughtered. There was simply no way to win against six-to-one odds.

He yelled for his men to get to their horses. Then he dispatched the man in front of him and struggled to reach his own mount. Blood poured from his side. The acrid scent rose in the chill and filled his nostrils. Already his vision had dimmed, and he knew if he didn't get himself on his horse, he was done for.

He whistled and his horse bolted forward just as another warrior made his charge at Alaric. Weakening fast from the loss of blood, he fought without the discipline Ewan had instilled in him. He took chances. He was reckless. He was fighting for his life.

With a roar, Alaric's opponent lunged forward. Gripping his sword in both hands, Alaric swung. He sliced through his attacker's neck and completely decapitated him.

Alaric didn't waste a single moment savoring the victory. There was another attacker bearing down on him. With the last of his strength, he threw himself on his horse and gave the command to run.

He could make out the outline of bodies as his horse thundered away, and with a sinking feeling, Alaric knew that they weren't the enemy. He'd lost most, if not all, of his soldiers in the attack.

"Home," he commanded hoarsely.

He gripped his side and tried valiantly to remain conscious, but with each jostle as the horse flew across the terrain, Alaric's vision dimmed.

His last conscious thought was that he had to get home to warn Ewan. He just hoped to hell there hadn't been an attack on the McCabe holding as well.

CHAPTER 2

Keeley McDonald was up before dawn to tend her fire and ready herself for the day. She was midway between the wood pile behind her cottage and her cottage door when it occurred to her how ridiculous it was to imagine that she had a day filled with duties and activities.

She stopped as she came around the corner of her cottage and stared down into the valley that stretched to the distant crest several miles away. Smoke from the McDonald keep and the cottages immediately surrounding it rose like a whisper and floated lazily toward the sky.

How fitting that she should be afforded a prime view of the one place she was never welcome. Her home. Her clan. No more. They'd turned their backs on her. They didn't acknowledge her as kin. She was an outcast.

Was this her punishment? To be relegated to a cottage where she was forever reminded of her birthplace, close enough to see but barred from returning?

She supposed she should be grateful to have any place at all. It could be worse. She could have been forced from her home with no place to go and no recourse but to earn her way in life on her back.

Her lips grew thin and her upper lip curled into a snarl.

It was a trial to her good nature to dwell on such matters. It only made her bitter and angry. There was nothing she could do. She couldn't change the past. Her only regret was that she hadn't been able to seek justice against the bastard McDonald for all he'd done. And his wife. She'd known the truth. Keeley had seen it in her eyes, but the mistress of the keep had punished Keeley for her husband's sins.

Catriona McDonald had passed on four years ago, and yet Rionna hadn't sent for Keeley. Her oldest and dearest childhood friend hadn't come for her. Hadn't summoned her home. And Rionna, of all people, knew the truth.

Keeley sighed. It was stupid to stand here and dwell on past hurts and dashed hopes. It was stupid to have ever had the hope that when Rionna's mother died, Keeley might have been welcomed back into the clan.

The huff of a horse whirled Keeley around, and she dropped the armful of wood with a clatter. The horse clopped into view and came to a stop beside Keeley. Sweat gleamed from the horse's neck and there was a wildness in its eyes that suggested it had suffered a fright.

But Keeley's eyes were riveted to the warrior slumped over in the saddle and to the blood that dripped steadily onto the ground.

Before she could react, the man fell off the horse with a heavy thump. Keeley winced. Jesu, but that had to hurt.

The horse danced to the side, leaving the sprawled warrior at Keeley's feet. Keeley dropped down, pulling at his tunic as she sought the source of all the blood. There was a huge rend in the material at his side and when she pushed aside the tatters, she gasped.

There was a cut that ran from his hip to just underneath his arm. The flesh was flayed open and the wound was at least an inch deep. Thankfully it wasn't deeper, for surely it would have been a mortal blow.

It would certainly need needle and thread and a lot of praying that he didn't succumb to a fever.

She ran her hands anxiously over his taught abdomen. He was a strong warrior, lean and well muscled. There were other scars, one on his belly and one on his shoulder. They were older and didn't look to have been as severe as his current injury.

How was she to get him into her cottage? She glanced back at her doorway with her bottom lip stuck solidly between her teeth. He was enormous and no match for a lass her size. It would require cunning to solve this dilemma.

She rose and hurried into her cottage. She stripped the linens from her bed and wadded them into her hand. She ran back outside letting the material unfurl in the wind.

It took her a moment to position the sheet just so, and she had to place rocks on the end to keep it from billowing up in the wind. When she was done, she went around to the other side of the warrior and pushed at him to roll him onto the sheet.

It was like pushing a boulder.

She grit her teeth and put more muscle into the effort. He bobbed a bit but remained in his position.

"Wake up and help me!" she demanded in frustration. "I can't leave you out here in the cold. 'Tis likely to snow today and you're still bleeding. Have you no care for your life?"

She poked him for emphasis and when he didn't stir, she smacked his cheek with the flat of her palm.

He stirred and frowned. A growl escaped his lips that nearly sent her back into the safety of her cottage.

Then she scowled and bent closer so he could hear. "You're a stubborn one, aye, but you'll find I'm even more so. You won't be winning this battle, warrior. 'Tis better if you surrender now and help me in my endeavor."

"Leave off," he snarled, his eyes never opening. "I'll not aid you in taking me to hell."

"'Tis hell you're going to if you don't stop being difficult. Now move!"

To her surprise he grumbled but rolled as she pushed him.

"I always knew there would be women in hell," he muttered. "'Tis only appropriate that they should be there causing as much difficulty as they do on earth."

"I'm fair tempted to leave you out here to rot in the cold," Keeley snapped. "You're an ungrateful wretch, and your opinions of women are as deplorable as your manners. 'Tis no wonder you find women so repulsive. I've no doubt you've never been able to get close enough to one to change your opinion."

To her astonishment, the warrior laughed and then promptly groaned when the action caused him pain. Some of Keeley's irritation fell away as she saw his face grow ashen and sweat bead his forehead. He was truly in agony and here she sat debating with him.

She shook her head and then gathered the ends of the sheet in her hands and hauled them over her shoulder.

"Give me strength, God," she prayed. "I've no chance of dragging him into my cottage without your aid."

She pursed her lips, ground her teeth together, and then pulled with all her might. Only to be jerked backward. She nearly toppled to the ground. Her warrior hadn't budged an inch.

"Well, God never promised you extraordinary strength," she muttered. "Perhaps he grants only reasonable requests."

She stared at the problem before her and then glanced

at the warrior's horse who stood in the distance munching on grass.

With a disgruntled sigh she marched toward the horse and gripped the reins. At first he refused to budge, but she planted her feet and coaxed, pulled and begged the monstrous animal to do her bidding.

"Have you no loyalty?" she accused. "Your master is lying on the ground, gravely wounded, and all you can think of is your belly?"

The horse didn't look impressed with her speech, but finally he clopped toward the fallen warrior. He leaned his snout down to nuzzle against his master's neck, but Keeley pulled him away.

If she could just secure the ends of the sheet to the horse's saddle, then he could pull him into the cottage. Not that she wanted a dirty, foul-smelling animal in her home, but at the moment she didn't see an alternative.

It took her several long minutes before she was satisfied she had a workable plan. After the sheet was secure and she was reasonably sure the warrior wouldn't roll off the material, she urged the horse in the direction of the cottage.

To her delight it worked! The horse dragged the warrior along the ground. It would take a week to wash the dirt from her bedding, but at least the man was being moved.

The horse clopped into her cottage. There was barely room to maneuver around the animal and the warrior. They filled the tiny interior of her home.

She hastily untied the ends of the sheet and then set about getting the horse to go back the way he'd come. The stubborn horse evidently decided he liked the warmer interior of her cottage. It took half an hour to budge the stubborn beast.

When she finally had him outside where he belonged, she slammed her door and leaned heavily against it. She needed to remember next time that good deeds often went unrewarded.

She was fair exhausted from her efforts, but her warrior needed tending if he was to live.

Her warrior? She snorted. Her pain in the arse, more likely. No need in entertaining stupid, fanciful thoughts. If he died, she'd likely be blamed.

Upon closer inspection, he obviously wasn't a McDonald. She frowned. Was he an enemy to the McDonalds? Not that she owed them her loyalty, but she was a McDonald and as such their enemies were her own. Was she even now saving the life of a man who was a threat to her?

"There you go again, Keeley," she mumbled. Her flights of fancy often veered dramatically to the absurd. The tales she spun in her head would make a bard look boring.

His colors were unfamiliar to her, but then she had never been farther than McDonald land in her life.

She had no hope of getting him to her bed so she did the next best thing. She brought her bed to him.

She arranged the blankets and pillows around him so that he would be comfortable, and then she added wood to her dying fire. Already the room had gone chilly.

Next, she collected her supplies and gave thanks that she'd traveled into the neighboring village a few days past to replenish her meager stock. Most of what she needed, she gathered herself. And thank the good Lord that she had superior healing skills, because it was all that had sustained her for the last years.

Though the McDonalds were quick enough to toss her out of the clan, they had no compunction about seeking her out when one of them needed healing. It wasn't uncommon for her to stitch a McDonald warrior after a training mishap or a wee one's head after taking a tumble down the stairs.

McDonald keep had its own healer, but she was aging and her hand was no longer steady at stitching. 'Twas said she did more damage than good when putting her needle to flesh.

If Keeley were more mean spirited, she'd turn them away just as they'd turned her away, but the occasional coin they provided for her services kept food on her table when hunting was lean and it enabled her to purchase supplies that she couldn't gather herself.

She mixed herbs and mashed the leaves, adding just enough water to make a paste. When she was satisfied with the consistency, she laid it aside and set about preparing bandages from an older linen sheet she kept for just such emergencies.

When everything was in order, she went back to her warrior and knelt by his side. He hadn't regained consciousness since being dragged into her cottage. For that she was grateful. The last thing she needed was a man twice her size to become combative.

She dipped a cloth into a bowl of water and gently began to cleanse the wound. Fresh blood seeped from the wound as she brushed aside the crusted, dried parts. She was meticulous in her task, not wanting to leave even a speck of dirt into the wound when she closed it.

It was a jagged wound and it would leave a great scar, but it wasn't anything he should die of if he didn't take a fever.

After she was satisfied that it was clean, she pressed the flesh back together and took up her needle. She held her breath as she slid the needle in the first time, but the warrior slept on and she quickly set her stitches, making sure they were tight and close together.

She worked down, hovering over him until her back ached and her eyes crossed from the strain. She estimated the wound to be at least eight inches in length.

Perhaps ten. At any rate, it would pain him to move in the days to come.

When she set the last stitch, she sat back and sighed her relief. The hard part was over. Now she needed to bandage him and bind it in place.

By the time she was done wrestling with the warrior, she was exhausted. Wiping the hair from her eyes, she went to wash and to stretch her aching limbs. The inside had grown overwarm and she welcomed the brisk cool air of the outside. She walked down to the bubbling stream not far from her cottage and she knelt by the edge to scoop the water up in her hands.

She filled a bowl full of fresh water and then headed back to the cottage. Then she washed the wound down once more before applying the thick poultice to the stitched flesh. She folded over several strips of material to fashion a thick bandage and then holding it to his side, she awkwardly wound the much longer strips around his waist to hold the bandage in place.

If only she could sit him up, it would make the task much easier. Deciding there was no reason she couldn't lift him to a sitting position, she tugged at his head and then put her entire body behind him to shove upward.

He sagged forward and more blood seeped between the stitches. Working quickly, she wound the strips tightly around his midsection until she was satisfied that everything would stay as she'd positioned it.

Then she eased him gently back to the floor until his head rested on one of the small pillows. She smoothed the hair from his brow and fingered the braid that hung from his temple.

Drawn by the beauty of his face, she ran her finger over his cheekbone and to his jaw. He truly was a beautiful man. Perfectly formed and fashioned. A strong warrior honed by the fires of battle.

She wondered about the color of his eyes. Blue, she

speculated. With that dark hair, blue would be mesmerizing, but it was just as likely they were brown.

As if deciding to answer her unspoken question, his eyelids flipped open. His stare was unfocused, but she was mesmerized by the pale green orbs surrounded by dark lashes that only added to his beauty.

Beauty. Clearly she needed to come up with a better term. He would be mortally offended by a woman calling him beautiful. Handsome. Aye. But handsome didn't begin to aptly describe the warrior.

"Angel," he croaked out. "I've gone to heaven, aye. 'Tis the only explanation for beauty such as this."

She felt a prick of pleasure until she remembered that just earlier he was likening her to hell. With a sigh she smoothed her hand over the warrior's unshaven chin. The bristle abraded her palm and she briefly wondered what it would feel like on other parts of her body.

Then she promptly blushed and pushed the sinful thoughts from her mind.

"Nay, warrior. 'Tis not heaven you've found. You're still of this world, although you might be feeling as though you've been gripped by the fires of hell."

" 'Tis not possible for an angel such as you to reside in the bowels of hell," he said in a slurred voice.

She smiled and soothed her palm over his cheek again. He turned and nuzzled into her hand, his eyes closing as an expression of pleasure settled on his features.

"Sleep now warrior," she whispered. " 'Tis God's truth you have a long recovery ahead of you."

"You mustn't leave, lass," he murmured.

"Nay, warrior. I won't leave you."

CHAPTER 3

Alaric became aware of burning pain in his side that grew stronger with each second he was conscious. It became so much that he stirred and shifted in an attempt to alleviate the unbearable tension.

"Be still, warrior, lest you rip your stitches."

The honeyed voice was accompanied by gentle hands that scalded his already overwarm skin. The heat was nigh unbearable and yet he stilled, not wanting his angel to stop touching him. 'Twas the only semblance of pleasure he had.

How he could straddle the fires of hell and the pleasures of the sweetest angel, he didn't know. Perhaps he was betwixt the two worlds and it was as of yet undecided which direction he would venture.

"Thirsty," he said hoarsely. He slid his tongue over his dry, cracked lips, craving the soothing balm of water.

"Aye, but just a bit. I'll not have you retching all over my floor," the angel said.

She tucked her arm underneath his neck and lifted his head. It shamed him that he was as weak as a newborn kitten. He'd have never been able to hold himself up if it weren't for her firm grip.

The rim of a goblet pressed to his lips, and he drank greedily, nearly inhaling the cool water. It was a shock to his system, so cold and refreshing, that a shiver stole over his body. The contrast was nearly painful. Ice to the fires that burned over his flesh.

"There," the angel soothed. "'Tis enough for now. I know you suffer. I'll make a tisane for the pain and 'twill make you sleep a little easier."

But he didn't want to sleep. He wanted to remain there in her arms, cradled to her bosom. 'Twas a very nice bosom. Pillowy and plump, just as a woman should be. He turned, nuzzling into her softness. He inhaled her sweet scent and felt the fires of hell recede. Peace surrounded him. Ah. He'd taken a step toward heaven surely.

"Tell me your name," he ordered. Did angels have names?

"Keeley, warrior. My name is Keeley. Hush now. You must rest so you can regain your strength. I've not worked this hard for you to be arbitrary and die on me."

Nay, he wouldn't die. There were important things he must do, though at the moment his bruised mind couldn't grasp exactly what it was that was so pressing.

Maybe she was right. He should rest for a while. Perhaps when he next awakened, he'd know the right of things.

He inhaled deeply again and let himself go limp. He was vaguely aware of his angel lowering his head. He inhaled one last time, absorbing her scent. It was like drinking the sweetest of wines. A warm, soothing buzz flowed through his veins and lulled him.

He stopped fighting. His angel wouldn't allow him to die.

"Nay, warrior. I won't allow you to die."

Soft lips brushed over his brow, lingering at his temple. He turned his face, wanting her mouth on his own. He thought he *might* die if she didn't kiss him again.

There was hesitation, what felt to him like an eternity, before finally, her mouth touched his. Just a simple, innocent gesture that a child might bestow.

He growled low in his throat. Damn if he wanted a simple peck.

"Kiss me, angel."

He felt more than heard her sound of exasperation, but then her breathing hitched and it blew warm over his mouth. He could smell her. He could feel her vibrating against him. The tiny puff of air signaled that she was close. So very close.

It took all his strength, but he lifted his arm and delved his hand into her hair, gripping her nape to hold her in place. He raised his head and their lips met in a breathless, heated kiss.

Lord, but she was sweet. Her taste filled his mouth, slid over his tongue like smooth honey. He pushed impatiently at her lips, demanding her to open to him. With a sigh she gave him what he wanted. Her lips parted and he delved inside, probing and tasting every part of her mouth.

Aye, 'twas heaven. Because, if this was hell, there wasn't a man in the whole of Scotland who'd ever tread the path of righteousness.

His strength gone, he slumped back, his head hitting the pillow with a thud.

"You've overtaxed yourself, warrior," she reprimanded in a husky voice.

" 'Twas worth it," he whispered.

He thought she smiled, but the room was so blurred around him that he couldn't be sure. He was vaguely aware of her leaving, but he didn't have the strength to protest. A moment later, she returned and pressed a goblet to his lips again.

The brew was bitter and he coughed, but she didn't

relent. She poured the liquid into his mouth until he had no choice but to swallow or choke.

When she was done, she lowered his head once more to the pillow and brushed her fingers over his brow.

"Sleep now, warrior."

"Stay by me, angel. I find it doesn't hurt so much when you're near."

There was faint rustling and then she pressed into his uninjured side, her body soft and so warm, a shield against the chill that gripped him more with each passing moment.

Her scent surrounded him. The feel of her against him soothed the savage fires. He breathed easier as peace enveloped him. Aye, she was his own sweet angel come to guard him from the gates of hell.

Just in case she thought to leave him, he wrapped his arm around her, pulling her in tighter to his side. He turned his head to the side until her hair tickled his nose. He inhaled deeply and gave in to the darkness creeping over him.

Keeley was in a predicament. Aye, she was trapped against her warrior, his arm like a band of steel surrounding her waist. She'd been there for hours, hoping after he fell asleep that his hold would loosen, but she was melded tight against him.

She could feel every tremor of his body. Every time he shook with the chill from his fever. Several times he mumbled in his sleep and she swept her hand over his chest, up to his face in an effort to soothe him.

She whispered words of nonsense, pitching her tone low so as to offer comfort. Each time she spoke, he seemed to settle and relax once more.

She pillowed her head in the crook of his arm and rested her cheek against his broad chest. 'Twas sinful how much enjoyment she gained from lying against him, but there was no one to see it, and surely God would forgive her if she managed to save the warrior's life.

A glance at her window had her grimacing. Dusk was upon them and it was growing chillier with each passing minute. She needed to get up to cover the window and she also needed to stoke the fire if they were to be warm the night through.

There was also the matter of the warrior's horse, if the animal hadn't already ambled off. Few things would make a man angrier than to have his horse neglected. He'd probably sooner forgive her neglecting his injuries before forgiving insult to his horse. Men had their priorities, after all.

With a sigh of regret, she set about extricating herself from the warrior's grasp. No simple feat when he seemed just as determined that she stay.

He frowned in his sleep and even mumbled a few words that pinkened her cheeks and scorched her ears. But in the end, she won out and managed to slip underneath his arm and roll free.

She struggled to her feet, stretching her stiff muscles, before heading to the window to pull down the covering and secure the sides. The wind had picked up and whistled through her thatched ceiling. If it didn't snow soon, she'd be surprised.

After fetching her shawl and wrapping it securely around her, she stepped outside and looked for the horse. To her surprise, he was right outside the window, as if he'd been checking in on his master.

She patted his neck. "I've no doubt you're used to better care than I can offer, but 'tis the truth I have no place to shelter you. Think you that you'll weather the night out here?"

The horse snorted and bobbed his head up and down, blowing warm air out his nostrils. He was a huge animal and surely he'd dealt with worse before. At any rate, she could hardly board the animal in her cottage.

With one last pat, she left the horse and went to fetch more wood for the fire. Her pile was dwindling, and in the morning she'd need to chop some more if she was to keep her fire ablaze.

She shivered when the wind howled over her, picking up the ends of her shawl and pulling as if trying to upset her balance. She hurried inside and stacked the wood by the hearth. After making sure the door and the window were both secure, she added more logs to the fire and poked until the blaze burned high and bright.

Her stomach growled, reminding her that she hadn't eaten since she'd broken her fast before dawn. Settling on a piece of salted fish and a leftover heel of bread, she sat cross-legged by the sleeping warrior and ate by the warmth of the fire.

As she absently chewed, she stared down at his features, illuminated by the orange glow of the flames. Ever fanciful, her mind began to paint images. Pleasing images. She sighed as she imagined belonging to this man. The two of them eating after a hard day's work. Or perhaps her welcoming him home after a fierce battle. He would have, of course, been victorious, and she would have given him a hero's welcome.

He would be glad to see her. He'd sweep her into his arms and kiss her until she was breathless. He'd tell her he missed her and thought of her often in his absence.

A faint smile brought on by distant memories made her chest ache. She and Rionna had daydreamed as girls about the day they'd marry their warriors. That dream had been cruelly torn away from Keeley, and the friendship that had meant so much to her had gone by the wayside.

There wasn't much chance of Keeley ever making a match. She was taboo to the McDonald clan, and Keeley had never traveled beyond her cottage.

Still, a handsome warrior falling at her doorstep had to be a sign, right? Maybe this was her one chance. Or maybe he was just fodder for more flights of fancy until he became well enough to leave again. Whatever the case, Keeley decided she was going to enjoy her dreams. Even if they were foolish and a waste of time. Sometimes dreams were all that sustained her.

She smiled again. He'd called her an angel. He thought her beautiful. Oh, so his mind was clouded by fever. It still made her chest swell just a bit that such a handsome, fit warrior insisted on kissing her at great cost to himself.

She touched her fingers to her lips, still able to conjure the tingling warmth from his kiss. 'Twas the truth that she'd made no effort to avoid his affection, and maybe that made her the whore the McDonalds had branded her. But she refused to feel guilt. There was no one left to think good of her anyway, so it wasn't as if she could fall any further in esteem.

Put that way, her sudden wickedness didn't feel quite so sinful. A mischievous grin widened her mouth.

Who was to know anyway? A few stolen kisses and a head full of girlish dreams wouldn't hurt anyone. She was tired of always telling herself to put away her silly notions of love. She'd do her duty and nurse the warrior back to health. And if he chose to steal a kiss or two in the process . . .

Wiping her hands down her skirts, she eyed the sleeping warrior and then decided that the best way to monitor his condition was to sleep right where she'd done so before.

She gently moved his arm aside and crawled against

his side. Immediately his arm clamped around her and he turned his head as if seeking her.

It warmed her to her toes when he murmured, "Angel."

She smiled and snuggled a little closer to his warmth. "Aye," she whispered. "Your angel has returned."

CHAPTER 4

How quickly the angel became the devil. As the warrior's fever raged throughout the next day, he alternated cursing Keeley as the devil's handmaiden sent to drag him into the bowels of hell and believing she was the sweetest of angels.

She was exhausted and was never quite sure from one moment to the next if he'd try to kiss her senseless or try to cast her as far from his side as he was able. She could only give thanks to God that he was so weakened from his injury and the fever that he wasn't able to do much more than flail his arm at her.

She felt bad for him. She truly did. She soothed. She wiped his brow. She murmured over and over, stroking his hair and even pressing kisses to his brow. He liked the kisses.

Once he moved his mouth up and caught hers in a hot, lusty kiss that stole her breath completely away. The man surely had a hearty appetite for loving because when he wasn't cursing her, he spent all his time trying to kiss her senseless.

To her shame, she didn't try to dissuade him. He was, after all, a very sick man. That was the excuse she used, and she refused to countenance any other reason for her tolerance of his affections.

As the afternoon got on, she separated some broth from the venison stew she prepared. She'd been extremely pleased when a grateful recipient of her healing had left half of a venison carcass at her door. It would feed her for days to come and feed her well.

Carrying the broth in a small cracked cup, she knelt by the warrior's side and went about the arduous task of getting him to sip the warm liquid.

Thankfully he wasn't in a combative mood and was back to thinking her the sweetest of angels. He sipped the offering as if it were ambrosia offered by God himself. And maybe in the warrior's fever-riddled mind it was.

She nearly spilt the broth all over his chin when a knock sounded at her door. Fear gripped her stomach as she hastily looked around for some way to hide the warrior. Hide such a man? He took up her entire floor.

She laid the cup aside and put a soothing hand on the warrior's forehead, hoping he wouldn't choose now to start muttering blasphemies. Then she rose and hurried toward the door.

She opened it just a crack and peered out. It was nearly sunset. The sun was barely visible over the distant mountaintop. She shivered as the wretched cold wind blew over her.

She breathed a little easier when she saw it was simply a neighboring crofter. That is, until she remembered the warrior's huge horse that had taken up residence on the side of her cottage.

She stepped outside with a smile and glanced left and right, frowning when she saw no sign of the animal. Where had the beast gone? The warrior surely wouldn't be pleased if he'd lost such a fine animal. Perhaps the horse had even been stolen. It wasn't as if all her attention hadn't been consumed by caring for the warrior. Guarding a contrary animal wasn't part of her duties.

"I'm sorry to be bothering you, Keeley, on such a cold day at that," Jane McNab began.

Keeley snapped her attention back to Jane and forced a smile to her lips. " 'Tis no problem at all. I just ask you keep your distance. I find I'm ailing, and I wouldn't want you to be similarly plagued."

The other woman's eyes rounded and she took a hasty step back. At least now she wouldn't expect Keeley to invite her inside her cottage.

"I wondered if I could trouble you for some salve for Angus's chest. He's coughing something fierce. Happens every time there's a turn in the weather."

"Of course," Keeley said. "I made a fresh batch just two days ago. Wait here and I'll fetch it."

She hurried inside and rummaged in the corner where she kept her mixtures and potions. She'd made an extra supply of the thick paste Angus used because she had several regulars who suffered the same affliction. Using one of her cracked cups, she portioned out enough of the concoction to last a week and then brought it back out to where Jane shivered in the cold.

"Thank you, Keeley. I'll pray you are back to rights soon," Jane said. She pressed a coin into Keeley's palm and before Keeley could protest, Jane turned and hurried off.

With a shrug, Keeley went back inside and secured the coin in the knotted piece of linen where she kept the rest of her meager funds. With the coming winter, she'd have need of all the coin she could rummage for when the food supplies ran low.

Her warrior was quiet and seemed to be resting even if fitfully. He twitched and stirred in his sleep, but he'd ceased his ramblings. She heaved a sigh of relief. 'Twas the truth she hadn't had to fake the weary, half-sick look to convince Jane that she was ailing. She was exhausted.

Probably looked on the verge of death herself, and she'd give anything for a restful night.

She knelt by the warrior and laid her palm over his brow, frowning at how dry and hot his skin was to the touch. He gave a light shiver and his muscles coiled and tensed as if trying to ward off the cold.

She eyed the hearth and knew she'd have to venture out once more to replenish the wood stock for the night ahead. Already the wind howled and whistled by her window, ruffling the skin covering the opening.

Knowing it was better to have done with it so she could spend the rest of the night in the warmth of her cottage, she pulled her shawl around her tightly and ventured out to collect another armful of wood.

By the time she returned, her shawl had ripped away from her and blew in the wind, held only by one corner. She shoved inside, dumped the wood on the floor by the hearth, and set about stoking the fire until the blaze licked high up the chimney.

She was hungry but was simply too tired to eat. All she wanted was to lie down and close her eyes. She surveyed the sleeping warrior and pondered the likelihood of getting a sleeping draught down his throat.

Thrashing about did his injury no good, and neither of them got much-needed rest when he flopped around in the throes of God knew what kind of delusion.

Wondering if she'd ever take her bed this night, she mixed the draught and knelt back down, curling her arm underneath the warrior's neck. She hoisted him as far up as she could muster and held the cup to his lips.

"Drink now," she said in a soothing voice. " 'Twill set things to right for this night. You have need of a peaceful sleep."

And so do I.

He drank it down docilely, grimacing only as the last washed down his throat. Blowing out her breath, she lowered him back down, arranged a fur over him to keep him warm, and then settled beside him, her head resting in the crook of his arm.

It wasn't the most modest of accommodations. If anyone saw her, they'd be scandalized and she'd be labeled a whore all over again. But no one was here to judge her, and she'd be damned if she allowed it under her own roof. She'd given up her warm bedding for the warrior. The least he could do was share his body heat.

Some of this trembling eased as she melded closer to his body. He even gave a sigh of contentment and turned blindly, his arm sliding over her waist. He smoothed his hand up her back until his palm was splayed wide between her shoulder blades. Then he simply tucked her into the shelter of his body and pulled her head into the hollow of his neck.

It was like being surrounded by a blazing fire. Heat seeped into her flesh until her muscles were bathed in it. She was careful not to touch his side, though she longed to throw her own arm possessively over his side as he was holding her. She contented herself instead with tucking her hand between their chests, feeling his heart thud against her palm.

"You are a beautiful man, warrior," she whispered. "I know not where you hail from or whether you are friend or foe, but you are the most beautiful man I've ever encountered."

As she drifted into a blissful sleep, warmth surrounding her like a blanket, the warrior smiled in the darkness.

CHAPTER 5

An uneasy prickle skittered over Keeley's skin a bare moment before she opened her eyes. She gasped and would have screamed, but a huge hand clamped over her mouth.

Terror swept through her when she took in the warriors gathered around where she and the injured warrior lay. They didn't look at all pleased.

They wore fierce scowls, and it dimly registered that two of them bore a striking resemblance to her warrior.

She didn't have time to give it much more thought before she was hauled to her feet by a man wielding a sword easily capable of cleaving her in two.

She was about to demand what they were about when the warrior fixed her with a glare so fierce, she promptly swallowed and clamped her lips shut.

It appeared the warrior had questions of his own.

"Who are you and what have you done to him?" he demanded as he pointed to where her warrior lay on the floor.

She gaped, unable to call back her gasp of indignation. "Do? I've done nothing, good sir. Well, except save his life, but I suppose that's paltry."

His gaze narrowed and he pressed in closer to her, gripping her arm until she gave a small cry of pain.

"Leave off, Caelen," the apparent leader barked.

Caelen scowled but eased his grip and shoved her a foot away so that she bumped into the chest of one of the other men. She turned, intending to scramble away, but he took over where Caelen had left off and grasped her arm, albeit much more gently.

The leader knelt by the sleeping warrior and concern darkened his features. He ran his palm over the warrior's fevered brow and then over his chest and shoulders as if seeking the source of his illness.

"Alaric," he called out, his voice enough to wake the dead.

Alaric? 'Twas a fine name for a warrior. But Alaric didn't so much as flinch. The man kneeling over him turned his worried gaze toward Keeley and then his green eyes, so much like Alaric's, turned cold and stormy.

"What has happened here? Why won't he awaken?"

She turned and glanced pointedly at the warrior holding her arm and then down to where his hand clamped around her flesh until he got the message and released her. Then she hurried over to where Alaric lay, determined that whoever this man was, he wouldn't bully Alaric while he lay so riddled with fever.

"'Tis a fever he's taken," she said huskily, trying to ward off the fear that surrounded her just as these men surrounded her.

"That much I can surmise on my own," the warrior growled. "What happened?"

Keeley reached to push aside the remnants of Alaric's tunic where she'd stitched his side. There were several quick intakes of breath and Caelen, who'd squeezed her arm so hard it had nearly broken, advanced to stand over Alaric as he looked down at the stitched wound.

"I don't know what happened," she said honestly. "His horse bore him here, and he fell onto the ground outside my door. It took all my wits to get him inside so that I could tend his wounds. 'Twas a nasty cut to his side. I stitched it the best I could and have tended him well and kept him warm ever since."

"She did a fine job of stitching him," Caelen said grudgingly.

Keeley bristled but held her tongue. What she'd like to do is give him a swift kick in his arse. Her arm still hurt where he'd gripped her.

"Aye, she did," the leader said softly. "I only wish I knew what transpired for him to arrive so grievously injured." He turned his seeking gaze on Keeley, probing, as if he considered whether she was being truthful with him.

"If I knew, I'd tell you," she grumbled. "'Tis shameful. He must have been ambushed or fought unfairly. He seems fit enough to handle himself in a fight."

The leader's eyes glimmered for a moment and she swore he almost smiled.

"I am Laird McCabe and Alaric is my brother."

Keeley cast her eyes downward and bobbed an awkward curtsy. He wasn't her laird, but still, a man of his position commanded respect, and it wasn't as if her laird was a man deserving of any.

"To whom do I speak?" he asked impatiently.

"Keeley," she stammered out. "Keeley . . . Just Keeley." It wasn't as if the McDonalds claimed her as kin any longer.

"Well, just Keeley. It would appear I owe my brother's life to you."

Her cheeks pinched tight as heat gathered and pooled there. She shifted uncomfortably, unused to such praise.

Laird McCabe began issuing orders to his men about how to transport Alaric back to their lands. Aye, she knew they'd want him home, but she felt pressing sadness that her warrior would no longer occupy her hearth.

"His stupid horse left," she blurted, not wanting the blame for not taking better care of his steed. "I did what I could."

Again, something that looked remarkably close to a smile flickered over Laird McCabe's features.

"That stupid horse alerted us that Alaric was in trouble," he said dryly.

She listened idly as they made plans for immediate departure and almost missed the mention of her. Nay, there it was again. A distinct reference to her.

She whirled around, gaping at Caelen, who obviously had to be another McCabe brother. He looked nearly identical to Alaric, though to be honest, Alaric was more pleasing to look at. Caelen frowned so ferociously, that she couldn't imagine a woman wanting to go anywhere near the man.

"I'm not going with you," she protested, sure she'd heard incorrectly.

Caelen didn't respond to her statement, nor did he look impressed with her ire. He simply plucked her up, threw her over his shoulder, and began walking from the house.

In her outrage, she was momentarily stunned. Speechless and motionless. By the time he got to his horse, she understood his purpose and she began to kick and fight.

Instead of forcing her onto his horse, he promptly dropped her onto the ground and then loomed over her with a look of sheer annoyance.

She reached underneath her skirts to rub her bruised behind and glared up at the warrior. "That hurt!"

Caelen rolled his eyes. "You have two choices. You can get yourself up off the ground and give in gracefully. Or I can tie you up, preferably with a gag, and throw you over my saddle."

"I can't just leave! Why on earth would you want me to? I've done nothing against your brother. I saved his life. Where is your gratitude? I have people who rely on my healing skills here."

"We have more pressing need of a healer at McCabe keep," Caelen calmly explained. "You did a fine job at stitching my brother and keeping him alive. You'll continue to do so on McCabe land."

She leveled a mutinous stare at him, though she had to crane her neck to do so. "I'll not ride with you." She crossed her arms stubbornly over her chest for emphasis.

"Fine."

He plucked her up off the ground and strode over to where one of his men had already mounted. She had no warning before she was literally tossed up for the other warrior to catch.

Caelen stared up at her. "Happy? You can ride with Gannon."

Gannon didn't look pleased with the task.

She scowled her own displeasure and then decided she'd inform Caelen just what she thought of him.

"I don't like you. You're a complete boor."

He shrugged, clearly telling her he had no care whether she liked him or not, but she could swear she heard him utter "good" under his breath as he turned and stalked away to see to the litter that was being fashioned for Alaric.

"You be careful not to rip his stitches," she called.

She strained forward and Gannon gingerly wrapped his hands around her waist to prevent her from tumbling from his lap.

" 'Tis a better idea if you sit still," he suggested. " 'Tis a long way to the ground for a lass as small as you."

"I've no wish to leave!" she protested.

Gannon shrugged. "The laird has decided to keep you. 'Tis better if you accept with good grace. The McCabes are a fine clan. And we have need of a healer since ours passed on just weeks ago."

Her gaze narrowed and it was on the tip of her tongue to tell the daft man that they couldn't just go around stealing people, but his words took hold and she quieted.

He seemed to relax, and she felt a sigh of relief release from his chest.

A clan. A position in a clan. Was it really that simple? She frowned. Would she have status in the McCabe clan, or would she be a prisoner with no more privilege than a captive? Would she be treated well until Alaric's recovery and then turned out?

And what if he didn't recover? Would she shoulder the blame?

A shiver took hold at the thought, and she instinctively burrowed closer to the warrior's warmth. The wind had a bite, and she was ill-prepared for the elements.

Nay. She wouldn't allow Alaric to die. She'd determined it from the moment she'd laid eyes on the handsome warrior.

Behind her Gannon cursed.

"Get the lass something to shield her from the cold," he called out. "She'll freeze before we hit McCabe land."

One of the other men tossed up a blanket and Gannon carefully arranged it around Keeley. She clutched the ends and stayed close to his chest, despite the fact that he was captor and she was captive.

Nay. He wasn't her captor. He didn't look any more pleased with the arrangement than she. Nay. She had Caelen and the laird to blame.

She sent a glare in their directions just so they'd know how displeased she was with their daring. Neither man spared her more than a cursory glance as they secured Alaric to a makeshift litter.

"Be vigilant," the laird directed as the men readied for their departure. "We know not what transpired during Alaric's journey, but none, save him, survived. We must return to McCabe keep without delay."

Keeley shivered at the ominous sound of the laird's declaration. Someone had indeed tried to kill her warrior. He was the lone survivor.

" 'Tis all right, lass. We won't allow any harm to come to you," Gannon said, mistaking her shudder.

Somehow she believed him. As ludicrous as it was to place any stock in these men when they were abducting her from her own home, she did believe that no harm would come to her as long as she was with them.

With that in mind, she relaxed in Gannon's hold and leaned her head over as they started forward at a slow pace. Her sleepless nights tending Alaric were beating a dull rhythm in her skull. She was tired, cold, and hungry, and there was absolutely nothing she could do about any of it. So she did the only thing that made sense.

She slept.

CHAPTER 6

"You could have at least found a more accommodating woman to steal," Caelen grumbled to his brother Ewan.

Ewan grinned and glanced sideways where his men bore Alaric's litter between them. Alaric hadn't woken once, and it concerned him, but it was obvious the little spitfire had cared for him well. Which made her perfect for what he had in mind.

"She has a fine hand at healing and that's all that matters," Ewan said, not wanting Caelen to begin a diatribe against women.

As he spoke, he looked over to where Gannon rode with the woman in front of him. She sagged all over Gannon's chest, and it was all Gannon could do to keep the limp burden on the saddle before him. The lass was fairly drooling out one side of her mouth in her deep sleep.

"It would appear she's gone without rest in her vigilance with Alaric," Ewan murmured. "We need that kind of dedication. With Mairin's time drawing ever near, it would make me feel better to have a competent midwife on hand. I'll take no chances with her safety or that of our child."

Caelen frowned but nodded his agreement.

Gannon slowed his horse as the lass shifted and nearly fell out of the saddle. Gannon grasped her at the last moment, and her eyes flew open as she righted herself.

Her disgruntled look made Ewan want to laugh. She was a prickly little thing. And not at all happy with the honor he afforded her. Why she'd want to continue living alone and in squalor was beyond him. Not when he offered her a revered position with his clan.

"Have you experience with birthing children, lass?" he called out to her.

She shot him a frown and her eyes narrowed. "Aye, I've delivered a babe or two in my time."

"Have you any skill at it?" he persisted.

"Well, none have died if that's what you're asking," she said dryly.

Ewan pulled up his reins and held up a fist for Gannon to do the same. He pinned the little wench with the full force of his glare.

"Listen to me, you little harridan. Two people who are more important to me than my life have need of your skills. My brother is grievously injured and my lady wife will bear my child this winter. I need your skills, not your disrespect. While you are on my lands and in my keep, my word is the law. I am the law. You will recognize me as your laird or so help me, you'll weather the winter with no shelter and no food."

Keeley pinched her lips together and gave a short nod.

"'Tis better not to anger the laird, lass," Gannon whispered close to her ear. "He's on edge with Lady McCabe so near her time. Our entire clan depends on the healthy arrival of the babe."

Keeley swallowed, feeling contrite for her flippancy. Still, she couldn't conjure up too much guilt. She'd been stolen from her home and expected to take up with the McCabes. She hadn't been asked or given a choice. Why, if the laird had only outlined his problem, she might have accepted the offer to travel to his keep. Too much in her life had been beyond her control and too long had she not been given a choice in her destiny.

"I've delivered well over twenty babes safely into this world, Laird," she said grudgingly. "I've never lost one. I'll do my best by your lady wife, and I'll not let your brother die. I've already set my mind to his survival, and you'll find, I'm not one to give up."

"Imagine that. A stubborn lass," Caelen muttered. "She and Mairin should get along famously."

Keeley cocked her head. "Mairin?"

"The laird's wife," Gannon supplied.

Keeley studied the laird with interest because it was evident that he'd spoken the truth. His brother and wife meant a lot to him. She could see the worry in his face, and her romantic heart took over.

How sweet that the laird would spirit away a healer just so his wife would have someone when her time came.

Keeley nearly groaned. How ridiculous was it to wax poetic about how romantic the laird was. He'd abducted her, for the love of all that was holy. She should be screaming the forest down, not dwelling wistfully on the laird's obvious affection for his wife.

"You are a simpleton," she muttered.

"I beg your pardon?"

Gannon sounded positively affronted.

"Not you. 'Tis myself I'm referring to."

She thought she heard him make reference to daft women, but she couldn't be sure.

"How long is the journey to your keep, Laird?" she called out.

The laird turned in her direction. "Barely a day, but with Alaric having to be carried, we can count on it taking longer. We'll travel as far as we can and camp as close to McCabe land as possible."

"And when I've cared for your brother and delivered Lady McCabe's babe safely, then may I return home?"

The laird's gaze narrowed. Caelen looked very much like he wanted to shout aye!

"I'll consider it, aye. But I make no promises. Our clan has need of a skilled healer."

She frowned, but she supposed it was better than an outright refusal.

Bored and restless from the slow pace the warriors set, she leaned back against Gannon's chest again, uncaring of whether it was proper or not. It wasn't as if she'd asked to be abducted, and it certainly hadn't been her idea to be tossed from man to man like foul-smelling rubbish.

She set her sights on the countryside, trying to muster excitement for seeing beyond the area that she'd grown up and resided in since her birth. In truth, it wasn't so different. Rugged landscape. Rocks scattered across the ground. They rode in and out of densely forested areas to valleys that were richly green and etched a path between rugged peaks.

Aye, 'twas beautiful, but not the difference she'd always imagined.

When they approached a stream that connected two lochs, Laird McCabe called a halt and ordered his men to secure the perimeter of their encampment.

Like a well-honed operation, they each took a different task, and soon tents were set, fires were built, and guards were posted.

As soon as Alaric was settled close to the fire, she hurried to him, feeling his brow and laying her head close to his chest to listen to his breathing.

His prolonged lack of consciousness bothered her immensely. He hadn't woken once during their travels. She strained to hear his breaths. They were shallow and his chest barely rose with the effort.

His forehead burned to the touch. His lips were dry and cracked. Grimly she turned her head in the direction of his brothers, knowing they were watching.

"I need water and I need one of you to assist me in getting him to drink."

Caelen went for the water himself while Ewan knelt on Alaric's other side and put his arm underneath his brother's neck. Ewan lifted as Caelen handed a tin down to Keeley.

She carefully put it to Alaric's lips, but when she dribbled the water into his mouth, it spilled right back out again.

"Stop being stubborn, warrior," she scolded. "Drink so that we may all sleep this night. I've gone long enough without sleep because of you."

"Devil," Alaric mumbled.

Ewan's mouth twitched and Keeley glared at him.

"You can call me whatever you like if you'll just drink," she said.

"What did you do to my angel?" Alaric slurred.

She took advantage of his open mouth and tilted the tin so the water spilled past his lips. He choked and coughed but swallowed most of it down.

"Aye, that's it. More now. You'll feel better for it," Keeley crooned as she dribbled more water into his mouth.

Alaric obediently swallowed, and when Keeley was satisfied he'd taken enough, she motioned for Ewan to lower Alaric back down.

She tore off a piece of her tattered skirts and dipped it into the remaining water. Then she wiped it over Alaric's brow, easing the taut lines that gathered at his forehead.

"Rest easy now, warrior," she whispered.

"Angel," he murmured. "You came back. Was worried the she-devil had done something evil to you."

Keeley sighed. "So 'tis an angel I am again."

"Stay next to me."

Keeley glanced over her shoulder to see Caelen frowning while amusement glimmered in Ewan's eyes. She narrowed her eyes at both of them. They wanted their brother to regain his health. Part of that was keeping him calm and noncombative. If that meant sleeping next to him, then she'd do so.

Ewan stepped forward. "I'll get blankets so that you're both comfortable. I appreciate you staying close to him when he's so ill."

In that moment, Keeley decided the laird couldn't be all bad. Caelen she would reserve judgment on, but the laird knew she was discomfited by what she considered her duty, and he was putting her at ease and giving her an excuse for remaining by Alaric's side.

Still, she glanced quickly around to gauge whether the laird's men had heard or had any understanding of where she was going to sleep.

None of them seemed bothered, and in fact, they began positioning themselves in a tight circumference around Alaric so that he was protected on all sides.

Two of the men brought blankets and rolled one of them into a cushion.

"For your head," one of the warriors explained. "So the ground won't be so hard to sleep on."

Touched by his thoughtfulness, she smiled and took the blankets. "By what name are you called?"

He returned her smile. "Cormac, mistress."

"Thank you, Cormac. 'Tis the truth I've spent the last nights on the floor and would welcome a barrier to the ground."

She arranged the blankets and then quickly positioned herself next to Alaric, careful to keep a respectable distance between them. With her head cushioned on the rolled up blanket and the furs between her and the ground, she found that she was quite comfortable.

Despite her nap during the day's ride, she yawned as soon as she settled the blankets over her and Alaric. 'Twas important to keep him warm. She could feel him shiver.

For a long while she lay in the darkness, watching and listening to Alaric. The fires died down but were tended through the night by the posted guards. Eventually she could keep her eyes open no longer.

As she drifted into sleep, she realized that on the morrow, she would begin a completely new chapter in her life. And she wasn't sure quite what to make of that.

CHAPTER 7

When Keeley opened her eyes, all she could see was the broad chest of a man. Warmth surrounded her, as did two steel bands she finally figured were arms. She let out a sound of exasperation. So much for keeping her distance from Alaric McCabe. During the night he'd pulled her against him so that not even a breath separated them.

Resigned to her circumstances, she wiggled her arm between them and ran her fingers over his forehead. She frowned and pressed her lips together in worry. He was still hot. Far too hot for her liking.

She twisted and turned her head, staring up at the sky to see that it had just begun to lighten with the first shades of dawn. Around her the camp stirred and men moved quietly, readying the horses and packing the equipment.

When she caught sight of Laird McCabe, she called out softly to him. He stopped and then walked over to stand over Alaric.

"We must hasten," she said. "He needs a warm chamber. He'll not get better until we can see him out of this cold, damp air. His fever still burns this morning."

"Aye, we'll leave immediately. We aren't far from McCabe land. We'll have him to the keep by midmorning."

As he walked away, Keeley relaxed against her warrior and allowed his warmth to bleed into her flesh. 'Twas a pleasurable sensation to lie in his arms. She sighed and ran her hand over his chest.

"You must get better, warrior," she murmured. "Your kin won't like it if I'm unable to make you well again. 'Tis the truth I've suffered enough trouble. I'd like very much to have a peaceful life from here on out."

"Mistress, 'tis time to go," Cormac said.

She twisted again to look up at the man standing over her and Alaric. She frowned when she saw his impatience. As if she'd just been content to lie about all day.

She glanced pointedly down to where Alaric's arms circled her body and then back up at Cormac.

Soon Cormac, aided by Caelen, gently pulled Alaric away and positioned him on the litter that he'd been borne on the day before. Before Keeley could do more than push herself to her feet, she found herself tossed up to Gannon who was already astride his horse.

She huffed in irritation as she bounced against the warrior's chest. "I do wish the lot of you would quit tossing me around like a caber. I'm more than capable of mounting a horse myself."

Gannon grinned. "'Tis much quicker this way, lass. Just stay where we put you and there'll be no trouble."

She sent him a look of disgust before settling into the saddle for the short journey ahead.

The wind kicked up and Keeley swore she could smell snow coming. The sky was cast in gray and the clouds swelled, puffy and ready to drop their moisture at any moment.

She shivered as they rode steadily forward. Gannon pulled the blanket tighter around her with one hand while he guided his horse with the other. She clutched gratefully at the ends and pushed back against him so she could absorb his warmth.

To the side, Laird McCabe halted his horse and issued an order for Cormac to ride ahead and alert the keep of their return. Around her the cry went up from the group of warriors. They'd entered McCabe land.

"Make sure my wife stays in the keep where she belongs," the laird ordered Cormac.

Cormac sighed wearily and the other warriors gave him looks of pity as he rode ahead.

Gannon chuckled and Keeley turned, eyeing him curiously.

Gannon shook his head. " 'Tis an impossible task our laird has charged Cormac with, and he well knows it."

"Is Lady McCabe not accommodating of the laird's wishes?"

Around them several men laughed. Even Caelen wore a hint of amusement at her question.

"It would be disloyal of me to answer your question," Gannon said solemnly.

Keeley shrugged. She knew from experience that when women were heavy with child they tended to be more headstrong. Being trapped inside the keep would probably drive any pregnant woman insane. She couldn't fault the laird's wife for wanting a bit of freedom now and again.

An hour later, they topped a rise, and Keeley looked down at the dark waters of a loch spread across the valley and butting into the dramatic hills. Nestled in the bend was a keep in various stages of repair, or disrepair, although it looked as if the men were working hard to rebuild the walls.

The McCabes looked as though they were on hard times. While she herself could hardly be considered wealthy, she was self-sufficient and she never went without food.

As if sensing the direction of her thoughts, the laird turned and fixed her with a steely stare.

"You will be well provided for on McCabe land. As long as you do the tasks we've brought you here for, you will be amply rewarded with a place to live and food on your table."

She almost snorted. He made it sound so civilized, as if they'd hired her services. Snatching her from the warmth of her blankets at dawn could hardly be construed as an invitation.

"Will you work through the winter, Laird?" she asked as they rode down the incline toward the bridge that led over the loch and into the courtyard of the keep.

Ewan didn't respond. His attention was focused ahead, his sharp eyes taking in every detail. It was as though he was looking for someone.

As they neared the bridge, Keeley could see inside the stone wall. Warriors gathered, concern etched on their faces. Behind them, women and children also gathered, silent and waiting.

When they rode into the courtyard, Ewan frowned, and he let out a great sigh. Keeley followed his gaze to where a visibly pregnant woman hurried past the warriors standing at attention. Another man followed closely on her heels, his expression haggard.

"Ewan!" the woman cried. "What has happened to Alaric?"

Ewan dismounted just as the woman reached the litter. "Mairin, you were instructed to remain inside the keep. Not only is it cold out here, it isn't safe."

Mairin raised her gaze to Ewan and frowned just as ferociously as he was scowling at her. "You must bring him inside so we can tend to him. He doesn't look well!"

"I've brought along someone who will care for him," Ewan soothed.

Mairin turned sharply to survey the riders who were slowly dismounting around Keeley. Then Mairin's gaze rested on Keeley and her eyebrows went up in surprise.

Her eyes narrowed and a thoughtful frown spread across her face.

"Is she qualified to tend to Alaric's injuries?"

At that, Keeley's back went up and she struggled to free herself from Gannon's hold. He lifted her down and as soon as her feet were planted on the ground, she faced Mairin with an indignant huff.

"I'll have you know I'm sought out regularly for my healing abilities. Furthermore, I had no desire to come with Laird McCabe. I wasn't given a choice! Am I qualified? Certainly. But the question that should be posed is whether I'm *willing* to tend to Alaric's wounds."

Mairin blinked and her mouth fell open. Her brows drew together in confusion just before she rounded on her husband who was glaring holes through Keeley.

"Ewan? Is this true? You abducted this woman?"

Ewan's lips twisted in a snarl. He pointed at Keeley and advanced. Keeley clamped her legs together to keep her knees from knocking. She wouldn't show fear even if she was terrified to her toes.

"You will address Lady McCabe with respect. You have two choices. You can accept your fate or you can die. And if you ever show my wife such blatant disrespect again, you'll regret it. I have no time for petulance. My brother's life is hanging in the balance. You *will* tend to him and you'll not begrudge your duty. Are we clear?"

Keeley's lips tightened into a line and she bit her tongue to prevent herself from saying what she really wanted. Instead she issued a short nod.

Mairin glanced between Keeley and her husband, clearly befuddled. "Ewan, you can't just abduct this woman. What of her home? Her family? Surely there's another way."

Ewan placed his hand on his wife's shoulder, but Keeley didn't miss the gentleness in his gesture. Why, his face even softened. He truly did love her.

Keeley wanted to sigh but held it in.

"While we stand here arguing, Alaric worsens. Go and hurry. Have his chamber prepared so my men might carry him in. Keeley will have need of supplies. Make sure the women give her what she needs for Alaric's care. She'll also have need of a chamber. Give her the one next to Alaric so that she will be close at all times."

There was clear exasperation in his voice, but his expression completely belied it.

Mairin tossed one last look Keeley's way, and her eyes darkened with regret. Keeley could swear there was an unspoken apology in her gaze. Then Mairin turned and hurried into the keep, shouting for Maddie.

As soon as his wife was gone, Ewan rounded on Keeley, his expression black.

"You will obey me without question, and you will do everything in your power to aid both Alaric and my lady wife when her time is here."

Keeley swallowed and nodded.

Ewan turned his back dismissively on her and motioned for his men to carry Alaric inside the keep. For a moment she stood there dumbly, unsure of what she was supposed to do.

Gannon nudged her elbow and gestured for her to follow the men inside. He remained just a step behind her all the way up the winding, narrow staircase. He pulled her back to stand outside the chamber door until the men who'd carried Alaric filed back out. Then Gannon ushered her forward.

Mairin and another older woman stood by the fire that blazed in the hearth. The room was still chilled so the fire had just been laid. Ewan stood by Alaric's bed and he motioned impatiently for Keeley.

"Give an accounting of what supplies you need to Maddie. See to his wound and make sure the stitches haven't torn."

She bit her tongue again, tempted to snap back at him that she knew well how to do her duty without him instructing her. Instead she gave a crisp nod and shoved past him to where Alaric lay.

She cupped her palm over his forehead, heartened by the fact he didn't feel quite as hot as he did earlier. Of course being exposed to the much cooler air outside had probably done the deed, and now that he was within the warmer confines of his chamber, she had to concern herself with his fever worsening.

"Will he recover?" Mairin asked fearfully.

Keeley turned to the laird's wife. "Aye. I'll not have it any other way."

The woman beside Mairin raised her brows. "You're young to be so arrogant, lass."

"Arrogant?" Keeley was honestly surprised by the other woman's assessment. "I've never considered myself arrogant. Not when other's lives depend on me. I find what I do very humbling. I fear all the time that I'll be unable to provide the care that is needed. But I'm stubborn—not arrogant. I refuse to allow someone to suffer if 'tis within my power to prevent it."

Mairin smiled and closed the distance between them. She grasped Keeley's hands and squeezed. "Whether 'tis arrogance or confidence, I care naught. I only care that when I look at you, I see such determination in your eyes that I know you'll not allow Alaric to die. For that I thank you, mistress. You'll have my undying gratitude if you set Alaric to rights."

Keeley's cheeks warmed at the other woman's praise. "Please. Do call me Keeley."

"And you must call me Mairin."

Keeley shook her head. "Oh nay, my lady. It wouldn't do. And your laird wouldn't like it one bit."

Mairin chuckled. "Ewan's bark is much worse than

his bite. He can be gruff and growly, but he truly is a fair man."

Keeley arched one brow at the other woman.

Mairin flushed. "What he did was reprehensible. I can't imagine what he was thinking. Perhaps concern for Alaric blinded him to all else."

"I imagine his concern for you had something to do with it," Keeley said dryly.

"Me?"

Keeley's gaze dropped to Mairin's swollen belly. "He intends that I remain to deliver your babe."

"Oh dear," Mairin murmured. "The man is addled. He cannot go about abducting people because he fears for my safety. 'Tis madness."

Keeley smiled. " 'Tis a good husband who worries for his wife. I find after meeting you, I don't have an aversion to remaining for the winter to see your child safely born."

"You've a kind heart, Keeley," Maddie interjected. "We have need of a good healer. Lorna passed on some weeks ago and the laird, while skilled with a needle, has no knowledge of herbs and poultices. He has no experience with childbirth either."

Keeley's eyebrows went up again. "The laird has been acting as your healer?"

"He stitched my wound when an arrow struck me," Mairin said. "He did a fine job."

"Tell us what you need," Maddie urged. "I'll make sure you have it as soon as possible."

Keeley thought a moment as she surveyed the sleeping warrior. She'd need a whole host of herbs and roots, but she preferred to find those herself. She didn't trust others to recognize the plants she used.

Instead she asked Maddie for water and bandages and broth so Alaric would have some sustenance. It was important for him to keep up his strength. A weakened man didn't fight off illness as well as a strong and fit warrior.

She instructed the older woman on what she wanted done for Alaric in her absence.

"But where are you going?" Mairin asked with a frown.

"I must go forage for the roots and herbs I need for my medicines. If I don't go now, I'll have to wait until the morrow and that might be too late."

"Ewan won't like that," Mairin murmured. "He's very firm on going outside the walls of the keep."

"If he wants his brother to survive, he won't make a fuss."

Maddie grinned. "'Twould seem our laird may have met his match in you, Keeley."

"Still, it would be better if you were to have an escort," Mairin said. "I'd go with you myself—'tis God's truth I'd welcome a walk and some fresh air—but Ewan would never let me hear the end of it."

"You aren't allowed even a wee walk outside the keep?" Keeley asked incredulously.

Mairin sighed. "'Tis not the sentence you think it is. Ewan isn't overbearing. He's worried, and with good reason. We have many enemies, and until I deliver this babe safe and sound, I am a target."

When Keeley continued to stare at her in puzzlement, Mairin let out a long breath. "'Tis a long story. Perhaps I'll tell you all about it tonight as we tend to Alaric."

"Oh nay, my lady. 'Tis not your duty to stay awake with Alaric. He'll be just fine in my care. A woman in your condition needs all the rest she can get."

"Still, I'll sit with you awhile. If nothing more, it will be a way to pass the time. I won't sleep for worrying over Alaric anyway."

Keeley smiled. "Very well then. Now if I may, I must be off before I lose good light."

"Maddie, see to the supplies and do as Keeley instructed. I'm going to walk her down to the courtyard and ask Gannon and Cormac to accompany her on her search. Ewan won't allow anything less, I'm sure."

Maddie chuckled. "You know our laird well, my lady."

Maddie turned and hurried out of the room. Keeley brushed her hand over Alaric's forehead one last time before she followed Mairin from the chamber.

As Keeley expected, the laird argued only as long as it took her to inform him that if she didn't gather the things she needed, his brother would suffer. Grudgingly he sent three of his men with her, though none looked pleased with the chore.

"They never like looking after women," Mairin whispered next to Keeley. "I am the bane of their existence, for they are assigned regularly to me."

Keeley grinned. "I heard a lot about you during our journey."

Mairin scowled. " 'Twas disloyal of them to speak behind my back."

"They didn't speak as much as they hinted," Keeley corrected. "And Gannon refused to answer a direct question. He said 'twas disloyal."

Mairin laughed outright, earning her suspicious frowns from the men.

"Come, mistress," Gannon said in resignation. "Let us hasten to the forest so we can return quickly."

"No need to act as though a death sentence is being carried out," Keeley muttered.

Mairin laughed softly. "I'll wait for you in Alaric's chambers, Keeley. In the meantime I'll make sure he is comfortable and that your instructions are carried out."

Keeley nodded and fell into step behind the group of warriors assigned to watch over her. Despite her initial irritation at the idea that she couldn't simply leave the keep alone, it gave her a tiny thrill that she was considered important enough to warrant the watch of three highly trained warriors.

She'd never felt safer than she did right now with three such brawny men surrounding her as they walked beyond the stone skirt and toward the patch of trees in the distance.

Perhaps coming to McCabe keep wasn't the inconvenience she'd first thought. The laird's wife wasn't at all what she'd expected, and despite the circumstances of Keeley's arrival, she was being treated well.

It was entirely possible that she could grow to like life here. After all, it wasn't as though she had a clan to return to.

She pursed her lips and shook her head. No sense putting the cart before the horse. She was entirely too fanciful for her own good. The laird hadn't brought her here out of the goodness of his heart. He had no desire to make her feel at home or make her feel a valued member of his clan. He wanted her skills. Nothing more. It would behoove her to remember that. When she no longer served a purpose, she might well find herself turned out.

The one thing she'd learned in life was that family was a fickle concept. There was no loyalty. If she couldn't expect such a thing from her own clan, how could she expect it from complete strangers?

She nodded grimly to herself. Aye, she needed to pull her head from the clouds and view her mission with more objectivity.

She was a captive. Nothing more. To forget such was to open herself up for more disappointment.

CHAPTER 8

By the time Keeley returned to the keep, the sun had already slipped beyond the horizon and cold permeated her bones. She was weary and aching from all the bending and kneeling, but she'd been successful beyond her expectations. The McCabes had an excellent stock of plants and roots, and now her skirt was full as she trudged toward the door.

She shivered and curled her fingers a little tighter into the material of her dress as she clutched the ends so the tiny shoots didn't fall. Her hands were numb with cold and her teeth had long since stopped chattering. She could barely feel her chin.

She stumbled going up the steps and Cormac caught her elbow to steady her. She mumbled her thanks and continued on, welcoming the warmer air of the interior.

"'Tis growing colder," Gannon said. "It looks like snow this night."

"It's looked like snow for two days," Cormac argued.

"Aye, he's right. It will snow before the morn," Keeley said as she mounted the stairs to Alaric's chamber.

"Thank goodness our stores are full," Gannon said. "We look to be in for a long winter. It will be nice to not worry where our next meal will come from."

Keeley paused on the stairs and glanced behind her to

where Gannon stood. "What happened here? The keep is in disrepair and you speak of hard times."

Gannon grimaced. "I spoke out of turn. 'Tis not something I should have spoken freely about. I was merely thinking aloud. My laird would not be pleased that my tongue got away from me."

Keeley shrugged. " 'Tis not as if I asked you for battle secrets. I would think I'm entitled to know what I've been thrust upon."

" 'Tis of no consequence," Cormac offered from below Gannon. "All is well now that the laird has married Lady McCabe. Our clan thrives again thanks to her. We are blessed to have her."

Keeley smiled at the obvious affection in his voice. Mairin McCabe was a most fortunate woman for she was dearly loved by not only her husband but her clan as well.

"Is there a reason you dally on the stairs when my brother is sore in need of aid?" Caelen snapped from above.

She turned and cast a baleful look in his direction. "Is there a reason for your surly disposition? I've spent the last hours searching your forest for all manner of herbs. I'm tired. I'm hungry. I've not slept in days. And yet even I have more manners than you. Think you there is something amiss about that?"

Caelen blinked and then scowled, not that she expected any less. He opened his mouth as if to say something but then quickly snapped it shut. Smart man. He didn't intimidate her, and she'd not let him get away with his rudeness. 'Twas true. She was exhausted to her core and the last thing she needed was him hovering over her, criticizing her every move.

She pushed by him once she reached the top of the stairs and leveled a scowl at him that was every bit as impressive as his. She entered Alaric's chamber and shut it firmly behind her.

"Keeley, you're back!" Mairin exclaimed from Alaric's bedside.

Keeley glanced over to see Mairin carefully bathing Alaric's forehead while Maddie stood to the side. The fire had been stoked and wood added, and Keeley immediately went to stand in front of it, soaking in every bit of the heat she could.

"Here, lass, let me take your findings. Do you have any special instructions or can I leave them all together?" Maddie asked as she came over to help Keeley.

Keeley glanced down at the pile in her gathered skirts. "Aye, you can leave it all together. I'll sort it out after I can feel my hands again. I'll need a bowl or two and something to grind the leaves and roots with."

"You heard the lass," Maddie said to Gannon who stood in the doorway. "Go fetch her bowls and a mortar and pestle."

Gannon looked extremely disgruntled to be ordered about by a woman, but he turned to do her bidding although not before allowing his displeasure to cross his face.

Mairin frowned in Keeley's direction. "Keeley, are you certain you are up for caring for Alaric this night? You look exhausted, and you're shaking with cold."

Keeley offered a faint smile. "I'll be warm in no time. If you have food to spare, I'd be most grateful for something to eat."

"I'll go fetch something from Gertie," Maddie said.

As Maddie left the chamber, she met Gannon on his way back in with the items Keeley had requested. Keeley carefully deposited the herbs into one of the bowls and straightened her skirts. Now that her hands were free, she turned and held them out to the fire, wincing when feeling began to race through her veins again.

"You have need of proper clothing if you are to stay here," Gannon said gruffly. "I'll speak to the laird about it straight away."

"Oh, you're right," Mairin said, remorse heavy in her voice. "'Tis something I should have thought of. You could hardly have prepared for a journey if my husband snatched you from your home. I'll speak to the women at once. Between us, we can surely remedy the problem."

Keeley fidgeted under their scrutiny. "'Tis thoughtful of you both. I'm most appreciative of your regard."

"Is there anything else you require?" Gannon asked.

Keeley shook her head. "Nay. Thank you for your aid. I have all I need."

Gannon dipped his head in acknowledgment and then turned and left the chamber.

Relieved to have rid of most of the occupants of the chamber, Keeley wearily seated herself on the small stool next to Alaric's bed. Mairin hovered at a distance, watching as Keeley carefully examined Alaric's side.

She touched the long cut, frowning at how swollen and red it was. She closed her eyes and issued a curse under her breath.

"What's wrong, Keeley?" Mairin demanded. "Is he worsening?"

Keeley opened her eyes and stared down at the inflamed wound. She sighed. "I need to reopen his wound to rid it of its poison. It'll require cleaning and then I'll have to stitch him up again. 'Tis no easy task, but it must be done."

"Should I stay to assist you?"

Keeley eyed the slight woman and the bulge at her waist. Then she shook her head. "I've no wish for you to come to harm if Alaric becomes combative. 'Tis a better idea if one of his brothers is present in case there is need to hold him down."

Mairin frowned and stared over at Alaric. "If he tries to fight, 'twill take more than one man to hold him. Perhaps I should call for Ewan and Caelen both."

Keeley's lips twisted in distaste. Mairin laughed softly. "Caelen is truly a good sort. I used to swear the man did nothing but frown. He's really not so terrible once you've grown accustomed to his manner."

"Manners? He has none," Keeley muttered.

Mairin's eyes twinkled with amusement. "I like you, Keeley . . ." Then she frowned. "By what family name are you called?"

Keeley froze and refused to meet Mairin's gaze. She could feel the other woman assessing her, probing her with her stare. She glanced down at her hands and twisted them in her lap.

"McDonald," she whispered. "I used to be, but no more. Now I just call myself Keeley."

"McDonald?" Mairin echoed. "Oh dear. I wonder, does Ewan know he's stolen the healer from the clan Alaric was to be laird over?"

Keeley's head snapped up. "Laird? But the McDonalds have a laird." She should know. The bastard was directly responsible for her banishment. If something had happened to the worm, shouldn't she know? Was she forever doomed to live on the outside of her family? Never welcomed to their hearth and into their fold?

Tears burned her lids and she'd be damned before she'd let a single one fall. The lot of them could rot, Gregor McDonald included. *Especially* Gregor McDonald.

"'Tis a long story," Mairin said with a sigh. "Alaric's marriage to Rionna McDonald has been arranged. He was traveling to McDonald keep to make it official and formally ask for Rionna's hand. Laird McDonald has no male heir and he wants the man Rionna marries to take the mantle of leadership."

Married to Rionna. Her childhood friend. Her only friend. But she, like everyone else, had turned their back on Keeley. It shouldn't still hurt her, but it did. Keeley had dearly loved her cousin and friend. She still occupied a special place in Keeley's heart, and she missed her sorely.

She glanced over at her sleeping warrior. Her warrior. Nay. He belonged to Rionna. How fitting that a man she'd allowed herself to spin girlish fantasies about was forbidden to her. If any of the McDonalds knew that Keeley had given sanctuary to Alaric, the accusations would abound once more.

"Did I say something wrong?" Mairin asked softly.

Keeley shook her head. "So he is to be married to Rionna."

"Aye. Come spring. 'Tis a fact I hate the idea of Alaric leaving our lands, but 'tis a good opportunity for him to have something of his own. A clan to lead. Lands to own. Children to pass on his legacy to."

It was silly, the sadness that crept into her chest. She had naught but ridiculous fantasies of a strong, fit warrior riding into her life and sweeping her away.

"I better tell Ewan what he has done," Mairin said in a worried voice. "He must set this to rights."

"Nay!" Keeley said as she shot to her feet. "I am not claimed by the McDonald clan. Truly. No one will miss me. 'Tis true I have healing skills and I am sought out regularly by some of the McDonald clan, but I don't live within their walls. I am free to go where I please."

Mairin regarded her with open curiosity. "If you have such a gift, they would be fools not to keep you. Why do you no longer call yourself McDonald?"

" 'Twas not my choice," Keeley said in a low voice. "I didn't turn my back on my clan. They turned their back on me."

They were interrupted when Maddie swept back into

the room bearing a trencher of food. She set it on the small table a mere foot from where Keeley stood.

"There now, eat up, lass. You must keep your strength up as well if you are to tend to Alaric through the night."

As hungry as she'd been, Keeley found she no longer had an appetite after learning of Alaric's impending marriage. Still, she forced herself to eat and found that the fragrant stew and fresh-baked bread was the best meal she'd had in longer than she could remember.

"I'll go summon Ewan and Caelen," Mairin said. "Come, Maddie. Leave Keeley to her meal. She has an arduous task ahead of her."

The two women traipsed out the door, leaving Keeley alone with Alaric. Keeley's gaze traveled over the lean, hard lines of the sleeping warrior.

"Why couldn't you have belonged to another?" she whispered. "Rionna is the sister of my heart, no matter that she betrayed me. It shouldn't hurt me that you are betrothed, but I find the disappointment almost too keen to bear. I know you not, but you have fast found a place in my heart."

Alaric stirred and opened his eyes, the green startling her with its brilliance. For a long moment he stared as if he had no understanding of who she was or where he was.

Then his lips moved and he whispered, so soft she almost didn't hear. "Angel. My angel."

CHAPTER 9

It seemed that Keeley had no sooner laid her head on her pillow than a knock sounded loudly at her door. She opened her eyes and blinked to try and orient herself.

It had to be near to dawn. She'd spent two hours meticulously cleaning and restitching Alaric's wound with the aid of his two brothers. She'd been bleary-eyed and near unconscious by the time she'd stumbled to her chamber.

She was tempted to pull the pillow over her head and ignore the summons at the door, but before she could do anything, it burst open.

She yanked the covers to her chin despite the fact she was fully clothed and stared in irritation at her intruder— or intruders, she should amend.

Ewan and Caelen McCabe stood in her doorway and they didn't look any happier to be there than she was at their presence.

"Alaric is calling for his angel," Caelen said in disgust.

Keeley blinked and then let her gaze rest on Ewan. "You know as well as I that I'll be the demon in the next breath."

Ewan sighed. "He is in a state of supreme agitation. I'm worried he'll rip his stitches and the wound will bleed again. We must keep him quiet and allow him rest. The only way I see to do that is if . . . you're with him."

Keeley's mouth dropped open. "What you're suggesting isn't proper at all. You may have abducted me without care, but I refuse to allow my reputation to become more tarnished than it already is. The last thing I need is your clan to think me a woman without morals."

Ewan held up a placating hand. "My clan will say nothing. No one will know. I'll make sure no one but myself or my wife is allowed inside Alaric's chamber—or yours for that matter. I would not ask if it wasn't important, Keeley. Right now I'll do whatever it takes to calm my brother and ease his distress."

Keeley propped herself up on one elbow and rubbed a weary hand over her face. "What I need is sleep. I haven't slept since Alaric came to my cottage wounded. If I go to his chamber, can you make sure I am undisturbed?"

She knew annoyance was reflected in her tone, and at the moment, she just didn't care. She'd do whatever it took for these people to leave her alone.

"In fact, what I'd really appreciate is for everyone to leave me alone to tend to Alaric. If I have need of something, I'll call."

Already Keeley was dreaming of several hours of uninterrupted sleep. If she had to agree to share Alaric's chamber in order to achieve it, then that's what she'd do.

The corner of Ewan's mouth twitched. "Aye, Keeley. You'll have your sleep. I'll make sure you are undisturbed. We won't come to see about Alaric's progress until the afternoon. You have my word."

Keeley threw off the covers and slung her legs over the bed, careful to keep as much of her tattered dress covering her as possible. She struggled to her feet, smoothing her snarled hair from her face.

"Let's get on with it then," she grumbled.

She trudged into Alaric's chamber to find the covers twisted in a ball at his feet. His arm was thrown over his head and sweat beaded his brow. He moved his head from side to side, mumbling unintelligible things under his breath.

Sweat gleamed on his chest and on his side as well, and she could see the stress the stitching on his wound was undergoing.

Stifling her curse, she hurried to his side, her fingers probing the stitched cut.

He stilled immediately and his eyes opened, bleary with confusion. "Angel?"

"Aye, warrior, 'tis your angel come to soothe you. Tell me now, will you rest if I remain by your side?"

"Glad you're here," he croaked. "Not the same when you're gone."

She went soft from head to toe and leaned in closer, allowing his seeking hand to touch her arm.

"I won't leave this time, warrior. I'll stay with you."

His arm curled around her, pulling her until she was forced down to his side. "I'll not let you go this time," he vowed.

Keeley refused to look at Alaric's brothers. She had no desire to see the irritation or condemnation in Caelen's eyes. She'd seen enough of that to last her a lifetime. If he had a single word to say to her after dragging her from her bed, she'd belt him right across the face and damn the consequences.

Luckily she heard no sound from that quarter. Only the soft shutting of the door alerted her to the fact that she and Alaric were alone.

She snuggled into his side and smoothed her hand over his taut belly. "Sleep now, warrior. Your angel will be ever close. This I swear."

He made a sound of contentment and his body went

slack, all the fight leaving his muscles. He squeezed his arm around her until not a single part of her wasn't touching him in some way.

He went immediately to sleep, but despite Keeley's overwhelming fatigue, she lay awake for a long time, savoring the sensation of lying in her warrior's arms.

When she next opened her eyes, sunlight was straining around the furs covering the window. The fire had died down in the hearth and only a few glowing embers remained. Despite the chill that she knew was probably present in the room, she was bathed in warmth. So cozy and comfortable that she didn't move a single muscle.

Alaric's arm was still wound tightly around her waist and she was pressed up tight to his side, her head resting in the hollow of his shoulder.

Her hand glided over his chest and finally up to rest against his cheek. To her delight, his skin was much cooler and not as dry as it had been over the past hours. Cool sweat shimmered on his forehead and she pried herself out of his arms to rise excitedly.

As she looked down at his face, she was surprised by how clear his eyes were. No haze of confusion darkened the light green orbs.

Then he smiled up at her and to her utter shock, he reached up and pulled her down on top of him.

"You're mad!" she hissed as she struggled to move to his uninjured side. "You're going to tear your stitches and I spent the better part of two hours setting them!"

"So my angel is real," he murmured, not letting her wiggle out of his grasp.

"Your assessment of a demon was more accurate," she gritted out.

He chuckled and then winced.

"See? You should be lying still, not dragging me over your body," she said in exasperation.

"But I like you on my body," he purred. "I like it very much. In fact, I barely feel my injury now. All I feel is your softness against my flesh. Your breasts pressed into my chest."

Heat crept over her shoulders and up her neck over her cheeks. She refused to meet his gaze and focused instead on his shoulder.

"Do you know what would make me feel even better?" he husked out.

She chanced a peek at him to see him studying her intently, his eyes glowing in the faint light that bled through the furs.

"What?" she asked nervously.

"A kiss."

She shook her head even as she tried to wiggle off his chest again. He caught her against him and then reached with his free hand to cup her chin.

Ignoring her protests, he raised his head and fit his lips to hers. It wasn't clear who had the fever. Him or her. Heat seared through her body. 'Twas a wondrous sensation. Heady. Sinfully sweet.

Her head spun and she felt incredibly light, like she'd taken flight and drifted among the clouds. She let out a sigh and melted into his strong body.

His fingers splayed out over her back and he rubbed up and down. When they reached her nape, he gripped her neck and delved his fingers into her hair, pulling her down to meet the intensity of his kiss.

"Alaric," she whispered.

"I like the sound of my name on your lips, lass. Now tell me yours so I may know the name of my angel."

She sighed in exasperation at how quickly he turned away her objections.

"My name is Keeley."

"Keeley," he murmured. "Such a beautiful name. Fitting for such a beautiful lass."

"You must let me up," she said firmly. "Your brothers will be up any moment now. They're most concerned about your injury. I need to look at the stitches to make sure they're holding, and if you feel strong enough, you should eat."

"I'd rather kiss you."

Foregoing her gentle reproach, she balled her fist and gave him a thump on the chest. To her surprise, he laughed but relinquished his hold on her.

She scrambled off his chest and smoothed her wrinkled clothing and disheveled hair. She probably looked like she'd been dunked in the loch and then dragged behind a horse.

Her gaze kept creeping to his broad, naked chest. Not that a man's chest was a mystery to her. Nor was the rest of the male anatomy. She'd seen more than her fair share of naked males thanks to her skill at healing. But this man took her breath away. He was . . . magnificent.

Her eyes ate him, and she wasn't being entirely discreet about it. She hoped that his fever and pain kept him from noticing her avid attention.

"I must look at your wound," she said, damning the husky catch to her voice.

He glanced down and then slowly rolled onto his good side so that his injury was outward.

"I must thank you, Keeley. I don't remember much about the day I was injured, only that I knew I would die if I didn't seek aid immediately. When I opened my eyes and saw you, I knew that God had sent me an angel."

"Sorry to disappoint you," she said lightly. "Angel I'm not. I'm merely an ordinary woman who is skilled in the healing arts. 'Tis nothing more than knowledge gleaned from other women who've come before me."

"Nay," he denied. He reached up and caught her hand when she moved closer, bringing her fingers to his lips.

Tingles shot up her arm and her chest tightened in pleasure. It was hard not to smile at the handsome warrior who wielded pretty words as surely as he did a broadsword.

She caught his wrist and gently pushed until his arm was over his head at an angle. Then she leaned in to survey his newly stitched wound. It pleased her to see the redness had abated and that it no longer looked quite so raw and angry.

"What's the verdict? Will I live?" he asked in amusement.

"Aye, warrior. You'll live a long, healthy life. You're fit, which will aid you in a complete recovery."

"Glad to hear it."

When she allowed him to lay his arm back down, he rubbed at his belly and grimaced.

"Hungry?"

"Aye. Fair to starving."

" 'Tis a good sign," she said with an approving nod. "I'll ask for a trencher to be brought up."

"You don't leave."

She raised her brow because it wasn't a request. The command in his voice was evident.

"Please."

At the lowering of his voice, she all but melted again. "Aye. I'll stay."

He gifted her with a smile even as his eyelids lowered. He blinked, fighting the urge to sleep. She laid her hand over his forehead. "Rest, warrior. I'll have your food to you in a moment."

She rose from the bed and smoothed her skirts, wishing she didn't look so bloody awful. She'd made it to the door and was about to open it when it swung open. She scowled at the intruder, letting him know his bursting in wasn't welcome.

Caelen scowled back, letting her know he wasn't impressed with her ire.

"How is he?" he demanded.

She swept her hand toward the bed. "See for yourself. He was awake a few moments ago. He's hungry."

Caelen strode past her and she made a face at his back. When she turned around to exit, she nearly ran into Ewan.

"I don't suppose you'll forget you saw that," she muttered.

Ewan's lips twisted in amusement. "Saw what?"

Keeley nodded her approval and then walked past, not really knowing where she was going, but she could definitely use some air. She could still feel Alaric's mouth on hers. She could still taste him.

CHAPTER 10

Alaric kept his gaze fastened on the lass until she dis-appeared from view. Then he shot his brothers the full force of his glare.

"Is there something you wanted?" he asked irritably.

"Aye," Caelen drawled. "For instance, to know whether you were still alive or not."

"As you can see I am. Isn't there something else you could be doing?"

Ewan shook his head and sat on the stool next to the bed. "Forget your fascination with the lass for a moment. There are things we must know. Starting with who did this to you."

Alaric sighed. His side ached. His head felt as though he'd spent the last week drowning in a tankard of ale, and he was hungry and grouchy to boot. The last thing he wanted was an inquisition.

"I don't know," he said honestly. "They ambushed us in the middle of the night. It was a slaughter. We were outnumbered at least six to one. Maybe more. I barely managed escape and don't remember much beyond waking up feeling as though I was being burned by the fires of hell but with an angel soothing the pain."

Caelen snorted. "More like a she-demon likely mated to Satan himself."

"She saved my life," Alaric said.

"Aye, she did," Ewan agreed. "She has a fine hand at healing. I plan for her to attend Mairin's birth."

Unexpected pleasure—and excitement—coursed through Alaric's blood, stirring desire he hadn't felt for a woman in a long time. He had plenty of dalliances. A quick tup now and then was good for a man's disposition. But Keeley fired his senses like no other. He was on edge, his skin way too tight, all because she wasn't near.

"She agreed to come here and be our healer?" Alaric asked casually.

Caelen chuckled. "Not exactly."

Alaric narrowed his eyes. "What does that mean?"

"It means we didn't give her a choice in the matter. You needed her skills and so will Mairin. So I brought her here," Ewan said with a shrug.

Typical Ewan. He made a decision and acted on it. Though he liked the idea of Keeley being near, it didn't sit well that his brothers had manhandled her. It would explain her sharpness with him.

"Forget the woman," Caelen said darkly. "Unless you forget, you have an agreement to wed McDonald's daughter."

Nay, he hadn't forgotten. He may have pushed it from his mind temporarily, but he hadn't forgotten why he'd embarked on the journey where he'd lost several of his best men.

"I received a missive from Gregor a few hours ago," Ewan said. "He was concerned that you hadn't arrived yet. I held off sending him word of what transpired until I knew myself what exactly had happened."

" 'Twas as I said," Alaric said wearily. He raised his hand and rubbed his aching temple. "We'd stopped for the night. Six men were standing guard. In the middle of the night we were attacked with speed and ferocity I haven't witnessed since the attack that decimated our keep eight years ago."

"Cameron?" Caelen asked with a scowl.

Ewan blew out his breath, his eyes as dark as a winter storm. "Who else? What purpose would anyone else have to launch such a vicious attack? This was no demand for ransom. You don't slaughter people you have hopes of collecting a bounty for."

Caelen leaned against the wall, his lips set into a grim line. "But why Alaric? Mairin and Neamh Álainn have been his focus. Killing *you* makes sense, Ewan. That gets him closer to his aim of having both Mairin and her inheritance. Killing Alaric does nothing to further his crusade."

"He has a vested interest in keeping our clans from allying themselves," Alaric pointed out. "'Tis not just the McDonalds. 'Tis the fact we would control a vast portion of land and that neighboring clans would readily join with us. They'd be afraid not to."

"I'll send word to McDonald of what occurred. I'll alert him so that he will be on guard against a possible attack by Cameron. We'll determine what is to be done about your marriage to Rionna."

Caelen nodded his agreement. "For now our focus should be on Mairin's safety and seeing her through the delivery of her child. All else can wait."

Alaric also nodded, relief rushing through his body until the sensation left him light-headed. He knew their clan needed this alliance with the McDonalds. Their future depended on making strong ties with neighboring clans. He even coveted the position of laird of his own clan. But that didn't mean he was in a rush to leave everything he held dear. It didn't mean he was ready to rush into marriage with a woman who inspired nothing within him.

Perhaps that explained his unreasonable attraction to

Keeley. Not only did the lass save him, but proximity and the fact that he was hesitant to bind himself to another woman might account for him wanting her near him. She was a distraction. Aye, nothing more.

Feeling better now that he'd explained away his odd fascination with her, he returned his attention to his brothers.

"I won't be down for long. It's naught but a cut to my side. I'll be up and on the training field in no time. And then we can turn our attention to staining the countryside with Cameron's blood."

Caelen snorted. "A wee cut? You nearly died from that scratch. You'll rest and do as Keeley instructs even if I have to tie you down and sit on you."

Alaric scowled at his younger brother. "This cut won't prevent me from giving you a sound beating."

Caelen rolled his eyes and Ewan scowled at them both. "You act like a bunch of children."

"So says the old married man," Alaric retorted.

Caelen snickered and nodded his agreement. Behind Ewan's back, he made a gesture that signaled Mairin had Ewan by the cock. Alaric choked back his laughter and then groaned at the flash of pain that soared through his midsection.

"'Tis obvious you'll need to spend the next days in bed," Ewan said grimly. "Caelen is right. If we have to tie you down, we'll do it. Don't test me on this, brother."

Alaric blew out his breath. "I've no need of your coddling. Leave off. I'll get out of the bed when I'm good and bloody ready. As it happens, I'm in no hurry. I intend to allow Keeley to wait on me hand and foot."

Caelen shook his head. "I've no idea what you see in that prickly lass. She has the appeal of a hedgehog."

"Then I won't have to warn you off her, will I?" Alaric said with a grin.

"Remember your duty and your forthcoming marriage," Ewan said quietly.

Alaric sobered. " 'Tis all I can think of, Ewan. I'm not likely to forget."

Ewan rose. "We'll leave you to rest now. Keeley should be back up with your meal in a moment's time. Then perhaps you should allow the lass to go to her chamber and rest. She has attended you for the last days without sleep."

Alaric nodded, but he had no intention of allowing her to sleep alone in her chamber. She would remain with him. In his arms.

As his brothers went to exit, Keeley came in bearing a trencher in one hand and a goblet in the other. Alaric stared at her flushed face. Aye, she looked tired. Worn through. She'd been diligent in her care of him.

He was still ailing. He wasn't even close to feeling himself no matter what he'd told his brothers, but from this moment on, he was going to take care of Keeley and make sure she had the rest she needed.

Keeley eyed his brothers with irritation, which amused Alaric. She stepped around them and didn't spare them another glance as she walked over to Alaric's bedside.

"I have broth and some ale. I wanted water, but Gertie insisted that a braw man should drink ale if he wants to regain his strength."

"Gertie has the right of it. Good stout ale will cure damn near anything."

Keeley wrinkled her nose but didn't argue. "Can you sit up?"

Alaric glanced down, then gingerly planted his elbow in the mattress to give himself a shove upward.

Agony lanced up his side, stealing his breath. He froze, panting softly as a red haze settled over his vision.

Keeley made a sound of alarm and then suddenly she was there. Surrounding him with her arms and her softness. Some of the vicious pain subsided and he drew in steadying breaths as he leaned into her.

She jerked several pillows behind him, then eased him back until he was propped against the wall. "Slowly, warrior. I know it hurts."

He lay there panting, a sheen of sweat on his forehead. Nausea welled in his belly and it was all he could do not to lean over and heave. Jesu, but that little cut in his side hurt like the devil.

He started to protest when she moved away, but before he could open his mouth, she was back, trencher and ale in hand. She gave him the goblet and then slid onto the bed beside him, her curvy body nestling against his side.

"Sip slowly until your stomach has settled," she murmured.

How she knew he was on the verge of retching his guts up he didn't know, but he made sure to follow her advice and took wary sips of the strong brew.

After a few swallows, he grimaced and set the goblet away. "I think you had the right of it, Keeley. I think plain water would be easier on my stomach. 'Tis the truth the ale seems to sour it all the more."

"Here," she said in a gentle voice. "Sip at the broth from the trencher. See if that does the trick. I'll go down and fetch some water for you in a moment."

"Nay, don't move." He threw back his head and bellowed Gannon's name.

Keeley jumped beside him and drew in her breath.

"Sorry, lass," he said. "I didn't mean to frighten you."

They had only a moment to wait before the door burst open and Gannon stuck his head in. Keeley shot him a bemused look and Alaric chuckled.

" 'Tis his duty to remain outside my chamber in case I have need of anything. I knew he wouldn't be far."

"Was this merely a test?" Gannon grumbled.

"Nay, I require water and didn't want Keeley to have to fetch it herself. She's tired and has galloped up the stairs more than enough already."

"I'll return in a moment," Gannon said as he withdrew.

"Think you that you can down some of the broth now? If you're finished bellowing at your men?"

Alaric grinned at the sour note in her voice. "I might have need of you to help me. I'm feeling rather weak."

Keeley rolled her eyes, but she turned into him, balancing the trencher in her palm as she guided it to his mouth. "Sip at it," she directed. "Not too fast. Let it settle in your stomach before you take more."

Alaric sucked some of the liquid into his mouth and savored the soothing warmth as it slipped down his throat. More than the comfort of the broth, Keeley's tender regard brushed over his senses and soothed the incessant ache at his side.

Her knuckles grazed his lips as she maneuvered to get closer to him. She knelt up and leaned over, giving him an eyeful of her cleavage. The delectable mounds peeked above the neckline of her smock, and his gaze was riveted. He held his breath, waiting to see if the dress would move lower.

He could fair taste her already, and it was all he could do not to lean in and nuzzle the sweet, soft flesh.

She palmed his chin and lifted until his gaze met hers again. Brown. Rich brown pools with tiny flecks of gold and green. Thick lashes fringed her eyes, making them larger and more exotic looking.

"Drink," she directed.

He allowed her complete control. Whatever she dictated, he obeyed. She stroked his cheek as she tilted the trencher to allow him more of the broth. With each brush of her flesh against his, his body stirred and tightened uncomfortably. He wouldn't have thought his cock would possibly react when he was in so much pain, but he strained the limits of his trews. The ache was becoming intolerable and as uncomfortable as the pain in his side.

Before he realized it, he'd drained the trencher of the broth and Keeley slowly pulled it away, and with it her palm.

His protest bubbled on his lips and escaped in a throaty growl.

"Do you want more?" she asked huskily.

"Aye," he whispered.

"I'll call for more."

"Nay."

"Nay?"

" 'Tis not what I want."

Her eyes glowed and she stared at him, her gaze stroking over his face. "What do you want, warrior?"

He reached down and threaded his fingers through hers. He raised her hand and cradled his cheek in her palm. He rubbed back and forth until the pleasure was nearly too much to bear.

"I want you near me."

"I've already said I won't leave," she chided softly.

The door opened again, and Alaric cursed when Keeley all but leapt from his arms. She straightened her skirts and busied herself with putting the trencher and goblet away while Gannon handed Alaric the tin of water.

He drank thirstily, wanting Gannon to be gone as quickly as possible. When he had drained the tin, he thrust it back at Gannon. "Be sure we aren't disturbed. Keeley must rest."

"Me?"

Keeley's mouth dropped open and her eyes narrowed. "If I'm not mistaken, 'tis you who have suffered serious injury."

Alaric nodded. "Aye, and you've gone without rest ever since."

She closed her mouth and he smiled at the weary set to her eyes. She was fierce with regard to her duties, but she was also exhausted and she wasn't going to further argue the need for her rest.

Her shoulders sagged and Alaric motioned for Gannon to come closer.

"Have a bath drawn for Keeley," he murmured to his man. "You can have the tub brought up here and placed in the corner so she has privacy."

Gannon raised one eyebrow but didn't argue. He turned and left the chamber and Alaric settled back onto the bed, content to watch as Keeley puttered around the room doing this and that in a clear effort to avoid him.

When another knock sounded, Keeley frowned but went to answer. Alaric grinned when she backed away, eyes wide at the men who carted the large tub into the room. They were followed by a parade of women, each bearing a steaming bucket of water.

Keeley shot Alaric a frown. "You cannot wet your stitches."

" 'Tis not for me."

Keeley's brows drew together. "Who is it for then?"

"You."

Her eyes widened and she glanced between where the water was being emptied into the tub and Alaric, as if she had no idea what to say. When she opened her mouth, he brought his finger to his lips in a motion to silence her.

She marched across the room and perched on the edge of his bed. "Alaric, I can't bathe in here!"

"I won't look," he said innocently.

She glanced longingly at the tub. Steam rose as the last of the water was poured in.

"If you don't hurry, the water will grow too cool," he said.

Gannon came in then with a tall wooden barrier that folded in the middle. "I've borrowed Mairin's privacy board," he said to Keeley.

Alaric shot him a glare, but Gannon made certain not to meet his gaze.

"Privacy board?" Keeley stared at the contraption in puzzlement.

"Aye, she had it built to shield her tub so she could bathe in private," Gannon explained.

Keeley smiled in delight as it was set up and completely obscured the view of the tub. "It's perfect!"

Gannon returned her smile and then extended a bundle of clothing toward her. "Mairin sent you a new dress to change into. She said to tell you that on the morrow the ladies will have more to give you."

Warmth suffused Keeley's eyes and cheeks. "Thank Mairin and the other women for me," she said softly.

Gannon nodded and turned to follow the women out, shutting the door behind him.

Keeley fingered the material of the dress, a wistful expression on her face. Then she glanced up at Alaric. "I'll hurry."

Alaric shook his head. "No need. Take as long as you like. I'm feeling much better after taking sustenance. I'm just going to lie back and get comfortable."

He broke into a cold sweat when Keely ducked behind the screen and moments later her dress flew over the top, hanging on the edge.

She was naked behind that piece of wood. He cursed Gannon for his interference because now he was stuck in bed imagining long slender legs, perfect breasts, and curvy hips shielding curls that were likely as dark as her hair.

He closed his eyes when he heard the splash of water.

Her sigh of contentment tightened his scrotum and his cock strained relentlessly upward, so hard and erect that he thought he might split his flesh.

He reached down with his left hand, shoving impatiently at his laces. His fingers bumped into his rigid flesh and he circled the base, gripping tight. Up and down he worked, nearly groaning aloud at the wicked tightness.

She made little humming noises, and he closed his eyes as he imagined her picking up one leg at a time and running a washing cloth down the length and back up again.

Jesu. He couldn't finish this.

The hell he couldn't. He'd take her leftover bath water. He needed to scrub the blood from his side anyway. She'd done an excellent job of keeping him clean. Even his hair. He remembered every minute of her washing his hair. Never before had a woman tended him in such an intimate manner.

He'd give anything to be able to slip behind her and return the favor. He'd wash every inch of her delectable body and run his fingers through her silken strands.

He exerted firmer pressure around his shaft, rolling the foreskin over the head, pressing and then sliding down again. His breaths came rapidly. He closed his eyes and imagined her on her knees in front of him, her lips parted to accept him.

His hands delving into her hair, holding her tight as he guided his cock into the velvet heat of her mouth. Sinking deep. Back and forth, her tongue rubbing erotically over the crown.

Fire gathered in his groin. His sac tightened unbearably and his release boiled like a cauldron low and then rising. Racing up his shaft. Faster and harder he worked his hand. Ignoring the screaming pain in his side, he bowed his back and arched upward, his toes curling as his semen spurted onto his belly.

It was painful in its intensity. The most violent release of his life. Jesu, and he hadn't even touched her yet. How much more incredible would it be if he was deep in her body or her mouth surrounded him?

The sound of water raining down alerted him to the fact that she was rising from the tub. He moaned and slowly worked the last vestiges of his release from his shaft before finally allowing his cock to fall limply to the side. He pulled his trews back over his groin, wincing as the material brushed over his sensitive flesh.

Keeley peeked her head around the side of the wood barrier. "Are you all right? I thought I heard you."

"I'm well," he croaked. "If you are finished, I'd like to wash as well. I'll be careful not to wet my stitches."

She frowned but didn't argue. She disappeared behind the wood again and he heard the rustle of material as she finished drying and then dressed. A few minutes later, she reappeared, clad in a fresh dress, her cheeks flushed from the heat of the water. Her long hair lay in a damp trail down her back, resting just above the small of her back.

"While you bathe, I'll dry my hair by the fire," she said.

He started to push himself upward but caught his breath and remained still when his side protested.

She rushed forward, reaching for his arm. "Let me help you. Lean into me. Take hold of my waist and let me pull you until you can gain your footing."

He needed no invitation to curl his arm around her waist and bury his face in the softness of her belly. He inhaled her clean scent, and the lingering smell of roses tantalized his nose. It was Mairin's soap, but it had never enticed him as it did now on Keeley's skin.

"Come now," she urged in her sweet, husky voice.

He allowed her to pull him forward, but he held her so she didn't stumble. His weight was far too much for her to bear on her own. When he turned so that his feet grazed the floor, he paused for a moment, gathering his strength to rise.

As soon as he stood, the room swam in circles and his knees threatened to buckle. It took everything he had not to go down in a heap. He also became aware of a most pressing need.

With a grimace he wrapped an arm around Keeley's shoulders to steady himself.

"I have need of the chamber pot," he said gruffly. "Perhaps 'twould be best if you stepped from the room a moment." He had no desire to horrify her with his personal needs.

Her expression softened and she smiled up at him. "Who do you think has helped you accomplish your needs for the past days, warrior?"

Heat crept up his neck until he was sure he was blushing like a maiden.

"I'll forget you said that."

She laughed and slipped from underneath his arm. "Are you certain you'll be all right? I'll just be right outside. If you have need of me just holler. I'll give you a moment to get into the tub and then I'll return."

Alaric nodded and watched as she walked to the door. Once there, she turned and gifted him with a shy smile that sent a shiver of pleasure down his spine. Then she exited and closed the door behind her.

Feeling like an old, decrepit man, Alaric completed his business and then went about the task of easing into the tub. He found it easier to kneel on one knee instead of sitting all the way down. He never understood the pleasures of a bath. He much preferred a swim in the loch with his brothers. The basin seemed much too small for a man his size and it was awkward as hell to maneuver in.

Still, he managed to wash himself the best he could. When he was satisfied that he'd done an adequate job, he braced his palms on the sides of the tub and pushed upward with a grunt.

"Alaric?"

Keeley's voice drifted through the wood barrier and he went still, a drying cloth in his hand.

"Aye."

"Are you well? Do you need help?"

He was sorely tempted to tell her aye, but he couldn't bring himself to be that underhanded.

"Look in my chest at the foot of the bed and bring me a clean pair of trews."

A moment later she put her hand around the side of the barrier and held out his trews to him.

"Are you sure you'll be able to get them on?" she asked doubtfully.

"I'll manage."

Several painful minutes later, he trudged around the side of the barrier, sure he was as white as a sheet. She took one look at him and immediately wrapped her arm around his waist, taking care not to touch his wound.

"You should have let me help you," she chided. "You're in pain."

He eased onto the bed with her help and positioned himself on his back. His strength was flagging, but he held up his hand to her.

"Lie with me, Keeley. We both have need of rest. I'll sleep better with you by my side."

Her eyes glowed and her cheeks pinkened, but she slipped her hand into his and allowed him to pull her down to the mattress.

"'Tis the truth I'm tired," she whispered.

"Aye, you have every reason to be."

He slid his hand up and down her back and rested his chin on the top of her head. Gradually she relaxed until she was limp and soft against him.

"Keeley?"

"Aye?" she asked sleepily.

"Thank you for giving me aid and for returning with my brothers to tend me."

She was silent for a moment, and then she slipped her hand into his. "You're welcome, warrior."

CHAPTER 11

Keeley sighed and burrowed closer to the source of heat. She gave a lazy yawn and nearly purred at the large hand rubbing up and down her back. 'Twas a wondrous way to awaken.

Then she remembered that she was in bed with Alaric McCabe and it could only be his hand wandering aimlessly across her back.

She lifted her head and found him staring down at her. His hand moved up to her hair and he gently massaged her nape. She was hesitant to speak, to break the peaceful still that had invaded the chamber.

Soft light poured through the gap in the furs at the window, and the fire had once again died down to a bed of glowing embers.

Alaric was propped above her, his long hair streaming over his broad shoulders. He looked deliciously savage, but content as well. No pain darkened his gaze. Nay, something else entirely blazed in his depths. Something that made her itchy and warm inside and out.

She licked her lips nervously and his gaze darkened further, until the green of his eyes was a slim ring around the dilated black of his pupils. His mouth parted and his breaths came in uneven jerks. His hand tightened around her nape and before she could process the situation, he pulled her to him, bending his head to meet her lips.

It was a gentle kiss. Barely a brush across her tingling mouth, but how sweet it tasted. He came back again, this time pressing his mouth to the corner of hers. His tongue lapped out, warm and rough, dragging over the curve of her mouth and then running along the seam, demanding her lips to part.

Unable to deny him anything, she opened and allowed him entrance. He probed cautiously as if savoring the first meeting of their tongues. In a delicate dance, the tips dueled, withdrawing and then advancing more boldly, brushing over the other in a heady rasp.

"You taste so sweet," Alaric whispered.

His voice sent shivers down her spine, but it also awakened her to what they were doing. She was lying in his bed, half sprawled atop him while he kissed her senseless.

And he was betrothed to another.

That last thought was as effective as dousing her with cold water.

"Keeley, what is it?"

She pried herself from his grasp and put space between them, though she was still perched on his bed.

" 'Tis wrong," she murmured. "You are betrothed to another."

Alaric frowned. "Who told you of this?"

She frowned back. " 'Tis no matter who told me. 'Tis what is true. You belong to another. It isn't right for you to kiss me and hold me so."

"I am not betrothed to her yet."

Keeley sighed. " 'Tis a rotten excuse and well you know it. Do you have plans not to marry her?"

Alaric's lips thinned, but he shook his head. "Nay. 'Tis a marriage of necessity. A union needed to secure our alliance with the McDonalds."

It shouldn't hurt her to hear what she already knew. What was this man to her, after all? He was naught but someone who needed her aid. Nothing more. A few shared kisses did not a future make. Surely she didn't fancy herself in love with him?

She shook her head to rid herself of such an absurd notion. Rionna was a laird's daughter. Keeley was nothing. She had naught to bring to a marriage save herself. No connections. No dowry. Not even the support of her clan.

"Then 'tis the wrong woman you're kissing," she said lightly.

Alaric sighed and leaned his head back on his pillow. "You cannot expect me to ignore this attraction between us, Keeley. I couldn't even if I wanted. 'Tis the strongest reaction I've ever had to a woman. I burn for you, lass."

Keeley closed her eyes. Her throat tightened and she swallowed against the restriction. When she reopened them, she saw answering agony in Alaric's gaze.

"Tell me, warrior. What happens to me?" she asked softly. "Am I to give myself to you only to watch you wed another? What becomes of me when you become laird of the McDonald clan?"

Alaric reached out to touch her cheek. "I would see you well cared for. You have to know that. I would do nothing to cause you shame or disgrace."

She smiled faintly. Shame and disgrace were things she was well accustomed to. "If you care for me at all, you'll not pursue whatever is between us."

He looked as if he would argue, but she pressed her finger over his lips in gentle reproach.

" 'Tis dawn now. We've slept the night away. I must see to your wound and call for a meal to break your fast. Then I must see your laird to determine my place in this keep."

"He'll see to your care," Alaric said tightly. "If he doesn't, he'll answer to me."

She let her hand fall away and then she busied herself inspecting the stitches on his side.

"The redness is almost gone," she said. "A few more days' rest and I'll allow you out of bed as long as you don't go back to fighting the moment your feet hit the floor."

Her attempt at levity was wasted. Alaric still stared at her, his eyes bleak and full of regret. She looked away and then pushed herself from the bed.

She went to the window, and pushed aside the furs to allow fresh air and the morning sun in. For a moment she stood there, cursing fate and its inevitable grasp. She gripped the sill until her knuckles were white and faced sunrise with all the sadness and regret in her heart.

Her life—her future—had been determined by the actions of others. She'd sworn that never again would her fate be left up to others. But now, deciding her own had a decidedly unsatisfactory feeling.

She'd done what was right. She'd taken a stand to protect herself . . . from what? Unhappiness? Disgrace?

It should feel better. She alone decided the course of her fate. Instead, she was left with a hollow ache in her chest and a fleeting sense of unfulfilled desires.

She chanced another glance at Alaric to see his eyes closed, his head unmoved from his pillow. Aye, 'twas for the best. He could never be hers. If she agreed to an affair, it would only hurt her more to let him go. Better she never know the joys of his loving.

Taking a deep breath, she squared her shoulders and crossed the chamber to the door. It was time to determine the rest of her destiny. Ewan McCabe had abducted the wrong person. He was going to tell her of his plans and offer some guarantees if she was going to remain for Lady McCabe's birthing.

She left the room and nearly stumbled over Gannon who sat in the hallway, his head resting against the wall. He came to attention immediately and scrambled to his feet. Alaric hadn't exaggerated when he'd said that his man would remain outside in case he was needed.

"Is there something I can do for you?" Gannon inquired politely.

She shook her head. "Nay. Alaric is doing well. I'm going belowstairs to speak to the laird and to ask for a meal so that Alaric may break his fast."

An uneasy expression flashed on Gannon's face. "Perhaps it would be best if I went to the laird with any requests you have."

She narrowed her gaze at the much bigger warrior. "*I* don't think it's best. If you want to help, you can go down to the kitchens and have a meal brought up to Alaric's chamber. I'll be with the laird if you need me."

Not giving the warrior a chance to argue his point, she strode past him to the stairs and hurried down. Once in the great hall, she surveyed the interior curiously. There was a flurry of activity as women passed back and forth doing their duties.

Though she'd spoken bravely to Gannon, she had no idea where to seek out the laird. And she was nervous, despite her earlier bravado.

"Keeley! Is there something I can help you with?"

Keeley turned to see Maddie approaching from the kitchens.

"Where might I find the laird?"

Maddie frowned. "He's out training with his men in the courtyard."

Keeley smiled. "My thanks."

As she turned to go, Maddie called after her, "The laird doesn't like to be disturbed when he's training!"

"Aye, well I don't like to be disturbed when I'm in my cottage asleep in my bed," Keeley grumbled under her breath. That didn't stop the laird from bursting in and spiriting her away.

She paused in the doorway leading to the courtyard and sucked in her breath at the sight of so many warriors, all engaged in sparring, swordplay, and archery. There were hundreds, and the sounds of their fighting nearly deafened her.

Holding her hands to her ears, she descended into the courtyard and warily skirted the perimeter looking for the laird. She stopped when a snowflake drifted by her nose and she looked up to see that it was indeed snowing. She hadn't even noticed, so intent was she on finding the laird.

Shivering, she hunched her shoulders forward and resumed her search.

When she rounded the side of the wall of men, she came face-to-face with the laird and his brother, both of whom stood surveying their men's progress.

Caelen's scowl was instantaneous, but the laird wasn't far behind once he caught sight of her.

"Is something amiss?" the laird demanded. "How does Alaric fare?"

"Alaric is well. His wound is healing and his fever has abated. I didn't come to speak to you of Alaric."

"I'm busy," the laird said shortly. "Whatever it is can wait."

He turned his back on her dismissively and Keeley's blood boiled.

"Nay, Laird. It will not wait." She stamped her foot for emphasis and made sure her voice could be heard above the din.

The laird stiffened and then turned slowly back to stare at her. Around them, activity ceased. Swords were lowered as the men stopped to look at Keeley.

"What did you say?" he asked in a dangerously low voice.

Caelen stared at her in disbelief and then looked to his brother as if confirming that she'd dared argue with the laird.

She raised her chin, refusing to back down. Even if her knees were quaking abysmally. "I said it won't wait."

"Is that so? Tell me then. What's so important that you would interrupt my men in training? You have all our attention now. Don't be timid."

"I've never been accused of being timid," she said dryly. "And what is important is that I know of your plans for me. You've taken me from my home to care for your brother and you expect that I attend Lady McCabe at her time. I refuse to be treated as a prisoner. I would know my place in your clan."

Ewan McCabe arched one eyebrow as he continued to stare at her. "Have you been treated with anything but respect thus far? I assure you, I don't give my prisoners their own chamber nor do I give them leave to make requests of my serving staff. I have a dungeon where my prisoners are made welcome."

She refused to be cowed by the sternness in his voice. She met his gaze and stiffened her spine. "I would know exactly my position here, Laird. So there is no misunderstanding at a later date. I've had to give up the only home and security I know. I'm used to living on my own and abiding by only my rules. I find I don't obey the dictates of others so easily."

Ewan's expression darkened until she was sure he might explode. Then to her utter amazement he threw back his head and laughed. "Tell me, Keeley, have you been speaking to my wife? Did she put you up to this?"

Around him, his men began laughing. Even Caelen lost his scowl for the barest of moments.

She looked at them all in bewilderment. "Why would Lady McCabe have me talk to you? I haven't seen her this morn."

Ewan's shoulders heaved in an exaggerated sigh. "Jesu, I'm cursed to have two women who insist on defying me at every turn."

"Just remember it was your idea," Caelen muttered.

Ewan raised his hand as laughter rose again from his ranks. Keeley viewed him anxiously. They seem to think it was all a jest. She was entirely serious, and it infuriated her that they could laugh when she'd been abducted and forced from her home—and worse, her independence.

Her face tight and teeth clenched, she whirled around and stalked back toward the keep. It crossed her mind that she wanted to go up to Alaric and unload her frustration and anger, but it would only cause dissention between him and his brothers. The last thing he needed right now was that.

She was almost to the keep when a strong hand clamped down on her shoulder and turned her around. She balled her fist and swung. Caelen's eyes widened in shock just before he dodged his head to the side and popped up his hand to block her blow.

"God's teeth, woman. Stand down."

"Remove your hand from my person," she snapped.

"Keeley, I would speak to you," Ewan said in a grim voice.

She looked beyond Caelen to see Ewan standing a foot behind his brother. She wrenched her hand from Caelen's grasp and took a step backward.

"I think you've said enough, Laird."

"Nay, I don't think so. Come inside. We'll speak in the hall while I break my fast. Have you eaten yet? It's my practice to eat with my wife. She sleeps longer now that she's heavy with child."

Keeley issued a short nod and waited for the laird to precede her into the keep. Caelen backed away and with a last glance in Keeley's direction returned to where the men were training.

When they entered the hall, the places were being set and Mairin was already at the table. Her face lit up when she set eyes on Ewan and she started to rise.

"Nay, sweeting, don't get up," he said, placing a hand on her shoulder as he walked past her. He paused and dropped a kiss on her temple and gifted her with a smile that made Keeley wistful to her toes.

As he sat, he motioned for Keeley to sit on his other side across from Mairin.

"Good morning, Keeley," Mairin said, offering a smile in her direction.

"Good morning, Mairin," Keeley returned.

"How is Alaric?" Mairin asked.

Keeley gave her a reassuring smile. "He is much better this morning. His fever has abated and I've instructed him to rest for the next few days."

" 'Tis wonderful to hear, and we owe it all to you," Mairin said.

Ewan cleared his throat and glanced up at Keeley as the serving women came in with trenchers of food. "While the circumstances of your coming here were less than desirable, 'tis my wish that you stay on with us, at least until Mairin has safely delivered our child. She means everything to me. I want the best care I can give her."

"Your regard is admirable, Laird. Your lady wife is fortunate to have a husband so concerned with her welfare."

"I sense a but in your statement," Ewan said dryly.

"I want your guarantee of my status here," Keeley returned. "I want the freedom to come and go as I please."

Ewan sat back and studied her for a long moment. "If I give you these freedoms, do I have your word that you won't leave my lands?"

Keeley sucked air through her nose. Once given, her word would not be broken. Which meant she would stay the winter with the McCabes. She'd been in constant proximity to Alaric and temptation like she'd never known.

She glanced at Mairin who looked both delicate and tired, and she looked at the love and concern in the laird's eyes. He truly loved his wife and feared for her welfare. If Keeley could alleviate that worry and see Mairin through the birth of her child, it would please her.

"Aye. You have my word."

Ewan nodded. " 'Tis important for you to know that your freedoms come with conditions. You aren't ever to leave the keep unescorted. We have enemies who would use whatever means necessary to strike at us."

"I can live with those conditions."

"Aye, Keeley. You will have a respected and revered position in our clan. Though I brought you here to tend to Alaric and to deliver my child, 'tis the truth we have no healer and the members of my clan will have need of your services between now and the time Mairin delivers. I would hope that you see fit to help them. If you give your allegiance willingly, you will be treated as a McCabe, which means you never have to want for whatever we can provide."

His speech was earnest and sincere. He didn't look to be a man who offered deceit. Nay, he was a man of honor. She'd wager all she owned on it.

"I will do as you wish, Laird," she murmured.

Mairin clapped her hands together in delight. " 'Tis wonderful news! 'Twill be nice to have another woman in the keep. Perhaps you can teach me some of your skills, Keeley."

"As if we don't have enough women," Ewan grumbled. "You already shamelessly run over the men of the keep."

Mairin covered her mouth with her hand, but her eyes twinkled merrily in Keeley's direction.

"After the meal, Maddie and I will show you the clothes we've gathered for you. Then I'll show you around the keep and introduce you to the clan. Everyone is excited to learn we have a new healer," Mairin said.

Keeley smiled at the other woman. "Thank you. I'd like that."

After a light repast, Ewan pushed away from the table and leaned down to kiss Mairin's cheek. "I must return to the men. Make sure you keep Gannon and Cormac with you while you give Keeley the tour."

Mairin rolled her eyes as Ewan walked away.

"I saw that, Mairin," Ewan growled.

Mairin grinned and waved her hand in dismissal. "Do you need to check in on Alaric before we begin?" she asked Keeley.

"He'll be fine," Keeley said quickly. "He was resting comfortably when I left his chamber, and Gannon was bringing him up something to eat. I'll check in on him once we've finished touring the keep."

Mairin nodded and then rose clumsily from her seat. "Come then. I'll introduce you around to the women."

CHAPTER 12

Throughout the tour of the keep and the cottages that
dotted the hillside just outside the stone skirt, Mairin
kept up a steady conversation. Keeley's head spun
through most of it, but she tried to hone in when people's names were mentioned.

Mairin didn't give Keeley's surname, and many of the
McCabes viewed her with suspicion, though some were
warm and welcoming.

Christina, a young girl perhaps a year or two younger
than Keeley, was vivacious with sparkling eyes and a
ready smile. It was nice to feel an immediate kinship
with the other woman.

Keeley smothered a smile at the obvious flirtation between Christina and Cormac. Neither could keep their
eyes from the other but both fiercely pretended disinter-
est.

They circled to the back of the keep where a group of
children were valiantly trying to scrape up the smatter-
ing of snow on the ground. The flakes had stopped falling for now, though a look at the sky told Keeley they
would begin falling again at any moment.

One of the boys looked up and when he saw Mairin,
he left the crowd of children and ran straight toward
Mairin and Keeley.

"Mama!"

The child threw his arms around Mairin while Mairin hugged him close. Keeley watched with interest. Mairin looked far too young to have birthed a child of this age.

Mairin scrubbed the top of the boy's head and then turned to Keeley, an indulgent smile on her face. "Crispen, I'd like you to meet Keeley. She'll be staying with us for a while and lending us her healing skills."

Keeley extended her hand in a solemn gesture. " 'Tis wonderful to meet you, Crispen."

He cocked his head and looked up at Keeley. Keeley was surprised to see anxiety flashing in the boy's eyes.

"Are you here to attend my mama when her time comes?"

Keeley's heart softened at the worry she heard for Mairin. What a sweet boy. She wanted to gather him in her arms and hug him tight. Mairin looked close to doing the same.

"Aye, Crispen. I've delivered many a babe. I'll be attending your mother when 'tis her time to deliver."

Relief washed through the child's eyes and he grinned broadly. " 'Tis good, that. Papa and I want her to have the best. She's carrying my brother or sister!"

Keeley smiled. "Indeed she is. Do you have a preference as to boy or girl?"

Crispen wrinkled his nose and then glanced back at the group of children who were shouting for him to return. "I wouldn't mind a sister as long as she wasn't like Gretchen. But a brother would be nicer to play with."

Mairin chuckled. "I think we've established that Gretchen is one of a kind, dearling. Run back and go play. I must finish showing Keeley around the keep."

Crispen gave her another quick hug and then bounded back to the noisy pack in the distance.

Keeley shot Mairin an inquisitive look, not knowing where to start with the questions. Mairin shook her head. "Gretchen is a strong-minded young lady who will no doubt rule the world one day. She is the bane of Crispen and the other boys' existence. When she's not besting them in mock war play, she insists that she will one day become a warrior."

Keeley grinned, easily searching out the girl named Gretchen in the group. She was sitting astride one of the boys, holding his arms to the ground while he shouted his protests.

"Crispen is Ewan's son from his first marriage," Mairin explained. "His wife passed when Crispen was but a babe."

" 'Tis obvious he holds you in high regard."

Mairin's face softened. "I am heavy with a child of my own, but Crispen will always be my first. The child of my heart though he didn't come from my womb. He is the reason I came to Ewan. He brought me here."

Impulsively Keeley reached over and squeezed Mairin's hand. "You are a very fortunate woman. 'Tis obvious the laird loves you dearly."

"You must stop. You'll have me all weepy." Mairin sniffed. "I cry over the least little thing these days. It drives Ewan daft. All his men avoid me for fear of doing or saying something to make me cry."

Keeley chuckled. "You aren't the only lass who suffers so. Many of the women I've attended find themselves overly emotional. Particularly as their time draws near."

They continued to walk along the hillside farther from the children and as they circled around the keep, Cormac at their heels, the courtyard came into view. At first Keeley paid little attention to the goings on. Men spent their time fighting. 'Twas the life of a warrior. A man had to be prepared to defend his home at all times.

But then a particular warrior caught her eyes. He wasn't practicing. He didn't even hold a sword. He stood to the side with the laird watching as the other men sparred.

"That bloody fool," Keeley muttered.

"What?" Mairin asked in a startled voice.

Ignoring both Mairin and Cormac, Keeley charged down the hill toward the courtyard, fury bubbling with each stomp.

"Ignorant, stubborn, impossible fool!"

She hadn't realized that the men had paused the moment she came into the courtyard or that her words flew like arrows. Ewan tilted his head heavenward as if praying for patience while Alaric grinned and put his arms out to ward off her impending attack.

"You were saying?" Alaric asked when she came to a stop in front of him.

"What do you think you're doing?" she demanded. "I told you to stay abed. In your chamber. To rest! You shouldn't be outside in the cold. You shouldn't even be on your feet. How can I tend you when you won't listen to even the most common sense directives?"

Alaric winced while Caelen chuckled. Alaric shot his brother a dark look.

"I believe the lass just suggested you're lacking in common sense," Caelen drawled. "Clearly I didn't give her enough credit. She is an astute lass, indeed."

Alaric turned, fist raised when Keeley grabbed his wrist and forced him to face her. Then she rounded furiously on the laird and Caelen.

"You two are just as guilty of lacking in common sense. Why didn't you insist your brother return to his chamber the moment he stepped outside?"

"He isn't a child to be coddled," Ewan growled. "You'll stop with your insults immediately."

"This has nothing to do with being a child. The man clearly has no judgment. It's up to you to lay down the law. You are laird, are you not? Would you allow one of your other warriors to endanger his health by rising too soon from his sick bed? Would you then explain a defeat in battle away by saying that the warrior wasn't a child to be coddled when he wasn't present to help you defend your keep because he lies in a cold grave?"

"The lass has a solid point," Caelen pointed out. "And I'd also like to offer that 'twas me who suggested you were a dolt for being up."

Ewan scowled. He clearly had no liking for being reprimanded by a woman. By this time, Mairin and Cormac had arrived in the courtyard and Ewan looked even less happy that his wife was present.

"Mairin, you should not be out in the cold," he said sternly.

Keeley gaped at him. "Oh, so you'd reprimand your wife who is hale and hearty, but not your brother who has only just recovered from his fever and has many days to go before he is well enough to be out of his bed?"

"God spare me," Ewan muttered.

Keeley returned fiercely to Alaric. "Are you trying to kill yourself? Have you no care for your well being?" She poked him in the chest and rose up on tiptoe so she could look him more squarely in the eye. "If you tear my stitches, I'll not repair them. You'll have to bleed to death. The wound will fester and your flesh will rot away, but don't expect any help from my quarter. Stubborn, infuriating man."

Alaric placed both hands on her shoulders and squeezed gently. "Keeley, lass, please. Calm down. I'm feeling quite well. My side still pains me. I know I'm not fully recovered, but if I spent one more moment behind the closed door of my chamber, I'd go mad. I needed but a bit of fresh air."

"Well you've had your fresh air," Ewan grumbled. "Now get your arse back to your chamber so that we can restore peace around here." He pinned Mairin and Keeley both with the full force of his glare. "And the both of you will return indoors immediately. When I agreed to a tour, I didn't mean the whole of our lands, Mairin."

Mairin smiled serenely but didn't look in the least intimidated by her husband.

"And you!" Keeley said, directing her outrage toward Gannon who was standing on Alaric's other side. "Was your duty not to make sure Alaric didn't do anything foolish?"

Gannon's mouth popped open and his lips flapped up and down but nothing came out. He looked to Ewan for help, but the laird was too busy shaking his head.

Keeley didn't waste a moment longer. She latched on to Alaric's arm and began pulling him toward the steps entering the keep. Alaric chuckled but followed behind her and allowed her to guide him inside and up the stairs.

All the way up to his chambers, she lectured him about taking better care of himself. How else was she to impress upon him the seriousness of his injuries? 'Twas no small scrape he'd suffered. If the cut had gone any deeper, it would surely have gutted him. He would have bled to death long before he could have sought aid from her.

She shoved him inside his chamber and then slammed the door behind them.

"You're mad," she said. "Completely and utterly mad. Now we must get those boots off you. How on earth did you get them on? It must have been agony. And your tunic."

Alaric eased onto the edge of the bed and extended his foot to her.

"You want me to take your boots off? You put them on. You can bloody well take them off."

"Has anyone ever told you that you have what could possibly be the most outrageous, delectable, enticing, incredible mouth?"

She halted her tirade and stared dumbly at him. "I—you—what?" she sputtered.

He grinned, making a dimple appear in the side of his cheek. Lord, but the man was simply irresistible.

"Come here," he ordered, crooking his finger at her.

Too befuddled to do anything but obey, she closed the distance between them and came to stand between his thighs.

"That's better," he murmured. "Now come closer."

He wrapped his arms around her waist and pulled her in until his mouth was a breath from her bosom. That knowledge did peculiar things to her nipples. They hardened and stabbed relentlessly at the bodice of her dress, and they ached as if they'd been stroked by fire.

"You won't ignore me and pretend I'm not here," he reproached. "You won't shut me out."

She placed her hands on his shoulder and looked down at him with a look of consternation. "Is that why you came out of your chamber?"

" 'Twas the only way to get you to attend me again," he said lazily. "Think you I'd put on those boots just to get a breath of fresh air when it's fair freezing out there? You were right, lass. Those boots damn near killed me."

Something twisted in the region of her heart and she shook her head helplessly. "You sore try my patience, warrior. I had tasks to attend to this morn. Including getting the right of things from your brother, and then Mairin showed me around the keep. 'Tis important to meet the people I'm expected to tend to."

"Your first priority is me. I find I don't like it when you're away, lass. You've become as important as the air I breathe. Don't venture far next time. I find I think daft thoughts when left to my own devices."

She sighed. "I think what you are is spoiled. Has anyone ever told you nay?"

"I'm sure they have but at the moment I cannot remember."

"I'll tend you, warrior. You give me no choice if you are to survive. Your impulsiveness is going to kill you."

The triumph in Alaric's eyes sent a giddy thrill down her spine. He pulled at her waist, running his hands up to her nape, grasping and then lowering her until his mouth was on level with hers.

"I know you told me not to kiss you, lass, but I should warn you that I've never been good at taking directions."

CHAPTER 13

He sensed her surrender after a short hesitation, and he took full advantage, pulling her closer until their lips touched. For a moment he remained still, simply absorbing the sensation of her delectable mouth against his. Then he pressed in, moving sensuously over her mouth, harder, deeper until they both gasped for air.

He swallowed her breath, savored it, and then returned it. It was as if he breathed *her*. Absorbed her into his body and she became a living part of him.

Light and delicate, her hands smoothed over his shoulders before cupping his nape. Whether she realized it or not, she gripped him and pulled him into her. She kissed him greedily, fanning the already out-of-control flames licking over his body.

He rubbed his tongue over her upper lip and then flicked inward to run along the inside seam of her mouth. Her tongue crept out cautiously to touch his and he moaned when they finally met and rolled. Playfully at first but then more urgent as if they couldn't get enough and wanted more.

His hands slipped to her face, cupping her and holding her as his fingers delved into her hair. He had too firm a grip. He held her too tightly but he couldn't let go.

He took her whole, devouring her mouth. His tongue thrust deep in a perfect imitation of what he wanted to do with his cock. As hot and moist as her mouth was, as heavenly as she felt, he could only imagine how her tight sheath would surround him with fire and welcome him into her depths.

He had to drag himself away. He was perilously close to spinning her around and pinning her to his mattress. He'd throw up her skirts and have her right here and right now. It was no way to treat her. She deserved a slow and gentle wooing. A lover's kisses and sweet words. She deserved to be told how beautiful she was and how she made him feel as though he were the only man in the world. The last thing he wanted for her was a quick and brutal rutting.

His pulse pounded as he pulled his mouth from hers. "What you do to me, lass," he whispered, each word painful through his tight throat.

It was as though he'd swallowed shards of glass. His skin felt too tight. His body was too heavy. His cock was about to burst out of his trews, and his wound ached like hell fire. And he wanted more of her with every breath he had.

This wasn't him. What he felt bordered on obsession. Nay. Not bordered. It was true obsession. He'd nearly gone mad when she'd left his chamber and hadn't returned. He'd gotten up from his bed, sweating and swearing with each movement. He'd paced his chamber, looked out his window, listened at the door, anxious to hear her light footsteps.

Finally it had been all he could bear. He simply had to get out of his chamber. Outside where he could breathe. Where he could feel more himself and shake off the insanity that gripped him whenever he thought of her. It had to stop.

She unmanned him. She made him feel like a boy who hadn't proved his mettle.

"We can't continue to do this," she whispered back. "Please, Alaric. I don't seem to have the ability to deny you anything."

Her eyes burned bright with a multitude of emotions. Regret. Desire. The tiny golden glints glowed against the brown of her eyes, and her dark brows were drawn together in clear consternation.

They were the words he wanted to hear but not with the distress so evident in her voice. She looked to be near tears and it was his undoing. That she was so close to begging flayed his chest open. He hugged her to him, content to simply hold her as he cursed fate and duty and all the things that conspired to tear this woman from his arms.

"I'm sorry, Keeley. I find I haven't the ability to deny myself the pleasure of your touch. You are an addiction. One I can't readily be free of. I listen to your arguments and I understand them well, but then you look at me or I look at you and all reason flies out the window. I only know that if I don't touch you, if I don't kiss you, I'll go mad."

She cupped his face in her hands and gave him a look so sad that it clenched his stomach into a ball. "So sweet are your words and how heavy they fall on my ears. I take them into my heart and am filled with gladness and longing all at the same time and yet I realize how hopeless such feelings are. You will never be mine, warrior. Just as I'll never be yours. 'Tis madness to continue to torment ourselves."

"I can't—I won't—accept that we cannot be together even for a little while," he whispered. "Isn't any time better than none at all? Isn't a taste of sweet better than a lifetime of bitter regret?"

" 'Tis like a wound. 'Tis better to make a quick, clean

cut and be rid of the pain rather than wait for it to become agonizing."

He closed his eyes at the conviction in her voice. She truly believed what she spoke. It made sense to him, aye. But he didn't agree. Any time to savor her sweetness was better than naught. He just had to convince her.

Slowly he released her. "I'll let you go . . . for now. I do not want to distress you. The last thing I want is to make you sad. I much prefer you reprimanding me or ordering me about with that saucy smile of yours. So smile, Keeley. Smile for me."

The corners of her mouth lifted, but her eyes dripped all the sadness he himself felt. 'Twas madness. Never had he failed to take what he wanted. Never had he been denied by a woman. But Keeley . . . Keeley was different and it was important to woo her patiently. He'd settle for backing away for now. He wanted her willing. He wanted her complete surrender.

"Now if we are finished speaking of things we shouldn't, you need to be back in your bed," she said crisply, all signs of her distress gone.

He stared at her beautiful face and at the stone set to her features. But the truth was in her eyes. They never lied.

"Aye, healer. 'Tis back in my bed I'll go. I find all this activity has drained me of strength."

He leaned cautiously back, resting his head on the soft pillow. His eyes closed as weariness assailed him. And then he felt her warm breath blow over his forehead and the sweet press of her lips against his forehead.

"Sleep then, warrior," she whispered. "I'll be here when you awaken."

He smiled and allowed himself to drift away, her promise held tight to his heart.

CHAPTER 14

Having Keeley in such close proximity was driving him to his wits' end. Though she was careful to keep a respectful and modest distance between them at all times, simply being across the room from her or dining at the same table in the hall was an exercise in frustration.

His wound had taken several more days to heal, and in that time, Keeley had become an expert at erecting a barrier between them. The better he recovered, the more distant she became and the less time she spent with him in his chamber.

In the end, it was the drive to be out of his chamber where he could see more of her that spurred his recovery the most.

He was still sore. His side ached, and if he turned too quickly, he was rewarded with a bolt of pain through his midriff. But he refused to spend another moment staring up at his ceiling, seeking ways to make the hunger go away.

Even now, as he tried to sit and listen to what his brothers were discussing, his gaze kept drifting across the hall where the women of the keep sat in front of the hearth sewing baby clothing for Mairin's child.

Outside, the snow fell and had accumulated on the

ground in small drifts that would grow larger through the night. Everyone had taken shelter indoors and in their cottages. The men were drinking ale and discussing warfare and alliances and, of course, their most hated enemy, Duncan Cameron.

But Alaric heard none of it. He watched as Keeley laughed and her eyes glowed in delight as she chattered with the women in the circle.

Ewan occasionally cast glances in Mairin's direction. It didn't go unnoticed by Alaric, and when Mairin looked up and caught her husband's gaze, in that moment, Alaric envied Ewan with everything he had. Their obvious love and regard for each other made the ache in Alaric's chest grow until it was all he could do not to bolt from the table.

"Snap out of it, Alaric."

Alaric blinked and then glared at Caelen for intruding so rudely on his thoughts.

"What the hell do you want?"

"For you to pay attention. 'Tis important matters we discuss and you're busy mooning over the lass."

Alaric curled his fingers into a fist but didn't respond to Caelen's ribbing.

Ewan frowned as he stared between the brothers. "I was saying that I received a missive from Laird McDonald. He sorely regrets that your travel was interrupted. He sought to seal our alliance as quickly as possible. He grows more uneasy over the idea of Cameron taking over his borders. There is much unrest among our neighbors. They all fear Cameron's might and are looking to us for aid and support."

Alaric glanced at his brother, unease growing in his chest.

"He doesn't want to wait until spring to join our clans through marriage. He also knows I refuse to leave the keep with Mairin's time so close nor will I leave thereafter. He has offered to travel with Rionna after Mairin's babe is born and have the wedding ceremony here."

Alaric forced himself not to outwardly react. He went completely still until he could hear his heart beat against his chest. He wouldn't look at Keeley. He wouldn't think of what he wanted when the future of his clan rested in his hands.

"Alaric? What say you?" Ewan asked.

"'Tis good he is willing to travel here," Alaric said evenly. "We can't afford to leave the keep unguarded nor can we afford to split our defenses by sending a contingent with me. We've already lost a dozen good men."

Ewan stared thoughtfully at Alaric. "So you are willing still to go through with the marriage?"

"I've never said anything to make you think differently."

"It's not what you've said or not said," Ewan said quietly, as his gaze lifted from Alaric and went beyond to where the women sat. "I know you want her."

Alaric refused to turn and follow the direction of Ewan's stare. "What I want is inconsequential. I agreed to the match. I won't go back on my word."

Regret briefly flickered over Ewan's face before he schooled his features and dropped his stare. He faced his two brothers. "'Tis done then. I'll respond to McDonald's message and let him know that we'll receive him after my son or daughter is born. 'Tis likely you and your new bride will have to spend the winter here. The McDonalds' travel here will be arduous enough. 'Tis no reason to risk a return trip until the snows thaw."

The idea of marrying Rionna left a sour enough feeling in his belly but having her here, living as man and wife and him having to see Keeley on a daily basis, was unbearable.

"I'll send her away as soon as she's safely delivered Mairin's babe," Ewan murmured.

Alaric's head snapped up. "Nay! You'll not turn her out in the midst of the winter with no place to go and no home to call her own. I vowed to her that you would provide for her. Swear to me that she'll have a home here for as long as she desires."

Ewan sighed. "Aye, then. I swear it."

"You torture yourself needlessly, brother," Caelen hissed. "Have the lass. Take her and rid yourself of this obsession. Sate yourself and by the time the McDonalds arrive, your blood will be rid of this need."

Alaric stared bleakly at his brother. "Nay, Caelen. I fear I'll never be rid of my need of her. It runs too deep and too hot. And I'll not use her thus. She deserves my respect. She saved my life."

Caelen shook his head but didn't argue further. He drained the rest of his ale and muttered under his breath as he stared into the fire that blazed in the hearth.

Across the room, Mairin rose and instantly put her hand to her back. She looked tired, something that didn't go unnoticed by Ewan. He frowned and quickly stood up. He was across the room in a moment, and leaned down to murmur in her ear. She smiled up at him, and soon Ewan was walking her toward the stairs leading to their chamber.

Alaric gripped his goblet and stared at the swirl of ale still left. He set it down on the table, unable to stomach the thought of swilling more of the stout brew.

"I hate seeing you like this," Caelen muttered. "Go have a tumble with one of the women more than willing to warm your bed. You'll forget the healer. 'Tis unseemly to allow a woman so much power over you."

Alaric smiled faintly. "Clearly you've never wanted a woman in the way I want Keeley."

Caelen's expression darkened and Alaric immediately wished he could call back the ill-spoken words. 'Twas the truth that years ago Caelen had been thoroughly besotted by a woman. He'd declared his love openly for her. He would have died for her. Instead, she betrayed them to Duncan Cameron and their clan lost all, Ewan's young wife and their father. Caelen had never allowed himself to fall under the spell of a woman again. Alaric wasn't even sure if Caelen ever bedded a woman. If he did, he was extremely discreet.

"I'm sorry. That wasn't well done of me," Alaric said.

Caelen raised his goblet to his mouth and stared stonily toward the fire. "'Tis no matter. My mistakes should serve as a warning to you never to allow a woman to lead you about by the cock."

Alaric sighed. "Not all women are of Elsepeth's ilk. Look at Mairin. She serves Ewan well. She is loyal and steadfast. She is a good mother to Crispen and would die for Ewan."

"Mairin is a woman above others," Caelen said stubbornly. "Ewan is fortunate. Most men go a lifetime and will never find a woman who places her husband and clan above herself."

"And Keeley did none of those things by caring for me? How was she to know I wasn't some monster who'd rape and abuse her? She was abducted from her home and brought to live with strangers and yet she still tended me to exhaustion."

Caelen made a sound of annoyance. "'Tis clear you're besotted, and nothing I saw will sway you on the matter. Take my advice, brother. Stay away from the healer. You'll have a wife before winter's over. Nothing good can come of your dalliance with another woman. These are precarious times. You cannot afford to offend McDonald. Too much depends on strong alliances so that Duncan Cameron can be wiped from the face of the earth. As strong as we are, we cannot go after him alone with Mairin close to her time. Once she is safely delivered of the heir to Neamh Álainn, our thoughts and efforts can turn to ridding us of his threat. We need our neighboring clans to unite with us into a formidable force. We may not face just the threat of Duncan Cameron but of Malcolm as well, should Duncan join forces with him to oust David from the throne."

Alaric's lips twisted into a fierce snarl. Caelen acted as though Alaric was a senseless dolt. "You have no need to remind me what is at stake here, Caelen. I'm well aware of the implications of my marriage to Rionna McDonald. I've said I would do my duty. You insult me by suggesting anything less."

Caelen nodded. "My apologies. I'll not broach the subject again."

"Good," Alaric muttered.

He drained the rest of his ale anyway and promptly grimaced as it swirled and bubbled in his gut. He'd partaken too much and his head already ached. Unable to resist, he chanced another look over at Keeley just as she turned her head slightly in his direction.

Their gazes met and locked, and she froze like a doe about to bolt. Her eyes were wide and expressive, and for a moment he saw everything he knew she didn't want him to see. The same longing he felt. The same desire. The same regret.

He dragged his gaze away and swore under his breath. Then he held up his goblet and signaled the serving woman to bring him more.

Suddenly he decided he hadn't had enough to drink. He needed more and then maybe he wouldn't feel the horrible ache that swelled in his belly and thrust upward into his chest.

Maybe he'd forget.

CHAPTER 15

Keeley bundled the heavy fur cape around her as she trudged through the snow toward Maddie's cottage. The afternoon sun was high overhead and glistened off the snow-covered landscape, casting a shine that hurt Keeley's eyes.

Mairin had been ordered to remain inside the keep by the laird, a fact Mairin was none too happy about. Keeley felt disloyal but in this she agreed with the laird. Ewan was afraid that Mairin might fall on the ice and injure herself. She was large and ungainly with the babe and had already nearly fallen down the stairs twice, both times giving Cormac, who was attending her, failure of the heart.

As a result she was now forbidden to walk up or down the stairs without someone holding her arm.

And since Mairin was confined to the hall and about to go mad with boredom, Keeley was trekking across the snow to collect Maddie and Christina because Mairin wanted their company.

Keeley smiled. 'Twas no burden to summon the other women. 'Twas the truth that Keeley enjoyed their company and Mairin's as well. They spent many a night in front of the fire, sewing, gossiping, and teasing Christina about her infatuation with Cormac. Thankfully no one had picked up on Keeley's interest in Alaric or his interest in her, or if they had, they had the grace to remain silent, a favor Keeley was grateful for.

Cormac had increasingly made more excuses to remain in the hall at night, usually to drink ale with the men and discuss the day's training, but his attention was focused on Christina. The two played a game of cat and mouse that amused Keeley. They weren't as direct as she and Alaric had been, but then what had admitting their attraction gained Keeley and Alaric except heartache and regret?

She knocked on Maddie's cottage door and then blew warm air onto her cold fingers. The door swung open and Maddie immediately exclaimed, "Keeley! Don't stand there in the cold. Come warm yourself by the fire."

"My thanks," Keeley said as she pushed inside to stand by the hearth.

"What brings you out on a cold day such as this?"

Keeley grinned. "Mairin is at her wits' end. She wishes for you and Christina to come sit with her and keep her company. The laird has forbidden her to leave the confines of the keep."

"As well he should," Maddie said with an approving nod. "In the snow and ice is no place for the lass to be walking in. She could fall and hurt the babe."

"She offered no argument, but she's not happy about it. She asked that if you weren't busy with your own duties, would you mind sitting with her awhile?"

"Of course not. Let me get my shawl and my boots. We'll stop by and collect Christina on our way back to the keep."

In a few moments' time, both women bundled back up and stepped into the biting wind.

"Have you all you need for the coming winter?" Maddie asked as they approached Christina's parents' cottage.

Keeley shook her head. "Nay. There are a few herbs I must look for. 'Twill require digging into the snow but I know what trees to look under. Many will come down with a cough and aching chest as it grows colder. Especially the children. There is a paste I make that eases the ache and helps with the cough. 'Twill be useful to have this winter."

Maddie frowned. "When will you collect these herbs?"

Keeley grinned ruefully. "Not until it stops snowing and the wind dies down. 'Tis too cold to go digging about in the snow right now."

"Aye, you're right. Be sure to bring a man or two to help you. 'Tis no easy task for a lass to take on herself."

"Now you sound like the laird with all his dictates," Keeley teased.

Maddie stopped and knocked at Christina's door. "The laird is a wise man. 'Tis no insult to be compared to him."

Keeley rolled her eyes. "I was offering no insult."

Christina opened the door and her face brightened when she saw Maddie and Keeley standing there. When they told her Mairin would like her to come to the keep, she pounced on the opportunity.

"I love my mother dearly," Christina said as they hurried toward the keep. "But 'tis God's truth, the woman is driving me daft. I can't take being sequestered in the cottage with her any longer."

Maddie chuckled. "Complaining about the weather, I imagine."

"When doesn't she complain?" Christina asked in exasperation. "If it's not the weather, it's my father, or me, or some imagined ailment. I was near to screaming before you knocked on my door."

Keeley smiled and squeezed the young woman's hand. "I'm sure the opportunity to see Cormac again never entered your mind."

Christina blushed and Maddie hooted with laughter. "She has you there, lass."

"Do you think he'll ever try to kiss me?" Christina asked wistfully.

Maddie pursed her lips. "It seems to me that if he hasn't been trying to kiss you then maybe you should take the matter into your own hands and kiss him."

Christina's mouth dropped open and her eyes widened with shock. "Oh I couldn't! Why, that would be brazen. He'd think me . . . He'd think me . . ." she sputtered to a halt, clearly unable to voice the word floating through her mind.

"I wager he'd be too knocked off his feet to have such thoughts," Maddie muttered. "Some men need a shove every now and again. A stolen kiss does not a harlot make. No matter what your mother might preach."

"I agree with Maddie," Keeley said.

"You do?" Christina turned to look at Keeley just as they stepped into the keep and were greeted by much warmer air. "Have you ever . . . kissed a man?" Her voice dropped to a whisper as she looked around to make certain they weren't overheard. "I mean did you do the kissing?"

"Aye," Keeley said softly. "I've kissed and I've been kissed. 'Tis not a shameful thing, Christina. If it doesn't go too far. Cormac is a good man. He won't take advantage, and if he does, you scream loudly and I'll kick him betwixt the legs."

Maddie dissolved into laughter while Christina looked so shocked that Keeley wondered if she and Maddie should have counseled the younger woman at all.

But then a speculative gleam appeared in her eyes and Christina's expression grew thoughtful. As soon as they entered the hall, Mairin rose from her chair in front of the fire and hurried toward them.

"Thank goodness you're here. I am driving myself daft with boredom. Ewan won't allow me out of the keep but everyone else must still go about their duties."

Then Mairin stopped and studied them curiously. "What is amiss? And Christina, why do you have such a peculiar look on your face?"

Maddie chuckled. "The lass is conspiring."

Mairin's brows shot up. "This, I must hear. Come, sit in front of the fire with me and tell me all. If there is mischief to be had, I want a part in it."

"Oh sure, make the laird furious with us all for leading you astray," Keeley grumbled.

Mairin grinned cheekily and settled back in her chair, her palm molding to her protruding belly. "Ewan won't touch a hair on your head. At least not until our babe is safely delivered."

"It's afterward you need to worry," Maddie teased.

Keeley sobered, for after she delivered Mairin's babe, her future was indeed precarious. She had no idea if she even had a cottage to return to at this point. With her disappearance, naught would be known of her fate and her cottage would surely be taken over by someone in need of a sturdy shelter. She had no champion to back her claim, and in fact the cottage didn't really belong to her. It was a McDonald holding.

"Did we say something wrong?" Mairin asked anxiously. "You look so . . . sad, Keeley."

Keeley offered a valiant smile. " 'Tis nothing. I was thinking of my fate after your babe is born."

The other women looked shocked and a little appalled.

"Surely you don't think you'd be turned out," Maddie exclaimed.

Mairin shifted forward in her chair and clutched Keeley's hand to hers. "Ewan would never allow such a thing to happen. You do know that, don't you?"

"'Tis the truth I know nothing of my future," Keeley said softly. "More likely than that, I don't have a home to return to. Such as it was."

"You don't like it here?" Christina asked.

Keeley hesitated. Once Alaric married Rionna, 'twas true that being here would take her further away from Alaric than returning to the McDonald land where she might very well be called to deliver Rionna's first child. With Alaric. The thought was too much to bear. And yet staying here would also put her into close proximity with both Alaric and Rionna when they came to visit. 'Twas a conundrum that promised hurt for her no matter what the course of her fate.

"Aye, I like it here," she finally said. "I never realized how lonely I was before I had all of you to laugh and talk with."

"Keeley, will you tell us what happened to you?" Mairin asked quietly. "If 'tis none of our business, feel free to say so, but I wonder so why you no longer carry the McDonald name and why it is you say your clan turned their back on you."

"'Tis shameful that," Maddie offered with a scowl. "Family is family. A clan is all a person has. If they won't stand behind you, who will?"

"Who will indeed?" Keeley asked ruefully.

She sat back and drew in her breath, surprised by how angry she still felt after so long. Resentment festered just underneath her skin, looking for a crack in which to spill out.

"I grew up as a close friend to Rionna McDonald, the laird's only child."

"Alaric's Rionna?" Mairin asked with a gasp.

"Aye, Alaric's Rionna." It took her all not to flinch when saying those words. "It was common for me to be around the laird and Lady McDonald. They indulged Rionna and me and gave us run of the keep. As we grew older and became more womanly in look, the laird began watching me. So closely it discomfited me."

"The lecher," Maddie muttered.

"It became so uncomfortable that I started to avoid him entirely and started spending less time with Rionna inside the keep. One day when going to summon Rionna from her room, the laird caught me alone and he began saying horrible things. He kissed me and I was appalled. I told him I would scream for help and he asked who would go against him? He was laird. He could have what he wanted. No one would gainsay him.

"I was terrified, for he spoke the truth. He would have raped me in his daughter's chamber, but Lady McDonald walked in."

Mairin looked horrified. "Oh, Keeley."

"I thought the worst of it was having the laird attack me so. I was wrong. The worst of it was when Lady McDonald labeled me whore and accused me of enticing her husband. I was banished from the keep and forbidden to return. I suppose I was fortunate that they allowed me to take a cottage a distance from the keep, but 'twas a lonely existence for a young girl."

"That's despicable!" Christina exclaimed. "How could they have done that to you?"

All three women's faces were creased with horror and it sparked gladness in Keeley's heart. It felt good to have someone be outraged on her behalf.

"The loss of Rionna's friendship hurt the most. I didn't know at first if she believed what was said about me. After Lady McDonald passed and she made no effort to see me or allow me back into the clan, I realized that everyone had indeed believed the worst."

Mairin clumsily got up and enfolded Keeley in a hug, squeezing until Keeley was breathless. "You cannot return there. You'll stay here with the McCabes. We don't turn on our own and we'd certainly never cast a young girl out for the sins of a lecherous old man. The laird visited here some months past. I wish I had known then. I would have spit in his eyes."

Keeley laughed. Once she started she couldn't stop. Her shoulders shook as she imagined Mairin spitting on the laird. She looked helplessly at the other women and soon they were all laughing uproariously.

They wiped tears from their eyes and gasped for breath, and then they looked at Mairin's disgruntled features and laughed all over again.

"I cannot tell you how much better that made me feel," Keeley confessed. "'Tis the truth I've never told anyone the source of my shame."

"'Tis not your shame," Mairin said fiercely. "The shame is Laird McDonald's."

Maddie nodded her agreement while Christina still looked dumbstruck by Keeley's tale.

"And 'tis why you simply must stay here," Maddie announced. "You might not be a McCabe born, but a McCabe you'll be and stay. Your healing skills are needed here and no one will dare treat you as you were treated on McDonald land. Our laird doesn't stand for such injustice."

"I've been so angry for so long," Keeley admitted. "It felt good to tell someone. Thank you for not judging me."

"Men are pigs," Christina spit out.

The three women turned to the younger girl in surprise. Christina had remained largely silent through the telling, and now her cheeks were flushed and her eyes glittered with anger.

"I don't know why any of us tolerate them," she continued.

Mairin laughed. "They aren't all pigs. Your Cormac has a good head on his shoulders."

"If he had such a good head then why hasn't he tried to kiss me yet?" Christina muttered.

Maddie laughed. "You see, lass, this is why you should take matters into your own hands and kiss him first. The lad is probably scared spitless to make a wrong move and offend or frighten you. Men take on the strangest notions sometimes."

Mairin groaned. "Don't get Maddie started about men. She'll summon Bertha and they'll scorch your ears with all their knowledge."

"Aye, but lass, you and the laird benefited well from our advice," Maddie said smugly.

Mairin blushed furiously and waved a hand in front of her face. " 'Tis not me we should be discussing. Christina, I agree. You should kiss Cormac and see how he reacts."

All the talk of kissing and intimacy started an ache in Keeley's chest. Watching young Christina so in love and alive with joy and curiosity made her yearn for things she couldn't have.

Christina leaned forward in her chair, her gaze darting cautiously left and right. "But when? I'll not want anyone seeing us, to be sure. If it got back to my mother, I'd never hear the end of it."

"Well, if your kiss has the impact you're hoping, you won't be your mother's responsibility any more," Maddie said with a smile. "Perhaps this will hasten Cormac to ask to wed you."

A wistful, hopeful smile crept over Christina's features, softening her eyes until they glowed in the light of the fire.

"Do you think he will?"

Keeley and Mairin exchanged looks and smiled at the younger girl.

"Aye, I do," Mairin said. " 'Tis obvious he's smitten with you. Be bold. And if he rebuffs you, I'll kick him, and we will convene to mutter all manner of blasphemies against men."

Keeley grinned broadly as Maddie chortled with laughter. Christina smiled and all but bounced excitedly in her seat.

"I still must know when. It must be a private moment."

"Tonight when the men have done drinking their ale, I'll suggest that Cormac walk you back to your cottage," Mairin said. " 'Tis up to you to do the kissing as soon as you've left the hall but not outside in plain view of the watchmen. In the meantime, I'll send a message to your mother explaining that you'll be eating in the hall with me tonight."

"Oh, I'm so nervous!" Christina exclaimed.

"Don't be nervous, lass. Cormac will be nervous enough for the both of you once he learns he's to escort you home," Maddie teased.

"Wife, my men and I heard your laughter all the way out to the courtyard," Ewan said from the entrance. "They're all terrified that you're plotting against them again."

Mairin looked up to where her husband stood and grinned mischievously. " 'Tis a fact we are, husband. You may of course tell them that, if you wish."

Ewan scowled. "I'm not daft. They'll all abandon their duties and hide like women if I tell them that."

Mairin smiled innocently while Maddie and Keeley found something else to focus their attention on.

"I'll not have you interfering with my men and their duties, Mairin," Ewan said sternly.

"Of course not," she soothed.

He cast a suspicious glare in her direction and then turned and left the hall. No sooner had he exited than the women all burst into laughter once more.

CHAPTER 16

Dinner was a lively affair as many of Alaric's men supped with him in the great hall. A fire roared in the hearth and the furs were all rolled down over the windows with extra bindings to seal the gaps.

Keeley sat on Mairin's left with Christina on Keeley's other side. Cormac had been strategically placed across the table from Christina, and watching the two dodge the other's gaze but take peeks when they thought the other wasn't looking was amusing.

On either side of Cormac sat Alaric and Caelen, and despite her best efforts, Keeley found her gaze traveling to Alaric. Tonight Ewan discussed Alaric's upcoming marriage, and it took all of Keeley's strength to remain in her seat, smile in place, and act as though she hadn't a care in the world.

Her cheeks ached. Her head throbbed.

Alliances. Bonds. Talk of impending war. Naught mattered but the fact that Alaric would marry another and move to McDonald land to take the position of laird.

The usually flavorful food was dry and unremarkable. She ate because there was naught else to do but eat and smile. Another bite. Another smile. Nod in Christina's direction. Laugh at a jest from Mairin. Watch Caelen scowl. And then look in Alaric's direction again.

She sighed and moved the venison around with her cutting knife. She just wished the meal over with so she could retire to her chamber and try to lose herself in a few hours sleep.

She chanced another peek at Alaric and sucked in her breath when she found his gaze resting on her. He didn't move away or try to pretend he hadn't been watching her. His eyes like green ice delved past her defenses and threatened to crumble her on the spot.

He didn't smile. In his eyes she saw all that she felt. And yet she couldn't make herself look away. Nay, if he could brave allowing her to see his torment, then she could offer her own in return. She wouldn't pretend to feel naught.

Beside her Mairin cleared her throat, jerking Keeley from her locked gaze. Keeley glanced swiftly around, but all eyes were turned toward the mistress of the keep as she prepared to speak.

"The meal is done and 'tis nigh time for Christina to hasten back to her cottage. Her mother will worry, with the weather so raw out."

She glanced over at Cormac and gifted him with a sweet smile. "Cormac, would you kindly escort Christina? I'd hate for her to brave the weather by herself."

For a moment, Cormac looked as though he'd swallowed his tongue. After casting a quick glance in Christina's direction, he hastily stood.

"Of course, Lady McCabe."

Ewan shot Mairin a long-suffering look while Caelen just frowned as Cormac walked around to offer his arm to Christina.

The table went quiet and it seemed everyone in the hall watched as Cormac awkwardly guided Christina from the table. As soon as they were gone, Ewan let out a sigh and pinned his wife with his stare.

"What mischief are you up to now, wife?"

Mairin smiled and exchanged a conspiratorial look with Keeley before facing her husband.

"Would you have Christina walk to her cottage alone? Why, she could slip and fall on the ice and then what would we tell her mother? That our laird sent a young girl into the weather unescorted?"

Ewan sent his gaze heavenward. "Why do I even ask?"

"Come now, husband. Have another serving of ale and tell me of your day," Mairin said with an innocent smile.

"You know well how my day went. I've just spent the last half hour with the retelling."

"Have you yet sent a message to McDonald agreeing to his terms?" Caelen asked.

He looked directly at Keeley, pointedly, as he spoke. Keeley held his gaze, refusing to react to his words.

"Aye, two days past," Ewan said. "I don't expect to receive a response until the storm has passed and the snows have stopped."

"Then we should expect him closer to spring," Caelen pressed. "He and Rionna."

"Caelen."

Alaric said only the one word, but his tone was glacial and as frigid as the winds outside. It was a clear warning to his brother to stop meddling, but it didn't make Keeley feel any better.

Caelen was warning her. He knew of the attraction between her and Alaric. Keeley wanted to crawl under the table and die of shame.

Instead she nudged her chin up and looked down her nose at Caelen as if he were an annoying insect she was about to squash. That image cheered her considerably. 'Twas the truth she'd enjoy nothing more than giving Caelen a good stomping.

Caelen's eyebrow went up as if surprised by her daring, and she narrowed her eyes to tell him she knew precisely what he was about.

To her further surprise a slight smile lifted one corner of his mouth. Then he went back to his goblet and promptly ignored her.

Keeley was just about to excuse herself when Cormac returned to the hall, a dazed expression on his face. She arched an eyebrow at Mairin, who looked utterly delighted. Mairin reached under the table and squeezed Keeley's hand.

Cormac bumped into his chair as he attempted to retake his seat. His color was heightened and his hair . . . looked decidedly unkempt. Mairin's smile grew even broader.

Ewan grunted in disgust and Caelen rolled his eyes. Alaric just stared at Keeley until her cheeks warmed under his scrutiny.

"Laird, I have need to speak with you," Cormac said in a low voice. "'Tis of utmost importance."

Ewan cast a resigned look at his wife and then nodded in Cormac's direction. "Speak then."

Cormac cleared his throat and looked nervously around at the people still remaining at the table. Most of the men had gone on to their quarters, but Gannon, Alaric, and his brothers along with Keeley and Mairin yet remained.

"I would ask permission to seek Christina's hand in marriage," he blurted out.

Mairin nearly bounced out of her chair and Keeley found herself unable to hold back the smile at the other man's stunned expression.

"I see. Have you thought this through?" Ewan asked. "Is she truly the one you would marry? And are you sure she wishes to marry you?"

"Aye. 'Tis the truth she said I wouldn't be kissing her again until we were formally betrothed."

At that, Keeley and Mairin could hold in their laughter no longer.

"God save us from interfering women," Ewan muttered. " 'Twould seem there is much matchmaking afoot in the keep. Aye, Cormac. You have my permission to speak with her father, but I'll not have your duties disrupted. Your first duty is to see to the safety of my wife. If I find you distracted even once, I'll dismiss you."

"Of course, Laird. My loyalty is to you and your lady above all else," Cormac said.

"Then prepare your speech for her father. We'll have a priest out as soon as weather permits, and provided, of course, her father is agreeable."

Cormac fought his grin but the relief and . . . happiness in his eyes made Keeley go soft all over. She swallowed back her longing and the brief surge of jealousy. She was truly happy for Christina. The young woman would be giddy when Cormac proposed.

She glanced over at Mairin to see that her excitement was mirrored in the other woman. Mairin leaned over and whispered, "We'll have to query Christina about that kiss on the morrow."

Keeley put a hand to her mouth to stifle the laughter. "It must have been a kiss for the ages," she whispered back.

"I've had a few of those," Mairin said wistfully. Then she cast a glance in Ewan's direction. "Maybe more than a few."

It was on the tip of her tongue to confide that she, too, had experienced a kiss like no other, but she remained quiet. Instead she glanced Alaric's way again only to find his gaze caressing her as surely as if he touched her with his hand.

It was as though someone gripped her throat and squeezed. Each breath was torturous, until her chest ached with the effort. She dragged her gaze away and then bolted from her seat at the table. She turned to Ewan first and bobbed an awkward curtsy.

"With your permission, Laird, I would retire above stairs. I find I'm quite tired this eve."

Ewan nodded and continued his conversation with Alaric.

Keeley then turned to Mairin. "I'll see you on the morrow. Good eve."

Mairin shot her a look of sympathy that told Keeley she wasn't immune to the undercurrents between Keeley and Alaric.

Keeley hurried away but felt the weight of Alaric's stare the entire time. She couldn't be away from the scrutiny of those at the table fast enough. She'd already make a fool of herself with all the stolen glances at Alaric. Someone would have to be blind and daft not to sense what was going on.

The climb up the stairs seemed interminable. Her chamber was cold when she let herself in, and shivering, she went about reviving the fire from the nearly dead coals. After adding fresh wood, she stood by the flame a moment to instill warmth in her hands and then went to check the fur covering the window.

Satisfied that all was as it should be, she donned her night dress and slipped beneath the furs on her bed. The only light in the darkness was the vibrant, orange glow of the fire. It cast shadows on the walls and made her feel every bit as alone as she was.

Outside, the wind whistled and groaned, like an old

man bemoaning his fate. Keeley wrapped the furs tighter around her and stared at the dancing flames on the ceiling.

If only things were as simple as stealing a kiss. If only she'd take matters into her own hands as Christina had done. Keeley smiled a sad, rueful smile. If only a kiss could solve all the ills. Christina had kissed her man and now they would forge a life together.

She had no life to forge with Alaric. But she could cherish a few stolen moments in his arms.

She went utterly still as the thought took hold. Her breath caught and held and her hand flew to her throat, massaging as if to take the tightness away.

What if she did go to Alaric? How would it change any aspect of her life when she was already thought a woman of no virtue?

She closed her eyes and shook her head in mute denial.

But she couldn't even use the excuse that Rionna was her friend. Friends didn't turn their backs. And no one ever had to know.

Just one night.

Was it possible?

Alaric wanted her. He'd make that plain enough. And Keeley wanted him with every breath she breathed. She wanted him so much that it was a physical ache.

What would his hands feel like on her flesh? His mouth against hers?

Aye, it would hurt to walk away from Alaric. It would hurt to have him but for a short tryst, but she was beginning to believe that he was right. A taste of sweet was better than a lifetime of bitter regret. And right now she'd regret going to her cold grave a virgin still.

For so long she held her virtue tight. So tight that

naught else mattered. It was her only proof that she wasn't the whore she'd been labeled. And yet it hadn't brought her justice. There was no one to stand for her. There would never be anyone to stand for her. Only she knew the truth, and that's how it would stay.

How much comfort did the truth bring her on cold nights?

She nearly laughed at the lengths her mind went to in order to rationalize her desire to indulge in an affair with her warrior.

Her warrior. Always hers. But not. In her heart, though, there was no other. There never would be.

"Do stop being so dramatic and fanciful, Keeley," she murmured. "The next thing you know, you'll be throwing aside the furs covering the window and threatening to hurl yourself onto the snow-covered heath."

She would laugh, but tears stung her eyelids and she swiped at them to alleviate the burn.

Nay, now was not the time for silly and idyllic dreams. She needed to be a realist and decide what was acceptable to her. No one else. For once, she would place her own wants and desires above others. For if she didn't see to her happiness, no one else would.

One night in Alaric's arms.

Once spoken aloud in her mind, she couldn't push the thought away. It consumed her. It tempted and tantalized her as nothing else ever had.

She'd never even been kissed until Alaric, save the brutal mouth of the laird and she didn't consider that a kiss. A kiss was something given, and the laird had taken. She had never given him *anything* willingly.

She pressed her palms to her eyes and plunged her fingers into her hair.

It was too late for her to turn back. It had become

more than some hopeless dream. The idea had taken root. It burned so brightly in her mind that she knew she couldn't go another day under the unbearable strain that existed between her and Alaric.

Tonight it had to end.

CHAPTER 17

Alaric stood and stared moodily out the window into the night. Above, the moon gleamed bright and reflected boldly off the snow-covered terrain. In the distance the loch glistened and shone like silver with nary a ripple to disturb the pristine surface.

'Twas a tranquil sight and yet his insides were in complete turmoil.

His brother's words whispered to him, an insidious thought that once seeded had taken root and it shamed him that he gave it more thought with each passing day. Take her. Use her. Be rid of this madness.

But he couldn't. Because he knew that what he felt wasn't simple lust. What it was, he couldn't say. It was new and fresh. He was on the cusp of something alarming and exhilarating all at the same time. 'Twas as if he prepared for battle and his blood soared in preparation.

He wanted her, aye. Not a doubt. But he wouldn't take what wasn't willingly given. The last thing he wanted to do was cause her pain. Seeing the torment in her eyes had hurt him in a way he hadn't thought it possible to be hurt by a woman.

The sound of his chamber door opening whirled him around, a blistering set down-poised and ready to fly at whoever dared to enter without knocking.

When he saw Keeley standing in the shadows, uncertainty etched on her features, he forgot to breathe.

"I thought you would be abed," she said in barely above a whisper. "'Tis late. We took to our beds hours ago."

"And yet here we both stand, unable to sleep. Why is that, Keeley?" he asked softly. "Are we going to continue to deny what it is we both want?"

"Nay."

He went still. So still that the room went deathly quiet and only the howl of the wind could be heard. Cold rushed through the room, blanketing it in frigid layers. Keeley shivered and gathered her arms around her. She looked so vulnerable that every instinct in him cried out to protect her from harm. To cherish her and lavish on her all the patience and understanding he had in him.

Then he cursed when another blast of cold air rushed through the room. The flame in the hearth flickered and sparked higher, fed by the draft. He hurried to the window to pull the furs down and then went to Keeley and pulled her into his arms, shielding her from the chill.

Her heart beat frantically against his chest, and she trembled from head to toe.

"Come over to the bed so you can wrap up in one of the furs while I build up the fire," he said gently.

Carefully he tugged her away from his chest and led her to his bed. She sat on the edge, tense and nervous as he tucked one of the furs around her body.

Unable to resist, he kissed the top of her head and smoothed his hand over her long tresses. He wouldn't taste her lips yet. If he started, he wouldn't stop and she'd freeze.

His hands trembled while he added logs to the fire. He curled and uncurled his fingers in an attempt to dispel the quiver but to no avail. He was shaken to the core and so afraid of making a wrong move that he was nearly paralyzed.

At last he turned to see Keeley watching him with wide eyes from her perch on the bed. He crossed the room and went down on one knee in front of her.

"Are you sure about this, Keeley?"

She reached up to fan her fingers over his lips. She stroked over his mouth and then down his jaw line. "I want you. I can't deny you—us—any longer. I know 'tis your destiny to marry into the McDonald clan and become laird and 'tis a noble destiny. I'll not deter you from that end. I want tonight. One night in your arms so that I can hold the memory tight once you've gone from this place."

He caught her hand and dragged it across his mouth, settling his lips into her palm. He kissed the smooth skin and then tucked each fingertip into his mouth, kissing them in turn.

"I want you too, lass. So much I ache. I want to burn the memory of you in my arms into my mind so that it never leaves me no matter how old I may grow."

She smiled, her eyes glinting with sadness as she cupped his cheek. "Give me tonight so that we make just such a memory for the both of us."

"Aye, lass. I'll love you well."

When he would have gotten to his feet, she put out a hand and he paused on one knee.

"There is something I would say before we go any further."

He cocked his head, studying her sudden nervousness and the quick intake of her breath.

He smoothed the hair from her face and tangled his fingers in the long tresses in an effort to soothe the worry creasing her brow. "Speak then."

She looked briefly away before returning her gaze to

his. The beauty of her eyes was dampened by worry and . . . shame.

" 'Tis important you know this. I was cast from the McDonald clan. They are my family. I was a McDonald born."

His brow furrowed with confusion as he grappled with what she'd said. A McDonald? He hadn't given much thought to where he'd ended up after being injured. The whole time was a blur. His brothers hadn't mentioned how close they'd been to McDonald land when they'd come to take him home.

And she'd been cast out? Anger pricked at him. He touched her chin to stop the silent quiver and nudged upward until she stared him directly in the eye.

"Why, lass? Why would your own kin turn you out?"

"The laird made improper advances toward me when I was but a young girl, barely on the cusp of womanhood. His wife walked in as he tried to rape me, and she cried me whore. I was turned out for trying to seduce the laird."

Alaric was momentarily speechless. His hand fell away from her chin as his mind grappled with the implications.

"Sweet Jesu," he whispered.

His nostrils flared and he clenched his jaw as he imagined his sweet Keeley, a much younger Keeley, trying to fend off a much older, stronger man. It made him ill.

It made him furious.

"It wasn't true," she said in a fierce whisper.

"Nay!" he denied, his hand flying back to caress her cheek. "Of course it wasn't. I hope you don't think I thought so even for a moment. I'm furious that you were treated so unjustly and that you paid the sins of the laird. His job is to protect his clan. To be deserving of the mantle of leadership. To prey on a young girl is a betrayal of all he is foresworn to do."

She closed her eyes as relief washed in a clear line across her face. Alaric's heart twinged for what she'd endured. But more than that, he had a strong urge to hie himself to McDonald keep and beat Laird McDonald until he was incapable of ever forcing himself on another woman. To think he'd supped with the man in the McCabe hall. He'd welcomed the man on his land as an ally and as a future father through marriage. His lips curled in disgust and his head ached when he realized there was naught to do. He couldn't set aside an alliance by making an enemy of McDonald.

It was a damnable position to be in.

Determined not to dwell on things beyond his control, he turned his attention to the one thing he could.

He stroked his palm over Keeley's silken flesh, his thumb lingering over her full lips and to the slight indention at her chin. His fingers stroked down the slim column of her neck to rest on her chest just above the swell of her breasts.

He could feel the slight flutter of her pulse, and he heard the swift intake of her breath when he lowered his hand to cup the swell through the thin material of her night dress.

"I wonder if you have any idea of your beauty, lass. Your flesh is soft and as pale as moonlight on the snow. 'Tis unmarred by a single blemish or defect. I could spend forever just touching you."

She sighed and moved closer, filling his palm with her warmth. Her nipple tightened against his thumb and he brushed over the tip, bringing it to a hardened bud.

Their mouths hovered precariously close. His gaze slid over her face, meeting the piercing beauty of her eyes just as he touched her lips with his.

It was a shock. Like kissing the moon and being illuminated by a thousand silver rays. Desire snaked down his spine and spread through his limbs until they were laden.

He licked over her mouth and delved between her lips to the sweetness inside. Hot and damp and so sinful that it sent shivers of intense desire quaking over his body.

She was breathing hard, little huffs blowing over his face as she pulled away, her eyes glazed with tiny little sparks of green and gold that reminded him of the highlands in the spring.

" 'Tis the truth I've never lain with another man. No one has ever touched me as you have."

Her admission awoke a primitive, possessive urge deep inside him. At the same time he was filled with tenderness and the desire to make this night one she'd never forget.

"I'll be gentle, love. I swear it."

She smiled and cupped his face in her hands as she drew him close. "I know you will, warrior."

He pulled her into his arms, trapping her against his chest. She smelled sweet and delicate, so much female flesh, soft and supple. He nuzzled against her neck, inhaling her scent and marking her with his teeth. Gentle nips, she shivered with each one.

"Aye, you taste sweet, lass. The sweetest I've ever tasted."

He felt her smile against his temple.

"And you have honeyed lips, warrior. The sweetest I've ever heard."

" 'Tis not pretty words in which to woo you. 'Tis the truth as I've never spoken it."

She looped her arms around his neck and melted into him with a sigh. "I like the kissing part very much, but something tells me there's a whole lot more to the matter of loving."

He smiled and brushed his lips across her brow. "Aye,

you are right there. 'Tis much more and I plan to show you in great detail."

Her lips found his again, this time at her instigation. Her breathy sigh spilled into his mouth and he swallowed her breath, taking her deep into his chest.

He allowed her to take the direction of the kiss, allowed her to take as much as she would from him.

Always before, a quick tup had been to his liking. He took lasses to his bed who enjoyed a fast, playful romp. But here and now, he wanted to savor every moment. He wanted it to last forever. He'd take his time and show her the delights of the flesh—and the heart.

Rising before her, he lowered her onto the bed and pressed his palms into the mattress on either side of her head. Her hair spread out over the sheets like a silken mass. The strands glowed like spun gold in the light from the fire. He ran his fingertips over the glints of color and the varying shades intermixed in the thick pelt of her hair.

She stared up at him, her eyes aglow with trust. It humbled him that she offered him what she'd never granted another man. That she had such faith in him staggered him.

She stretched and twisted beneath him before raising her arms invitingly. Gently he gathered her hands, kissed her knuckles and then lowered them back down to her belly. He slid his hands up her arms, caught her sleeves and slowly pulled them over her shoulders, baring the creamy flesh.

Unable to resist such a temptation, he bent down and kissed the top of her shoulder and teased a line to the curve of her neck. Chill bumps broke out over her skin and danced beneath his lips. He chuckled softly when he took the lobe of her ear between his teeth and she shuddered violently.

"You have a wicked mouth, warrior."

"I've only just begun."

He pulled at her dress until it hung precariously over the tips of her breasts. He held his breath, and his body tightened like the string of a bow. His cock swelled and pushed hard against his trews, straining to be set free and find her sweetness.

He cursed under his breath and clenched his jaw in a frantic effort to maintain control. For several long seconds, his chest heaved as he breathed in and out.

"Is something wrong?"

He yanked his gaze down to see the worry in her eyes and he kissed her, long and leisurely, to chase the fears away. "Nay, lass. Nothing is wrong at all. Everything is right. Just right."

He left her mouth, nipping lightly at her chin on his way back to her chest. He paused just above the valley of her breasts and then nuzzled into the hollow, taking the hem of her bodice over the tips.

Her dress gathered at her waist and he stared down at the pebbled nipples, a delectable pink, so taut that they beckoned his mouth—an urge he was powerless to fight.

He licked one bud and she cried out, her voice hoarse and thin. She gripped his shoulders, her fingers digging into his flesh.

She bowed underneath him when he found her other nipple and sucked it strongly into his mouth.

She was so taut, straining upward, her fingers dug so tight that she looked to be near pain. When he loosened his hold on her breast, she whimpered and stirred restlessly beneath him.

"Shh, lass, 'tis just beginning. Be at ease. Let me love you."

He moved back until his feet were once again on the floor. He pulled at her dress until it came away, leaving her bare to his gaze.

He swallowed. In all his life, he'd never seen a lass

more beautiful. Her skin glowed in the firelight. Creamy and smooth with nary an imperfection. She was perfectly fashioned, her hips rounded, her waist narrow, and generous breasts to fill a man's hand and mouth.

Her belly was flat with a tiny, shallow indention at her navel that he was dying to run his tongue around.

His gaze drifted lower to the small patch of curls nestled at the apex of her legs, guarding her innocence and the sweetness found within.

He hadn't thought it possible to grow harder than he already was. His cock strained against his trews until the very feel of the material drove him mad.

He didn't want to frighten her, but if he didn't shed his clothing soon, he was going to claw it from his flesh.

"Lie there while I undress," he said in a low voice.

Her eyes widened as his fingers fumbled with the laces of his trews. Then he peeled the material away and his cock sprang free. The relief was so acute that he nearly went to his knees right then and there.

He yanked at his tunic and sent it sailing across the room. When he returned his gaze to Keeley, he saw that her gaze was fixed on his groin. He wasn't sure whether she was appalled or curious. Her expression was a strange mixture of both.

He stepped between her thighs, and her hands rose automatically as if to ward him off.

He caught her wrists and held them as his thumbs caressed the soft pads of hers.

" 'Tis nothing to be afraid of, Keeley. I won't hurt you. I'll be as gentle as a newborn lamb."

And if it killed him, he wouldn't break his word.

CHAPTER 18

Keeley held her breath until she was light-headed and near to fainting. When she let it out, it came out in a rush that unsteadied her.

Before her stood a man—a warrior—that had no equal. He was honed by the fires of battle. Muscled. Scarred. Lean. No spare flesh on any part of his body.

He towered over her, his strength a tangible thing in the small space of the chamber. He could so easily hurt her, and yet she trusted him fully. His gentleness soothed her and made her ache with longing.

But looking at his groin with his . . . appendage . . . jutting upward like a battle flag, she cast a doubtful look upward. "Are you sure . . . Are you sure we'll . . . it'll . . . *fit?*"

She nearly groaned with her humiliation. How was she supposed to act like a grown woman who'd been on her own for the last years when she swooned at the mere sight of a man's shaft. It wasn't as though she hadn't seen one before. She'd seen his for that matter, but they'd all been at rest. Not flagging upward like a battle-ax.

It amazed her that something soft and unremarkable could grow to such a size and appear so menacing.

Alaric laughed softly, and his eyes gleamed with amusement as he gazed down at her.

"Aye, it'll fit. 'Tis your duty to accommodate me."

She arched an eyebrow at his arrogance. "'Tis my duty? Who made this rule, warrior?"

He grinned. "You'll soften and grow damp. 'Tis my duty to make that happen."

"I will?"

She tried to keep the confusion and question from her voice, but it came out breathy, almost excited.

He moved in close and then leaned over her, his body so close to hers that his heat surrounded her and seeped into her flesh. "Aye, you will. I'll make certain of that."

He settled onto her, scorching her as their skin molded and her body melted into his. The hair on his chest lightly abraded her skin and his hair fell over his shoulders and onto hers.

"'Tis unseemly for a man to have such beautiful hair," she murmured.

He levered up and scowled down at her. "'Tis unseemly to tell a man he has beautiful hair."

She smiled. "Oh, but I love to run my fingers through it. Do you remember me washing you when we were still in my cottage? I dried it and put a brush to it and then I rebraided the strands at your temples. 'Twas like silk, the finest I've ever felt."

"I remember an enchantress with her hands sliding through my hair. 'Twas like a dream I never wished to waken from."

She reached up to capture his hair with her fingers and let the strands twine around the tips.

"And this is a dream I never want to waken from," she whispered.

He captured her mouth. Fierce and hot. Not as gentle as he'd been before. He stole her breath. Demanded it and her kiss. His body moved urgently against hers, roughly as their legs twined and he branded her flesh with his.

His arousal was bold and hard, butting against the juncture of her legs. Instinctively, she parted her thighs, and then she gasped when the length of him slid along her most intimate flesh.

Indescribable sensations jolted through her body as his thick shaft rubbed along the tiny nub of flesh between her folds. She lifted her thighs, wanting more, but he pushed himself off her and slid down her body.

She would have protested, but his tongue swirled around her navel, and she promptly forgot all but his sinful mouth. But when he dragged his tongue even lower, she raised her head in alarm.

When he looked up at her, his eyes glittered, reminding her of a predator about to charge his prey. She shivered at the sheer intensity in his gaze. And the promise.

Slowly he lowered his head as his fingers gripped her thighs. He spread her, gently, but with enough force that she was helpless in his grasp. He pressed a tender kiss just above the thatch of curls and her entire belly quivered in reaction.

Her mind was afire with naughty, delicious thoughts of him touching her even more intimately with his tongue. She tingled from head to toe, and the room was so hazy around her that it felt as though she were swimming in waters heated by the sun.

"Oh," she gasped when his fingers gently parted the delicate folds between her legs.

His thumb brushed over the sensitive little nub, and he trailed a single fingertip to her opening where he continued to tease.

When he touched his tongue to where his thumb had rested, the most peculiar, spectacular sensation thrilled through her pelvis and into her limbs. Her belly tightened with unbearable pleasure. It flooded her, tightening every muscle until her body quivered with the strain.

He continued a slow, decadent dance over feminine

flesh, lapping and licking like she was a sweet treat. Her legs shook uncontrollably. Her senses spiraled out of control.

She reached down and thrust her fingers into his hair. Her breaths came in ragged, painful bursts, burning a path up her throat before exploding into the quiet.

"Alaric!"

He continued to nuzzle between her legs, kissing and tonguing her until she begged him to stop, not to stop, for more. And more.

She had no inkling of what was happening or what she should do. So she put herself into his care, gave her trust to him, and she let go of her fears and reservations.

Never had she imagined such a beautiful, physical manifestation of loving between a man and a woman. She knew the mechanics. She knew what had to occur, but somehow she'd thought it would be baser and faster. A quick penetration and maybe a cuddle afterward.

His hands explored her body, every inch, every secret was revealed to him. He kissed and caressed until she was near sobbing, desperate for something just out of her reach.

"Shh, lass," he murmured as he rose up to position himself between her thighs once more. "I've got you. Trust me now. 'Twill hurt a bit at first, but stay with me. 'Tis a fleeting pain, I'm told. And I'll take care with you."

There was an odd, aching pulse between her legs. An unfulfilled ache that throbbed endlessly. She twisted restlessly, knowing she needed something more. Her hands flew to his chest in a silent plea for him to ease the ache.

His features drew into a tight, harsh line as he reached down to grasp his erection and guide it to her opening. The brush of his shaft against her entrance sent wave after wave of exquisite anticipation coursing through her.

He paused and their gazes met and held. The muscles in his arms bulged as he lowered himself over her body.

"Hold on to me, lass," he whispered. "Hold me tight."

She twined her arms around his neck and pulled him down to meet her lips. As they kissed, he pushed his hips forward the slightest bit. Her eyes flew open at the stretching sensation.

"Does it hurt?"

She shook her head. "Nay. 'Tis a full feeling. 'Tis wondrous. We're joined."

He smiled. "Aye, that we are, lass."

He pushed again and her fingers curled into his back.

"Just a bit more and the worst will be over," he soothed.

"Worst? But it hasn't been bad so far," she murmured.

He grinned as he kissed her. He withdrew and some of the pressure lessened. Then he probed gently once more and the sense of fullness, of stretching so tightly around him was back. She loved that feeling. She wanted more.

"Now, Alaric," she whispered into his ear. "Make me yours."

He groaned and moved so his forehead was pressed to hers. Their mouths were a breath apart and their gazes fastened to the other. Just as he thrust forward, he pressed his lips to hers and swallowed her startled gasp of pain.

She felt her body give way, could feel her maidenhead tear as he pushed through. The sudden burn of his complete possession unsettled her.

She became aware of him murmuring to her in a low voice. Sweet, soothing words. Praising her and telling her how beautiful she was.

"'Tis over, lass. You're mine now." His voice drifted

over her ears, warm and husky. "I've dreamed of this moment when you take me deep into your body."

He remained still as her body adjusted to their fit. Then he looked down into her eyes and in between kisses, he asked, "All right now? Is the pain gone?"

" 'Twas naught but a twinge," she reassured. "I feel nothing but pleasure."

With a groan, he withdrew, and she sighed as her body tugged relentlessly at him. Tiny ripples of intense pleasure streaked through her blood, heating her veins until the room seemed overwarm.

Then he eased his way back inside her, watching her all the while as if worried he still caused her pain.

She reached for him and then wrapped her legs around him. "Take me. It doesn't hurt. Please. I need you."

It seemed it was all he needed to hear. He dropped down and gathered her tight in his arms and then he plunged forward, his hips meeting hers in a forceful thrust.

She closed her eyes as he rocked over her, their bodies undulating in perfect rhythm. The unbearable tension was back, only this time it didn't lessen as it had when he'd stopped using his mouth on her.

There was no space between them. Only his hips and buttocks moved as he worked in and out of her body. Deeper and harder. She went slick around him and he moved with greater ease. The friction was so sweet, but it made her desperate for something she wasn't sure of. Release. She needed release. But how?

"Don't fight it, lass. Hold on to me and let go. Trust me."

His words soothed the growing anxiety. She relaxed and did as he asked. She gave him herself. Her trust.

Faster and faster, they raced up a seemingly endless peak. Just when she was sure she could take no more and would beg him to cease, it was like stepping off into empty space.

The world around her blurred. Her body spasmed and wave upon wave of wondrous, mind-numbing pleasure splintered and fell over her.

His hold tightened around her. He drove into her and then held himself deep just before tearing himself away. She reached for him, afraid he was leaving her, but he collapsed back onto her and she felt hot spurts on her bare belly.

He lay atop her, heaving for breath. She dragged air into her lungs, but they burned with the effort. She simply couldn't process what had just happened. Was this normal? Was this what happened every time a man and woman indulged in loving? Surely it couldn't be, otherwise no one would ever get out of bed.

Alaric rolled them both to the side so that his weight was off her but she was still clasped tightly to his body. She felt his shaft pulsing against her belly and could feel sticky warmth on her skin.

It finally dawned on her what had occurred, and she was both grateful and sad all at the same time. He'd taken care not to leave her with child. She wouldn't have to bear the shame of an illegitimate child while he married another and bore legitimate issue.

Yet the idea of having a part of him, his precious child, was bittersweet. She'd never take another man to her bed after Alaric. She'd never bear children.

She sighed and snuggled into his embrace. Perhaps 'twas too dramatic to be thinking such thoughts, and perhaps once Alaric was long gone, she'd think differently about another man. A lifetime of loneliness was hardly a balm for a broken heart. But those matters were for another time. For now, she couldn't even think of ever being so intimate with another.

Alaric gathered her close and kissed her forehead. "Did it hurt over much, love?"

She shook her head against his chest. "Nay, warrior. You were true to your word. You were gentle, and I felt hardly a pinch when you pushed inside me."

"I'm glad. The last thing I ever want to do is cause you pain."

Her heart ached just a bit at his words, for she knew that eventually, despite his best intentions, his marriage would cause her pain.

Determined not to allow the future to cast a pall over the present, she laid her head on his shoulder and pressed a kiss to his hard muscles.

"Tell me, warrior, how soon can we do this again?"

He tensed against her and then tucked a finger under her chin, forcing her gaze upward. His eyes gleamed with anticipation, and the heat in his gaze made her heart pound faster.

"As soon as you tell me aye."

"Aye," she whispered.

CHAPTER 19

Alaric rose on his elbow, blinking away the sleep, and stared across the chamber to the hearth where Keeley had placed another log on the fire. She sat back on the bench, her nude body silhouetted by the orange glow, and for a long moment she stared into the flames just as he stared at her.

She was beautiful. Feminine and yet strong. She was soft and silken, but she had an inner thread of strength that astonished him in light of her past.

Not many lasses could have survived on their own after being cast out of their clan. Many would have adopted the very life she'd been accused of. There weren't many ways for a woman to survive on her own and yet Keeley had done so.

She flipped her hair over her shoulder and turned her head to look in Alaric's direction. Her eyes widened in surprise for a moment before she broke into a shy smile.

He could barely swallow. She was so incredibly lovely that his teeth ached.

"Come here," he said as he held a hand out to her.

She rose and awkwardly covered her breasts in an effort to maintain her modesty. She looked adorably shy as she slid onto the bed next to him.

He pulled her into his arms, loving how easily she fit. "How are you feeling?"

She nuzzled against his neck and pressed a kiss to the column of his throat. "Much better now."

"And you say I have a honeyed tongue."

She tilted her head and smiled. "Aye, you do. There's no doubt after earlier."

"I'm glad I pleased my lady."

"Aye, you please me, warrior. You please me well."

He leaned in to kiss her. He meant for it to be a brief embrace, but he couldn't pull himself away. Their lips made a soft smooching sound in the room. Their tongues met and dueled. This time she was more confident and much more passionate, willing to meet him halfway and demand her due.

"We have a few hours before dawn. Come back to bed with me, Keeley. Let's not waste the time we have left."

Her smile lit up the entire room. Then her eyes glinted and her smile turned mischievous. She put her hands to his shoulders and pushed until he reclined on the bed.

"Granted I have no experience with these matters, but it seems to me that 'twould be just as easy for me to do the loving as it is for you."

He lifted an eyebrow but his eyes gleamed devilishly. "That's an arrogant statement, lass. Seems to me you have to back up that statement with action."

Her hair fell in a curtain over her shoulder as she straddled his naked body with her own. His approval of her arrogance was evident in his straining arousal. The idea of her covering him with her softness and of taking the initiative in loving tested the bounds of his discipline and control.

He was a patient man, but at the moment he felt the insane urge to tumble her over and drive between her thighs until it was all either of them knew or could feel.

He glanced up her body as she sat astride him, following the line over her flat belly to her full breasts and then back down to the slim curve of her waist to her fuller hips.

His cock strained upward, thrusting against her soft curls nestled at his base. His breath caught and wheezed out in a strangled gasp when she lowered her hands to grasp his cock.

Her expression was one of wonder as she gently caressed his length. Up and down, she drew the skin tight and then rolled it back down until the blunt crest had widened and blood had rushed to the tip.

It was nearly painful. Each touch drove him more daft by the minute. She was exquisitely gentle, almost as if she feared hurting him.

Finally, he was able to take it no longer, and he curled his hand around hers, tightening her grasp.

"Like this," he rasped out.

He worked from the bottom up and then down, tightening and loosening until moisture formed at the tip and slipped over their linked hands.

"Ah, lass, you drive me mad."

"'Tis a good thing, I hope."

"Aye, the best."

Her hand still wrapped around him, she leaned down, her breasts bobbing like tempting apples in front of him. Then she lifted her hips upward but then seemed at a loss. She had good instincts, but she simply didn't have experience. He found that it gave him great satisfaction to have to offer instruction. She was his. She'd never been with another man. It was up to him to teach her all she needed and to give her ultimate pleasure.

He grasped her hips and aided her in lifting up. "Like this, lass. Just like this." He fitted her over his cock and carefully began to pull her down.

They both gasped when he found her heat and sank

slowly into her. She paused and chewed nervously at her bottom lip as her body spasmed around him.

He raised one hand to stroke her hair, wanting to soothe her worries. "Easy. Nice and slow," he murmured.

She trembled as she began a slow descent once more. It was the most excruciating agony of Alaric's life and he wanted to die from the pleasure of it.

She surrounded him. Bathed him in her fire. Her velvety softness grasped him and sucked him deeper. She stroked his cock with liquid satin. She sheathed him whole.

Gingerly she settled her tiny rounded bottom over his groin as flesh met flesh. He was embedded as deeply in her as he could go, and still it wasn't enough.

His flesh felt alive. Like a thousand insects crawled just below the surface. He needed to move.

Sweat broke out on his forehead and on his upper lip. His breaths came ragged, harsh in the silence.

Smooth, silken flesh seduced his fingers as he caressed her slim back and stroked over her hips. He wanted to give her as much time as she needed to grow accustomed to being on top.

She gave a tentative rotation, and he groaned aloud.

She stopped instantly, concern flashing in her eyes.

"Nay, don't stop, lass. God, please, don't stop. 'Tis wondrous."

Placing her hands on his chest, she levered up, his cock gliding through her damp heat. Then she sheathed him again, pushing downward until her bottom met his groin once more. Then she rotated in a tight circle, watching his face all the while.

"You are a temptress," he said raggedly.

"Angel no more. Am I back to being a demon from hell?"

"Wicked angel. The very best kind." He rose up and

circled her in his arms, the action pushing her further onto his cock. "My angel."

She cradled him against her and then tilted their heads and took him in a savage kiss. She took his breath away. Possessive. Like he belonged only to her. And in this moment he did. No other woman existed for him. He doubted one ever would.

He reached down to curl his fingers around her hips. He needed her. Needed to push deep. To demonstrate his possession again. He lifted and then drove deep, arching his hips. They both cried out.

Her hands flew frantically over his shoulders, seeking purchase. With a growl, his lips found her neck, nipping and biting at the delectable flesh.

She arched her back, plumping her breasts against his chest. The chords in her neck strained and bulged as he lifted and thrust over and over.

" 'Twas I who was supposed to love you," she said breathlessly.

"Oh aye, you were and you did. If you love me any harder, I'll die from the effort."

"Please," she begged. " 'Tis burning, Alaric. I can't . . . I must . . ."

"Do what you must," he urged.

She gripped his shoulders and began lifting herself out of his hands, pushing downward, harder and faster until she rode him as surely as he would his steed.

Unable to keep the position any longer, he lay back, hitting the mattress as she came down over him. He helped her, but she was a wild thing in his arms, her hips undulating as she took him over and over.

He'd never been so aroused by a woman. He'd never thought a woman so beautiful or giving. He'd never wanted a woman to be his as he wanted her.

His release boiled in his loins, rising like a tumultuous storm. Building, burning. Oh God, he wouldn't last.

He slid his hand between their bodies, finding her slick heat. He stroked her pleasure spot and shuddered in ecstasy when she tightened spasmodically around him.

"I can't last," he cried hoarsely.

"Then let go," she said, echoing his words from earlier. She leaned down and cupped his face in her hands. "I'll be here to catch you, warrior."

Her sweetness flooded his soul. With a strangled gasp, he let go and arched up. He barely managed to grasp her hips and tear himself from her sheath. He erupted in great liquid spurts as her hand cupped over him, holding him against her belly.

He continued to pulse against her flesh, his hands curled into tight balls at his sides. He twitched and thrust against her, unable to hold still as pleasure tore through his bones.

As he slowly lowered himself down to the bed once more, her grasp gentled and then she let go. She gazed curiously at his cock, now only partially erect and wiped her finger over a drop of liquid on the head.

She glanced back up at him before carefully sliding her finger into her mouth. Her tongue danced over the tip before letting it fall free, and he groaned all over again.

She lifted one delicate brow as his cock twitched and became instantly erect.

"I wondered at your taste," she said huskily. "You liked me tasting you." She cocked her head to the side in concentration. "Before, when you loved me with your mouth and tongue . . . is that something men like for women to do to them?"

"Oh aye," he breathed. "Just imagining your sweet mouth around my shaft is more than I can bear."

"Oh. 'Tis something I've never given thought to before."

He chuckled. "I should hope not. Where would you have gotten such thoughts from?"

She smiled. "Only a few hours in your company and I find myself completely debauched. Surely other lasses don't dwell on such things."

"I don't care what other lasses think about," he murmured. "Just one particular lass, and I'm awfully glad she's thinking what she is right now."

"Is it too soon?" she asked hesitantly. "I mean for me to . . ."

"Let me clean myself. Then I'll lie down so you're comfortable."

She reclined on her elbow and watched as he strode naked across the chamber to the pitcher and basin by the window. It was intensely arousing to watch him carefully clean the stickiness from his shaft. She glanced down at the smear on her belly and realized that she, too, needed cleaning.

She looked up, prepared to rise but Alaric had returned, a wet cloth in his hand. He reclined on the bed next to her and gently wiped away his semen from her belly.

His shaft distended stiffly from his groin, and he didn't look comfortable. How could he be? It looked . . . painful. Swollen and thick.

Tentatively, she reached out to touch him. He jerked against her and made an odd sound in his throat.

"I'm not certain what to do. I don't want to do it . . . wrong."

Alaric smiled and cupped her cheek. "I guarantee you won't do it wrong. Well, unless you use your teeth."

She giggled and then trailed her hand over his abdomen and up to his chest. "Perchance, you could instruct me on the way of it."

He kissed her, then nibbled at the corner of her mouth.

"Aye, lass. I'll show you the way of it, and then I'll die a happy man inside your mouth."

He rolled from the bed and stood at the edge. He held out his hand and when she took it, he pulled her to a sitting position. Then he arranged her legs so that her feet were planted on the floor and she was perched on the edge of the straw mattress.

She caught on immediately when she saw that his shaft was on perfect level with her mouth. He reached for her head, tangling his fingers in her hair as he positioned her just so.

"Open your mouth, lass. Let me inside."

He dropped one hand from her head and grasped the base of his cock. Slowly he guided himself forward, past her parted lips and over her tongue.

The sensation startled her. He was incredibly hard, blunt and probing, and yet the skin was silky soft, the sensation intoxicating.

"Relax. Trust me and breathe through your nose."

She hadn't realized how tense she was until his words settled over her. Heeding his instruction, she willed herself to relax and she sucked in air through her nostrils.

He framed her head with his hands and held her firmly while he eased forward, deeper than before. His fingers trembled. It was the only sign of how affected he was by her attentions.

Never had she imagined such an explicit act. It seemed tawdry, a whore's trick, something a lady would never contemplate, much less do. But it aroused Keeley. She wanted to please him—was desperate to please him. Her body did such odd things. Her breasts plumped and swelled. Her most feminine parts throbbed and pulsed, so much so that the slightest touch would send her spiraling out of control.

His taste was as masculine as his scent. Strong. A hint

of wood and smoke. She inhaled deeply, wanting his taste and his scent embedded into her memory.

A tiny spurt of liquid seeped onto her tongue. For a moment she savored it and allowed it to lubricate the deeper thrusts. Then she tenderly slid her tongue over the tip, sipping until there was nothing left.

He rocked up on his toes, straining forward as his fingers tightened on the sides of her head.

"Let me deeper. Swallow. Aye, that's it, Keeley. Just like that. Take me whole."

She swallowed against him and sucked him deep. For a moment she struggled to breathe, but he adjusted the angle so she was more comfortable.

He was inside her. All she could taste, breathe, or see was him. His heavy sac rested against her chin and the rough hairs at his groin tickled her nose.

When he retreated, he breathed so raggedly that the tortured sound was loud in the room. For a long moment he stood there, panting, his cock still distended a mere inch from her mouth while she, too, gasped for breath.

"Turn around," he ordered.

She blinked in confusion and looked behind her. She was on the bed. What did he mean?

"On your hands and knees. Face away from me," he said.

Even as she went to do his bidding, he helped her get awkwardly on her knees as she turned to face the wall. He urged her backward, easing her knees along the soft mattress until her lower legs dangled in midair.

As soon as he was satisfied with her position, he slid his hands over the curve of her behind. It was an odd sensation being in such a position. Her mind conjured all sorts of naughty images, but she wasn't sure such things were possible.

He squeezed and fondled the globes before moving

lower to spread her folds. He ran his fingers through her wetness, sliding easily inside her. His entry shocked her and she bucked upward to meet the movement of his hand.

"I would take you like this, Keeley. Like a stallion covering a mare. Would you like that?"

She closed her eyes and let her chin fall to her chest as she sucked in deep, steadying breaths through her nose.

"Aye," she whispered.

Her knees trembled and threatened to buckle underneath her. She braced her palms against the bed in an effort to keep from falling.

She felt extremely vulnerable in this position. She had no defense. He could take her as he liked, do anything he wanted, and there was naught she could do.

Again his hand smoothed over her backside, caressing and rubbing until she sighed with pleasure. Then his other hand grasped her hip and he held her in place.

The tip of his cock bumped against her entrance, moved away, and then back again before he finally plunged forward, burying himself in her damp heat.

She threw back her head and would have cried out if he suddenly hadn't covered her mouth with his hand.

"Shh, lass. Easy now," he soothed.

She let out a whimper as he pushed even deeper. It didn't seem possible that she could take him so deep. She felt full to bursting, stretched so tight around him, it was almost painful.

"I'm going to ride you hard, Keeley." The words came out as a near growl. His voice was hoarse and raspy as though he hung on to control by a mere thread. "Just lie still and take it. I'll take care of you."

She had no choice. Her head was bent to the mattress and her arms were splayed out, her fingers curled into the covers. Her knees were her only means of support as he drove into her again and again.

Images battered her mind. How must he look mounted over her? Her mouth went completely dry, and she closed her eyes as pleasure quaked over her body.

He was deep, so much deeper than he'd been the previous two times he'd taken her. She was much more sensitive now after having endured his possession twice already. His movements were part pain, but raw, edgy pleasure as well.

After a few moments, the cloud of pleasure dissipated and she became aware of the raw twinges with every one of his thrusts. He was too thick, too big, too deep this way.

He plunged deep, his hips slapping against her buttocks. She let out a soft cry and flinched away.

He froze and carefully withdrew, but even that elicited a tiny sound of pain.

"Keeley, what is it? Have I hurt you?"

He turned her around, sat on the bed, and pulled her into his arms. He kissed her brow and stroked her hair as he stared anxiously into her eyes.

She grimaced. "I'm a bit tender."

He cursed softly, self-recrimination burning brightly in his eyes. "You were a virgin and yet I've used you like a woman well accustomed to matters of the flesh. 'Tis inexcusable. I wanted you so much that I paid no heed to your comfort."

She rubbed her hand over his cheek and smiled. "I wanted you as much as you wanted me. I still do. 'Twas just uncomfortable for a moment."

Alaric shook his head. "You should have a long, hot, soaking bath to soothe your aches and pains. I'll have one brought up to your chamber so you can have the care you deserve."

Again she smiled and pushed her mouth up to his to kiss him. "A bath sounds heavenly, but right now, we have but another hour until dawn. And I want to spend that time in your arms. Could we lie in your bed and rest for the remainder of our time?"

His gaze softened and he pushed a stray tendril of hair behind her ear. "Aye, lass. There's nothing more I want than to hold you against me. When the morning comes, I'll have your bath brought up to your chambers. No shame will be visited upon you for this night."

She grasped his hand and squeezed. "It would be worth any shame to have spent this night with you, Alaric. I want you to know that. I have no regrets."

"Me either. No regrets. I'll hold this night close for the rest of my days."

She allowed him to lay them both back onto the bed. Alaric reached for the furs and pulled them over himself and Keeley until they were bundled up warm against each other.

"I'll not sleep this night," she said. "For I don't want to miss a single minute in your arms."

Alaric kissed her brow and gently rubbed his hand repeatedly down the side of her hair.

"I'll not pretend I've not loved you, Keeley. In public, aye, I'd never do anything to bring you shame. In private, however, don't expect me to pretend you didn't give your innocence to me."

Her smile was sad. "Nay, Alaric. I'll not pretend either. But 'tis for the best not to dwell on impossible matters."

"Let us cease this kind of talk. I find it makes my heart heavy."

"Then wrap yourself around me and keep me warm until I must rise and return to my cold bedchamber."

"Aye, lass. I can do just that."

CHAPTER 20

Dawn was creeping across the sky, bringing with it ugly fingers of regret that the night was over. Keeley lay sleeping against him, her head nestled in the crook of his arm.

Her arm was thrown possessively over his midriff and her breasts were flattened against his side.

Slowly he grazed his fingers up and down her bare arm as he inhaled the scent of her hair just an inch from his nose. He loved touching her. Loved her smell. Loved the feel of her next to him. It was a feeling he'd enjoy waking to for all his days.

Instead he had to look forward to another woman in his bed. Someone who didn't have Keeley's sweetness or her fire. Or her infuriating stubbornness that amused him to no end.

He turned into her, gathering her tight as he buried his face in her hair. She stirred quietly next to him and stretched, her body tightening against his as her back bowed.

As he drew away so he could look down at her, her lips split into a wide yawn and then her eyelashes fluttered as the lids opened. At first her eyes were cast in cloudy sleepiness, but then they warmed as she smiled up at him.

Unable to resist, he stroked the line of her cheek with his fingertip. At her lips, he paused and she kissed the tip before returning her gaze to his eyes.

"Good morn," he murmured.

She snuggled closer to him. "I hate 'tis morning already."

Dread pulsed in his throat. "Aye, I hate it, too. But we must hasten you back to your chamber before 'tis discovered you're here."

She sighed and rose up on her elbow, her hair spilling over her shoulder, covering her plump breasts. When she would have pushed herself even farther away from him, he caught her by the waist and rolled her until she was atop him.

Raising his head, he caught her lips, so full and sweet. Soft like the finest silk. He kissed her as he'd never kissed a woman, allowing the full force of his desire and his regret to spill over.

As she pulled away, her eyes dark with all the things he felt most, he smoothed a hand over her cheek, then thrusting his fingers into the thick pelt of her hair. "You have no equal, Keeley. I want you to know that."

She smiled and lowered down to kiss him one last time. "You have no equal either, warrior."

He sighed. The time had come. She must return now before the keep came alive with activity and the halls were filled with those attending the needs of the laird and his lady.

"Dress quickly, lass," he urged. "I'll give Gannon his instructions."

As she hurried over to slip her dress back on, Alaric went to the door and cracked it open. Only Gannon was outside in the darkened hallway. Nary a window or a torch illuminated the path.

"Gannon," Alaric whispered.

Trained to be alerted by the slightest of noises, Gannon roused himself and was on his feet in a mere moment.

"Is something amiss?" Gannon demanded.

"Nay, I have need of something."

Gannon waited.

"Take the tub from this room into Keeley's. Have water brought up for a hot bath. Make sure no one knows where she spent her night. While you are belowstairs, I'll return her to her room."

Gannon nodded, and Alaric looked back to make sure Keeley was fully dressed. He didn't want her embarrassed by Gannon's appearance so he strode across the room, shielding her from view with his large body while Gannon set about dragging the tub from the chamber.

Keeley lay her cheek against his chest and he rested his chin atop her head. When the chamber door closed behind Gannon, Alaric drew away and clasped her shoulders.

"Come. I'll see you to your chambers. You should be abed when the water is brought up so it appears you have just awoken."

She bit her bottom lip and then nodded. Before he gave in to the temptation to hold her a moment longer, he guided her toward the door and into the darkened hallway.

They ducked quickly into the chamber just as Gannon was exiting. Alaric held up a finger for him to await him before urging Keeley toward the bed.

She climbed beneath the covers and Alaric sat on the edge, simply watching her for a long moment. Then he bent and pressed his lips to her forehead.

"I'll treasure last night forever."

"As will I," she whispered. "Go now, Alaric. Parting is all the more difficult for the hesitation."

He swallowed and stood abruptly. She was right in

that regard. The longer he tarried, the more tempted he was to say to hell with everyone.

Without a backward glance he left the chamber. Gannon awaited him, and Alaric gave his instructions in a terse voice.

"See to her bath. Make sure she is undisturbed. Pass the word that she is tired and feeling unwell and will remain in her chamber for the day. There is no work for her to be done this day."

"Aye," Gannon said with a nod.

Alaric watched him go and then stepped back into his chamber. He closed the door behind him and leaned heavily against it, his heart thudding like an ax to wood.

Being with Keeley had been the sweetest of pleasures, but having her and knowing he was forbidden her was an agony that surpassed any wound of the flesh.

Keeley hunkered lower in the now cooling water and drew her knees to her chin. The heat had soothed the aches in her body, but naught could be done about the ache that still resided in her heart.

She shook her head and turned to lay her cheek on her knees. Last night had been the single most wonderful night of her life. It was a moment to cherish. She'd spend a lifetime reliving every touch. Every touch.

There was no place for sadness now.

And yet she couldn't shake the heavy feeling in her chest.

A knock sounded at the door, and Keeley closed her eyes, hugging her legs a little closer. If she ignored the summons, they'd go away surely.

To her horror, the door swung open. Just as she was frantically searching for a way to preserve her modesty, Maddie stuck her head around.

Keeley slumped against the back of the wooden tub. "Oh, 'tis you. I nearly had failure of the heart."

"I heard you were ailing. I wanted to come up and see if there is anything I can do."

Keeley smiled, or tried to. The result was her eyes stinging and watering. She sniffed but as soon as the first tear trickled down her cheek, she was done for.

Maddie look horrified and then her features crinkled in sympathy. "Oh lass, whatever is the matter? Now, now, let me get you out of that tub. 'Twill be all right."

Keeley allowed Maddie to help her from the tub, and then wrapped in a drying linen, she sat in front of the fire while Maddie dried and combed out her hair.

"Now tell me what's prompted your upset," Maddie said gently.

"Oh Maddie. I fear I've made a huge mistake, but 'tis the truth I don't regret a minute of it."

"Would this have something to do with Alaric McCabe?"

Keeley turned her tearful gaze to Maddie. " 'Tis so obvious? Does everyone know of my shame?"

Maddie enfolded her into her arms. "Shh. None of that." She rocked back and forth, soothing Keeley with motherly noises.

"I gave myself to him," Keeley whispered. "He's to marry another and I went to him anyway. I couldn't resist any longer."

"You love him."

"Aye. I love him."

Maddie made a sound of sympathy. " 'Tis no shame in giving yourself to a man you love. But I must know, did he take advantage of you, lass?"

There was an edge of anger to Maddie's tone and Keeley ripped herself away from the older woman. "Nay! He is as tortured as I am. He knows he must marry Rionna. We've both tried to ignore what is between us. 'Tis I who went to him last eve."

Maddie reached to trail her fingers down the locks of

Keeley's hair in a soothing manner. "'Tis hard when the heart must be denied. I don't have words to tend the hurt. I wish I did. But you are a good lass, Keeley. You mustn't allow the ills done to you in the past to influence you now. You aren't a whore. You have a good and loyal heart. The McCabes are fortunate to have you."

Keeley threw herself in Maddie's arms and hugged the other woman fiercely. "Thank you, Maddie. 'Tis the truth I've never had dearer friends than you and the other women of the keep. I'll never forget your kindness—or your understanding."

Maddie stroked Keeley's hair and returned her hug. "Gannon has told the others that you're tired and ailing. We all agree you've done much in your time here. Why don't I go down and ask Gertie to send up something to eat. I'll come sit with you if you like, but you should go to bed and have a long rest."

Keeley nodded and slowly pulled away. "I'd like that. 'Tis the truth I'm tired and sick at heart. I haven't the strength to smile this day and pretend naught is the matter."

Maddie patted her hand. "Hie yourself to bed and let me take care of the rest. Your secret 'tis safe with me. I'll not even be telling Lady McCabe. 'Tis your concern who you share your affairs with."

"Thank you," Keeley said again.

Maddie rose and gestured toward the bed. "Go now. Make yourself comfortable. After a night of loving, I imagine your appetite 'tis monstrous."

Keeley blushed and then laughed. "Aye, it is to be sure."

Maddie smiled and exited the room, closing the door behind her. Keeley pulled on her nightdress and then burrowed under the covers. It was a cold day and her chamber had a chill despite the fire Gannon had thoughtfully tended.

As she waited for Maddie, she stared up at the ceiling, grateful she wouldn't bear the day alone. Her heart already ached enough without the burden of solitude. Sometimes 'twas best to share with a friend. She missed the friendship that she and Rionna used to share.

Keeley had lived a long time alone, but now that she'd found the companionship—and camaraderie—of other women, the idea of going back to the silent cottage was more than she could bear.

She wanted to be part of the McCabe clan. As painful as it would be, knowing Alaric was close but never to be hers. But she wasn't willing to be a coward and flee to sulk and lick her wounds in solitude. She was tired of being alone.

She wanted to belong.

Moments later, Maddie returned, not only with Mairin but Christina as well. The women burst into Keeley's chambers, their smiles warm, their laughter vibrant.

Christina was ablaze with joy as she recounted Cormac's marriage proposal. Maddie glanced over at Keeley and then reached to squeeze her hand. Keeley squeezed back and smiled fondly at Christina.

The lass was overjoyed, and Keeley allowed that happiness to seep into her soul, bringing with it a measure of comfort she desperately needed. She gathered the blankets to her chest and watched as Maddie added another log to the fire. Food and ale were delivered, and soon the women's laughter filtered into the hall and beyond.

At his chamber door, Alaric paused and listened to the honeyed sound of Keeley's amusement. He closed his eyes and rubbed the bridge of his nose between his thumb and forefinger. Then he turned and strode rapidly down the hall toward the stair, ignoring the increasing discomfort in his side.

CHAPTER 21

"Keeley! Keeley!"

Keeley turned her head to see Crispen bolting across the great hall toward her. She braced herself, having become well acquainted with the way Crispen "greeted" her.

He flung himself around her, nearly knocking them both to the floor, but Keeley's preparation kept them upright.

She laughed and pried him away from her. "What are you about, Crispen?"

"Will you go outside and play with us in the snow? Will you, Keeley? Mama can't go. Papa has forbidden her outside the doors. She's not happy, but Maddie says 'tis good because Mama is ungainly and as round as a pumpkin and she might fall on the ice."

Keeley hesitated, nearly laughing at the flood of words from the lad's mouth.

"The storm is over and the sun's out. 'Tis a beautiful day. Papa has been out training since dawn. We can play on the hill and Gannon and Cormac can come along."

"Slow down," she said with a chuckle. " 'Tis the truth I'd welcome a bit of fresh air."

Crispen's face lit up. "Then you'll come? Really?" He all but danced out of her reach and around the hall.

"If you'll give me a moment to don warmer clothing, I'll be glad to come out with you as long as you have the laird's permission."

Crispen nodded eagerly. "I'll go ask him now."

"Very well. I'll meet you back belowstairs in a few minutes' time."

She watched as Crispen dashed out of the hall at full speed and then shaking her head, she headed toward the stairs to don clothing appropriate for the bitter cold.

When she returned, both Cormac and Gannon stood in the hall surrounded by Crispen and several other children. They looked wearily in her direction as she approached.

Grinning, she made it a point to enthusiastically greet each of the children and then she asked if they were ready to proceed outdoors. Surrounded by their lively chatter, she stepped into the cold and shivered as chill bumps prickled up her spine.

" 'Tis cold today!" she exclaimed.

"Aye, 'tis," Cormac grumbled. "Too cold to be standing still watching over children."

Keeley slanted a sly smile in Cormac's direction. " 'Tis likely Christina will be joining us."

His expression brightened and then he glanced rapidly in Gannon's direction and adopted a more bland look.

"Come on!" Crispen urged. He tugged at Keeley's hand until she gave in and hurried up the hill toward the area where the children played.

Teams were quickly formed and Keeley groaned when she realized the game was tossing balls of snow at one another with as much force as they could muster.

Thankfully for her, Gretchen was on Keeley's team and she was quite adept at hitting her target. The boys howled with outrage every time Gretchen pelted one of them in the face.

Breathless with exertion after an hour of steady warfare, they called a truce and stood, hands on hips, gasping for air.

Crispen and Gretchen were whispering in low tones and kept staring over at Cormac and Gannon.

"You ask," Crispen muttered.

"Nay, you ask," Gretchen demanded. "'Tis your father's men. They'll more likely do it for you."

Crispen jutted his chin out. "You're a girl. 'Tis fact girls always get what they want."

Gretchen rolled her eyes and then punched him hard in the arm.

"Ow!"

Crispen glared at her and rubbed his arm. "We'll both ask."

Gretchen smiled serenely and the two ran in Gannon's direction. Keeley watched with interest when the two warriors visibly recoiled. Then they began shaking their heads and making negative gestures. They frowned, then scowled, and the children argued on.

It wasn't until Gretchen's expression turned from fierce determination to pitifully woeful that the men began to look uneasy. Her big eyes shimmered with tears and her chin quivered.

"Oh dear. They don't stand a chance now."

Keeley turned to see Christina approaching, her eyes twinkling with amusement.

"Gretchen isn't opposed to using womanly wiles if it gains her what she wants. A more clever lass I've never met," Christina said ruefully. "If she can't beat capitulation from someone, she'll turn on the pitiful eyes."

"I'm dying to know what they want," Keeley said.

"Whatever it is, it looks like they've been successful."

Cormac looked up and his eyes brightened when he saw Christina. Gannon turned in the direction of the keep while Crispen and Gretchen trailed Cormac as he walked over to where the two women stood.

"Gannon's going to fetch his shield!" Crispen crowed.

"His shield?" Keeley asked.

"Aye," Gretchen said. "To slide down the hill on."

"'Tis a sin to abuse a shield thusly," Cormac muttered.

"'Tis good fun to ride down the hill atop them," Crispen piped in.

Gannon appeared in the distance, the sun glinting off the large shield that he bore up the hill. When he reached the crowd of children they cheered.

Intrigued by the notion of sliding down a hill on a warrior's shield, Keeley leaned closer to examine the object. 'Twas certainly large enough to hold a child or even a small adult.

"How does it work?"

"'Tis placed down like so," Gannon said, placing the outward face onto the snow. "Then someone climbs atop and another gives them a push down the hill."

Keeley's eyes widened. "Is it safe?"

Gannon sighed. "Not if we allow them to slide into the loch or the courtyard where the men are training. The laird would be furious."

"Then we must go the other way," Keeley said, pointing away from the keep and the stone skirts.

Cormac eyed the next hill, sloping upward from the slight crest they were standing on. "Aye, the lass is right. We'll need to go over the top of the next so we stay away from harm."

"Yay! 'Tis a much steeper hillside to ride down," Crispen cheered as they slogged up the rise through the snow.

"Me first!" Robbie cried as soon as they were looking down at the valley below them.

"Nay, 'twas my idea and I did the asking," Gretchen protested. "'Tis only fair I go first."

"Let her go first," Crispen muttered. "'Twill be her who is killed if 'tis not safe."

Robbie grinned. "'Tis a sound plan that. All right, Gretchen. 'Tis agreed. You go first."

Gretchen stared suspiciously at both boys but gladly took position on the shield that Gannon positioned in the snow.

"Now hold your skirts tight and don't let go of the sides," Christina said anxiously.

"All set?" Cormac asked.

"Aye, send me off," Gretchen said, her eyes wide with excitement.

Gannon gave her a gentle push, but the polished iron of the shield was slick on the surface and she quickly picked up speed. Soon she was flying along the ground, barely skimming the surface.

At one point she turned sideways, gave a delighted squeal, and then was able to set herself to rights by using the weight of her body.

"'Tis a clever lass," Gannon said in resignation. "I've no doubt that one day she'll lead her own army."

Christina and Keeley exchanged smug glances.

Gretchen landed at the bottom, coming to a skidding halt barely inches from one of the large trees that guarded the entrance to the forest. She waved her hand excitedly to let them know that all was well, not that they couldn't tell that from the broad grin covering her face.

Dragging the shield behind her, she struggled up the hillside until Gannon went down to help her.

Crispen was next to go and he shouted all the way down, his laughter ringing over the snow. He spun in several dizzying circles at the bottom before coming to a halt in a particularly deep drift.

Robbie was next and he howled his displeasure at tipping over halfway down and rolling like a runaway snowball for the rest of the way.

Thinking it looked like good fun, Crispen and Gretchen threw themselves in the snow and began rolling down the hill after Robbie.

"Would you like to try it, Keeley?" Gannon offered politely as he pointed at the empty shield.

Her first instinct was a vehement refusal, but she swore she saw challenge in the warrior's eyes. Her gaze narrowed and she fixed him with a glare. "You think me too cowardly to try."

Gannon shrugged. "It does seem rather fearsome for a slight lass as yourself."

Christina choked and covered the sound with rapid coughing.

"That sounds remarkably like a challenge, warrior, but I have one of my own to make. If I go down the hill without tumbling from the shield, you and Cormac must also attempt it."

Cormac scowled. " 'Tis unseemly for warriors to indulge in child's play."

"Well, if you're afraid," she said innocently.

"Did you question our courage?" Gannon asked incredulously.

"Aye, I did. What think you to do about it?"

Gannon threw down the shield and pointed. "Get yourself on it and prepare to be soundly trumped."

Keeley rolled her eyes and settled herself onto the cold metal. " 'Tis so like a man to allow his pride to go before a fall."

Before she could say yay or nay, or anything else for that matter, Gannon gave her a mighty shove down the hill. She lurched back and grasped desperately at the edge of the shield and hung on for dear life as the slick metal flew over the ice-covered landscape.

Oh dear, this was indeed a lot more difficult than it

appeared, and she would need all her wits about her to complete the run without taking a huge spill.

Down the hill the children chanted her name and cheered wildly as she drew near. The problem was she raced right by them and into the trees beyond.

She squeezed her eyes shut and curled her arms atop her head just as she went flying through the air. She landed with a bounce in a snowdrift and ate a mouthful of snow.

Thank goodness she hadn't wrapped herself around a tree.

"Keeley! Keeley!"

It was hard to discern who shouted her name. It was a mix of the children and the roars of Gannon and Cormac. She glanced up in time to see the children fast converging while Gannon and Cormac—after instructing Christina to remain where she was—charged down the hill.

An uneasy prickle raced down Keeley's nape. Her nostrils flared and she sensed . . . Her head whipped up just as several warriors charged through the trees, bearing right down on her and the children.

"Attack!" she yelled. "We're under attack!"

Intrigued by the fact that Gannon had fetched an old shield from the pile of armor that needed repairing, Alaric followed after the other man as he trudged up the hill to where the children usually played. Only, no one was there. He knew that Keeley had taken the children to play as Ewan had given Crispen permission for her to do so.

He quickened his step to follow Gannon and when he reached the rise that Gannon had disappeared over, he saw Keeley, Christina, Cormac, and the children at the next peak. He quickly saw the purpose of the shield when Gretchen plopped down onto it and then went flying down the opposite side.

With a grin he started the long hike up the opposing side. He hadn't slid down a hill on a shield in many a year. It still sounded like a hell of a lot of fun though.

When he staggered to the top, he was shocked to see Keeley settle onto the shield and then Gannon give her a mighty push. One way too big for a lass her size. She went spinning down the hill, out of control and obviously headed for trouble.

She disappeared into the trees just as Gannon and Cormac turned and saw Alaric standing there.

The two men started down the hillside at a near run, slipping and sliding along the way. The children had already disappeared into the trees after her, when Alaric started after Gannon and Cormac.

The men froze when they heard Keeley cry, "Attack! We're under attack!"

Not wasting a moment, the three men drew their swords. Cormac shouted back toward the keep in hopes the men would hear, then he snarled at Christina to run for help.

As soon as they reached the trees, they were met by Robbie and Gretchen who stumbled out, tears streaming down their faces. They babbled incoherently as Gannon caught both of them against him.

"They have Keeley and Crispen," Gretchen cried. "You must hurry. They have horses."

"Christ's blood!" Alaric swore. "We'll never catch them on foot in these drifts."

Using their swords for leverage, they rammed through the snow, following the hoofprints as they led farther into the forest.

Anger and fear beat strongly in Alaric's chest. He'd nearly lost Ewan's son before. They'd thought him dead. And now Alaric was faced with not only losing a lad who was dear to the entire clan but also a woman who was more dear to him than any other human being.

When they rounded the corner beyond a particularly dense settings of trees, the landscape opened up to a wide path through clean snow. To Alaric's utter astonishment, Crispen jumped from behind one of the trees and threw himself into Alaric's arms.

"Uncle Alaric, you must hurry. They have Keeley and they think she's my mama. They'll kill her when they know the truth!"

"How on earth did you get free, lad?" Alaric demanded. For if Cameron thought he held Ewan's wife and his son, he'd truly have everything Ewan held dear in the world. He couldn't imagine them simply letting Crispen go.

"Keeley kicked two of the men betwixt the legs and told me to run. She tried to run too, but the third man, the one who wasn't rolling around on the snow, caught her by the hair and pulled her back. She screamed at me to go and that she'd never let me throw another snowball in my life if I didn't heed her instructions."

"The lass saved the boy's live," Cormac murmured.

Alaric nodded. "Aye, 'twould seems she has a habit of saving the McCabes."

He grasped Crispen by the shirt. "Are you hurt anywhere, lad? I need you to go back to the keep and tell your father what has transpired here. Tell him we need horses and men. Make sure he leaves enough behind to defend the keep and that Mairin is safely locked away."

"Aye," Crispen said, determination etched into his youthful features. Only now he didn't appear so young. He looked damned angry.

"Come," he ordered Gannon and Cormac. "We continue on foot until the others have reached us on horseback. We must stay on their tracks."

CHAPTER 22

Several long minutes later, Ewan thundered up, leading a horse for Alaric. Behind him, his men trailed, armor on, weapons at the ready.

Alaric threw himself onto the horse and ignored the scream of protest his side gave at the first time he'd remounted since his injury. Behind him Cormac and Gannon also mounted, while six of his men herded the children into a protective circle and took them back to the keep.

Not awaiting Ewan's orders, Alaric charged forward, sending his horse into the drifts. At first the horse struggled but then found his footing and charged over the terrain.

He followed the sets of hoofprints, his brothers and men close behind him all the while.

"Have more care, Alaric," Ewan called. "Could be an ambush."

Alaric's lips curled as he glanced back at his brother. "They thought they'd abducted Mairin. Think you that you would be telling me have more care if it was she who was danger?"

Ewan grimaced but fell silent.

"They couldn't think to get far in this weather. 'Twas

a risky abduction," Alaric muttered as he studied the terrain.

"Aye. They're desperate and hoped to strike when we least expected it."

Caelen spurred his horse through a particularly deep drift. "We shouldn't be leaving the keep unattended. 'Tis Mairin and the babe who are all important."

In that moment, Alaric would have struck his brother if he were close enough. As it was, it was all he could do not to launch himself across the distance and drag him from his horse. Only the knowledge that for every moment lost, Keeley would be farther away kept him from venting his rage.

"Enough," Ewan barked. "Keeley is important to the well-being of Mairin and the babe. We go after her. The keep is well guarded. Only a fool would launch a full attack in the dead of winter."

"Cameron has proved he's a fool tenfold over," Alaric pointed out. "Let's find her before it's too late."

Even as he said the words, dread filled his heart. He knew that as soon as it was discovered Keeley wasn't Mairin, her life would be forfeit. She'd be discarded. Of no use. Cameron was ruthless in his pursuit of his goal and he'd allow no one to slow him down.

He urged his horse onward, to the point of exhaustion. If their pace was quicker, they'd close the gap.

"'Tis madness for you to be out here," Caelen growled. "You're not fit to be riding a horse or going into battle."

Alaric stared hotly at his brother, rage bubbling like a cauldron. "If I don't fight for her, who will?"

"I won't leave her to Cameron," Caelen said. "I don't understand your fascination with the lass, but I'll not abandon her to her fate. You should return to the keep."

Alaric ignored his brother and pushed onward, snow flying up in great puffs. The longer they spent in pursuit, the more his spirits flagged. It had been an hour. Maybe longer. He had no sense of time. The sun was sinking lower, and soon dusk would be upon them. Any chance of tracking would be gone until torches could be brought forth to continue the search.

They rode on in silence, their gazes scanning the horizon for any sign of the attackers.

They almost rode by her.

Caelen was the one who first spotted the lump in the snow. He pulled up hard, his horse rearing. He'd dismounted and was wading through the snow before Alaric could process what was amiss.

"Alaric, 'tis her!"

Ewan and Alaric both slid from their horses, and Alaric's knees buckled from the sharp pain that splintered through his side. He gasped, yanked his arm against his body, and shoved all but the thought of Keeley from his mind.

Caelen knelt and began frantically brushing away the snow from her body. Alaric rushed forward and dropped to his knees beside her. He aided Caelen in clearing the rest of the snow from her clothing and then lifted her into his arms.

"Keeley," he whispered. "Keeley!" he said louder when she didn't respond.

She was cold. Her skin like ice. He pressed his ear to her nose and mouth and relief nearly crushed him when he felt the light brush of her breath.

He pulled away just enough that he could examine her for injury.

"She's bleeding from the head," Caelen said grimly, as he ran his finger through her hair. "Or she was. 'Tis too cold and the bleeding has stopped."

"We must hurry," Ewan urged. "Her attackers may still be about and it's growing colder."

As Alaric started to rise, she stirred and her features twisted in pain.

"Keeley?"

Her eyelids fluttered open and she stared up at him, her eyes dazed.

"Alaric?"

"Aye, lass. Thank God you're all right. 'Tis the truth you scared ten years from my life."

"We can't have that warrior," she teased. "You may only have a few years left if that's the truth."

Some of the tightness eased in his chest and he felt faint with relief. He squeezed her against him and hurried back toward his horse.

"I'll have the whole of the story but not now. We must hasten back to the keep," Alaric said.

Wordlessly, Caelen took her from Alaric's arms and waited while Alaric carefully mounted. Then he held Keeley up for Alaric to take. Further surprising Alaric, Caelen retrieved a blanket from his mount and held it up so Alaric could wrap her in the warmth.

"Thank you, Caelen," Keeley uttered in a raspy, weak voice.

Caelen nodded shortly and then leapt atop his horse and spurred him through the drifts. Alaric fell in behind Caelen while Ewan brought up the rear.

When they rode over the next rise, they were met by a contingent of McCabe soldiers. They quickly surrounded their laird and his brothers and escorted them back to the keep.

As soon as they entered the courtyard, Caelen swung down and simply held his arms up for Keeley.

"I can walk," she protested.

Caelen said nothing but neither did he relinquish her. He frowned when Alaric slid down and reached for her.

"Go ahead of us. You're in no state to be carrying the

lass. You'll reopen that damn wound when it's almost healed."

Not wanting to argue when Keeley shivered with cold, Alaric hurried inside, leaving Ewan to give orders to his men.

Caelen barked a series of orders and people scurried in all directions to do his bidding. He carried Keeley into her chamber as several serving women swarmed around him to build up the fire and add furs to the bed for warmth.

When he lay Keeley on the bed, she shivered from head to toe. Her teeth clattered violently, and Alaric shoved Caelen aside to climb onto the bed next to her.

Alaric wrapped his arms tightly around her and then directed Caelen to lay the furs over the both of them.

"C-C-Cold," she chattered. "S-So c-cold."

Alaric brushed his lips over her head. "I know, love. Hold tight to me. We'll have you warm in no time."

"Crispen," she said in alarm. "Is he safe? Did you find him? And the other children?"

"Aye, you saw to that. Crispen is well. Tell me, how did you escape, lass?"

To his surprise, she cracked a smile around her chattering teeth. "They thought me to be Mairin and as soon as they discovered their error, they tried to kill me."

Alaric swore. 'Twas as he thought.

Caelen's eyes narrowed. "And yet you survived. Were they inept?"

"Unfortunately for you, they were," she said dryly. "I know how fraught with disappointment you must be. But nay, I convinced them that I was a witch and I would curse them and their entire line to eternity if they murdered me."

Caelen scowled. "I have no wish for you to die, Keeley. 'Tis not well done of you to suggest so."

She raised an eyebrow.

Alaric cut in impatiently. "A witch? And they believed this nonsense?"

"Aye, well, I'd already caused them considerable pain. I fought them, allowing Crispen to run free. I bit the one who held me before him on his horse. He was already half convinced I was a demon from hell when I threatened to curse him."

Caelen chuckled. "You're an ingenious lass. 'Tis amazing you were able to think so quick on your feet. The men likely ran for their lives."

She snuggled farther into Alaric's arms, her eyes closing.

"Nay, lass, you must stay awake," Alaric said in alarm. He glanced frantically at Caelen. "Argue with her. Tease her or make her angry. She cannot fall asleep until we've warmed her and tended to her wounds."

Concern shadowed Caelen's eyes. He leaned over to where Keeley lay nestled in Alaric's arms. " 'Tis the truth I'm sorry I was nice to you, Keeley. You grow all soft and womanly on me given a bit of kindness. And here I thought you a much fiercer lass."

She cracked one eye open and stared balefully up at him. "I have no intention of dying, Caelen, so you may save your insults. 'Tis the truth, though, I prefer you surly, for I know not this man before me. Perhaps 'tis proof I have died and just don't have the sense to realize it yet."

Caelen threw back his head and laughed. "Aye, you're much too ornery to die, lass. I guess that much we have in common."

"God help me," Alaric muttered. " 'Tis the last thing I have need of. Two Caelens."

"Do you have plans to be nicer to me now?" Keeley murmured sleepily.

"Only if you stay awake and cease to worry my

brother," he returned. "Alaric looks like a worried mother."

"Don't be nice. It has me thinking I'm dying."

Her voice was growing fainter and it worried Alaric. Where were the serving women with the hot water? The warm broth? More blankets and dry clothing?

Caelen and Alaric exchanged concerned glances, and then Caelen abruptly stood and strode to the door. He bellowed down the hallway, making Keeley flinch in Alaric's arms.

A moment later, Maddie hurried in with Christina, Bertha, and Mairin on her heels.

"Mairin," Alaric reproached. "You shouldn't be up and about. Leave Keeley's care to the rest of us."

She pointed a finger. "You hush, Alaric McCabe. Keeley is my friend and she saved my son. I'll see to her needs until I'm satisfied all is well."

The tub and pails of water were borne into the room. Soon the tub was filled and the women began to shoo the men from the room.

Reluctantly Alaric rose. He didn't want to leave her, but his presence would only raise questions and make things uncomfortable for Keeley.

Still, he positioned himself outside the door and refused to budge while Keeley was being cared for. Caelen remained with him and soon Ewan joined the two men.

"I assume my wife is within," Ewan said in resignation.

"Aye, they're warming Keeley in the tub," Alaric said.

"Our watch has been doubled and the children have been forbidden to go beyond the first skirt. None of the women are to leave the keep unescorted."

Caelen nodded his agreement. "The sooner spring arrives and our alliances are sealed, the sooner we can turn our eyes to destroying Cameron. Our clan will never know peace while he's alive."

Alaric swallowed and leaned his head back against the wall. Aye, he knew there was urgent need of his marriage to Rionna McDonald. The sooner the better. And yet he dreaded her arrival with everything within him. He prayed for a harsh winter and frequent snows. Anything that would keep the McDonalds within their walls.

Keeley's door opened and Mairin stepped outside. Ewan's arm instantly wrapped around her, and she lay her head on his shoulder.

But it was Alaric she looked at when she spoke. "Keeley is doing well. We've warmed her and she's abed. There was a wound to her head where one of her attackers struck her, but 'tisn't a serious injury. It won't even require stitching."

Alaric's chest collapsed in relief. He watched as the other women filed by him and ignored the inquiring look that Maddie sent his way. As soon as everyone had left the room, he turned to go in.

At the door he paused and looked back at his brothers. "See that we aren't disturbed."

CHAPTER 23

Keeley opened her eyes to see Alaric standing by the bed, his expression brooding and inquisitive.

"How are you feeling?" he asked.

"Warm. Finally warm."

But even as she spoke, a shiver rolled over her body, setting off another round of uncontrollable chills.

With a muttered curse, he slid onto the bed next to her and pulled her into his arms.

He was heaven. Like a stone warmed in an oven. She pushed every part of her body into his and absorbed his heat to her bones. It was so exquisite that she moaned.

"Are you in pain?" he asked quickly.

"Nay. 'Tis a wondrous sensation. You are so warm. I may never want to move."

He kissed her brow and soothed a hand over her face. "If 'twas my choice, you never would."

"Can I sleep now? Maddie said the injury to my head wasn't serious. I find myself unable to hold my eyes open."

"Aye, Keeley, sleep. I'll remain ever near to watch over you."

His promise gladdened her heart and spread warmth into areas still numb with the cold. Although she knew he shouldn't be here, she hadn't the power—or the desire—to turn him away.

She rubbed her cheek over his broad chest and sighed in contentment. The night was hers, and she'd not spend a single moment lamenting what couldn't be changed. Instead she'd enjoy whatever she could have, while she could have it, and tomorrow would take care of itself.

During the night, Alaric was awakened by Keeley's restless movements. It took him a moment in his deep sleep to realize that she was still asleep herself.

Rousing himself, he studied her in the dim light as she twisted fretfully next to him. Fear took hold and he cupped a hand over her forehead.

He cursed as he registered the warmth radiating from her.

"'Tis cold," she said in a small voice. "I can't get warm. Please, the fire, I need the fire."

Shivers wracked her body, and as hot as she felt to his touch, she seemed equally freezing on the inside.

"Shh, love. I'll warm you."

Even as he said the words, he recalled the knowledge that extra warmth only added to a fever. Was he supposed to strip her of the furs and her clothing and bathe her in cool water, or at least wipe her brow with a cool rag?

Helplessness gripped him. He hadn't the skills to nurse someone with a fever. Battle was his skill. Killing and defense. Repairing wounds? He had no experience.

Gently he pried her body away from his and rolled from the heat of the furs. He was glad for the slight chill in the room, for Keeley burned with a fever, and where he'd warmed her earlier, she now had heat enough for the both of them.

He bent to brush his lips across her hot brow. "I'll return in a moment. I promise."

Her slight whimper tightened his chest, but he turned away and hurried out of the chamber. The hallway was dark and quiet. The keep was asleep. He walked all the way down to where Ewan's chamber was located.

He knocked, knowing Ewan was a light sleeper, but he didn't go in, not knowing what he'd interrupt between the laird and his wife if he did.

Only when he heard the gruff summons, did he crack the door and stick his head around.

" 'Tis I," Alaric whispered.

Ewan sat up in bed, careful to keep the furs covering Mairin.

"Alaric?" Mairin asked sleepily. "Is anything amiss? Is it Keeley?"

"Go back to sleep," Ewan said gently. "You have need of your rest. I'll see to the matter."

"Nothing is amiss," Alaric reassured. "I have need to speak with Ewan, 'tis all."

Ewan hurriedly dressed and joined Alaric in the hallway.

"What is the matter?" Ewan demanded.

"I didn't want to speak in front of Mairin because I knew she wouldn't sleep this night. Keeley has taken a fever and I know naught of healing skills."

"I'll come have a look," Ewan said.

The two men returned to Keeley's chamber. When they entered, Alaric saw that Keeley had managed to kick all the furs from the bed and she tossed back and forth, small sounds of distress escaping her lips.

Ewan frowned and went to the bed. He bent over and placed his hand over her forehead and then down to her cheeks.

"She's burning up," he said grimly.

Fear knotted in Alaric's throat. "How can such a thing be possible? She is unharmed for the most part. Just a small bump on the head. It didn't even require stitching."

"She lay in the snow for several hours," Ewan pointed out. " 'Tis enough to sicken even the stoutest warrior."

"So 'tis a minor ailment."

Ewan sighed. "I won't offer false reassurance, Alaric. I have no idea how ill she is. Only time will tell. For now we need to try to cool her skin no matter how chilled she might feel. I'll send down for a basin of water and some rags to bathe her forehead. 'Tis possible you'll need to submerge her in a bath of water. Our father used to swear by the method, as strange as it may sound, to cure a high fever. I can remember a time when he ordered snow packed into a tub for a warrior who'd raged with fever for four straight days. 'Twas not a comfortable experience for the warrior, but it saved him. He lives to this day."

"I'll do whatever it takes to save her."

Ewan nodded. "Aye, I know it. Stay with her. I'll go belowstairs to see to the supplies. 'Twill be a long night, Alaric. It could last for days."

"She nursed me through my worse," Alaric said quietly. "I can do no less for her. She has no one. We are her family now. 'Tis our duty to see to her needs just as we would any other member of our clan."

Ewan hesitated only a moment before nodding again. "I owe her a great debt for your life and now for my son. My debt will only grow if she sees Mairin through the delivery of our child. I can do no less than see to her every need."

Relief coursed through Alaric's blood. The last thing he wanted was to be in constant conflict with his brother. Keeley was important to him and even if any future between them was doomed, he would still do everything in his power to care for her.

Once Ewan departed the chamber, Alaric returned his

attention to Keeley, who lay limply on the bed, quiet now and still.

He eased down beside her and smoothed his hand over her side and up to her neck. She turned into his caress, her flesh dry and hot. Even her lips were hot and cracked against his palm.

She burrowed under him and then entwined her legs with his as if seeking every bit of his body heat.

"Cold," she murmured. "So cold."

Cupping the back of her head in his palm, he drew her into his neck and kissed her temple. "I know, love. I know you're cold. I'll care for you, I swear it. Even when you curse me with every breath, I won't waver."

She sighed against his flesh, and it sent a shiver down his spine. Then she kissed him, her mouth hot and erotic against his pulse. His entire body tightened as she stirred restlessly against him.

The top of her leg rubbed enticingly over the juncture of his legs, and he cursed low and hard when his cock swelled in response.

"I love the way you taste," she rasped out against his neck.

As if testing the veracity of her words, her tongue swept out and she licked against the thudding pulse that bumped even harder as her mouth closed wet and hot over the flesh of his neck.

Before he could extricate himself from her hold, she rose up and fused her mouth to his, so sweet and fiery that he couldn't breathe. He didn't want to move, so caught up in the feel of her, the smell of her.

Lusty and demanding. Hot, open-mouthed kisses that shattered every bit of his control. Surely God was testing him in this moment. He could feel the fires of hell licking at his ankles as he briefly contemplated sliding between her legs and giving them what they both so desperately wanted.

Not only would Ewan shortly return, but he simply wouldn't allow himself to take advantage of Keeley in a reduced state of awareness.

Keeley was about climb atop him and continue to kiss him senseless when Ewan returned to the chamber bearing two pails of water and several rags.

"You'll need to disrobe her and only use a light sheet as a covering. Nothing that will trap the heat within her body or create more."

Alaric scowled.

"I'll look away," Ewan muttered. "You forget I'm a man very devoted to my wife. I have no desire to see another woman's body."

As soon as Ewan began busying himself with dampening the clothes in the basin across the room, Alaric set about removing Keeley's gown—an act she was not happy about and determined to fight him at every turn.

"Nay!" she cried.

Tears thickened in her throat, making her already-hoarse voice all the more husky.

"Please, 'tis not seemly. You should not do this. 'Tis wrong!"

Her hands batted outward, connecting with Alaric's cheekbone. It stung, but she was as weak as a kitten and didn't pack much of a punch. Thank goodness.

"Shh, lass. I'm not going to hurt you. I swear it. Be at ease. 'Tis Alaric, your warrior."

When he continued to ease the dress over her shoulders she began weeping. Silent tears slid seamlessly down her cheeks. There was resignation in her posture as if she'd given up fighting off her unknown demon.

"'Tis my home," she said brokenly. "You can't turn me away from my home. I did nothing."

Alaric's rage knew no bounds. He realized now that she was reliving her treatment by the hands of Laird

McDonald and her subsequent banishment from the McDonald clan.

He wanted to march over and kill the whole lot of them.

"Jesu, what happened to her?" Ewan demanded quietly.

"She has had all manner of injustice heaped upon her," Alaric said in a tight voice. "If 'tis up to me, the debt owed to her will be repaid."

"Alaric . . ." Ewan trailed off and stared up at his brother while he rung out a series of cloths. He stopped and dropped the last over the edge of the pail. "Don't make her fall in love with you. 'Twould be cruel. She feels for you. Any fool can see that. Don't encourage her in this foolishness. It will only hurt her later when you marry another. If you care at all for her, you'll spare her that devastation and humiliation."

"You ask the impossible, Ewan. I can't . . . I can't just give her up because it's the right thing to do. Of course it's the right thing to do. I have no desire to hurt either woman even if I have no knowledge of Rionna McDonald. I would visit no shame on either of the women."

"This can't end well," Ewan said softly. "Whether for you or Rionna or Keeley. Someone will be hurt unless you end it here and now."

"Could you let go of Mairin? If the king came to you tomorrow and told you that she would be given in marriage to another man to seal an alliance with the throne of Scotland, would you simply say aye and accept that you could never have her?"

"That's a ridiculous comparison."

"I've not pushed aside my duty. I only know that as long as I have her, I refuse to pretend I'm not filled with gladness as soon as she comes into a room. I'm not going to waste a single second, so that when it comes time for us to part, we'll have a lifetime of memories to hold us into our old age."

"Fool," Ewan bit out. "Stay away from her. Make a clean break *before* you become too involved. 'Tis the best way."

Alaric smiled sadly. " 'Tis too late to tell me not to become too involved."

"Tread lightly then. We cannot afford to anger Gregor McDonald. Nay, he isn't the strongest of allies, but he's key in our quest to ally ourselves with the neighboring clan."

" 'Tis Gregor who is better not to anger me," Alaric hissed. "He has a lot to pay for on his deathbed. I'd like to hasten him to it for his treatment of Keeley."

Keeley began to moan and toss again, fretting in incoherent phrases and babbling nonsense. Ewan tossed Alaric one of the cool cloths and Alaric applied it over her forehead.

She quieted for a moment, but when Alaric placed the second cloth over her neck, she began to shiver violently.

"C-C-Cold, Alaric. Please. I don't want to be cold."

"Shhh, love, I'm here," he crooned.

"Do you want me to stay?" Ewan asked.

Alaric shook his head. "Nay, Mairin will wonder why you are up. If I have need of water for the tub or snow, I'll call for Gannon and Cormac."

Ewan squeezed his shoulder and then let himself out of the chamber. Alaric returned his attention to bathing Keeley.

With each stroke of the cloth down her skin, chill bumps erupted and danced across her flesh. She accompanied each outbreak with a violent shiver and a soft moan.

Finally it was too much for him. Her flesh had cooled a significant amount, and he knew that if he went too far in the other direction, she could die of exposure as well.

Leaving her naked, he climbed into bed beside her and curled her into his arms. Her body was a shock of cold, her hands clumsy as they skittered across his chest seeking warmth.

Finally they tucked beneath his tunic and found his skin, and she sighed in contentment as she burrowed her head in the crook of his arm.

Gradually the shaking stopped and she went limp against him. He reached down to pull one of the furs and settled it over the both of them, but was careful not to seal their heat under the covering.

He kissed her still warm forehead and whispered, "Sleep, love. I'm here to watch over you."

"My warrior," she murmured.

And he smiled. Aye, just as she was his angel.

CHAPTER 24

Keeley awoke feeling like she was trapped under a boulder. Even breathing hurt. Her head was so heavy she couldn't lift it, and she positively rattled when she tried to draw in air.

She opened her mouth, but her lips were cracked and her tongue was so dry it felt as though she rubbed it across sand.

Then she made the mistake of trying to move.

She whimpered and tears welled in her eyes. How could she feel so miserable? What had happened to her? She was never ill. She prided herself on being hale and hearty.

"Keeley, love, don't cry."

Alaric's usually soothing, deep timbred voice, crackled over her ears like the sound of swords clashing.

Her vision blurred by tears, she could barely make out the outline of his face as he peered over her.

"Sick," she croaked.

"Aye, lass, I know you're ailing."

"Never sick."

He leaned in closer and smiled. "You are now."

"Ask Maddie for the paste for my chest. 'Twill lessen some of the rattle and discomfort."

Alaric slid his palm over her cheek, and his skin felt so

cool against her burning face that she nuzzled and rubbed back and forth.

"Not to worry. Maddie has already been in your chamber three times this morning. She's clucking like a mother hen. Mairin has been forbidden access, and she's voicing her displeasure to anyone within hearing distance."

Keeley tried to smile, but it hurt too much.

"Hungry," she complained.

"Gertie is bringing you some broth."

She blinked to try and bring Alaric's face further into focus, but he was still blurry around the edges. But she could see his eyes. His beautiful, crystal green eyes.

She sighed. "I love your eyes."

He grinned and she blinked in surprise.

"Did I say that aloud?"

"Aye, you did," he said in a tone heavy with amusement.

"Am I still gripped with fever? 'Tis the only explanation for my wayward tongue."

"Aye, the fever still rages high within you."

She frowned. "But I'm no longer cold. The sign of a fever 'tis a chill. I find I'm overhot."

"Your flesh still burns and your eyes are dull. 'Tis a good sign I'm told that you are not racked by chills any longer, but you are sick still."

"I don't like being ill."

She knew she sounded like a petulant child, but she couldn't control the urge to sulk. She was used to tending the ill, not joining their ranks.

Alaric grinned and then pulled her into his arms.

"Why are you tending me?" she asked, her voice muffled by his chest. " 'Tis not proper at all."

"But then we've not been very proper together," he murmured.

She smiled but then sobered. "What will everyone think? Say?"

"If they value their well-being, they'll say nothing at all. They'll think what they think. We cannot control that."

She frowned. He was right. She well knew it. But she also knew that suspicion led to gossip and gossip led to accusations and then action.

He kissed the top of her head and she closed her eyes against the sweetness of his embrace.

"Ewan will want to know what occurred. Are you feeling well enough to face his questions?"

'Twas the truth she'd rather face an angry mob flinging stones than have to think back over the events with the way her head throbbed and her throat ached. But she also knew that the laird needed to know whatever she could tell him. He had a wife and a child to protect. He had the whole of the clan to protect.

"As long as I have water to sip at, I can speak with the laird."

"I'll make sure he doesn't keep you long," Alaric soothed.

Just then the door burst open and Maddie stuck her head around the door. Even though the older woman knew of Keeley's feelings for Alaric, Keeley stiffened and tried to pull away.

Alaric caught her to him and relaxed against the bed as he waited for Maddie to come to them.

"I have hot broth and water. The broth will soothe your sore throat, lass. The water will help the fever I hope. 'Tis important you drink enough."

Alaric took the steaming broth and carefully put it to Keeley's lips. "Just sip. 'Tis hot."

Grateful for the support of his arm, she carefully took a little of the broth into her mouth. She felt as weak as a kitten and would surely have flopped over were it not for Alaric holding her up.

He was infinitely patient, holding the trencher each time she took a bit of the liquid onto her tongue. At first it hurt going down. Her throat felt like it had a thousand scratches in the swollen flesh.

When she could take no more, she leaned back against Alaric's arm and closed her eyes.

"I'll be back up in a little while, lass," Maddie said in hushed tones. "If you have need of anything before that, summon me. I'll come at once."

Keeley was barely able to nod. Just consuming the broth had taken all the strength she had. And she still had to speak to the laird.

She closed her eyes and focused on breathing to keep the room from spinning. Alaric pressed his lips to her temple and curled her tighter into his side.

His warmth seeped into her bones and she gave a sigh of contentment. 'Twas the best she'd felt since she'd awakened.

She groaned when a knock sounded at the door. Alaric's command to enter sounded distant, like he was underwater. Or maybe it was she who was underwater. 'Twas clear that one of them was.

She roused herself when she heard the laird's quietly voiced question. Then she frowned. Alaric was arguing with his brother. He wanted Ewan to leave her alone and leave the questioning to later.

"Nay, 'tis all right," she said. Her throat protested the few words, and she put her hand to her neck to massage away the discomfort.

Ewan sat right on the bed at Alaric's feet, which Keeley thought a bit improper, but he was the laird and as such he could do what he wanted.

Ewan grinned. "Aye, lass, 'tis a perk of being laird. I do get to do what I like."

"I didn't mean to say that so loud," she muttered.

"Are you feeling well enough to tell me what happened in the woods? I've spoken to Crispen and the other children, and God's teeth, but they each give a different accounting."

She smiled but groaned when it hurt. "I don't understand why I feel so badly."

She tried not to sound so cross, but she was sure she failed, judging by the amused looks on Alaric's and Ewan's faces.

Ewan's expression sobered and then he leaned forward. "I feel I'm forever thanking someone for saving my son's life. 'Tis the truth he seems to find trouble wherever he goes. He told me you fought for him. I owe you a debt that can never be repaid."

She shook her head drowsily. "Nay. You've already repaid it."

His brow furrowed in confusion. "What do you speak of, lass?"

"Your clan," she said hoarsely. "You made me a member of your clan. 'Tis payment enough."

Alaric's arm tightened around her shoulders and he stroked his fingers over her arm in a soothing pattern.

Ewan's expression softened. "You will have a home here for as long as you wish it. You have my word."

She licked her cracked lips and burrowed a little closer to Alaric. The chill was returning and already her bones ached.

"I fear I'll be of no aid to you. It all happened so fast. I know they thought me your lady wife and they were most eager to spirit me away. They called you a fool for leaving Lady McCabe unattended."

Ewan scowled at that, his face growing as dark as a thundercloud.

"They crowed over the fact that they had managed to capture both your son and wife."

Ewan leaned forward, his eyes intense. "Did they say anything else? Did they identify themselves? Did you recognize their crest?"

Slowly she shook her head. Then her brows knit together in concentration. "There was one thing. They said that Cameron would reward them handsomely for their bounty. 'Twas all I remember. When they discovered I was not pregnant, they meant to kill me for they realized their error."

"Mercenaries," Alaric spat. "Cameron has posted a reward for the capture of Mairin."

Ewan let loose a string of blasphemies that had Keeley cringing. "There are many men without coin and nothing to lose by attempting to abduct Mairin and my child."

"If they are mercenaries, they have no clan or keep to call home," Alaric said. "'Tis likely they are still nearby."

Ewan's lips curled and his nostrils flared. "Aye. 'Tis time to go hunting."

"I'll ready myself to accompany you."

Ewan paused and then shook his head. He stared down at Keeley and then back up to his brother. "Nay. I need you here. I want you to keep Mairin close. She can busy herself with Keeley. Caelen will accompany me."

As he rose, he glanced down at Keeley again. He inclined his head in a gesture of respect. "Again, you have my thanks for the life of my son. I hope you are feeling to rights again soon."

Keeley mumbled something appropriate and fought another yawn as he departed the chamber. 'Twas freezing again and she needed another fur. Why had Alaric taken it from her?

Alaric sank lower into the bed and cuddled her into his embrace. "Never have I been so frightened," he admitted. "When I heard what had occurred and then I could not find you. 'Tis not a feeling I want to ever have again."

"I knew you would come."

"Your faith humbles me."

She stroked his chest with her fingertips. Someday . . . Someday he would owe his protection to Rionna. And their children. Keeley would no longer be able to look to him to solve her ills or fight her battles. After so long of fighting her own, it was a wondrous feeling to have a man such as Alaric to stand for her.

"You should rest, Keeley. I can feel the fever burning through you."

She was already drifting off, cocooned in his heat.

Alaric paced the interior of the hall in darkness. Ewan had taken a contingent of men to track the mercenaries who'd attacked Crispen and Keeley, and it was nearing dawn. They'd been gone for hours and Alaric's impatience grew with each passing minute.

It angered him to be here when he itched for a fight. He wanted to vent some of the rage that smoldered in his system.

It wasn't only the fact that these men had dared to touch what he considered his—and Keeley *was* his— Alaric wanted to let loose his frustration with the fates that would deny him the woman he loved.

Instead he waited for his brothers to return while he kept silent watch over the women of the keep.

He should go back up to look in on Keeley, but Maddie had agreed to stay by her bedside while Alaric stayed belowstairs where he could hear the watchmen cry alarm.

The fire was dying in the hearth but instead of summoning someone to add logs, he set about the task himself and soon the flames licked over the dry wood and roared to life.

A cry went up from the courtyard and Alaric reared his head. He hurried to the door and down the steps into the brisk night air.

Ewan and Caelen led their party into the courtyard and Alaric silently took stock of the men. All were present and accounted for, which meant they'd either not been successful in tracking their quarry or they'd sustained no losses in the fight.

Ewan dismounted and absently wiped his hand over his tunic, leaving a smear of blood. Alaric strode forward. "Are you hurt?"

Ewan glanced down and shook his head. "Nay. We sustained no injuries."

"They are dead?"

"Aye," Caelen said in a dark voice. "They'll not be a bother to us again."

Alaric nodded. "Good."

"They would not talk and 'tis God's truth I wasn't patient with my questioning," Ewan said. "They were the same men who took Crispen and Keeley, and Keeley said they spoke of Cameron. 'Tis enough proof for me."

"How much longer must we wait?" Alaric asked in a quiet voice.

Around them, the men went silent. They all looked to Ewan, the question burning in their eyes. They wanted war. They were ready for war. They all despised Cameron and all he'd done to the McCabe clan. No McCabe would rest until Cameron and all his allies were wiped from the face of the earth.

"Soon," Ewan said tersely. "We must have patience. After my son or daughter is born, we'll claim Neamh Álainn as is our right. We'll unite the whole of the highlands through Alaric's marriage to Rionna McDonald. Then we'll spit Duncan Cameron on the end of our swords."

A roar went up from the courtyard. Torches and

swords were thrust skyward as the cry went from warrior to warrior. Swords clanked against shields, horses reared, and fists were raised as the din increased.

Alaric met the gazes of his brothers in the glow of surrounding torches. Ewan's eyes were alight with determination, and for the first time, Alaric felt shame for his frustration over his impending marriage.

Ewan had given all to his clan. He'd gone without so every woman and child could eat. He'd put his men above himself in every manner. Now they were poised to be the most powerful clan in all of Scotland.

If Alaric could do this one thing for his clan—for his brother, for Mairin, who'd rescued their clan from the brink of extinction—then he'd do it gladly and with pride.

He reached out with his arm, his hand splayed wide. Ewan grasped it and they locked arms. Sweat and blood gleamed on Ewan's flesh. Their muscles bulged as they held fiercely to each other.

There was understanding when their gazes met and held.

Caelen sheathed his sword and then gave the order for their men to dismount and retire to their quarters. Then he turned to his two brothers. "Anyone for a swim in the loch?"

CHAPTER 25

When next Keeley awoke, her head felt like an empty tankard and her mouth felt as though she'd dragged her tongue along the ground for a mile. She smacked her lips noisily and licked them, trying to infuse any sort of moisture into them.

She turned her head to the side and then groaned. Jesu, but moving hurt.

Her entire body was as limp as a well-used cleaning rag, and her skin was sticky from sweat. And she was naked. Not a stitch of clothing on, and the furs were in a bunch at her feet.

Embarrassment swept heat through her body once more. She was probably scarlet. Lord only knew who'd come and gone from her chamber during her fever.

A moan started to escape but she curled her lips and snarled. Enough was enough. How much more pitiful could she become? She'd already wasted who knew how much time abed acting like a sickling child. How many days had she lain here senseless? 'Twas embarrassing.

She raised one hand and then let it flop back to the bed. Her throat still pained her, but the fever was gone, though it had left her as a weak as a newborn.

And speaking of newborns, she needed to look in on

Mairin to see how things progressed with the babe. Which meant she had to get up.

It took several long, exhausting minutes before she was able to push herself to the edge of the bed and sit up. She'd love a full-blown bath, but she didn't have the strength to manage it.

She dragged herself over to the basin and wet a cloth. She took her time wiping down her body until she felt somewhat human again. She was tempted to go jump in the loch, frigid temperature and all.

After washing, she pulled out one of her dresses and faced it down like she was about to do battle. With a rueful smile, she realized she was. It took all her strength just to make herself presentable, and when she was done with all the trappings, she collapsed onto the bed and sat there girding her loins to go belowstairs.

By the time she staggered to the stairs, she prided herself of the fact that she hadn't fallen on her face. Indeed by the time she worked her way to the bottom, her blood had sped up from its sluggish rate.

Breathless, but pleased, she pushed her way into the hall and looked around to see who was about.

Mairin was seated next to the fire with her feet propped on a stool with a pillow. Keeley smiled and set off toward the hearth.

When Mairin looked up and saw her, she gasped. "Keeley! What are you doing out of bed? You've been quite ill. You should be resting still. You bent Alaric's ear for being up too soon."

Keeley settled into the chair next to Mairin. "Aye 'tis true, I make a rotten patient but a strident caretaker. I expect those under my care to do as I say and not as I do."

Mairin burst into laughter. "Well, at least you make no bones about it." Then she reached over and grasped

Keeley's hand. "Are you all right? You still look a bit pale to me."

Keeley grimaced. "My throat still pains me and my head has a hollow ache that unsettles me, but I couldn't take another moment of lying in bed. I feel much better now that I'm up and about."

Mairin fidgeted in her chair and repositioned her feet on the cushion. "'Tis the truth I'd love to lie in bed today. The babe is pressing on my back and I find it too much to even stand for more than a moment."

"You should go up to bed then. 'Tis important not to overtax yourself."

Mairin smiled over at her. "You sound so motherly and yet you won't take your own advice."

"'Tis a healer's prerogative," Keeley said cheekily.

Both women were startled when Ewan swept into the hall with the king's messenger directly behind him. Unsure of whether she was to show respect for the king's man, Keeley scrambled from her chair and stood ramrod straight as Caelen and Alaric entered the hall after the messenger.

Mairin struggled to push herself from her chair. "Ewan?"

Ewan crossed the room and pushed her gently back down. "Nay, don't get up." He looked to Keeley and nodded for her to also take her seat. He frowned slightly as if just noticing she was up and around, but he dismissed her with a glance and turned his attention back to the messenger.

"'Tis a missive from the king I bring you. He asks that I wait for a response," the messenger said.

Ewan nodded and gestured for the messenger to sit down at the table. He then motioned for refreshment to be brought from the kitchen.

He unfurled the scroll and spent a few moments reading before he looked up again. It was Alaric his gaze found.

" 'Tis a message about your forthcoming marriage."

Alaric's brow went up, and he glanced quickly at Keeley before returning his gaze to his brother.

"The king expresses his satisfaction with the match and his excitement over the alliances we'll form. He'd like to travel here for the marriage and for the neighboring clans to be invited so that he may hear their vows of allegiance in person."

The hall went quiet.

Keeley's chest tightened until she thought it might explode. She dare not look up at Alaric for she knew her expression must be tortured. She looked down at her tightly clasped hands, not wanting *anyone* to see her pain.

" 'Tis a great honor, Alaric," Ewan said quietly.

"Aye. Please convey my appreciation for the honor he bestows upon me," Alaric said formally.

"He asks that I send word as soon as we know the day the wedding will take place."

Out of the corner of her eye, Keeley saw Alaric nod stiffly.

Keeley heard Mairin's swift intake of breath and when she glanced up at the other woman, sympathy shone bright in her eyes. Keeley smiled bravely and lifted her chin.

"I've always wanted to meet the king."

'Twas not her being cowardly that forced Keeley to her chamber before the evening meal had finished being served. She shuddered to think what she looked like. She knew what she felt like, and Maddie had promised to have hot water for a bath brought up.

The prospect of soaking in a tub of steaming water made her moan in anticipation. She struggled up the stairs, so exhausted she could barely make her legs work.

When she entered her chamber, she was so grateful that the women had already started filling the tub, she was weepy.

Maddie bustled in a moment later, hands on her hips as she surveyed the progress. Then she turned to Keeley and plopped onto the bed beside her.

"Do you need help getting into the tub, lass?"

Keeley smiled. "Thank you but nay. You're wonderful to do this for me, Maddie. I know 'tis a burden to bring the water up the stairs."

Maddie patted her knee. "'Tis the least we can do for our healer. If we don't take care of you and keep you hale and hearty, there'll be no one to care for our sick!"

The two watched as the last pail was brought up and the tub brimmed with water. Steam rose in rapid puffs, and Keeley's eyes rolled back in her head as she imagined getting in.

"Well, I'll leave you to it, lass. Gannon will be outside, so call if you need anything."

Keeley's cheeks burned. "Gannon! I can't have him barging in here. Besides, 'tis his duty to see to Alaric's needs."

Maddie chuckled. "He won't barge in, not unless he fears for your life, then it won't matter if you've not a stitch on. But if you call out to him, he'll summon me or Christina for you."

"Whew," Keeley breathed.

Maddie laughed and left the chamber. Keeley wasted no time ripping her dress over her head. She sent it sailing across the room and hastened to the tub.

Every movement caused considerable ache, but she inched down into the water until it lapped over her body and finally to her chin as she settled back against the side.

This was heaven.

She closed her eyes and relaxed her tired, sore muscles. She let go of everything but the wondrous sensation of so much hot water. If someone would but dump a fresh pail of hot water into the tub every so often, she'd be content to remain here for days. She wasn't entirely certain she'd be able to get back out anyway.

She sighed and settled her arms along the sides of the tub then tipped her chin skyward so that her head rested against the back. The heat from the fire just a few paces away toasted her skin and relaxed her even more.

She was nearly asleep, her head tilting to the side, when her door opened. Startled, she looked up to see Alaric standing across the room, shrouded in darkness. The few candles ablaze in her chamber were all situated around her tub and dressing area. The rest of the light was cast from the fire in the hearth and it didn't quite reach to where Alaric stood.

For a long moment he stood watching and she returned his gaze, waiting, and absorbing the hunger in his eyes. There was something decidedly different about his demeanor this night.

Typically he was lighthearted and teasing. They'd laugh softly before making love and often talk about the events of the day.

Tonight his expression was fierce and his eyes glittered dangerously. She swallowed nervously as he advanced toward the tub, his gaze never leaving her.

She was struck by sudden vulnerability, and it excited her. Power rippled through his body and swelled through the room until it was a living, breathing thing.

He stood over the tub, looking down at her naked body, his gaze stroking possessively over her. When she went to cover her breasts with her arms, he knelt beside the tub and gently pried her arms away.

"Nay, do not shield yourself from me. This night you

are mine. Solely mine. You belong to me and only me. Tonight I take what is mine. I cherish what is mine."

Her chin trembled and she pressed her lips together to curb her nervousness. It wasn't that she was afraid. Far from it. She was excited. More so than she'd ever been, and she was about to fidget right out of the tub.

He took the cloth where it hung limply over the edge of the tub and touched it to her neck. Despite the warmth of the water and from the fire just a short distance away, chill bumps instantly dotted her upper torso.

They rushed over her chest to her breasts and beaded her nipples into tight nubs as he gently pulled the cloth over her shoulder.

The scent of roses wafted through her nostrils. Alaric took the bar of soap from its nook and massaged the cloth around it until suds formed.

"Lean forward," he commanded.

His quiet, sensual tone made her insides quiver. There was a dark promise in his voice that had her wound so tightly, she felt near to bursting.

When she was positioned as he wanted her, he began rubbing the cloth in lazy circles over her back.

"Oh that feels wondrous," she moaned.

He covered every inch, coming up to knead her shoulders before retreating to caress the line of her back down to the dimple just over the crease of her buttocks.

Her eyes were closed, her head bobbing forward as sweet lethargy—and pleasure—flooded her veins. But when he reached around to brush the cloth across her nipples, her eyes flew open and her breathing sped up and bounced erratically from her nostrils.

He paused then cupped both mounds in his palms. Slowly, his thumbs brushed over the peaks. Up and then down until each touch sent shards of exquisite pleasure bolting through her womb.

She flinched, not from pain but from the overwhelming shock of ecstasy when his mouth touched her nape. Just a simple, gentle kiss, but his mouth was like a bolt of lightning.

The dual sensations of his thumbs brushing her nipples and his mouth moving sensuously over her neck turned her bones to jam. She was helpless. Completely at his mercy, and that excited her all the more.

"You're so beautiful," he whispered against her neck. "I look at you and I'm overwhelmed by your fire, your gentle beauty, your determination, and your courage. I think there has never been another woman of your equal. There never will be."

Her heart swelled and the ache spread to her throat, tightening until words were impossible. What could she say anyway?

"Tonight I'm going to take care of you as you did for me."

His husky whisper hummed over her ears, and she shivered at the images his words invoked.

He wet her hair and then slowly and thoroughly washed every strand. He ran his fingers through the thick tresses, one by one, until every part was clean. Then he tilted her head back and rinsed so that the soapy water didn't wash into her eyes.

Over and over the warm water cascaded over her shoulders until finally he was satisfied that the job was done.

"Give me your hand."

She slipped her fingers over his and he lifted her to her feet. Water rushed down her body, leaving her sleek and shiny in the low light. Nervously she waited as his gaze swept up and down, heating every inch in his path.

His eyes glittered as he lowered his head. She caught her breath when his mouth hovered precariously over her breast. Then he pulled her nipple into his mouth and sucked strongly at the tip.

Her knees buckled and she would have collapsed back into the tub, but he grasped her around her waist and hauled her against him, his mouth still firmly around her nipple.

"I'm getting you all wet," she gasped.

"I don't care."

He moved to her other breast and flicked his tongue out. It rasped over the sensitive point, sending shivers of delight down her spine.

She was captivated by the picture they presented. Their bodies meshed together in the warm glow of firelight, his mouth at her breast and her skin gleaming from wetness. It was every romantic dream she'd ever hatched. He was her warrior. Though she'd saved him in the beginning, he saved her each and every day.

Her warrior. Her love.

"Love me, Alaric," she whispered.

"Aye, I do, lass. I do. And I will. Tonight is mine. You're my captive to do with as I see fit. Never will you feel more cherished and loved than you do this night."

He left her for the barest moment and returned with a drying blanket. As soon as she stepped from the tub, he wrapped her in it and guided her toward the fire.

Carefully he worked all the excess water from her hair until it lay damply against her back. Then he collected her comb and began patiently working the tangles from her hair.

No one had ever attended her thus. It was a marvelous feeling. She felt important. Like she was the lady of the keep and beloved by her laird.

He pressed his lips to the back of her head and kept them there a long moment. "Tonight you will obey my every command. Aye, I'll see to your every need because 'tis my wish. But this night you are mine and will cede to my wishes."

His hands slid up and down her arms, and his mouth

moved to the side of her neck. "Think you that you can agree to not say me nay?"

Her insides squeezed unbearably and she was breathing so rapidly that she was light-headed. The power and sensuality in his voice excited her beyond measure. Didn't he know she would never deny him anything?

She nodded, unable to voice a single word around the knot in her throat.

He turned her head so that their gazes met. His eyes burned into her and his expression was fierce, every inch the warrior he was. "The words, Keeley. I would have the words from you."

"Aye, I agree," she whispered.

CHAPTER 26

Alaric lifted Keeley into his arms and strode toward the bed. The linen that he'd wrapped around her body loosened and fell to the floor, leaving her naked. He eased her onto the mattress and took a step back, his gaze never leaving her.

She felt intensely vulnerable and she swallowed with nervous excitement as he slowly began to disrobe.

His arms and shoulders rippled and bulged, and his taut abdomen stretched over tightly corded muscles. Her fingers itched to trace the lean lines and explore every hard spot on his body.

"Spread your thighs for me, Keeley. Let me look upon your womanly softness."

Blushing, she relaxed her legs and then slowly drew them apart. Alaric reached down and circled her ankles with his fingers and then pushed upward until her heels were dug into the mattress and her knees were bent double.

The position bared her completely to him. Left her open and aching for his touch.

He knelt at the bedside and ran one finger through her damp petals, pausing at her entrance before pushing ever so slightly inside.

She gasped and arched her hips, wanting more. He withdrew and then lowered his mouth.

She held her breath until she was light-headed. Every part of her body tightened in anticipation of the brush of his lips.

But it wasn't his lips that touched her. He licked from her entrance to the tight, straining bud sheltered under the hood of flesh at her apex.

She cried out and her body convulsed. He gripped her thighs and held her in place as he continued to lap at her. The roughness of his tongue sent indescribable flashes of pleasure splintering through her belly up to her breasts where her nipples beaded painfully.

Gently he sucked at the tiny mound and then flicked his tongue back over it, coaxing it to a hardened point.

It was simply too much. Her body shattered. It was as if she were leaves scattered on a windy day. After so much pressure and unbearable tightening, suddenly she was so light that she floated, drifting downward in a gentle spiral.

Bewildered by the intensity of her release she raised her head. "Alaric?" she whispered.

But he didn't answer. Instead he gently turned her onto her belly and drew one hand behind her back. To her shock, he wrapped a linen strip around her wrist and then pulled her other arm back to bind her wrists together.

Butterflies swarmed in her belly and her knees trembled uncontrollably.

When he was finished, he tested the binding and it held firm. Then he pushed her onto her knees so that her cheek rested against the mattress and her behind was high in the air, her hands tied securely behind her back.

As he rose, his palm caressed the curve of her buttocks. Then he palmed both of her cheeks and pushed upward and out so that she was spread to him.

"I hurt you this way when you were nearly a virgin still. Tonight I'll only give you pleasure."

One hand left her and then she felt the brush of his knuckles as he positioned his cock at her opening. He pushed and his thickness filled her, stretching her around his shaft.

She moaned softly. It was a wondrous sensation as he forced himself deeper. Her body clasped tightly to him and rippled over his hardness. When he pulled back, her swollen tissues protested the movement and clamped wetly around his cock.

"Does it pain you?" he asked.

"Nay," she whispered.

He thrust into her, harder this time. Never had she felt so stretched, so full. After he was assured that she could take him this way, he began to ride her more vigorously.

He reached up and grabbed on to her bound wrists. Holding her tightly, he pulled back as he thrust forward.

The smacking sound of his thighs pounding against her bottom filled the air. As gentle as he'd been before, now he took her ruthlessly, setting a pace to please himself.

Faster and harder and then he paused, buried deeply inside her. She was opened wide and defenseless against whatever he wanted to do. It only heightened her excitement. She wiggled impatiently, but he held her still as he remained lodged inside her.

Then he withdrew and pounded forward. Much slower and methodical this time. He was in control, his thrusts measured. Hard. Deep. Over and over he retreated and then plunged forward until she was begging him to give her release. She needed more. She needed him to move fast and hard, to provide sweet friction.

"Have not I said that you are to obey me this night?" he asked huskily. "'Tis I who say the commands, Keeley. You will say naught but aye to whatever I ask."

She squeezed her eyes shut and clenched her teeth in sweet agony as he powered forward in a particularly forceful thrust as if to reinforce his words. Aye, he was in control. She had none.

She had to bite her lip to keep from protesting when he pulled from the tight clasp of her body. He pulled her to her feet and held her until he was sure she was steady. Then he grasped her shoulders and pushed her to her knees on the floor.

His cock was hugely erect, stiff and distended just inches from her face. It gleamed with her wetness and the skin was stretched tight over the broad tip.

"Open your mouth, Keeley."

He thrust one hand into her hair and cupped her nape, at the same time he grasped the base of his cock with his other hand and guided it toward her parted lips.

Her mouth stretched around his swollen girth and he pushed deep. At first she struggled to accommodate him, but he was patient, giving her time to adjust and to breathe from her nose.

Wanting to please him, she took more, but he pulled at her hair to prevent her action. "Nay, just remain still," he murmured.

Holding her head with both hands, he began to thrust inside her mouth. Slowly at first. He glided across her tongue and to the back of her throat. As she relaxed more, he became more demanding, pushing deeper and holding himself there before retreating so she could draw breath.

The only sounds that she could hear was the wet sucking noises as he powered in and out of her mouth and his own harsh breathing.

He groaned when a tiny amount of liquid spurted onto her tongue. Salty and tangy. She prepared herself for more, but he pulled himself roughly from her mouth and then pulled forcefully at his shaft with his hand.

Hot semen splashed onto her chest. He held her neck and tilted her head upward as he directed more over her breasts. His fingers tightened at her nape and he groaned as he worked the last of his release onto her skin.

He stood there, his breaths coming hard while she knelt in front of him trying to catch her breath as well. Never had she imagined such a thing between a man and a woman. It invoked a primitive response deep in her being. She felt owned by the warrior. His possession to do with as he wished. Never had she wished so hard for anything to be true.

He bent and kissed the top of her head and then helped her to rise. He led her over to the wash basin and gently cleaned his semen from her body.

He washed himself and she could see that he was still rigidly erect. She wasn't overly knowledgeable about such things, but she was sure this couldn't be normal.

Leaving her hands secured behind her back, he took her back over to the bed where he piled pillows on the side. Then he simply nudged her until she lay over the pillows, belly down, her legs splayed wide with her feet planted on the floor.

This time when he slid into her from behind, he lacked some of the urgency of before. Almost as if he'd sated himself and could be more patient this time.

He pushed back and forth, setting a slow and steady rhythm, almost exploratory in nature. He squeezed her plump bottom with both hands and massaged as his cock disappeared into her body over and over.

He worked into her until her body started to respond. Soon she arched upward to take him and she tingled in anticipation, her womb clenching with desperate need. She gasped and curled her fingers into tight fists in their bonds.

Then he reached between the pillow and her body and his fingers found the sensitive nub between her legs. He stroked and caressed until she was wild in her need for release. Still, he continued his relentless assault, never deviating from the steady pace he'd begun.

She was nearly weeping with her need. Her body was strung too tight. The pressure was painful.

And still, he pushed back and forth, infinitely patient.

His fingers stroked gently over her flesh until finally she was as taut as a bowstring at full draw. And then finally, all the tension released in one huge burst of exquisite, mind-numbing pleasure.

Her vision blurred. She cried out his name over and over until all she could hear were her own sobs. Wave after wave, seemingly unending until she melted into the pillows holding her up to him.

She lost awareness as she floated on some distant cloud. For several long moments she had no understanding of her surroundings or that he continued to push into her.

Gradually she became aware of the slapping of flesh against flesh and realized that he was still inside her, riding her ruthlessly.

She hadn't the strength to do more than lie there as he commanded her body. Unbelievably she felt the stirrings deep within her core as he continued to thrust.

He was less patient now. He grasped her hips, his fingers digging into her flesh. He pounded into her, now seemingly determined to build the fire within her anew.

It was sharper, faster, and more intense this time. He whispered her name. Then he leaned forward, his hips powering against her behind with bruising strength.

"You're mine," he uttered. "Mine. You belong to me. No man will ever have you as I've had you this night."

Warmth traveled through her blood, curling low in her pelvis. Nay, no man would ever lay claim to her in the way that Alaric McCabe had.

She gave herself over to the rising tide. She surrendered. She wanted nothing more than to belong to this man. She shuddered in the throes of her release and opened her body fully to receive him.

He pulled from her, his retreat nearly painful around her swollen, tender flesh. Then she felt his seed against her back as he lay against her, his chest heaving with exertion.

He kissed her nape and whispered soft words she couldn't even hear.

For a long moment he lay against her, his cock pulsing against her flesh. Then slowly he pushed himself off and untied her wrists. He held each one and massaged her hands until all the tingles had gone away.

"Stay here," he said as he left the bed.

He returned a moment later with a warm cloth and gently wiped the remnants of his passion from her back and buttocks. When he was done, he rolled her over and pulled her into his arms.

"Never have I acted thusly with a woman," he admitted as he stroked her hair. "'Tis something primitive within me that roars at me to claim you, to make you mine and to mark you in some permanent way."

She smiled and cuddled closer to him. She was deliciously sore and sated. "I like that you mark me yours. I never dreamed that something like this existed between a man and a woman."

"Neither did I," Alaric said ruefully. "You inspire me, lass."

She chuckled and then yawned. Alaric kissed her brow and pulled her even tighter against him.

"What do we do, Alaric?" she whispered. " 'Twas only supposed to be one night."

He ran his fingers through her hair and laid his cheek against her forehead. "We take it one day at a time and savor every moment together. When the time comes to say good-bye, we'll have these nights to look back upon and remember how fierce the passion was between us."

CHAPTER 27

Keeley was convinced that the birth of Mairin's child was not only a blessed event in the McCabe clan but in heaven as well. In January, when winter was usually at its harshest, what could only be considered mild weather settled in just a fortnight before Lady McCabe's birthing time.

It was as if the whole of the highlands waited with held breath for the appearance of the heir to Neamh Álainn.

Oh the weather was still cold to be sure, but the snows hadn't fallen in weeks and the wind hadn't howled. The sun seemed to shine brighter for the short period of the day it rose, and the nights didn't seem quite so dark.

Mairin was becoming increasingly impatient. In the evenings, Keeley gathered with Maddie, Bertha, and Christina and they took turns entertaining Mairin to keep her mind from her impending delivery.

Even Ewan joined in and spent many an evening sitting with his wife in front of the fire in the great hall. 'Twas a relaxed time, and more and more Keeley felt a part of the McCabe clan.

Though she and Alaric were careful to keep public contact to a minimum, their nights were spent behind the closed doors of her chambers.

He'd come to her late, once all were abed, and he'd make sweet love to her until dawn's rays spread across the sky.

After her illness, she hadn't tried to deny him. She was powerless to. Oh, she knew their time was drawing to an end, and the thought instilled a fierce ache in the deepest recesses of her soul, but not for one moment would she regret being with him. It was a joy she'd carry with her all the days of her life.

This morning they stayed abed longer than usual. It was typical for Alaric to go quietly back to his chamber before the rest of the keep awakened, but today they lay and he traced lazy lines up and down her arm as she snuggled against his chest.

"I should rise," he whispered before pressing his lips to her temple.

"Aye, you should."

He remained still. "I find it harder and harder with each passing day to leave your arms."

She closed her eyes against the ache and squeezed him to her a little tighter. 'Twas the truth she'd expected for him to grow tired of her after a few nights. She'd resigned herself to taking what he offered and not saying a word when he left her bed. But for the past weeks, he'd visited her bed with increasing frequency, until it was commonplace for him to spend every night with her.

"Do you train today?" she asked lightly.

He grunted. "Aye. And every day. 'Tis important not to grow fat and lazy in the winter. With Mairin's day drawing nigh, the chance of attack grows stronger by the day."

She sighed. "'Tis no way to live. Poor Mairin."

They rested in silence for several more minutes before Alaric turned and captured her lips in a hungry, carnal kiss. It caught her by surprise and before she could muster a response, he rolled, fitting himself between her legs.

There was no gentleness. Where before he was infinitely patient and loving, now he was urgent and demanding. It reminded her of the night when he'd commanded her complete obedience and had taken her over and over.

His cock slid over her entrance and then stabbed deep. She gasped at the overwhelming fullness and her eyes went wide at the savage look in his gaze. He was fierce. A predator intent on his prey.

Reaching down, he grasped the undersides of her legs and yanked upward, the motion seating himself fully within her.

Her fingers gripped his shoulders, her nails digging as he moved over her, his body covering hers completely.

His breaths came harsh, the sound explosive in her ears. "I can never get enough of you. I tell myself one more time. Just once. And it's never enough. It'll never be enough."

Her heart went soft at the pain in his voice. She'd spent so much time dwelling on her own despair and dread for when they were to be parted; she hadn't considered that he, too, was full of regret.

She reached for his face, cupping his strong jaw before pulling him down until his mouth was a mere breath from hers. She traced the lines of his cheekbone, feathering down to his mouth and chin.

"I love you," she whispered. "I told myself I wouldn't make it hard, that I'd never breathe those words. But 'tis harder for me to go without saying them. I need to give them to you."

His breath caught and anguish flooded his eyes. He stilled within her and gazed down at her with such emotion that tears pricked at her lids. When he started to open his mouth she pressed a finger to his lips.

"Don't say anything. 'Tis no need. I feel the very heart of you inside me, surrounding me. I carry you with me everywhere I go. Do not speak of forbidden things between us. Let it remain my sin alone."

He crushed her to him and rolled until she was atop him. He kissed her breathlessly, her mouth, her cheek, her eyes, and back down to her chin.

They took each other desperately, feeding as if starved, loving as if this would be their last time together. She knew not what fed the urgency, but she didn't fight it.

"Ride me," he whispered. "Take me. Make me yours, lass. Let me hold you in my arms and watch you fly. There's not a more beautiful sight."

Swallowing the knot in her throat, she pressed her palms to his chest and began moving over him, sensuously, watching his every expression as she took him deep inside her body.

His eyes glittered and became half-lidded, smoky with desire, and his lips curved into a satisfied smile.

Aye, he was hers. Her warrior. No one could ever take that from her. Another woman might bear his name and his children, but she would own his heart just as he would always own hers.

The power in his body mesmerized her. Every ripple and bulge of his muscles, the broad plane of his chest and the taut surface of his belly. He was all male, all hard, all beautiful.

She hoisted herself upward and then leaned her head down to run her tongue up the middle of his chest. He tensed and held his breath when she nibbled a path to his neck. She nipped playfully and then sank her teeth into the thickly corded column below his ear.

With a groan, he wrapped his arms around her and dragged her down, bucking his hips and driving deep into her softness.

"I love you. I love you."

It was a litany on her lips, a song from the depths of her soul. Tears swam and slipped down her cheeks as she gathered him in her arms.

His arms slipped around her body like bands of steel. They held tightly to each other as the storm swelled around them. Her release, when it came, was sweet and tender, not the tumultuous tide it had been so many times before.

Bittersweet and aching, it flooded her body, tightening until she came apart into a million tiny pieces.

As she came down, she became aware of him stroking her back, his fingers running through her hair as he murmured softly in her ear.

She lay atop him for a long moment, cuddled in his arms as he continued to stroke her. She knew it was late. Far later than they'd dared before. He would have to go soon.

As if following her thoughts, Alaric stirred beneath her. He gripped her and rolled until he was once more atop her, still buried deeply in her body.

He stared down at her, his eyes earnest and dark. "I love you too, Keeley. If I can give you nothing else, let me give you these words."

She bit the inside of her lip to prevent more tears from sliding down her cheeks. Instead she kissed him, just one reverent, loving kiss to his lips.

"You must go now," she whispered. "Before we are found."

"Aye. Lay here awhile and rest. If Mairin has need of you, I'll send someone for you. Until then, enjoy the rest."

She smiled and pulled the furs up as he slid from her body and backed from the bed. He dressed in silence and then left the room, pausing at the doorway for a long, heated glance back in her direction.

It was only after he'd long gone from her chamber, that she realized he'd spilled his seed inside her.

She closed her eyes, hopeful and dreading all at once. She had no wish for a child of hers to ever bear the stigma of being a bastard, but at the same time, she knew that if she were to become pregnant, it would be the only child she'd ever bear.

She rolled onto her side and clutched the covers tightly to her breast. "I don't know what to do," she whispered tearfully. "I love him. I want him. I want his children and yet all those things are forbidden me."

She closed her eyes and allowed the hot tears to disappear into the covers. She'd promised herself she wouldn't cry. That she'd be brave when the time came. But more and more she knew she was deluding herself. For when it came time for Alaric to marry another, it would destroy her.

CHAPTER 28

Keeley took her time dressing. She was in no hurry to go belowstairs and allow the dreamlike haze that surrounded her to evaporate once she greeted reality.

She hummed softly to herself as she braided her hair and then she straightened the furs on her bed. After giving the pillow a final pat, she turned and exited the chamber.

'Twas positively late, and she allowed herself a lusty yawn as she descended the stairs. It was a good day to stay indoors and enjoy the company of the other women. Mairin was becoming increasingly more restless as the days went by.

She was three steps from the bottom when the noise from the hall filtered to her ears. Frowning, she braced her hand against the wall and peered around to see what was about.

"Laird McDonald approaches our gates," the herald announced as Ewan stood before him.

Keeley gasped and faltered down the remaining steps. She stood rigid as she stared across the room to where Alaric stood with his brothers receiving the news.

"He brings his daughter and asks that you receive him in good faith."

Ewan nodded at the messenger. "Aye, tell him he may pass. I'll greet him in the courtyard."

He turned and barked out several orders. Serving women scattered in all directions as they set about preparing the table for refreshment.

Keeley stared numbly at Alaric, feeling as if her entire world had crumbled at her feet. Then he looked up and caught her stare.

His gaze was raw and expressed all the turmoil that rolled within her.

She should be strong. She should be a better person. She should be able to stand tall as if she didn't have a care in the world. She was none of those things. She couldn't face her childhood friend or the man who'd attacked her. She couldn't face the woman who would have the man she loved.

Covering her mouth to squelch the mounting sob, she whirled and fled back up the stairs.

Alaric watched Keeley rush back up the stairs and he turned away, not trusting himself not to go after her.

"What is McDonald doing here?" he hissed. "He isn't supposed to be here until closer to spring, after Mairin's child is delivered."

"I don't know," Ewan said grimly. "I intend to find out. 'Tis possible he received a missive from our king as well. He would be eager to do his bidding."

Alaric dragged a hand through his hair. The noose was tightening around his neck. Maybe he'd been living in denial of his reality. He'd pushed thoughts of his marriage to Rionna from his mind, content to savor each night in Keeley's arms.

Now . . . now his future was upon him, and Keeley was part of his past.

" 'Tis better to have done with it," Ewan murmured.

He cringed at the sympathy in Ewan's voice and the

disgust on Caelen's face. Alaric straightened his stance and pushed back his anguish.

"Let us go greet him," he said quietly.

Ewan tucked Mairin's hand in his and then pulled her into his embrace. "Wait here, sweeting, where 'tis warm and you're comfortable. Have the women attend you and stay off your feet."

He rubbed his hand over her burgeoning belly and kissed her one last time before he turned to Alaric.

Mairin frowned unhappily in Alaric's direction as he and his brothers left the hall to go greet the McDonalds.

The entire way out, Alaric wondered how he could pretend not to loathe the bastard. How was he supposed to stand in front of the man, embrace him and his clan, promise to care for his daughter, and assume the mantle of leadership when McDonald stepped down?

He wanted to spit in his eye and run him through with a sword on the spot. What kind of man preyed on a young girl barely past the cusp of womanhood? Who allowed her to shoulder the blame for his lust and be cast out of her clan by a jealous wife?

He couldn't dwell on the matter because his fury mounted with each breath.

"Ease your expression," Caelen murmured. "You look murderous."

" 'Tis disgraceful what he did to Keeley."

Caelen's brows drew together. The brothers stopped just inside the open gateway to await the approach of the McDonald riders.

"What is this you speak of?" Caelen demanded.

Alaric shook his head. " 'Tis not your matter."

"Still, I would know what manner of man he is before I blindly ally myself with him," Caelen responded.

" 'Tis not him you ally yourself with," Ewan cut in. " 'Tis your brother for he will be laird." He glanced sharply at Alaric as he spoke. "I know you care for

Keeley, but much rides on this alliance. Pull yourself together lest war be declared."

Ewan took a step forward as the McDonald riders appeared over the hillside in the distance. When Alaric would have done so himself, Caelen caught him by the arm and pulled him back.

"What do you speak of?"

Alaric's nostrils flared and his lips tightened. "He molested her when she was but a girl barely grown. His wife came upon them before he could rape her but cried her a whore and had her cast from the clan. She's been on her own ever since."

Caelen went silent. His jaw twitched, but he said nothing, as he stared ahead to the approaching riders.

Alaric took in a deep breath as McDonald and his daughter rode up side by side. She was first to slide from her saddle, and his brow rose when he saw that she was dressed in men's attire. 'Twas scandalous for a woman to be dressed thusly, and yet she didn't appear to have a care over the matter.

She boldly met his gaze, her golden eyes glinting in the sun.

Gregor McDonald dismounted with a grunt and pressed his lips together in displeasure as he approached his daughter.

"Ewan," he greeted with a nod of acknowledgment.

"Gregor," Ewan returned.

"You've met my daughter. Have a good look at the woman you wed with, Alaric," Gregor tossed in Alaric's direction.

"Rionna," Alaric said as he bowed his head respectfully.

Rionna offered an awkward curtsy in return then glanced over to where Caelen and Ewan stood.

Knowing it was expected of him to court the lass

while she was here—nay, until they married—he extended his hand to her.

For a moment she stared back at him with genuine confusion before her cheeks colored and she slipped her hand into his. He pulled it to his lips and brushed his lips across her knuckles.

" 'Tis my pleasure, my lady."

She cleared her throat and pulled her hand back, her discomfort keen.

"My lady wife is eager to see you again, Rionna," Ewan said. "She waits inside. Her time is near and she rests, but she wished me to convey her desire for you to go to her at your leisure."

"Thank you. I'm eager to see her again," Rionna said in a low voice. She glanced uncomfortably at Alaric again before walking past him toward the entrance to the keep.

Ewan turned to Gregor as soon as Rionna disappeared within. He stood, arms crossed as he stared down at the older man.

"You sent no word of your arrival. It was my understanding you were coming closer to spring after Mairin had delivered our babe."

Gregor had the grace to look discomfited by Ewan's bluntness. "With the break in the weather, it only made sense to make our journey sooner. 'Tis possible if the weather worsens, we wouldn't be able to make the journey until the spring, and I wished to seal our alliance at the first opportunity."

He blew out his breath and looked uneasily at Ewan. "I hear rumor that Cameron is gathering men and that he allies himself with Malcolm. David doesn't have the strength to win a war against the combined force of Malcolm *and* Cameron. If Cameron turns his sights on my lands or those of the neighboring clans, we won't be able to hold up under his might. An alliance is our only chance to defeat him.

" 'Tis the truth, Ewan, that the whole of the highlands holds their breath in anticipation of the heir to Neamh Álainn. That holding is at the heart of our stronghold. With the McCabes in control, we form an impenetrable wall that even Cameron will be unable to defeat."

Alaric listened to the laird's words with a sinking heart. 'Twas true, all of it. His marriage to Rionna was crucial, for not only did it seal an alliance between the McDonalds and the McCabes, but it would pull neighboring clans into that alliance. Clans that were otherwise afraid to defy Cameron—or choose the wrong side of the battle for the throne.

"Then you've come because you want the marriage soon."

Gregor nodded. "As soon as it can be arranged."

"Rionna is agreeable to this?" Ewan asked.

Gregor's lips twisted. "She is my daughter. She knows her duty. She will agree."

Ewan cast a long look at Alaric, almost as if he could reach inside his brother's head and pluck out his thoughts. Alaric hated that look. Hated knowing his brother pitied him.

"Are you willing, Alaric?" Ewan asked quietly.

Alaric swallowed. At his sides, his fingers curled slowly into tight balls. Then he looked up at his future father by marriage—a man from whom he'd take over the position of laird.

It was the hardest words he'd ever speak, but his brother, his king, Mairin, his clan . . . they were all depending on him.

And so he spoke the words that would force the woman he loved from his life.

"Aye. I'm willing."

CHAPTER 29

"I cannot face her."

Keeley whirled around to stare out her window, ignoring the chill that leaked into her chamber.

Maddie sighed and then walked up behind Keeley to slide an arm around her. "I know 'tis painful for you, lass. But there is naught to gain from hiding. Sooner or later you'll have to come out. Mairin is due to have her babe any day now. You can't miss that."

" 'Tis bad enough I once called her friend, but now I must stand aside and watch her marry Alaric. And Laird McDonald." She shuddered and closed her eyes. "How can I look at him after what he's done?"

Maddie gripped her arm and turned her around. "Come sit, lass. I want a word with you."

Numbly, Keeley followed Maddie over to the bed and sank onto the edge. The older woman settled next to her and then took her hand.

"You've done nothing wrong. You have nothing to be ashamed of. 'Tis the laird's sin and he'll answer to God for it in the end."

"I shouldn't be here," Keeley said with a moan. " 'Tis such a tangled mess. I gave myself to a man I can't have. The man who is to marry a woman I used to call sister.

And yet I sit here angry with her and her father. I'm not blameless when it comes to wrong."

Maddie wrapped her arms around Keeley and rocked back and forth. "'Tis true you're in an impossible situation. I don't dispute that. But you have to know that Laird McCabe won't allow any harm to come to you. Alaric won't allow it either. You're safe. Laird McDonald can do you no harm, and 'tis the truth, lass, he'll likely pretend he knows you not."

"I know you have the right of it," Keeley said. "I'm just afraid."

Maddie stroked her hand over Keeley's hair. "There, there, lass. I don't blame you for being afraid, but you have all the McCabes behind you. If you truly love Alaric, make this as easy as possible for him. Don't let him see how much you're hurting. 'Twill only add to his burden."

Keeley drew away and wiped the tears from her eyes. "You're right of course. I'm acting like a spoiled child."

Maddie smiled. "You're acting like a woman in love who knows she's going to lose. I'd say you're acting normal."

Keeley sent her a watery smile. "I'll be brave tomorrow. I promise. For today, I just want to remain above stairs."

"That seems fair enough to me. I'll let Mairin know what you're about. She'll understand. She worries for you."

"Summon me if she has need of me. I'll come immediately."

Maddie nodded and then rose from her perch on the bed.

Keeley flopped back to stare at the ceiling. Just this morn she'd lain with Alaric in this bed and told him she loved him. And he'd told her he loved her, too.

Tears leaked down the sides of her face. This wasn't

supposed to have been their last day. They were supposed to have known of the McDonalds' arrival ahead of time, and they would have time to say good-bye. One last time together. One more night in each other's arms.

She closed her eyes as the tears fell faster.

"I love you," she whispered. "I'll always love you."

Mairin McCabe fidgeted on the hard bench for the hundredth time and worked valiantly to control the yawn that threatened to crack her jaw. Her husband listened politely as Gregor McDonald recounted his tales of valor, also for the hundredth time, but Mairin's focus was on Alaric and Rionna.

The couple hadn't spoken more than a few words the entire dinner. It concerned Mairin that Alaric was so inattentive, and yet Rionna seemed perfectly satisfied for her future husband to say nothing.

The few times Mairin tried to draw Rionna into conversation, she was met with stubborn silence. She knew the girl to be friendlier, at least when the women were alone. Rionna had visited once already and the women had gotten along quite well together.

Alaric just looked . . . unhappy. Oh, he was stoic enough, and no one else would be able to tell he was anything but the warrior he was. Mairin knew better. Alaric wasn't as cold as Caelen and he didn't tend to be as fierce as Ewan. He could always be counted on to fill the gap in conversation and he was a sociable enough person. Tonight he sat in stony silence, picking at his food as if he had no appetite.

Keeley was noticeably absent, though Mairin couldn't blame her. It was enough to have to look upon the man she loved paying court to another woman, but the circumstances of Keeley's departure from the McDonald clan were enough to keep her sequestered.

Mairin wanted nothing more than to march over and

bash Laird McDonald's head in with a serving platter. If she thought she could move fast enough to get past Ewan, she might well attempt it.

"You are about to fidget right off the bench," Ewan said in a whisper. "What is amiss? Are you not feeling well?"

She glanced up at the concern—and exasperation—in her husband's eyes. "I'm ready to retire. I can see myself up. You stay and continue your talks with Laird McDonald."

Ewan frowned. "Nay, I'll go up with you. It will give Alaric some time to talk with the laird—and Rionna, should he choose."

Not waiting for her to respond, Ewan turned to Laird McDonald and smoothly interrupted the conversation. "If you will excuse us, my lady wife is ready to retire. She tires easily these days and I do not like her going up to our chamber without me."

Mairin couldn't control her look of distaste when Laird McDonald's eyes gleamed lasciviously. "Aye, I understand. If I had a wife as bonnie as yours, she'd not be retiring without me either."

Mairin shuddered. Poor Keeley. How awful it must have been for her when she was but a girl. The man was a lecher. And he ate too much. Gertie hadn't forgiven the man the last time he'd visited McCabe keep. Their stores hadn't been as plentiful as they were now, and the laird had eaten them near out of the keep.

"Come, sweeting," Ewan murmured as he helped her from her seat.

'Twas the truth she was weary, but then she was weary most days. There were times when she thought she'd carry this child to infinity. The bairn was particularly active at night. She and Ewan would lie in bed and quietly feel the tiny kicks and bumps.

She paused halfway up the stairs, already out of

breath. Ewan steadied her and waited until she was ready to resume.

"I vow I'm going to be pregnant forever," she complained as Ewan ushered her into their chamber.

Ewan smiled and helped her from her clothing. "It won't be long now. Think how exciting it will be to finally hold our son or daughter."

Mairin sighed. "I know it."

As soon as she had on her nightdress, she sank onto the edge of the bed. Across the room Ewan undressed and she could feel his gaze upon her as he returned to the bed.

He sat beside her. "What is it, Mairin? You look worried. Is it the babe that has you afraid?"

She smiled faintly and turned to look up at him. "Nay, I have complete faith in Keeley."

"Then what is it that has you so unhappy?"

"'Tis Keeley. And Alaric," she blurted.

Ewan blew out his breath and started to turn away, but Mairin caught his arm.

"They're unhappy, Ewan. Can't you do anything?"

Ewan grimaced and touched Mairin's cheek in a soothing gesture. "'Tis nothing I can do, sweeting. Too much rides on this alliance. Alaric is a man full grown. He's made his decision."

She huffed in exasperation. "But would he have made such a decision if our clan didn't have need of this alliance so much? He's a good man. He'd do anything for you. For the clan."

"He has a chance to be laird," Ewan pointed out. "A chance he'll never gain if he remains here. This is an opportunity as much as it is a necessity that we gain this alliance."

"Do we really need the McDonalds so much?" she asked incredulously. It didn't seem logical that they'd need the much weaker clan with the might the McCabes wielded.

"There is more to it than fighting force," Ewan said gently. " 'Tis a matter of politics. The king wants this match. This cannot pass your lips, but we both fear that McDonald could turn to Cameron's side and that would be disastrous, for he is all that lies between McCabe lands and Neamh Álainn."

Mairin's nose wrinkled. "Then 'tis more a strategic move than a need for his strength?"

Ewan nodded. "Add to that, there are still some clans who fear Cameron's might and have held off allying themselves with either side for fear of retaliation should Cameron and Malcolm prove victorious in the bid for the throne and control of the highlands. We need to appear an invincible force. 'Tis a never-ending cycle. To lure others to our cause we must have the alliances of many clans."

Mairin sighed. " 'Tis rotten business. I want Alaric and Keeley to be happy."

Ewan pulled her into his arms. "There's nothing to say that Alaric won't eventually be happy with the match. Rionna is a beautiful lass. She'll bear him strong sons and daughters."

"But what of Keeley?" Mairin whispered.

"She'll remain here with us, sheltered by the McCabe clan. There are plenty of men who'd count themselves fortunate to marry a lass such as Keeley."

"You make it sound so simple. Would you think the same if you were forbidden to marry me?"

Ewan pulled away, a scowl on his face. "There is no force on earth or heaven that would keep me from your side."

"Aye, and I love you for it. Maybe I think 'tis what Alaric should be willing to do for Keeley," she said quietly.

CHAPTER 30

Keeley was up at dawn, staring moodily over the terrain. The snows had almost fully melted during an unexpected warming trend, most unusual for January. She hadn't slept the night before and her eyes were dull and achy.

Maddie's counsel had been invaluable. Keeley needed to hear the other woman's wisdom. 'Twas no use in hiding in her chamber sulking. She was no longer the frightened young girl terrified to be on her own without the support of her clan.

She had the McCabes now. She had family. And friends. Good and loyal friends. Rionna and her father couldn't hurt her.

If it killed her, she would smile through Alaric's wedding. She'd send him off with all the love in her heart but with no weeping. No grief. Some things were private. As much as she'd love to shout her love for Alaric for all to hear, it was better kept to her heart where naught could be used against him.

Feeling marginally better after her all-night weep fest, she washed her face and straightened her hair. Then she took a deep breath and exited her chamber to go belowstairs. She really had no idea what she would do this day. For the past weeks, she and the other women of the keep gathered to keep Mairin company in the hall. With the McDonalds in residence, the women would likely seek a quieter spot for their visitation.

It was soon obvious to Keeley that most of the clan was still abed after a late night entertaining the McDonalds. The keep was blanketed in silence.

'Twould be a wonderful opportunity for a walk around the courtyard, at least since the laird forbade anyone from venturing farther.

She stopped into the kitchens to visit with Gertie and ask if there were any herbs she needed for her preparations. Gertie scowled and waved her away, mumbling something about being interrupted while she was trying to think.

With a grin, Keeley set off for the courtyard. A brisk chill met her as soon as she stepped outside, but she welcomed it on her skin. She drew in a deep breath and closed her eyes. The air just smelled cleaner and fresher in the winter. The bite of ice filled her lungs and when she exhaled, her breath came out in a cloud of steam.

Giggling like a child, she made a turn around the wall and ventured down the side of the keep. The loch was to her left and was so still, it resembled a looking glass. The sun bounced off the surface, reminding her of a shield held up in battle.

She was so ensconced in her view of the loch that she didn't notice the person coming toward her until she heard her name.

"Keeley? Keeley McDonald, is that you?"

Keeley whirled around, her heart leaping to her throat. Rionna stood but a few feet away, her expression stunned.

"Aye, 'tis I," Keeley returned in a low voice. She took a hesitant step back.

Pain creased Rionna's face. Her golden eyes turned dull until the ever-present shimmer had faded to amber.

"I thought you dead. When they told me you were gone, I looked. I waited. But when you didn't return, I thought you were *dead*."

Keeley's face crinkled in confusion. "Who did you speak with? I am fit as you can see."

"The women and men I sent to your cottage to ensure your well-being. How did you arrive here? What is it you're doing on McCabe land? It's been months since you were last seen at your cottage."

Keeley stared warily at the other woman, unsure of how to respond. " 'Tis where I am welcome."

A spasm of pain crossed Rionna's face. A McDonald man appeared in the distance and shouted Rionna's name.

"The laird is looking for you. He wants you present for the breaking of fast."

Rionna's hands curled into tight balls. She glanced back at Keeley and then to her father's man. "I must go. I would see you later. I have much to say to you."

Without further explanation, Rionna turned and hurried back toward the keep. Keeley watched her go, her stomach in knots. Her emotions were such a mass of uncertainty. Part of her wanted to throw her arms around Rionna and hug her senseless. Tell her how much she missed her childhood friend and tell her how beautiful she'd grown.

The other part wanted to demand an explanation. The hurt she thought she'd long buried bubbled to the surface. Maybe she would never be able to forget or forgive being forced from the only life and protection she knew.

She sighed and turned back to the loch. She walked to the edge and stared, mesmerized, into the crystal clear waters. She loved the water. It absorbed the moods and whims of nature and cast them onto the surface for all to see. 'Twas freeing, that. No pretending. No hiding. Just a reflection of what boiled right below the surface.

For how long she stood there, she wasn't certain. She stared across the loch, lost in her thoughts and the constant aching in her heart.

" 'Tis too cold a morn for a lass to be outdoors as long as you have," Gannon said gently.

She turned, startled by the warrior's presence. She hadn't heard him approach, but she'd been too absorbed with other matters.

She smiled faintly. " 'Tis the truth I've no awareness of the cold."

" 'Tis even worse then for you'll not know when you've grown too cold."

She wanted to ask him if Alaric had sent him, but she refused to speak his name. She had vowed to remain stoic, even if it killed her.

" 'Tis a beautiful morn," she said conversationally. "The snows are nearly gone. 'Tis not usually so warm this time of year."

"Aye, but it's still too cold for a lass such as yourself to be out alone without proper clothing."

Keeley sighed and cast another stare over the water. The calmness soothed her. Gave her peace when her insides were in turmoil. If only she could pull it around her like a cloak. Steel armor that no one could breech.

"You know the McDonalds were my clan."

The words were baldly spoken, laid out in brash fashion. She had no idea why she said them. Gannon was hardly a person to confide in. The warrior would likely rather have his arm cut off than to listen to womanly blether.

"Aye, I know it," he returned.

There was an odd note to his voice that she couldn't quite define.

"They are no more."

Gannon nodded. "Nay. You're a McCabe now."

She smiled at that. She couldn't help it. It filled her with such warmth that it was all she could do not to throw her arms around him and squeeze for all she was worth.

Her eyes went watery and he gave her such a look of horror that she had to laugh.

"Thank you for saying that. 'Tis a fact I needed to hear that this morn. I was . . . I was unprepared for their arrival as of yet."

"No reason to cry," he said gruffly. "A McCabe doesn't cry. They hold their heads up and don't allow others to trod on them."

This time the temptation was simply too strong. She flung her arms around him, making him stagger back as she hit him right in the chest.

"What the . . . ?"

He grasped her so they didn't both go down and stood as stiff as a boulder as she squeezed him. Then he sighed. "Between you and Lady McCabe, I swear the McCabe clan is becoming an emotional watering pot."

Keeley grinned against him. There was gruffness in his voice but there was also true affection. She drew away and smiled through her tears. "You like me."

He scowled. "I said nothing of the sort."

"Admit it. You like me."

"I don't like you very much right now."

"Ah, but you did before."

His scowl deepened. "You should come back inside the keep now."

"Thank you, Gannon. 'Tis a fact I was not feeling very well today." She glanced up again and was tempted to hug him once more, but he seemed to realize her intent and hastily stepped back. She grinned again. "I find I like my new clan very much. The McCabes recognize the importance of loyalty and family."

He looked offended. "Of course we do. There's no more loyal a clan than the McCabes and no better a laird than ours."

"I'm very glad I'm here," she said softly as they turned to walk back toward the keep.

Gannon hesitated a brief moment and then glanced sideways at her. "I'm glad you're here, too, Keeley McCabe."

CHAPTER 31

Bolstered by Gannon's escort, Keeley walked into the hall but was careful not to look at either Rionna or her father. Gannon led her to a seat next to Mairin and then took the place on the other side of Keeley.

She sent him a grateful smile at the same moment Mairin squeezed her hand under the table.

She refused to look at Alaric, who sat several places down between Rionna and Laird McDonald. Instead she focused on Mairin and Christina, who sat across the table next to Cormac.

The nervousness was making her ill. Her stomach was in knots. Surely Rionna would have told her father of her presence by now. Would he cry her whore in front of the McCabe clan? Would he try to ruin her position here? And what could Rionna possibly have need to say to her?

She ate in silence, nodding when Mairin spoke. At one point, Gannon leaned over and said, "You just nodded *aye* when Lady McCabe asked if you thought she'd be pregnant for months still."

Keeley closed her eyes and subdued the urge to smack her forehead with her fist. Then she turned to Mairin, apology in her eyes.

"I'm sorry."

Mairin grinned and shook her head. "I was just jesting with you. I knew you weren't paying attention because you nodded *aye* to everything." Then she leaned closer. "'Tis almost done with. No one would ever guess you're so ill at ease."

Keeley smiled gratefully at her but when she turned back, she saw Laird McDonald staring at her. His brows were drawn together and she could tell the moment recognition dawned. His eyes widened and he glanced down to where Rionna sat, a frown on his face. Then he looked back up at Keeley, but it wasn't anger or even shock that burned in his gaze.

It was lust, and that frightened Keeley more than if he'd stood up and shouted *whore*.

She couldn't look at him without remembering the utter helplessness she felt years earlier when she was sure he'd rape her.

The urge to bolt from the table and flee was so strong that she was nearly to her feet before she realized she was allowing something that had happened long ago to affect her.

As quickly as panic and fear rushed through her system leaving her weak and shaky, rage pushed its way through her veins. She relaxed into her chair and unclenched her fists.

She wasn't the young girl she'd been then. She was a woman full grown and she had the means to defend herself. The laird would find no helpless target now.

"You aren't alone," Gannon murmured.

She wouldn't embarrass either of them by shedding tears, but still she found her gaze a little watery when she glanced up at him.

"Nay, I'm not alone. Not anymore."

He smiled. "If you are done, I'll escort you above stairs to your chamber."

Keeley sighed in relief. It wasn't as if the laird or even

Rionna could run after her to her room without causing a scene, but still, she'd been afraid to draw notice to herself by excusing herself.

"Thank you. 'Twould be nice to retire early to my chamber."

Mairin, who'd been listening in, leaned forward and touched Keeley on the arm. "Aye, Keeley, why don't you go on up."

Keeley pushed herself up as quietly as possible, but despite her effort not to gain notice, the table quieted just then and all eyes cast in her direction.

Rionna, Alaric, and Laird McDonald all stared at her but with varying emotion. Concern brimmed in Alaric's gaze and it narrowed sharply when Gannon put his arm out to Keeley. Rionna looked at her with something that resembled sorrow, and the laird stared at her with avid interest, his gaze crawling over her until she shuddered visibly.

"Come," Gannon said in a low voice.

Keeley turned away and Gannon guided her toward the stair. They climbed in silence and when they reached her chamber, Gannon waited politely as she opened her door.

"I'll be outside should you have need," he said when she entered.

She turned, a frown on her face, and studied the warrior. "Your duty 'tis to the laird and his brothers."

"Aye, 'tis true. However, 'tis you who have most need of me at the moment."

It took a second for Keeley to realize that Gannon must have known of Laird McDonald's attack. Heat suffused her cheeks and she looked down, no longer able to meet the warrior's gaze.

"Thank you," she said in a low voice.

Before he could respond, she closed the door and leaned heavily against it.

'Twas an awful conundrum. She wanted Rionna and the laird gone from McCabe land as soon as possible, but when they'd leave, Alaric would travel with them as Rionna's new husband.

With a sigh she set about undressing and climbed into her bed. She lay there for a long time, staring into the dying flames in her hearth. Was Alaric thinking of her even now, or was he getting acquainted with his bride to be?

Keeley came awake and bolted upward, her heart pounding so hard 'twas painful. Her door was open and for a moment her nightmare took over and all she could see was Laird McDonald standing there and leering at her.

"Keeley, 'tis me, Ewan. I need you to hasten. 'Tis Mairin's time."

She blinked away the horror and gradually the laird came into view. He stood, framed in her doorway, awaiting her response.

"Aye, of course. I'll come right away," she babbled.

She scrambled from the bed and reached for her clothing then clutched them to her bosom while she waited for the laird to withdraw from her room.

She hurriedly dressed, nearly tripping on the hem of her gown in her haste. She was about to run from her chamber when she halted and clapped her hands to her head.

"Think, Keeley, think."

"Can I help?" Gannon asked as he pushed off the wall outside her room.

She massaged her aching temple, still battling the effects of her dreams. 'Twas ridiculous to have been so afraid when Laird McCabe burst into her chamber. Gannon was outside. He wouldn't have allowed anyone else to enter.

The reminder soothed her, and she closed her eyes to take a deep breath. "Aye, summon Maddie. And Christina. Have them bring water and fresh linens. I must gather my supplies and then I'll be to the laird's chamber."

Gannon nodded and strode down the hall while Keeley returned to her chamber to collect her forgotten supplies.

A few moments later, she approached the laird's chamber and knocked. The door swung open and Ewan stood in front of her, his expression fierce.

"Who is it, Ewan?" Mairin called. "Is it Keeley?"

Keeley pushed by Ewan and into Mairin's view. She smiled encouragingly. "Aye, 'tis me. Are you ready to have this babe?"

Mairin sat up on the bed, her hand clutched over her protruding belly. Her gown was bunched around her knees and her hair was askew. Some of the stress eased from her eyes and her lips turned upward into a smile.

"Aye, 'tis the truth I'm weary of carrying this child. I'm ready to hold him in my arms and not my belly."

Keeley laughed. "I hear that a lot when a woman's time comes."

She carefully set up her skirt full of supplies on the laird's dressing table and then returned to the bed and sat on the edge in front of Mairin.

"When did your pains start? And are they regular?"

Mairin frowned and glanced up at Ewan, her expression guilty. "They started this morn, but they came and went."

Ewan scowled and let out a breath. "You should have told me the *moment* your pains began."

"I had no desire to spend the entire day abed," Mairin muttered.

"When did they start to become more forceful and

constant?" Keeley asked. She stroked Mairin's hand as she spoke in an effort to soothe her.

"'Twas before the evening meal and they've gotten closer together since."

"'Tis hard to say how long you'll labor with the child," Keeley said as she rose. "Sometimes 'tis not over-long at all, but other times 'tis as if the child is determined to make the world wait."

Mairin laughed. "I'll hope for the former."

Her laughter died and a groan escaped her lips. She bent forward and gripped her middle as her face creased with pain.

Ewan bent over her immediately, his hands flying over her body. "Mairin, are you all right? Is it overly painful?" Then he yanked his gaze to Keeley. "What can I do? How can I help her?"

'Twas obvious to Keeley that the laird was going to drive them all daft if he remained. She laid a hand on Mairin's arm as she rose and said, "I'll return in just a moment."

She hurried out to the hall where she met with Gannon. "I need you to fetch Caelen or Alaric. Tell them to come for the laird and take him belowstairs. Give him some ale or something to soothe his nerves."

Gannon chuckled. "In other words, get him out of your and Lady McCabe's hair."

Keeley smiled. "Exactly. I'll summon him when 'tis time for the babe to be born."

As Gannon disappeared, Keeley returned to Mairin and had barely sat down when Maddie and Christina bustled in with the items Keeley had requested. Mairin looked extremely relieved to see the other women, and some of the tension fled from her face.

"By the looks of things, you have a while yet, lass," Maddie said to Mairin.

Mairin scowled.

Ewan had a faint lost look as he gazed around at all the women. It was obvious he was torn between fleeing for his life and remaining as a support to his wife. He was saved from making a decision when Caelen and Alaric arrived.

There was a brief argument before Mairin shooed Ewan and told him to leave her in peace. Caelen and Alaric each took an arm and all but hauled Ewan from the chamber.

At the doorway, Alaric stopped and glanced back at Keeley. His lips lifted in a half smile and she made herself do the same. Then the three brothers disappeared. Gannon stuck his head in and bowed his head in Mairin's direction.

"If you have need of anything, I'll be outside the chamber door."

Mairin smiled. "Thank you, Gannon." Then her face promptly spasmed in pain and she issued a grunt as Gannon backed hastily out.

"Ah now, that's better," Maddie proclaimed with a satisfied smile. "The birthing chamber is no place for a man. They're such babies when it comes to a woman's pain."

Christina chuckled and Mairin nodded her agreement.

"Ewan wants to be here. 'Tis important to him," Mairin said softly.

"I'll make sure he's here. I told Gannon to tell the others not to let him drink overmuch," Keeley teased. "You have a ways yet. 'Tis best if you're comfortable and have as little stress as possible."

For a few hours the women talked and jested with Mairin. They soothed her through her pains, wiped her brow, and offered her comfort.

"Jesu, 'tis hot in here," Mairin complained as Christina wiped the sweat from her brow for the tenth time.

"'Tis actually quite chilly," Maddie pointed out.

"You'll not want the babe chilled when he's pushed from the warmth of his mother."

"I think 'tis time to remove your gown and have you lie down," Keeley said. "Your pains are coming close and I'll need to check to make sure the babe's positioned correctly."

"And if he isn't?" Mairin asked anxiously.

"'Tis naught for you to worry over," Keeley soothed.

They helped Mairin to undress and then made her comfortable on clean linens. Mairin was a slight lass, but her hips weren't narrow, much to Keeley's relief. If the babe wasn't overlarge, she shouldn't have difficulty with the birthing.

A half hour later, the pains were nearly constant and Keeley looked up from her position between Mairin's legs. "Go fetch the laird," she said quietly. "'Tis nearly time."

Christina's eyes widened. "I'll go," she blurted, and was out the door before Maddie or Keeley could respond.

Not even a minute later, the laird burst into the room, his gaze fastened on Mairin. He knelt by the bed and gathered her hand in his.

"Are you all right, sweeting?" he asked anxiously. "Does it hurt overmuch?"

"Nay, not at all," Mairin said through gritted teeth. "It hurts like the fires of hell!"

"I see the head!" Keeley exclaimed. "With your next pain, I want you to take in your breath, hold it, and then push. Not too hard, just a steady, firm push."

Mairin nodded and gripped Ewan's hand harder.

"Oh!" Mairin began.

"Aye, that's it," Keeley encouraged.

When Mairin's breath escaped and she deflated against the bed, Keeley looked up. "Rest now and wait for the next. You'll do the same thing all over again."

"'Tis insane," Ewan muttered. "Why isn't the babe here yet?"

Maddie rolled her eyes. "Just like a man. He shows up and expects all to be done."

For the next several minutes, Mairin and Keeley worked together. She breathed when Keeley told her and pushed when instructed. The head eased forward and slipped into Keeley's waiting hands.

"This is it, Mairin!" Keeley said excitedly. "One more push and 'twill be done."

Mairin roused herself and with Ewan holding her up, she gathered in her breath and bore down, her eyes closed in concentration.

The babe slipped into Keeley's waiting hands, all gooey and warm and blessedly alive.

"'Tis a lass!" Keeley exclaimed. "You have a daughter, Mairin!"

Tears gathered in Mairin's eyes, and even the laird's were suspiciously wet as he gazed down at his wife.

"A daughter," he said hoarsely.

Keeley set about cutting and securing the cord. Then she quickly cleaned the baby and its small cry echoed over the quiet room.

Both parents were mesmerized at that first sound. They stared in awe as Keeley carefully wrapped the babe in a warm blanket and then laid her at Mairin's breast.

"She's beautiful," Ewan whispered. He kissed Mairin's sweaty brow and smoothed her hair from her face. "As beautiful as her mother."

Mairin eased the babe to her nipple and coaxed until the infant weakly latched on and began to suckle.

Tears burned Keeley's eyes as she watched the utter reverence in Ewan's eyes. He gathered both wife and daughter in his arms and held them as the babe fed. Neither parent could take their eyes from the delicate little girl in Mairin's arms.

"You did good, lass," Maddie whispered as she hugged Keeley. "I've never seen a birthing go so smoothly."

Keeley smiled at her and then motioned for Maddie to help gather the bloodied linens. They worked in silence, loathe to disturb the tender moment between the laird and his family.

They eased their way toward the door when suddenly the laird turned and rose from the bed. He closed the distance between himself and Keeley and stood before her, his eyes bright with relief and joy.

"Thank you. My wife means everything to me. I could not have borne to lose her or our child. You have my everlasting gratitude and 'tis a debt I can never hope to repay."

Keeley smiled. "I'll come back to check in on her in just a while."

Ewan nodded and quickly returned to his wife's bedside.

When Keeley and Maddie entered the hallway, Caelen, Alaric, and Gannon all pushed away from the wall to face the women.

" 'Tis done?" Caelen demanded.

Keeley nodded. "The laird has a daughter."

Alaric smiled. "A daughter. 'Tis fitting, that. She'll drive him as daft as her mother does."

Gannon chuckled. "Not to mention the rest of us."

"And Mairin? All is well with her?" Caelen asked.

Keeley raised an eyebrow. "Why, Caelen, I do believe you have a heart after all. Aye, Mairin is well. Ewan is with the both of them now, and I thought to give them a bit of privacy."

Caelen scowled and muttered something under his breath, but Keeley could see the relief in his eyes.

"If you'll excuse us, we must go belowstairs to clean

up, and 'tis truth I could use a bit of fresh air," Keeley said.

Without waiting a response, she walked by the men and went down the stairs, Maddie on her heels.

"Give me the linens," Maddie directed when they entered the hall. "You go take your fresh air. It's been an exhausting night for you."

Keeley offered no argument and headed for the courtyard, eager to feel the coldness on her cheeks. She closed her eyes as soon as the chill hit her. Exhausted to her core, she sank onto the steps. Birthing always scared her. Too many women died while trying to birth a child, and Keeley was determined that it wouldn't happen with Mairin. She needn't have worried though. It was one of the easiest births she'd ever attended. Still, relief was so fierce within her that her knees were weak.

So she sat there breathing in deep, steadying breaths.

"Keeley, are you all right?"

She yanked her head around to see Alaric standing in the shadows. Her pulse beat more rapidly as she drank in his appearance. 'Twas funny since it hadn't been overlong since she'd seen him at all, but still she soaked him in like a parched plant soaked in rain.

"Aye, I'm well," she murmured.

He took a step forward but stopped a respectable distance from her. "Keeley, I . . ."

She rose, moved by the discomfort in his voice. She pressed in close and put a finger to his lips. "Nay, don't say it," she whispered. "I've always known of your destiny—and mine. Yours is a noble one. You should have no regrets. You will be great, Alaric. You'll be a great laird. I am proud to have called you mine even for so short a time."

Alaric touched her cheek and then leaned in slowly and pressed a tender kiss to her lips. So sweet and fleeting. Brief. But she felt it to her soul.

"You, too, are great, Keeley McCabe," he whispered. "My clan is better for having you."

She leaned into his kiss, tipping her forehead to his. She closed her eyes, savoring the sweet contact. She breathed, allowing him to wash away the fatigue and grief.

Then she pulled away and steeled herself against the pain in her heart. "I must go now. I must see to Mairin and the new babe's needs."

Alaric stroked her hair away from her cheek and then cupped the side of her face in his palm. "I love you. Remember it always."

She covered his hand with hers and smiled achingly up at him. "Aye, I will."

Slowly, he pulled away and then stepped back so she could walk by him back into the keep. She went without looking back but felt the wetness on her cheeks before she mounted the first step.

CHAPTER 32

Laird McCabe stood atop the stairs to the courtyard, the tiny bundle of his daughter cradled in his massive arms.

"My daughter!" he proclaimed and held her high.

The gathered clan roared their approval. Swords thrust upward, shields banged, and a resounding cheer echoed over the land.

Ewan cradled her in his arms again, and his expression was so tender and proud that Keeley could barely swallow around the knot in her throat. Maddie smiled broadly beside Keeley and reached over to squeeze Keeley's hand.

" 'Tis a wondrous day for the McCabe clan."

The older woman wiped at her eyes and sniffed noisily even as she offered a loud cheer of her own.

Warmth traveled through Keeley as she realized that the clan's joy was her own. She was a part of the McCabe clan now. Their triumph was her triumph.

Surely there wasn't a better feeling. Acceptance. She *belonged*.

As the cheers died and Ewan returned inside with the babe, the clansmen went back to their duties. Maddie excused herself to the kitchens, and Keeley returned indoors, her intent to check on Mairin's well-being.

She hummed to herself as she mounted the stairs. The hallway was empty, a surprise since Gannon had become a permanent fixture outside the chambers. It seemed he rotated his duty. It was a great comfort to Keeley. She'd grown used to the gruff warrior and liked his company.

She hadn't taken more than two steps when a hand snaked out, grabbed her wrist, and she found herself yanked into one of the bedchambers.

Before she could cry out, defend herself, or even process what had happened, her lips were ravaged in a brutal kiss. The chamber door slammed behind her, and her back hit the closed door with enough force to knock the breath from her.

Through her muddled senses she recognized one thing: It was happening again, only this time there was no effort to woo a young, inexperienced girl. Laird McDonald had no care whether he hurt her or not or whether she was willing.

As soon as his lips left her, she opened her mouth to scream only to have his hand clamp over it with bruising force.

"I could not believe my eyes when I saw you here," he panted. " 'Twas fate. I always knew you'd belong to me. I've waited years for this moment, Keeley. *Years*. You'll not say me nay this time."

Keeley stared in horror at the older laird. He was daft. Mad! He would attack her inside the McCabe keep?

His free hand went to her breast and squeezed painfully. He loosened the hand over her mouth but before she could gather breath to scream, his mouth covered hers again.

With all her might, she jerked her knee into his groin and when he dropped his hands down to clutch himself in agony, she shoved hard. He stumbled back and went down on his arse.

She turned to fumble with the door, desperate to get into the hall. It was locked! She yelled hoarsely just as the laird grabbed her by the hair and threw her across the room.

She landed in a heap on the floor, all the breath knocked painfully from her chest. He stood over her, his eyes glittering with rage. Spittle frothed on his lips and his cheeks were red with exertion.

"You little bitch. You'll pay for your defiance."

Her eyes narrowed in fury and she flew at him. She hit him hard and he staggered back, shock reflected on his features. He actually held up his arms to ward her off, but her rage propelled her on.

The slovenly little bastard sickened her. For years she'd viewed him as some demon from hell. Larger than life. Evil. Powerful. She'd lived in fear of him, building him up in her mind to be something he wasn't.

"You're a pathetic worm who preys on children," she hissed.

She balled her fist and swung. Her knuckles exploded in pain as she connected with his nose. Blood splattered and the laird's head jerked back, his hand flying to his face.

He bellowed with rage and struck out at her. She ducked but not in time to keep him from striking her cheek. She reeled and tripped over the bed.

"Exactly where you belong," he spat as he advanced.

Several things happened at once.

The door splintered and exploded inward. The laird's eyes widened with fear. And then suddenly he flew across the room, hitting the wall with a loud smack.

Keeley stared in astonishment as Caelen advanced on the laird, his entire body bristling with rage. She scrambled backward on the bed, hoisting herself so she could see what went on.

Caelen hauled the laird to his feet and then flattened

him with a fist. Never had she seen someone so angry. If she didn't intervene, Caelen would kill the other man. Not that she particularly cared of his fate, but the implications would be far-reaching.

Ignoring the fiery pain in her jaw and the cold shock creeping over her body, she ran toward Caelen and latched on to his arm.

"Caelen, you must stop!"

Caelen dropped the laird and whirled around, cold fury brimming in his eyes.

"You would defend him?"

She shook her head, precariously close to tears. "Nay. Leave him, though. Please. Think of what you do. Think of the implications."

Her gaze skittered downward to the limp form of the laird and she shuddered in revulsion. Realization sunk in and her knees wobbled and she collapsed.

Caelen caught her and swung her into his arms. He strode from the chamber and down the hall to Keeley's door. Not hesitating, he bore her within and gently set her on the bed.

"Do you want me to summon Maddie or Christina?" he asked in a quiet voice.

She shook her head and cupped her hand to her aching jaw.

"I'll kill him," Caelen bit out.

She shook her head mutely, too stunned to do more.

Caelen swore and then turned. "I'm going to fetch Alaric."

At that, Keeley flew from the bed and grabbed Caelen. She pulled him back from the door and slammed it shut. "Nay! You cannot. Caelen, you mustn't say a word."

Caelen gaped incredulously at her.

"Think of what you do," she said hoarsely. "If you tell Alaric, he will be furious. He's already angry at what happened years ago. If you go to him with this, there is no telling what he'll do."

"Rightly so! No man tolerates such treatment of a woman," Caelen growled. "He deserves killing. 'Tis an insult he's offered to all McCabes. Ewan will never let him live."

"'Tis exactly why you cannot breathe a word. This alliance is important to your . . ." She broke off and thrust her chin upward. "'Tis important to *my* clan. What think you Alaric would do? He cannot afford to insult the father of the woman he is to marry. Alaric is to take over as laird of the McDonald clan. His destiny is a great one. If he knew of what happened, he would be furious. He would retaliate."

Caelen dragged a hand through his hair and made a sound of acute exasperation. "So you want me to do nothing?"

The question came out strangled, like he was close to exploding.

She raised her gaze, her eyes brimming with tears. She was holding on by a thread and very close to hysteria. It was either laugh or cry and she was unsure of which would win out.

Caelen sighed and settled on the bed next to her. He hesitated and then carefully put his arms around her in a hug.

"It's understandable if you need to cry," he said gruffly.

She buried her face in his chest and burst into tears. She cried noisily while he patted her awkwardly on the back. She cried until her eyes were puffy and her head ached vilely. After a while her sobs turned to painful hiccups.

She drew away and wiped at her nose with the back of her hand. Then she started laughing.

Caelen looked warily at her and she didn't blame him. He probably thought she'd lost her mind.

"I bloodied his nose," she said.

Caelen smiled. "I saw that. Very impressive. You're a fierce lass."

"I also kneed him between the legs."

He winced but nodded his approval. "Between the two of us, I don't think he'll be in any shape to accost any more lasses."

"Good," she said fiercely. "While I know we can't kill him, 'tis the truth I hope he suffers."

Caelen chuckled.

She sighed and looked up at him. "Thank you. I'm sorry to have sobbed all over you. Your tunic is wet."

"'Tis the least I can do after all you've done for my clan," he said quietly. "'Tis the truth I had little liking for you in the beginning. I thought no good could come of Alaric's infatuation with you. But 'tis the truth he is a most fortunate man. Even now when 'twould be easy to wreck his impending marriage to Rionna, you think only of the clan. You're a hell of a woman, Keeley McCabe."

Her eyes watered again. "Oh, you must stop. 'Tis the truth I tear up whenever I'm called by McCabe."

Caelen tucked his finger under her chin and forced it upward. "Are you all right? Did he hurt you badly?"

"I did more damage to him than he did to me. He struck me once on the jaw and it aches fiercely, but 'tis all he managed."

"Good. Now would you like me to fetch one of the women for you?"

He looked so hopeful that she had to hide her smile. "Nay. I'll be fine. You did a woman's job very skillfully."

He scowled, which amused her all the more.

"I'm jesting, but in all seriousness, thank you. It means much that you would come to my aid."

Caelen's expression darkened. "It displeases me that you would think I wouldn't."

She rose from her seat on the bed and swayed as her knees bobbled. Caelen caught her arm to steady her and frowned fiercely at her.

"You should remain on the bed. You've suffered a terrible fright."

"I must go tend to Mairin's needs and see how the babe fares. I need to go about my duties, or I'll sit here and cry."

"As soon as you've tended to Mairin, you're to return to your chamber and rest," he said sternly. "If you don't, I'll tell Alaric what occurred."

Her scowl was every bit as ferocious as his. "All right. I'll retire after I've seen to Mairin."

Caelen watched her walk from the room, noting her unsteady gait. She was daft if she thought he'd tell no one what happened. Ewan needed to be aware of the viper in his keep. He'd do as she wished and not tell Alaric only because she was right. There would be no calming his brother's rage if he knew of Gregor's attack on Keeley. War would be declared and everything the McCabes had worked for over the last years would be for naught.

For the first time he felt sadness for the position his brother was in. 'Twas obvious Alaric cared deeply for Keeley, and the lass cared for him in return. The fact that she didn't leap on the opportunity to ruin his match with Rionna earned her his deep respect.

Nay, Alaric could not know of what happened, but Caelen could step in and be her protector until the McDonalds were gone from McCabe lands. The sooner it happened, the better. For it was God's truth, Caelen wouldn't be able to look upon the bastard without seeing Keeley's tear-stained face, and then he'd want to kill him all over again.

CHAPTER 33

"Keeley, whatever happened to your face?" Mairin demanded.

Keeley touched the sore place on her jaw. "Does it look bad?"

Mairin frowned. "There's a bruise. I didn't see it at first until you turned a certain way in the light. What happened?"

"Oh, 'tis nothing," Keeley said brightly. "'Twas my clumsiness. 'Tis the truth I'm embarrassed. I wasn't looking where I was going. Thank goodness no one was there to witness it."

Mairin didn't look convinced but didn't pursue the topic.

"Now tell me, how are you feeling?"

"Tired but otherwise I feel well. 'Tis some soreness, but I'm eager to be up from my bed." She looked pleadingly at Keeley. "Ewan is about to drive me daft. I've told him that countless women have left their bed by now but he refuses to listen to reason."

Keeley smiled. "I don't see why a brief time to stand up and stretch your muscles would be amiss."

"I'd like to sit by the fire and nurse Isabel. I grow weary of lying abed."

"Oh, is that what you've named her? 'Tis a beautiful name."

Mairin's face shone with pride and love as she glanced down at the sleeping babe at her breast. "Aye. Ewan is going to announce it when the king arrives."

Keeley swallowed and looked away, busying herself with straightening items that didn't need straightening. "The king will be here soon?"

"Aye. Ewan sent word to him before Isabel was born. He wanted to attend Alaric's wedding. We expect his messenger any day to announce his impending arrival."

Steeling her features, Keeley reached for the babe. "Let me put her in her cradle and then I'll help you to the chair by the fire. Would you like me to help you wash and change into fresh clothing while I'm here?"

"Oh 'twould be wondrous," Mairin breathed.

After settling the babe in her cradle, Keeley helped Mairin sit up on the edge of the bed. She efficiently stripped the other woman down and helped her wash. Once Mairin was dressed in a clean, sweet-smelling gown, Keeley braced herself and helped the other woman to her feet.

"'Tis not so bad," Mairin said in triumph. "I don't feel weak at all."

"Wife, 'tis clear I'm going to have to post a guard on you at all times to make sure you stay where you belong," Ewan said from the door.

Keeley grabbed the startled Mairin and then turned to scowl at the laird. "Come in or go out, but shut the door and keep your voice down. The babe is sleeping."

Ewan didn't look happy to be ordered about, but he complied with Keeley's order and then returned to stand a few feet away from Mairin, his arms crossed over his chest.

"Oh, do quit standing there frowning," Keeley said in

exasperation. "Help her to the chair by the fire. She'd like to feed your daughter in comfort."

"She should be abed resting," Ewan said gruffly.

But he gathered Mairin gently to his side and eased her into the chair a short distance away. Keeley fussed around making sure Mairin was adequately covered, and then she went to fetch the baby and settled her into Mairin's arms.

"Do stop frowning, husband," Mairin said, echoing Keeley's order. "I'm perfectly fit. If I had to spend one more day in that bed, I was going to go mad."

"I just worry for you," he said. "I want you and Isabel to be hale and hearty."

Mairin smiled and patted Ewan's arm. "We are both perfectly well."

Ewan sat on the edge of the bed and watched as Mairin nursed Isabel. His expression was slightly awed and his eyes glowed with love. 'Twas a heart-squeezing sight to behold.

"You nearly made me forget what I came up to tell you," Ewan reproached. "Seeing you out of bed made me lose my purpose."

Mairin grinned. "'Tis not often you lose your purpose, husband."

He shot her a quelling stare. "The king arrives in two days' time. My messenger intercepted him with the news of Isabel's birth. He is most pleased to celebrate Alaric's wedding and the sealing of our alliance as well as to bestow the legacy of Neamh Álainn on our daughter."

Keeley froze but continued the task of collecting Mairin's soiled linens.

"I can't still be abed when the king arrives," Mairin wailed.

"You'll not overtax yourself," Ewan said sternly.

"I'll not miss Alaric's wedding. I don't care if you

must carry me belowstairs. 'Tis ridiculous that I've been stuck in this bed for so many days."

"You should have no difficulty going belowstairs for a short time, provided you rest in the meantime," Keeley interjected.

Ewan shot Mairin a smug look. Mairin turned to glare at Keeley. "Traitor," she whispered.

A knock sounded at the chamber door and Ewan rose with a frown. When he opened it, Rionna McDonald stood in the hallway. Keeley stiffened and looked away, though it was stupid. It wasn't as if Rionna couldn't see her.

"Your pardon, Laird McCabe," Rionna said formally. "I'd hoped to see Lady McCabe and her babe, if they are up to having visitors."

Mairin shot Ewan a helpless look and then glanced sideways at Keeley in apology.

"I'm quite finished with my duties," Keeley said loudly. "I'll be in to check on you later, my lady." She bowed to Laird McCabe and hurried past Rionna.

Rionna reached out to touch Keeley's arm. "Please, Keeley. I would speak to you later."

Keeley smiled brightly. "'Tis no need. There is nothing to discuss. I hear the king arrives in two days' time. Congratulations on your marriage. I'm sure you must be breathless with excitement."

She turned and hurried down the hall, Rionna's troubled gaze following her the entire way.

Alaric swung his sword in a wide arc and sent his opponent's shield flying through the air. 'Twas the fourth man he'd dispatched in as many minutes, and he whirled, looking for his next adversary.

His men stood at a wary distance, none stepping up to challenge.

Then Caelen stepped in front of him, flipping his sword in a casual manner that was blatantly mocking—and challenging.

"You're spoiling for a fight, brother. 'Tis the truth so I'm more than willing to oblige you."

Alaric scowled. "I'm in no mood for your baiting."

Caelen lifted an eyebrow. "Baiting? We both want the same thing. Quit wasting time and raise your sword."

Without pausing to wonder why Caelen was spoiling for a fight, Alaric lunged and swung his sword. Caelen easily danced out of the way and thrust his sword down to parry Alaric's thrust.

The clang of metal rang out over the courtyard and in a matter of moments an excited murmur rose. Both McCabe and McDonald men surged forward to form a circle around the two brothers.

At first Alaric took it easy, pacing himself and measuring his blows, but it quickly became obvious that Caelen had no patience for a simple sparring.

Rage glittered in his brother's eyes and his jaw was set in a line so tight that it bulged with every thrust of his sword.

With a savage sound of satisfaction, Alaric threw himself into the battle. All the frustration that had mounted over the last weeks came boiling out, and he took it out on his younger brother.

He needn't have worried. Whatever had Caelen so furious, it was fueling his strength, and the two men were snarling gladiators.

Their battle quickly became a matter of wagering, as sides were decided upon and shouts of encouragement rose above the clash of metal and the loud grunts of the two opponents.

A short distance away, Ewan watched the battle in silence. He made no effort to intervene. He wasn't a stupid man. His two brothers had blood in their eyes. He had every faith that they wouldn't actually kill each other. How badly they injured themselves was another matter entirely. But he wasn't about to step into the fray and risk a severed limb or broken bone.

He wasn't entirely certain what was driving Caelen's rage. But he'd find out.

The hour was late and most of the keep was solidly abed by now, and yet Keeley lay in her bed wide awake as the events of the day caught up to her. It had been an exhausting time and she wasn't sure how much longer she could hold up under the strain without cracking.

She'd heard of no controversy involving Laird McDonald, so she could only surmise that Caelen had kept his word and told no one of the laird's attack on her.

Her fingers curled into a fist and she had to make herself relax and filter the rage from her blood. She would have liked to have killed the bastard. Her only satisfaction was that he hadn't got the best of her and she hadn't been so paralyzed with fear that she hadn't been able to defend herself.

She would have leaped from the window before allowing Laird McDonald to violate her.

What she really wanted was to march down the hall to where the bastard had stayed sequestered in his chamber all day and hit him again.

A soft knock at Keeley's door had her sitting straight up in bed. She reached for a wrap and hastened to answer, worried that something had gone wrong with Mairin or the babe.

When she opened the door, she was stunned to see Rionna standing in the doorway, her expression indecipherable.

"Rionna?"

"Keeley," Rionna greeted softly. "Can I come in?"

Keeley gripped the door until her knuckles were white. She didn't want to have this conversation with Rionna. She didn't want to talk to the woman at all. 'Twas enough that she knew she would wed with Alaric in a little more than a day's time.

But she couldn't avoid the inevitable forever. 'Twas better to have the conversation in privacy where they wouldn't chance being overheard.

She relaxed her grasp on the door and opened it wider. "Aye, come in."

Rionna walked in and Keeley shut the door behind her. Keeley walked across the floor to sit on the edge of her bed. She wouldn't give Rionna the advantage and allow her to know how unsettled she was by her visit.

Rionna rubbed her hands down the men's trews she wore and flexed her fingers in a nervous gesture. "There is much I would say to you, Keeley. Beginning with the fact that I am overjoyed that you are alive and well. I feared so much that something terrible had happened to you."

Bitterness welled up and before Keeley could call back the words, she blurted out, "'Tis an odd thing to say given how I was turned from my home and left to survive on my own."

Rionna shook her head, pain glittering in her golden eyes. "Nay. Not on your own."

Keeley pushed herself from the bed and stood with trembling legs. "You did not even send for me after your mother passed, and you knew the truth, Rionna. You *knew*."

Rionna bowed her head. "Aye, I knew. I've always known. 'Tis a terrible thing for a lass to know about her father. Why do you think I always preferred to play outside the keep, away from my father? I saw the way he looked at you, Keeley. I knew and I despised him for it."

Keeley's mouth gaped open. She couldn't even form a response, so shocked was she by Rionna's words.

Rionna reached out and touched Keeley's arm. "Please, sit down and listen to what I have to say."

Keeley hesitated.

"Please," Rionna whispered.

Keeley slumped down on the bed and Rionna took the place next to her, though she kept a distance between them.

Rionna twisted her fingers nervously in front of her and focused her stare on the opposite wall.

"I was devastated when my mother labeled you a whore and turned you out of the keep. I *knew* what had happened and I was furious with her for blaming you. She was a prideful woman, and she would have died if anyone had known the truth. 'Twas no excuse. I was angry with her until the day she died for not protecting you as she would me. I always wondered . . ."

Rionna took a deep breath and closed her eyes. "I've always wondered what she would have done if it *had* been me. Would she have cried me whore? Would she have pretended it didn't happen? Would she have turned against her own daughter to save her pride?"

Keeley swallowed against the huge knot in her throat. There was so much pain and shame in Rionna's voice. She ached to reach out and enfold her in her arms.

"She pretended as though you didn't exist," Rionna said painfully. "I used to lie awake at night worried about how you fared and how you would survive."

"And yet you did or said nothing after your mother died," Keeley said bitterly.

Rionna sighed, her face creased with unhappiness. "The people who came to you for aid, the ones who always gave you coin or venison from the hunt, those were sent by me. 'Twas the only way I could be sure you were cared for and that you had what you needed."

Keeley called back the mounting grief and clenched her hands tight so she didn't break down. "What I needed was your love and support, the support of my clan. Have you any idea how it felt to be cast out and to know that I could never return, and that to the people who'd raised and loved me since birth I was now dead?"

Rionna reached over and gingerly took her hand, as if she were afraid that Keeley would jerk it away.

"I couldn't let you come back, Keeley."

Keeley's head jerked up and she stared in confusion at her cousin. "*Why?*"

Shame crowded Rionna's eyes and she looked away, tears brimming in the golden orbs.

"He was obsessed with you, Keeley. He would have never left you alone. The only way I could protect you was to make sure you stayed away from my father. You would have never been safe with him near."

Keeley's heart lurched. The truth of Rionna's words hit her with the force of a fist. She's seen the lust in Laird McDonald's eyes. She'd felt his desperation. 'Twas as if the last years hadn't existed and he'd waited this long to have his chance at her.

"Oh, Rionna," Keeley whispered.

" 'Tis part of the reason I agreed to the marriage with Alaric McCabe," Rionna continued. "If my father were no longer laird, I could have welcomed you back in your home. The McCabes are honorable. Alaric would have never allowed my father to harm you. We could be sisters again."

Keeley's eyes stung. Her throat throbbed with unshed tears and her heart ached for the lost innocence of two young girls.

"I've never forgotten you, Keeley. Not a day has gone by that I haven't worried for you. I've always loved you as a sister, and I know you have reason to be angry. I wouldn't blame you if you never forgave me, but I did the only thing I could do to keep you safe."

Keeley leaned forward and pulled Rionna into a hug. They gripped each other for several minutes, both of them sniffling as they battled their tears. Keeley didn't even know what to say. She'd harbored her hurt for so long but now she understood that Rionna had suffered just as much.

"I was so worried when I was told you were gone from your cottage," Rionna said as she pulled away. "How did you come to be with the McCabes?"

Guilt crowded uncomfortably into Keeley's mind. How could she tell Rionna of all that had transpired and of her affair with Alaric? How could she hurt her with the knowledge that her future husband loved another? She felt no guilt for the lie she quickly crafted.

"Laird McCabe had need of a healer, with his wife so close to her time. 'Twas a chance meeting, but he offered me a home and sanctuary and 'twas an opportunity I could not pass up."

Anxiety darkened Rionna's gaze as she stared back at Keeley. "Are you happy here? Are you treated well?"

Keeley smiled and took Rionna's hand in hers again. "Aye. I am. The McCabes are my family."

"I'm glad you'll be here for my marriage to Alaric," Rionna said. "There's no one I'd rather have near than you."

It took everything in Keeley's power not to react to Rionna's innocent statement.

Impulsively, Rionna tugged Keeley into her arms again and squeezed her in a hug. "I don't want to lose you again, Keeley. Promise me you'll come to visit and that you'll attend me at the birth of my first child. I don't want years to go by between us again."

Keeley closed her eyes and hugged Rionna fiercely in return. "Aye," she croaked out. "I promise."

CHAPTER 34

Keeley watched from her window as Alaric walked with Rionna along the shore of the loch. It wasn't the most private courtship. McCabes and McDonalds alike were posted as guards as the couple spent time together.

While certainly not warm, the unseasonable temperatures made it comfortable to be outdoors, and in fact, the courtyard was alive with wedding preparations.

With the king's arrival, word had flown through the highlands, and neighboring clans were arriving to set up camp outside the McCabe walls.

Gertie and the women of the keep ran themselves ragged trying to prepare enough food for the influx of visitors.

It seemed the whole of the highlands buzzed with anticipation. War was imminent, and each clan wanted to make sure they allied themselves with the winning side.

The king would openly declare his approval on the marriage between Rionna and Alaric and would also demand allegiance from the neighboring clans. With the bestowal of Neamh Álainn upon Ewan's daughter, the McCabes would control the largest holding in Scotland apart from the king himself.

It would be a day remembered for years to come.

Her gaze drifted over to Alaric, who stood listening

attentively to Rionna, though 'twas the truth it looked more like Rionna was lecturing him.

She'd known that Alaric was destined for greatness. As laird of the McDonalds, he would take his place alongside Ewan in the defense of the throne—and of their own clans.

At that moment Alaric looked up and the breeze caught his braid. Her fingers itched to thread their way through the thick pelt of his hair. Their gazes met and grief spasmed over his face.

Keeley withdrew, not wanting any witnesses to the exchange. She would do nothing to shame Rionna, no matter that her heart was breaking into a million pieces.

A knock at her door interrupted the maudlin direction of her thoughts and she went eagerly to answer it, grateful for the distraction.

To her surprise, Caelen loomed in her doorway. She stared up at him, unable to think of anything to say.

Caelen didn't look any more comfortable with the situation. He cleared his throat and scowled. "I thought you might like . . . that is, I thought you might not want to go down for the evening meal without an escort."

She lifted her eyebrow. "Are you offering?"

He frowned deeper. "Aye. I know 'tis overwhelming and the talk will be of Alaric's marriage on the morrow. But I don't think you should spend the eve alone in your chamber."

Her expression softened and she smiled up at him.

"For God's sake, just don't cry," he grumbled.

She smothered her laughter. "I'd be happy for your escort."

He held out his arm and stared pointedly at her.

The evening meal was noisy and boisterous, and it lasted long into the night. The high table was filled with lairds of surrounding clans, all jockeying for favor with the king.

Rionna looked bored and restless as she sat between Alaric and her father. Mairin looked as though she'd tip over at any moment, until Ewan put his arm around her and pulled her into his side, obviously uncaring of proprieties.

Caelen sat next to Keeley and quietly observed the hubbub around him. Though not talkative, he did lean in on more than one occasion and ask Keeley how she was faring.

His concern touched her. Beneath Caelen's surly disposition lay a man steeped in honor and loyalty. She knew not what had made him such a wary and cautious man with his affections, but 'twas equally evident that once earned, his devotion did not waver.

"I worry that this evening has been too much for Mairin," Keeley whispered to Caelen. "She'll not admit she's overtired because she wants to remain by her husband's side, especially with the king here."

Caelen glanced in Mairin's direction and frowned. "Ewan should have ordered her to bed an hour ago."

"Perhaps I can intervene and say the babe has need of her."

"I'll go up with the both of you so Ewan does not have to leave the gathering," Caelen said firmly.

Keeley smiled. " 'Tis glad I am of your escort."

"He'll not have the chance to be alone with you again," Caelen vowed as he stared pointedly at Laird McDonald.

Keeley rose without glancing in Laird McDonald's direction, though she did find Rionna and offered a small smile. Her gaze flickered over Alaric but she looked quickly away, afraid that her face would betray her.

Caelen led her to the head of the table and Keeley offered a curtsy to the king before turning her attention to Laird McCabe.

"I would take Lady McCabe above stairs if you give your leave. I'm concerned that she overtaxes herself so soon after the birth of your daughter."

The words were said for the benefit of the others seated close to Ewan and Mairin. Ewan shot her a grateful look and then rose to assist his wife to her feet.

Even Mairin looked thankful as she stepped to take Caelen's proffered arm.

Keeley was about to turn away when the king held up his hand. Keeley froze, uncertain as to what to do. Had she offered insult by interrupting?

"Ewan tells me you are the healer who attended my niece during her pregnancy and at her birthing time."

"Aye, Your Majesty."

The words stuttered out so shaky, she was unsure that they were intelligible.

"He tells me you have great skill and that you also saved the life of Alaric McCabe."

Keeley nodded, her discomfort growing as more people stopped eating to listen to the king's words.

"The McCabes are fortunate to have you. If Ewan was not such a valued ally, I would take you to tend me personally."

Her eyes widened and she gulped. "T-Thank you, Your Majesty. 'Tis a great honor to have you say so."

He lifted his hand in dismissal. "Go now. My niece has need of her rest. I charge you with her health and that of her newborn babe."

Keeley curtsied again, grateful she didn't trip and disgrace herself. Then she hurried after Caelen and Mairin as they headed toward the stairs.

"How are you faring?" Mairin asked Keeley when they were alone in Mairin's chamber.

Keeley's eyes widened. "'Tis you I'm concerned about. You looked fair to exhausted at dinner."

Mairin grimaced. "Aye, I was, and 'tis grateful I am for your rescue."

Mairin sat and Keeley took the babe from the woman charged with her care and handed her to Mairin. Mairin dismissed the nurse and then turned her attention back to Keeley.

"Are you all right? I know this can't be easy for you."

Keeley forced a smile to her face. "I'm fine. Truly. I had a chance to speak with Rionna. She has suffered as much as I have over the years. She is the sister of my heart. I have no wish for her to suffer more pain."

"And so you'll suffer instead," Mairin said in a low voice.

Keeley sighed. "I want her to be happy. I want Alaric to be happy. I believe she can make him so. She's a good woman. She'll be loyal and true to Alaric. She'll give him strong sons and daughters. She is a worthy mate to a laird."

"So are you, Keeley," Mairin said quietly.

Keeley smiled crookedly. "Maybe one day I'll find a laird of my own." But even as she spoke, she knew that no one would ever take the place of Alaric in her heart.

"Stay with me," Mairin invited. "Ewan will be late this night. It will surprise me if he finds his room before dawn."

Keeley agreed, because the thought of enduring her chamber alone was more than she could bear. Somehow the company of good friends alleviated some of the pain in her heart and she found it didn't hurt so much to smile.

A soft knock at her chamber door awakened Keeley. She rubbed her eyes and blinked in confusion. 'Twas not even dawn yet. She'd barely gotten to sleep after staying with Mairin through most of the night.

Hoping nothing was amiss, she rolled from the bed and went to crack her door.

When she saw Caelen there, she swung the door wider. "Caelen? Is something amiss?"

He held a finger to his lips. Then he leaned forward. "Alaric sent me to you. He'd like to see you. He didn't want to chance coming to your bedchamber."

Keeley swallowed. "Where?"

"Dress warmly. He's down by the loch where Crispen skips his stones."

"Give me a moment. I'll be ready."

She hurriedly dressed and went back out to where Caelen awaited her. Halfway down the stairs she stopped and frowned.

"You realize that if anyone were to see us, they'd assume that you and I—that we—were . . ."

"Aye," Caelen said quietly. "I know it."

Keeley bit her lips and resumed the trek down the stairs. Caelen hovered protectively as they exited the keep and walked toward the loch in darkness. They entered the small grove of trees and came out by the shore of the loch where several boulders jutted outward from the banks.

"Thank you, Caelen," Alaric said as he stepped forward.

"I'll wait for Keeley through the trees," Caelen said as he retreated.

Keeley turned nervously to Alaric. It felt as though it had been forever since they'd seen each other. Since they'd touched or kissed.

Alaric reached for her hands and grasped them gently in his. "I had to see you this night. One more time before I say my vows tomorrow. Once spoken, I'll never break them. I'd not betray my wife or my clan."

Tears shimmered in Keeley's eyes as she gazed upon the man she loved more than life. "Aye, I know it."

He raised her hands to his lips and pressed them to his trembling mouth. "I want you to know that I love you, Keeley McCabe. I'll always love you. I want you to find happiness. I want you to find a man who'll love you as I have loved you and who'll give you the family you deserve."

Tears ran unchecked down her cheeks. "I want you to be happy, too, Alaric. Rionna is a good woman. She'll make you a good wife. Try to love her. She deserves to be loved."

Alaric pulled her into his arms and held her tightly, his head rested atop hers. "I'll do anything you ask of me, Keeley."

"Then be happy," she whispered. "Remember me with fondness. I'll never forget our time together. I'll hold it to my heart always. You are a wonderful man and proud warrior. The McDonald clan will be all the more great with you as laird."

Alaric slowly pulled away, and she knew that the time had come to let him go. Her chest hurt so badly that each breath was agony. She steeled herself, determined that she'd be brave and would bear the parting with dignity and grace. Alaric deserved that much. The last thing he needed was a hysterical ex-lover on the eve of his wedding to another.

She reached up to touch his face and traced the lines of his strong jaw and the angles of his cheekbone.

"Live long and be happy, my love."

He caught her hand and pressed a kiss to her palm. When she pulled her hand back, it came away damp with his tears. 'Twas more than she could bear, the thought of her warrior grieving for what was not to be.

She turned and walked briskly toward the woods. "Caelen," she called softly.

"I'm here," he said as he stepped from the shadows.

"Please take me back," she said in as level a voice as she could manage.

Caelen took her arm and guided her toward the keep. With each step, the pain became so unbearable that she thought she might die.

They returned to the keep in silence. Caelen escorted her to her chamber and opened the door. For a long moment she stood, so numb she wasn't sure if she could even manage the short distance to her bed.

"Are you all right?" Caelen asked gently.

When she didn't answer, he led her into the chamber and closed the door behind them. Then he pulled her into his arms and hugged her tightly.

"There, there, lass. Cry if you'd like. No one will hear you but me."

She buried her face in his tunic as the tears began to fall.

CHAPTER 35

"Keeley, you must hurry! The priest is going to wed me and Cormac in the hall before he weds Alaric and Rionna in the courtyard at the noon hour," Christina said.

Keeley rubbed some of the weariness from her eyes and hoped that they didn't look red and swollen. She'd gotten no sleep after her meeting with Alaric, and 'twas the truth she had no desire to leave her chamber.

But she didn't want to dampen Christina's happiness. The girl was so excited for her wedding to Cormac that she was about to bounce right out of the beautifully sewn dress that Maddie and Bertha had gifted her.

She looked over at Christina and smiled. "You look beautiful, lass."

And she did. Her face was a wreath of happiness and her cheeks glowed. She hadn't stopped smiling the entire morning.

"Thank you," Christina said. "Now hurry! I don't want to keep Cormac waiting."

Christina reached for Keeley's hand and all but dragged her toward the stairs. Keeley had dressed with care and had even arranged her hair in a coiled braid for the occasion. She wanted no one to suspect that she was dying on the inside.

Indeed, Cormac was waiting for Christina, and the relief that crossed his face when she entered the room made Keeley smile. Ewan stood as witness for Cormac, and Christina pulled Keeley along.

"Mairin is resting before Alaric and Rionna's wedding so I wanted you to stand for me," Christina whispered.

Keeley squeezed the girl's hand. "Of course I will."

Christina shyly approached Cormac and his face lit up as he took her hand. They turned to the priest to exchange their vows. Keeley listened to the sacred words that bound them together as husband and wife. Their love for each other was evident as they stared into each other's eyes. No one else existed for the couple.

When finally Cormac leaned over to kiss Christina, the room erupted in cheers. Color bloomed in Christina's cheeks as they turned to face the gathered onlookers.

Keeley hesitated a moment to allow Christina and Cormac to step into the group of people waiting to congratulate them and then she skirted the perimeter, intent on escaping back to her chamber.

"Keeley, a word please," Ewan said as she passed.

He motioned her into the alcove behind the hall.

She looked questioningly at him and waited for the purpose of his command.

"Caelen told me of what occurred between you and Laird McDonald."

Keeley froze. "He shouldn't have."

"Aye, he should have. I'm sorry that it happened. I'm appalled that someone under my care was treated thusly. The laird will never be welcome into my keep again."

Keeley nodded. "Thank you."

"I also want to thank you for not going to Alaric," he said in a sober voice. "I know he cares deeply for you. This marriage is important. Caelen says you begged him not to tell Alaric because you knew it could possibly ruin the alliance between our clans."

Keeley swallowed and nodded.

"You have courage, lass. Perhaps the most courage I've ever witnessed in a lass so young. You have become dear to my wife—nay, to the entire clan. If there is anything I can do to ensure your happiness here, you have only to name it."

"I am grateful to call the McCabes my clan," she said. "I am proud."

Ewan smiled. "Go now. I'll not keep you further."

Keeley curtsied and hurriedly left the alcove and headed in the direction of the courtyard. She dodged through the throng of people and made her way to the hillside that overlooked the place where Alaric and Rionna would be wed.

Pulling her shawl tighter around her to ward off the chill, she settled down on the brown patch of grass that had been covered by snow for so long.

The brisk wind soothed her and numbed some of the pain that still clawed through her chest. The sun shone high overhead and warmed her face and shoulders. 'Twas a perfect day for a wedding. The near springlike conditions could only be a sign that this day was sanctioned by God himself.

The entire keep hummed with an air of expectancy. Banners from a dozen different clans flew high and rippled in the breeze outside the outer skirt. Smaller celebrations among the clans filtered through the air and she could hear musicians play lively tunes.

Today all eyes would be on Alaric and Rionna. Keeley smiled in fond remembrance of when she and Rionna were just girls, dreaming about their prince charming and one day when their wedding celebration would be held. Rionna deserved to have her dream come true, and Alaric would make her the best of husbands.

So immersed in her thoughts was she that she hadn't realized that everyone had started to gather in the courtyard. 'Twas not a large distance away and she could see every aspect of the ceremony.

She caught her breath when Alaric strode out, dressed in his wedding finery. He wore a velvet blue tunic and emblazoned on the hem was the McCabe crest. His hair fell below his shoulders and the ends lifted in the breeze, lending him a deliciously unkempt look.

He took position by the priest and waited for Rionna to make her appearance. A few moments later, Rionna arrived in the courtyard. Keeley felt a surge of pride at her friend's beauty. She shone like a million suns. Her golden hair looked afire in the sparkle of the sunlight.

Her dress was elaborately and intricately sewn and took the efforts of two women on either side to bear the hem in the back. She looked regal. She looked every bit a queen.

When Rionna was but a few steps away from Alaric, he looked in Keeley's direction. He stared for a long moment, and she knew he saw her on the hillside. Slowly she brought her fingers to her lips and then curled them into a fist and touched it to her heart.

Alaric raised his hand in a subtle gesture and splayed his fingers over his heart before returning his gaze to the approaching Rionna.

As he took Rionna's hand and they turned to face the priest, Keeley's heart seized. This was it. In a few moments' time, Alaric would marry another and be forever lost to her.

Twelve drums lined on either side of Alaric and Rionna began beating, a tribute to the marriage about to take place. The sound filled the air and echoed across the countryside.

Movement caught Keeley's eye and she frowned, leaning forward to focus on the figure laying atop the stone skirt behind the gathered crowd.

What was he about? What could he be doing?

The sun caught something in his hand and reflected, a quick shimmer, but it was enough for Keeley to see the crossbow cradled in his arms.

She surged to her feet and yelled loudly. But the drums continued to beat, faster and louder. She screamed but it was lost in the wind and then she began to run, sure she would never be in time. She wasn't even sure of the target. The king was present. Ewan was there as was Mairin.

All she knew was she had to issue a warning to all before it was too late.

The drums echoed fiercely in Alaric's ears. With each beat, the dread in his heart increased until it was all he could do to breathe.

He glanced down at his and Rionna's joined hands and then up at the beauty of his bride. Aye, she was beautiful. She would make a good wife. She would give him fine sons and daughters. She would be a credit to his leadership of her clan.

Then he looked to his brother, who stood with Mairin on one side and their king on the other. His brother who had sacrificed much over the years to ensure the survival of their clan. How could he not do the same?

He closed his eyes. Oh, God, he couldn't do this. He couldn't go through with it.

The drums stopped abruptly and the silence was so keen in the moment following that it was startling. Then he heard a scream. His name.

Rionna jerked around right as he did the same. Just in time to catch Keeley in his arms. Her eyes were wide with shock—and pain. Her mouth opened and then shut and she gasped, her face going white.

For a moment he didn't know what had occurred, but he heard the horrified screams behind Keeley. He heard the unmistakable sound of swords being drawn and then a shout went up.

Yet all he could see was Keeley's pain-stricken face as he held her in his arms, and then as she sagged, he saw the arrow protruding from her back, and he knew. The knowledge of what she had done struck him so hard that he staggered and his knees buckled. He sank to the ground holding her against his chest.

"Keeley, nay! *Nay!* Why did you do it? Oh, God, Keeley, nay. Nay. Nay."

It came out as a sob. He didn't care. He had no pride. No shame. Her face was ashen and she had the look of death in her eyes, the knowledge he'd seen in any number of other warriors' faces as they were struck down in the heat of battle.

Rionna dropped beside him, her face nearly as gray as Keeley's. "Keeley?" she whispered, her voice shaken and full of the same fear that gripped Alaric with unrelenting force.

Around them the world went mad. There were shouts and call to arms. Ewan ushered the king and Mairin to safety. Caelen and Gannon took position in front of Alaric, their swords drawn, ready to strike down any threat.

"Keeley, don't leave me, my love," Alaric whispered. "Hold on. I'll take care of you. Just as you did me."

She smiled shakily, her face creased with pain. " 'Twas worth it. You were destined to be great. I could not . . ." She broke off as another spasm of agony shook her body. "I could not allow you to die this day."

Alaric smoothed the hair from her cheek and held her gently to him as he rocked back and forth. He stared into her eyes, at the shadows that grew with each stuttered breath.

He cupped her face and forced her to look at him. Then he reached down and twined her fingers with his until their hands were tightly clasped.

"I, Alaric McCabe, wed you, Keeley McDonald McCabe. I take you as my wife until our last breaths are taken, until our souls are reunited in the hereafter."

Faint shock shone in her eyes and her mouth opened wordlessly.

"Say the words, Keeley. Give back to me what I was unwilling to give you before. Marry me here and now with all to bear witness. I love you."

A single tear trailed down her cheek. She closed her eyes as if to gather her strength and then she opened them and renewed determination shone in their depths.

"I, Keeley McDonald, now McCabe, wed you, Alaric McCabe. I take you as my husband forever and always until I've taken my last breath."

Her voice grew weaker with each exhale, but the words were spoken. They were handfasted before hundreds of witnesses. She was his wife. She belonged to him for as long as God saw fit to bestow such a precious gift.

He leaned down and kissed her forehead, choking as the cries of anguish threatened to pulse from his throat.

"I love you," he whispered. "Don't leave me, Keeley. Not now when I've summoned the courage to do what is right."

"Alaric."

Rionna's soft voice intruded on his grief.

He glanced up at the woman he'd nearly wed and saw no shock or horror. No judgment or resentment. He saw answering grief as tears trailed endlessly down her cheeks.

"We must take her inside. We must help her."

Alaric gathered her tighter in his arms and then stood.

The arrow protruded from her back, a stark reminder of what she'd sacrificed for him.

"Alaric, this way," Ewan barked at him. "Take her inside so that I may see to her wound."

The world tilted around him. It moved slowly as if suspended in time. Caelen and Gannon urged him forward, their swords providing a protective barrier to him and anyone who would venture near.

The roaring in his ears prevented him from hearing the voices around him. He staggered toward the keep as Keeley's blood dripped onto the ground below him.

He closed his eyes. *Don't take her from me, God. Not now. Don't let it to be too late to do what is right. Give me the chance to make amends.*

CHAPTER 36

Keeley's chamber was full of people when Alaric carried her inside. Ewan stood by the bed, his expression grim. Mairin and Maddie were at the foot of the bed, their eyes red from crying. Cormac stood to the side, comforting Christina, and Gannon and Caelen stood guard at the door, fury glinting in their eyes.

Alaric eased her down onto the bed, careful to put her on her side so the arrow would not be pushed farther into her body. He looked up at his brother, his chest tight with grief and dread.

"Can you help her? Can you fix this, Ewan?"

Ewan knelt beside the bed so that he was eye level with the shaft of the arrow. "I will try, Alaric, but you must know, this isn't good. The arrow is embedded deeply in her body. It might have struck something vital."

Alaric closed his eyes and sought to control the rage that threatened to overtake his senses. She needed him calm. She didn't need a raving lunatic, even though he wanted to scream and rage at the fates.

"I'll need to cut the arrowhead from her," Ewan said grimly. "'Tis the only way."

A commotion at the door yanked Alaric's head up.

Rionna, rid of her wedding finery, was held back by Caelen and she was none too happy.

"Let me by," she demanded. "She is my friend. I would help."

"Let her by," Alaric said hoarsely. He glanced at Rionna as she hurried to Keeley's bedside. "Can you help her? Do you have any skill at healing?"

"Not much, but I have a steady hand and a strong constitution. I'll not faint at the sight of blood and I'm determined that she'll not die."

"Let her stay. She can aid me," Ewan said. Then he looked in Caelen's direction. "Take him from here. 'Tis not something he should be present for."

For a moment Alaric didn't realize that his brother spoke of him. It wasn't until Gannon and Caelen reached for his arms that he understood they meant to remove him from the chamber.

He stumbled back and drew his sword, pointing it at his younger brother. "I'll kill the man who tries to take me from her. I'll not leave her."

"Alaric, be sensible," Ewan commanded. "Leave this place. You're only a hindrance."

"I'll not leave," Alaric snarled.

"Alaric, please," Mairin said as she rushed forward. She dodged around his sword and pressed a gentle hand to his chest. "Come with me. I know you love her. She knows you love her. Let Ewan try to save her. You do her no good standing over her bedside like a savage. It won't be pleasant to see and hear her when Ewan cuts the arrow from her back. Don't torture yourself needlessly."

Alaric stared down at his sister-in-law and saw the tears in her eyes, the grief shadowing her face. "I can't leave her," he whispered. "I'll not have her die alone."

"Damn it, Alaric. Get the hell out of here," Ewan

barked. "If things go badly, I'll summon you at once. If we are to have a chance to save her, we must act quickly."

Mairin reached and took his hand in hers then squeezed. "Come, Alaric. Leave them to their business."

Alaric closed his eyes, his shoulders slumping. He turned to where Keeley lay on the bed and then he went down on one knee. He touched her shoulder and gently caressed the soft skin before leaning over to kiss her ashen brow.

"I love you, Keeley. Be strong. Live. For me."

Caelen and Gannon pulled Alaric and this time he allowed them to push him from the room. He stumbled outside of the chamber, his heart hammering like a drum.

The door closed, bathing the hallway in darkness. He turned and pounded his fist into the stone wall. "Nay! God damn it, nay!"

Caelen wrapped his arms around Alaric and hauled him the rest of the way down the hallway to his own chamber. He kicked in the door and thrust Alaric inside.

Caelen's eyes glittered with anger as he shoved Alaric onto his bed. "You do her no good like this."

Alaric stared down at his swollen hand and at the blood seeping from the broken skin. He wanted to smash something else. He wanted the bastard who'd dared do this to Keeley.

He glanced up at Caelen as coldness crept over him.

"Did you apprehend the one who did this?"

"Aye," Gannon said from the doorway. "He is chained in the dungeon."

"Did he act alone?" Alaric demanded.

"We know not yet. We await the laird to question him."

Alaric sucked in air through his nostrils. "He is mine to kill."

Caelen sank onto the bed next to his brother. "Aye,

when we've extracted the necessary information from him, he is yours to kill. No one would deny you that right."

"She saved me again," Alaric said bleakly. "The arrow was meant for me. She stepped in front of it and gave her life for mine."

"She is a fierce lass. She loves you."

That Caelen spoke of love without derision in his voice was surprising. But there was only grudging admiration and truth in his tone.

Alaric buried his head in his hands. "I've made such a mess of things."

"Don't torture yourself, Alaric. You were in an impossible situation. You and Keeley handled it as best you could. Much was riding on your marriage to Rionna."

"I'm married to Keeley," Alaric said quietly.

"Aye, I heard it. I bore witness to the handfast."

"It brings me no comfort when she lies dying down the hall."

Caelen glanced at Gannon and then back to Alaric. "You sell the lass short, Alaric. She's tough. She's not a quitter. I confess I've never met another woman of her ilk. She's earned my respect and my allegiance."

Alaric pushed himself to his feet. "I cannot sit here not knowing what happens a few doors down. If she is brave enough to step in front of an arrow for me, the least I can do is stand at her side while she endures the worst. I know Ewan means well, but she needs me and I won't let her down."

Caelen sighed. "If 'twas my woman in her position, I'd not let anyone make me leave her side either."

Gannon nodded in agreement.

Alaric walked to the door but then paused and turned to face his brother. "I haven't thanked you for standing by Keeley during the last days. It's been hard for her, I know. It should have been me. It *will* be me from now on."

Caelen smiled. " 'Tis no hardship. 'Tis the truth the lass amuses me."

The corners of Alaric's mouth lifted in a half smile and then he left the chamber and strode down the hall. He paused at Keeley's door, afraid to open the door. There was no sound within. No cry of pain. Nothing to signal that she breathed still.

With a whispered prayer, he eased the door open and stepped within.

Ewan was bent over the bed, his face creased in concentration. Rionna was at Keeley's head, stroking her hair and murmuring soothing words.

Ewan cast a quick glance in Alaric's direction but didn't deviate from his task. When Alaric stepped closer, he could see that Ewan had cut around the shaft of the arrow to open the flesh enough for the arrowhead to be pulled free.

The cloths surrounding the arrow were soaked in her blood and it had seeped onto the bed.

"Let me hold her so you can concentrate more fully on the arrow," Alaric said. He barely recognized his own voice.

"You must hold her still. She mustn't move," Ewan said.

Alaric nodded and then carefully crawled onto the bed. Keeley faced away from Ewan and was scooted to the edge so that Ewan had access to her back. Ewan waited until Alaric lined his body alongside Keeley's and then carefully secured his arm over her hip. He slipped his arm underneath her head and carefully pulled her from Rionna's lap.

"You can help wipe the blood so I can see what I'm doing," Ewan said to Rionna.

Keeley's breaths were a mere whisper against Alaric's

neck. When Ewan returned the blade to her skin, she went rigid against Alaric and a whimper escaped her lips.

"Shh, love," Alaric murmured. "I'm with you. I have you. I know it hurts. Be brave for me. Fight as you told me to fight."

Ewan worked diligently through the next hours. He was afraid of the loss of blood, so he worked slowly and carefully extracted the arrowhead. When he finally worked the metal blade free, he swore when she started to bleed profusely.

Keeley had long since lost consciousness and didn't even rouse when Ewan pulled the arrow free of her flesh. Her blood seeped onto the floor while Ewan and Rionna both applied pressure to the wound.

Alaric ignored the resigned expression on his brother's face and focused only on Keeley's. He willed her to breathe. He willed her to live.

It took another two hours for Ewan to stitch the wound. 'Twas a difficult task because they couldn't staunch the bleeding. Ewan worked fast to close the wound and when he set the last stitch, he sat back on the floor, his face weary with exhaustion.

"Keep pressure to it," he directed Rionna. "The bleeding has slowed. 'Tis God's truth I don't know if we've managed to stop it, or if she's given her life's blood already."

With shaking fingers, Alaric felt for the pulse at her neck. It was weak and fluttered like the wings of a butterfly but she lived still.

Rionna stood after setting a bandage to the wound and wiped the back of her arm wearily over her forehead. "I need to clean her, Alaric. The linens need to be stripped. She should have a clean gown and I must wash the dirt from her body."

"I'll do it," Alaric said quietly. "I'll not leave her. 'Tis my duty to tend her. I'll not leave her alone."

The woman he almost married stared back at him, grief raw and aching in her eyes. "I'm sorry, Alaric. I did not know you loved her or that she loved you."

"Go now and rest," Alaric said gently. "I will see to Keeley."

After Rionna left, Ewan went to wash his hands in the basin and stood there for a long moment, his hands braced on the sides.

"I've done all I can, Alaric. 'Tis in God's hands now."

"Aye, I know it."

"I'll leave you. I have much to do."

Alaric nodded. "Thank you for saving her."

Ewan offered a small glimmer of a smile. "Your faith in my abilities is humbling. If the lass lives 'twill be because of her own stubbornness."

As Ewan was departing the chamber, Maddie hurried in. Alaric was grateful for her help. Together they stripped the bedding and Keeley's bloodied clothing. Alaric wiped her down with wet cloths until chill bumps dotted her flesh.

" 'Tis better if you leave her unclothed," Maddie advised. " 'Tis a large wound on her back and we'll need to check it often. Lay her on her side and we'll prop pillows behind her so she doesn't roll to her back."

Alaric did as Maddie suggested and when he was satisfied that she was as comfortable as he could make her, he stretched out beside her and gathered her in his arms.

He closed his eyes and pressed his lips to her soft forehead. "I love you," he whispered.

CHAPTER 37

For three days Alaric never left Keeley's side. She never regained consciousness no matter how much Alaric tried to rouse her. He begged, bullied, coerced. He promised her the moon. All to no avail. He worried that she wasn't taking in any sustenance, and after so much blood loss she surely needed every bit she could get.

And then the fever set in. Her flesh was dry and hot, so very hot. She twisted restlessly in her sleep and demons seemed to plague her without mercy. Alaric held and soothed her. He bathed her and at one point sat in a tub of water, holding her in an attempt to cool the raging fever.

A week after it all began, Alaric was losing hope. She grew weaker by the day and she lay so still, it was as if she'd already passed on but her body had refused to shut down.

On the seventh day, Ewan and Caelen came for him. Alaric's rage was a sight to behold. It took the combined efforts of his brothers as well as Gannon and Cormac to force him from Keeley's chamber.

Rionna and Maddie took Alaric's place as the men ushered Alaric outside the keep.

"Where do you take me?" Alaric snarled as he fought against their hold.

His brothers said naught but carried him to the loch and tossed him in.

The water was a shock. He sunk below the surface, all the air leaving his lungs in a rush of bubbles. How easy it would be to just breathe in and join Keeley. It killed him to think of her alone and afraid in some dark place, dead but not dead.

As the cold settled in, the instinct to live kicked in and he fought his way to the surface. He came above and gasped a deep mouthful of air.

"Glad you decided to stay with us," Ewan snapped from the shore.

Alaric treaded water for a moment and glared at his brothers. "What the hell was that for?"

"You're wasting away for nothing. You haven't left Keeley's chamber in a week. You won't eat. You haven't bathed. You haven't even changed clothing. If the injury doesn't kill her, 'tis likely your smell will," Caelen snarled.

Alaric swam to the shore and trudged out, shaking the water from his long hair. He bared his teeth just a moment before he leveled Caelen with a tackle.

The two men hit the ground with a thump and Caelen grunted as the breath was knocked from his chest. He recovered quickly and rolled, thrusting his arm over Alaric's neck.

Alaric slammed his fist into Caelen's jaw and Caelen reeled back. Before Alaric could jump to his feet, Ewan hit him hard, driving his shoulder into his belly.

"God's teeth, are you all trying to kill me?" Alaric demanded as Ewan pinned him to the ground.

"Just trying to knock some sense into your thick head," Ewan growled. "Are you ready to listen?"

Alaric head-butted Ewan in the nose and then rolled until he was atop his older brother. "You're getting to be an old man," Alaric taunted.

Caelen leaped back onto Alaric and the three men rolled, fists and curses flying. God but it felt good to beat the living hell out of something.

Several long minutes later, the three men lay sprawled on the ground breathing heavily.

"Ah damn," Ewan groaned.

Alaric looked over to see Mairin standing over her husband, her hands on her hips.

"You should be resting," Ewan growled.

"And you should be doing something other than beating each other into pulps!" Mairin snapped. " 'Tis disgraceful!"

"I don't know. It felt pretty damn good," Caelen offered from his position on the ground.

Alaric slowly picked himself up. "Is there any change with Keeley?"

Mairin's expression softened. "Nay, she sleeps still."

Alaric closed his eyes and then turned back toward the loch. Maybe a good swim would clear his head and he could bathe while he was at it. Ewan was right. Rotting next to Keeley did no one any good.

"Ewan, the king and all the lairds grow restless," Mairin said. "They want to know what is to be done."

"I know it well, Mairin." There was reproach in Ewan's voice, as if he had no liking for her bringing up the topic in front of Alaric.

Alaric ignored them both and waded back into the frigid water. He well knew that the king and the lairds waited for Keeley to die so that he could marry Rionna and seal the alliance.

Gannon tossed him a bar of soap and waited on the banks while Alaric completed his bath. Ewan and Caelen returned with Mairin, leaving Cormac behind with Gannon to see to Alaric.

He hadn't gone mad with grief yet. Yet, being the operative word.

When he returned to the keep a half hour later, Rionna greeted him, her eyes red and swollen. His heartbeat tripped and sped up, hammering against his chest. "What is it?" he demanded.

"You must come. She is calling for you. 'Tis bad, Alaric. I fear she'll not last the hour. She is so weak she cannot hold her eyes open, and the fever rages so high that she's delirious."

Alaric took the steps at a run and rushed down the hall, barreling past countless people. When he burst into Keeley's chamber, his heart seized.

She lay still, so still he feared he was too late. But then her lips twisted ever so slightly and she whispered his name.

He rushed to her side and knelt beside the bed. "I'm here, Keeley. I'm here, love."

He stroked his hand over her face, wanting her to feel his touch, wanting to reassure her that she wasn't alone.

She was so fragile, so very precious against his hands, so very breakable. He couldn't accept that she could be taken from him at any moment.

"Alaric?" she whispered again.

"Aye, love, I'm here."

"So cold. Don't hurt anymore. Just cold."

Alarm prickled up his spine.

She turned as if seeking his face. Her eyes opened to mere slits but she didn't focus on him. Her gaze was sightless as if she looked into a dark void.

"I'm afraid."

The admission gutted him. He gathered her in his arms and tears burned his eyelids. That a woman who'd feared nothing was now afraid was more than he could bear.

"I'm with you, Keeley. Do not be afraid. I'll not leave you. I swear it."

"Take me . . ." she broke off, her voice barely above a whisper.

"Take you where, sweeting?"

"To place . . . where we said . . . good-bye. Where you last . . . kissed me."

He buried his face against her neck and wept.

"Please."

Oh, God, he didn't want her to beg. The pleading in her voice completely undid him.

"Aye, Keeley, I'll take you. I'll take you wherever you want to go."

She smiled faintly and her eyes closed, as if the few words she'd spoken had completely spent her.

He gently gathered her in his arms and lifted her. He held her against his chest and pressed his lips to the top of her head. Tears slipped unchecked down his cheeks as he strode down the hall. No one tried to stop him. Mairin and Rionna openly wept as he passed. Maddie wore a stricken look and Gannon bowed his head in grief. At the top of the staircase, Caelen stood, his fingers curled into tight fists at his sides.

Then slowly he put his hand out to touch Keeley's hair and let his fingers slide over her cheek. He leaned down and brushed his lips over her forehead in a tender gesture. It was the first time Alaric had seen him show any open affection or regard for a woman since the woman he'd loved betrayed him so many years ago.

"Be at peace," Caelen whispered.

Then he backed up and strode away, his jaw clenched tight.

The entire clan gathered as Alaric bore Keeley through the courtyard and around to where the loch spread out to the east. He walked through the trees where he'd waited for her just a week earlier. He stopped at the water's edge and lowered himself to sit on one of the boulders.

"We're here, Keeley. Can you feel the breeze on your face? Can you smell the fresh air?"

Her eyelids fluttered weakly and she took in a deep breath. The action caused her immediate pain and a wicked spasm crossed her face. For several long moments she lay in his arms, her chest working up and down with exertion.

"Aye," she said finally. " 'Tis wondrous to feel the sun on my skin. I'm tired, Alaric. I've tried so hard to fight."

He could hear the ache in her voice, the grief over the knowledge that she was dying.

"I want you to know that I'll die happy. All . . . all I ever wanted . . . was to be yours. Your . . . wife. Even if for a while. You are mine and I am yours."

Alaric stared up at the sky, sorrow crushing down on him with the weight of a boulder. "You've always been mine, Keeley. From the moment you took me into your cottage. There's never been another woman who captured me, body and soul, the way you did. There'll never be another. I should have been willing to give you what was rightly yours before now. I tried to do what was right and in the end, none of it matters if I lose you."

"Hold me," she whispered. "Stay here with me and hold me until the time has come for me to go away. I can feel myself growing weaker. I don't think 'tis a long time."

A raw, gut-wrenching sound of agony ripped from Alaric's throat. His chest burned as if he'd swallowed fire. His hands shook so badly that he worried he'd let her fall.

"Aye, I'll hold you, Keeley. I won't let you go alone. We'll stay here together and watch the sun go down over the loch and I'll tell you every dream I ever had of our life together."

She smiled and shivered against him. She went completely limp in his arms as if she'd expended all her remaining strength to say what she needed. For a long moment she lay there until she roused herself, seeming to have one last thing that she needed him to hear.

"You're my dream, Alaric McCabe. And I love you. I've loved you from the moment your horse dumped you at my cottage. I spent so much time being resentful and lamenting the circumstances of my life, but 'tis true that I wouldn't change a single thing because then I would have never known your love."

He cupped her face in his hands and lowered his mouth to hers. Their tears mingled and the salt slipped onto their tongues as Alaric tenderly kissed her lips.

He closed his eyes and rocked her back and forth in his arms. The day faded to dusk and the evening grew colder. Gannon came out with furs and quietly wrapped them around Alaric and Keeley before leaving the two alone again.

The keep was already preparing to mourn. No one expected Keeley to live through the night.

Alaric settled into the furs and made himself as comfortable as possible on the face of the rock where he sat. He began to tell Keeley of all the things he loved most about her. How she made him laugh with her temper and her sharp wit. How she didn't back down from either of his brothers.

He told her of his dreams of their children and how he wanted girls as beautiful and as fierce as she was and boys with her fire and courage.

Night settled in and the stars popped overhead. The moon splashed onto the loch, illuminating the pair as Alaric hung on tightly, willing Keeley not to slip away from him.

She grew quieter. He could literally feel the change in

her as she grew weaker. The pain was too much for him to bear.

He laid his head atop hers and closed his eyes, wanting a brief moment of peace. When next he opened his eyes, the sky had paled with dawn's imminent approach.

Panic stabbed through his chest. How long had he slept? He was afraid to look down. He was afraid to focus in on Keeley. What if she'd died in his arms while he slept? How could he ever forgive himself?

"Keeley?" he whispered as he shifted on the rock.

To his amazement, she moaned and moved fretfully against him. Her forehead gleamed with . . . sweat. With shaking fingers he touched her clammy skin and felt the sticky moisture that signaled the end of her fever.

Oh, God, he couldn't function. He couldn't think. He couldn't process. He should get her back to the keep so that Ewan could look at her, but 'twas God's truth if he tried to stand now, he'd fall flat on his face.

He touched her face, her cheek, her eyelids even. "Keeley, Keeley, lass, wake up and look at me. Say something. Anything."

Her lips parted the barest amount and it was obvious she tried to say something but lacked the strength. Her eyes opened a crack but she couldn't keep them open.

"It doesn't matter," he soothed. "Your fever has broken. Do you hear me? Your fever has broken. 'Tis a good sign, Keeley. You'll not die on me now, do you hear? You've fought this hard and long and I refuse to let you die now that you've given me hope."

She whispered something he couldn't hear. He leaned down and placed his ear next to her lips. "What did you say?"

"Brute," she muttered.

He closed his eyes and laughed helplessly. 'Twas such a wonderful, exquisite feeling that he threw back his head and laughed until tears of relief streamed down his cheeks.

"Alaric, what is it?" Ewan demanded as he ran toward his brother.

Alaric turned to see his brother halt a few steps away, his expression wary and sorrowful. He glanced down at Keeley's still figure and then back up to the tears streaming down Alaric's cheeks.

"I'm sorry, Alaric. I'm so damn sorry."

Alaric grinned broadly. "She lives, Ewan. She lives! Her fever has broken and she just called me a brute. Surely 'tis a sign she has no intention of dying."

A broad smile split Ewan's face. "Aye, 'tis a good sign to be sure. Any lass who can muster the gumption to be contrary is surely not to die."

"I can't lift her, Ewan," Alaric admitted. "'Tis God's truth I'm so poleaxed that I lack the strength to stand."

Ewan hurried forward and lifted Keeley from his arms. It took Alaric a moment, but he was able to rise on shaking legs and walk alongside his brother back to the keep.

"They all think she's dead," Ewan explained. "Word went through the keep that you brought her to the loch to die."

"'Tis a miracle, Ewan. A miracle I can't explain but I'm so damn grateful for. She was dying. I could feel her dying in my arms. I held her through the night and I talked to her endlessly, telling her of my dreams and the children we'd have. I went to sleep and when I awoke, her fever was gone and she was bathed in a sweat. She's still weak as a kitten but the fever has left her."

"I'll have a look at her wound as soon as we get her to bed," Ewan promised. "Then we must address the issue of what is to be done about the alliance with the McDonalds. The king awaits as do the lairds of the clans who gathered here for your wedding. We cannot hold them off any longer."

Alaric looked at his brother with all the dread in his heart. Then he nodded, knowing he must face this issue or the result could be disaster for his clan.

"As soon as Keeley is settled, I'll go with you to meet with our king," Alaric said quietly.

CHAPTER 38

Alaric left Keeley with Maddie and Christina, and Mairin checking in as many times as she could slip past Cormac, who guarded her doorway.

Maddie burst into tears when Alaric told her of Keeley's fever breaking. "I'll take good care of the lass, Alaric. Go do what must be done. I'll have her washed and fed and well on her way to recovery by the time you return, I vow it."

Alaric smiled. "I know you will, Maddie."

He pressed one last kiss to Keeley's lips before he eased out of her chamber and headed belowstairs to where the others waited in the hall. Caelen met him just as he stepped off the stairs.

"I heard Keeley is recovering."

Alaric smiled. "Aye."

"I want you to know, you can count on my support no matter what is decided this day."

Alaric sobered. "That means a lot to me, Caelen. More than you'll ever know."

"Shall we go see what the king has to say then?"

Alaric walked in ahead of Caelen and the room immediately quieted. 'Twas quite an impressive gathering. At the high table sat Ewan and the king along with Laird McDonald and Rionna on his right.

The other lairds were seated at the two tables that flanked the high table in the middle of the room.

When the king saw Alaric enter, he rose and motioned for Alaric to come over.

"Your Highness," Alaric murmured as he came to a stop in front of the older man.

"We have a situation, Alaric McCabe. One that we must remedy with all haste."

Alaric stood legs wide apart, arms crossed over his chest as he waited for the king to continue.

" 'Twas admirable that you offered a handfast to the woman you loved after she saved your life and lay dying in your arms. The problem now arises that I've heard she may recover."

"She *will* recover," Alaric corrected softly.

"Then you find yourself married to the wrong woman."

Laird McDonald rose and thumped his fist onto the table. "This is an insult. 'Tis preposterous. The agreement was for him to marry my daughter, Rionna, not a whore who was cast out of the McDonald clan years ago."

Alaric snarled and started for the laird but Caelen got there first. He grasped the fleshy neck of Laird McDonald and slammed him back into his seat. The laird immediately went silent and stared up at Caelen in fear.

Alaric frowned. What had transpired between the two that would push Caelen to such anger, and why would the laird fear Caelen so much?

"Be silent, McDonald," the king reprimanded. "That whore you speak of saved Alaric's life twice and cared for my niece and safely brought forth the heir to Neamh Álainn. She is owed a great debt and 'tis my intention to make sure she never wants for anything in her life."

He turned his attention back to Alaric. "As I said, 'twas honorable that you sought to wed with her, but you must set her aside so the marriage to Rionna McDonald can go forth. I have a dozen lairds of surrounding clans ready to swear their allegiance to the crown and ally themselves with the McCabes as soon as you marry and take over as laird of the McDonald clan."

Alaric stared at the king, not believing that setting aside another so he could marry Rionna was so calmly suggested. He looked then to Ewan to see his response. His brother sat next to the king, his expression indecipherable. Did he too expect Alaric to set Keeley aside and go ahead with his marriage to Rionna?

He thought of all that rode on this marriage. The safety of his clan. His brothers. Mairin and her babe. Finally the ability to go to war and defeat Cameron.

And his marriage could do all that? He shook his head. "Nay. I'll not set her aside."

The king's eyes widened and the hall dissolved into chaos. Voices were raised. Angry statements were thrown. Threats were made and Laird McDonald was nearly apoplectic in his fury.

Alaric roared out an order for calm. When the hall finally quieted, he swept the gathered men with his gaze. "Only a man without honor would set aside the woman he loved to marry another. Only a man without honor would desert his woman when she lay so close to death after saving his life. I cannot be that man. I love her. I owe her my loyalty and my allegiance. I owe her my protection and all the happiness I can bring her for the rest of her life."

He turned then to face Ewan. "I know this will lower me in the esteem of my family. My brothers. My clan. My king. But I cannot be the man you've always known me to be if I do this thing. There has to be another way to make the alliance work. Me being laird of the McDonald clan should not be the hinge that holds us all together."

The king let out a deep breath, his eyes glittering with anger. "Think what you do. Cameron nearly destroyed your clan. This is your opportunity to finish him once and for all."

"With or without this alliance, Cameron is a dead man," Alaric said in a menacing voice. "What you seek is an alliance that will prevent Malcolm from a successful bid to the throne, and you would use our clan to achieve your means."

The king's scowl grew darker.

"I won't do it." Alaric glanced to Rionna, apology in his eyes. "I'm sorry, Rionna. I would not humiliate you for the world. You are a good lass who deserves a husband who does not love another. I cannot marry you."

"I'll marry her."

The hall went dead silent. Alaric turned, sure that it wasn't Caelen who'd spoken those words. When he saw that it was indeed his brother who'd stepped forward and made the declaration, he could only stare in astonishment.

Rionna gasped and raised a hand to her mouth as she stared in horror at Caelen.

Ewan rose from his seat, his expression guarded. "I don't think I heard you correctly."

"I said I'd marry her," Caelen repeated. " 'Tis the easiest solution. A McCabe still becomes laird of the McDonald clan. Our alliances are sealed. We pledge ourselves to the king against Malcolm and Cameron. Alaric stays married to Keeley. Everyone gets what they want."

"Except you," Alaric murmured.

Caelen twisted his lips. "It matters naught. As long as she can give me sons and daughters I'll be well satisfied with the match."

Rionna had gone pale and sank back into her seat

next to her father. The laird was nearly as pale as he stared in horror at the king.

"This cannot be allowed," Laird McDonald sputtered. "The agreement was for Alaric McCabe to wed with Rionna and become laird when I stepped down."

The king rubbed his chin in a thoughtful manner. "Ewan, what think you of this mess?"

Ewan stared hard at Caelen but Caelen stared back, his expression stubborn and unyielding.

"I think," Ewan said slowly, "that 'tis a reasonable solution so long as all parties agree."

"I don't agree!" Laird McDonald shouted.

"Father, sit down," Rionna said in a voice that sounded like the crack of a sword against a shield. She pushed forward and walked toward the center of the room where Alaric and Caelen stood before Ewan and the king.

"Your conditions?" she asked Caelen in a cool voice.

"Smart lass," Caelen murmured. "Aye, there are conditions. Your father leaves McCabe keep immediately and is never to return so long as Keeley McCabe resides here. When we return to McDonald land after our marriage, your father steps down as laird immediately and cedes power to me."

"This is an outrage!" Laird McDonald bellowed.

Several other of the McDonalds voiced their displeasure and soon the hall vibrated with angry shouts.

To Alaric's surprise, Rionna said nothing during the arguing. She stood completely still, studying Caelen.

"Your conditions do seem unreasonable," the king said.

Caelen shrugged. "They are mine. Unreasonable or not."

"I am not willing to give up the position of laird yet," Laird McDonald bellowed. "'Twas the plan to cede power to Alaric after the birth of Rionna's firstborn child."

Caelen offered a lazy smile. "I can assure you that your daughter will be delivered of a child within nine months of our marriage. What does nine more months buy you?"

Rionna flushed and Laird McDonald nearly exploded with rage.

Caelen then turned to the king. "I gave my word that I would not relate an event that happened some days past. But the reason for not telling is no longer an issue and I would want you and the other clans to know the kind of man Laird McDonald is and why it is my condition that he step down the moment I marry his daughter."

The king frowned. "Speak then. I give you leave to break this promise."

"When Keeley was a young girl, she was a McDonald. Cousin to Rionna and niece to Laird McDonald. He caught her in her chamber and tried to rape her. A girl barely on the cusp of womanhood. When his wife found them, she cried Keeley whore and cast her out of the keep. She was forced to live on her own and provide for herself as no young girl should have to do. She was without protection. It's a wonder she survived."

"That's crazy talk," Laird McDonald sputtered. " 'Tis as my lady wife said. The lass tried to seduce me."

Rionna whirled and pinned her father with a glare that made him pale and take his seat once again.

"That's not the whole of it," Caelen said softly. "Upon the laird's arrival here, when he found out that Keeley was staying here in the McCabe keep, he waited for her to pass his chamber. He pulled her into his room, locked the door, and tried to rape her again."

Alaric lunged across the table and slammed into Laird McDonald. The force sent them both over the back of

316 ### Maya Banks

the laird's chair and they hit the floor with a resounding thump that echoed throughout the keep.

"You son of a bitch," Alaric snarled. "You dared to touch her again? I'll kill you for this!"

He yanked the laird to his feet and smashed his fist into his face, satisfied when the laird promptly spewed blood and two teeth from his mouth. Alaric reared back to hit him again when Caelen caught his fist.

"'Tis enough," he said quietly. "I let you get in one, but now the laird is my problem, and I'll deal with him accordingly."

"You're the one who found her, weren't you?" Alaric said hoarsely. "And you didn't tell me. She was *mine* to defend. It should have been *me* to have repaid his insult."

Caelen smiled. "Your lass did a fine enough job on her own. She busted his nose and fair cracked his cods open. I merely finished the job for her."

The king rose, his expression dark as he stared at the goings-on. "Is this true, Laird McDonald? Did you try to rape a child under your own care and protection? And you attacked her once again under Laird McCabe's roof?"

The laird remained silent as he nursed his bloodied mouth.

"Aye, he did," Rionna said quietly. "I was there."

"Disloyal bitch!" the laird spat.

Caelen rounded on the laird again. "'Tis my future wife you insult. I would suggest you strongly reconsider any words you have to say to her in the future."

The king rubbed his fingers wearily over the bridge of his nose. "What think you of this, Ewan? Can we still salvage this alliance and will the others join with us in our cause?"

Ewan lifted a brow and then surveyed the occupants of the hall, most of whom had remained silent as they observed what had transpired between the McDonalds and the McCabes.

"Why don't you ask them?"

The king chuckled. "A sound idea indeed, Ewan."

He raised his hands for quiet and then addressed the crowded room. "What say you, Lairds? If Caelen McCabe marries Rionna McDonald and seals Neamh Álainn to the McCabe lands here via the alliance with the McDonalds, will you join with us in our fight against Duncan Cameron and Malcolm?"

One by one, the lairds stepped forward, the only sound, their boots scraping against the floor.

"I refuse to ally myself with a coward who preys on children," one laird called out. "If Caelen McCabe becomes laird upon his marriage to Rionna McDonald, then aye, I'll join and swear my allegiance to Your Majesty and to the McCabes."

The other lairds nodded and voiced their agreement.

"There is but one last question to ask," Caelen spoke up.

All heads turned in his direction, but he turned his gaze on Rionna, who still stood ramrod straight and pale in the center of the room.

"Are you willing to wed with me and not Alaric McCabe, Rionna McDonald?"

Rionna stared at her father and shook her head in a gesture of sorrow. Finally she looked up at Caelen and met his gaze with her captivating golden eyes.

"Aye, Caelen McCabe. You have proven a worthy and loyal friend to Keeley and brother to Alaric."

"And do you support me becoming laird upon our marriage and for your father to step down?"

This time she didn't even hesitate. "I do not want him on our lands."

The room buzzed with shock over her words. Laird McDonald blanched and then shoved himself upward again. "You ungrateful bitch! Where do you think me to go?"

"I care not. But you are not welcome on McDonald lands any longer."

Caelen lifted an eyebrow in surprise and then exchanged glances with Alaric. Neither of the brothers had expected such. It was evident from the McDonalds' earlier visits that there was tension between father and daughter, but they weren't prepared for Rionna's emotionless dictate.

"'Tis settled then," the king said. "'Twould appear we have a wedding to attend after all."

CHAPTER 39

Alaric met Caelen just as Alaric was about to enter Keeley's bedchamber. "Give her my love and tell her I never doubted her for a second," Caelen said with faint amusement.

"I will. And Caelen, thank you. I don't even know what to say. That you would step in like that for me and for Keeley. Neither of us can ever hope to repay you."

Caelen smiled. "I learned a lot from your lass, Alaric. I've never met someone as fiercely loyal and selfless as her. She refused to allow me to tell you of McDonald's attack because she knew what you would do and she worried it would ruin the marriage between you and Rionna. She knew how much this alliance meant to our clan, and since she considers the McCabes her family now, she was willing to put aside her own personal wants and desires to do what she thought was best for her family. How could I do anything less?"

"Have a care with Rionna," Alaric warned. "Mairin worried that I'd be too hard on her, and if she worried that about me, I can only imagine her fears of how you'll be."

Caelen snorted.

"Mairin seems to think we all want to handle her with

a strong hand and crush the part of her that makes her special." Alaric shrugged. "I have no idea what she means, but there you have it. I'm sure it has something to do with the fact that she goes around in man's clothing and can wield a sword and ride a horse better than most warriors."

"She'll do as I tell her," Caelen said lazily.

"I wish now I was there to witness it."

"Go now and see your lady. Your wife," Caelen amended.

Alaric clapped Caelen on the shoulder and then entered Keeley's chamber. To his surprise, Gannon sat on the bed next to Keeley, wiping her brow with a damp cloth.

He nearly laughed. Keeley had made conquests of them all. It wouldn't surprise him if the whole of the clan took a turn caring for Keeley.

Gannon looked up and saw Alaric. "Maddie took Mairin down so she could nurse the babe. I was to care for her until one of you returned."

Alaric nodded then motioned for Gannon to get up. "How is she? Has she been conscious?"

"She's sweating off the fever and has been so hot that we've had to open the window to let cooler air in. She drifts in and out, though I think she's more sleeping than being unconscious."

Alaric breathed in sweet relief and savored the taste on his tongue.

"You can go now. I'll take care of her from now on."

Gannon paused at the door. "What happened down there? There was talk of the king commanding you to set Keeley aside."

Alaric smiled. "Aye, he did."

Gannon scowled and his shoulders puffed up like he was about to explode.

"I declined."

Gannon lifted an eyebrow in shock. "You said nay to the king?"

"Aye, I did," Alaric said ruefully. "'Twas easier than I thought it would be."

"What will happen?"

"'Tis a long story and if you'll go find Caelen, I'm sure he'll be more than happy to fill you in. Right now, I have need to see my lady wife and tell her I love her again."

Gannon smiled and beat a hasty retreat from the room.

Alaric hastened to Keeley's side and tucked himself in next to her. She cuddled against his body and he absorbed the delightful sensation of her flesh against his, so warm and soft. Delicate and infinitely fragile against his much larger frame.

She was a miracle. His miracle. One he'd thank God for every day for the rest of his life.

"Alaric?" she whispered.

"Aye, love?"

"Are you setting me aside? Because I'll tell you 'tis a rotten thing to do after I live. I'll not go so quietly this time. You're my husband, and I won't just give up my husband so he can marry another."

The petulance in her voice made him chuckle. She sounded supremely irritated and aggrieved that such a thing was possible.

He kissed her nose and laid his cheek against hers. "Nay, love. You're stuck with me, I'm afraid. I've defied the king and my brother and about twelve other clans in the process, not to mention the bastard Laird McDonald who you did not tell me had attacked you just days ago."

"Mmm, you did all that for me?" she asked sleepily.

"Aye, I did."

She smiled against his neck. "I love you. Did I tell you that I strongly considered dying but that I couldn't stand the thought of never seeing you, even if you were married to another woman?"

He scowled down at her and touched her chin so that she'd look straight into his eyes. "You'll not ever even think of such a thing again, do you hear? I forbid you from dying."

"Very well then, since you forbid it, I should tell you that I plan to make a full recovery. The wound is very painful and 'tis the truth I feel like retching every time I move wrong, but I plan to be up and around in a week's time, mark my words."

He chuckled at the arrogant words and then hushed her with a gentle kiss to her mouth.

"I love you, Keeley McCabe. You are truly a McCabe now. We are married in the eyes of God and our clansmen. All that is required now is the consummation."

She groaned. "That part's going to have to wait awhile."

He hugged her to him as carefully as he was able and he just held on, absorbing the sheer joy of having her alive, belonging to him, of being able to tell the world he loved her.

"I'll wait as long as it takes, my love. We have the rest of our lives to consummate our marriage. In fact, I think we should make it a point to consummate it on a daily basis. After you are well, of course."

She sighed and pressed her cheek to his chest. "I love you, Alaric McCabe. And I'm willing to do a trial run of our consummation next week if you should so desire."

He laughed and maneuvered so he could capture her lips in a long, delicious kiss. "'So desire'? Lass, there isn't anything I desire more in this world than a life with you filled with love, laughter, and children."

She yawned and closed her eyes, and he watched her drift off to sleep against his chest. Surely there was not a more precious sight than her sprawled over his body, and no sweeter knowledge than the fact that she was truly his. For as long as they drew breath.

*Read on for an exciting preview
of Maya Banks's next novel*

NEVER LOVE A HIGHLANDER

The weather for her first wedding had been a splendor of nature. An unseasonably warm day in January. Quite balmy with nary a breeze to ruffle her carefully arranged hair. It was as if the world stood still to witness the joining of two souls.

A snort rippled from Rionna McDonald's throat, eliciting a raised eyebrow from her soon-to-be husband.

The weather for her second wedding? Gloomy and dank with a winter storm pushing in from the west. Already a brisk chill had set in and the wind blew in fierce, relentless sheets. As if the world knew just how uncertain she was about the man who stood beside her, ready to recite the vows that would bind him to her forever.

A shiver skirted up her spine despite the fact that they stood in front of the huge fire in the great hall.

Caelen frowned and stepped closer to Rionna as if to shield her from the draft blowing through the furs at the window. She took a hasty step back before thinking better of it. The man made her nervous, and not many people intimidated her.

He frowned harder then turned his attention back to the priest.

Rionna cast a quick glance around, hoping no one had witnessed that particular exchange. It wouldn't do for people to think she was afraid of her new husband. Even if she was.

Ewan McCabe, the oldest McCabe brother and the

first man she was supposed to have married, stood by his brother's side, his arms crossed over his broad chest. He looked anxious to be done with the whole thing.

Alaric McCabe, the man she'd very nearly wed after Ewan got himself married to Mairin Stuart, also looked impatient and kept glancing toward the stairs as if he might run out at any moment. Rionna couldn't blame him, though. His new wife, Keeley, was above stairs recovering from a wound that had nearly ended her life.

Third time was a charm, right?

King David wasn't standing for the occasion. He sat regally by the fire, looking on with approval as the priest droned on. Around him, also sitting, were the many lairds from neighboring lands. All waiting for the alliance between the McDonalds and the McCabes. An alliance that would be sealed upon her marriage to Caelen McCabe, the youngest—and last—McCabe brother.

It was important to denote last because if anything went amiss with this wedding, there were no more McCabes for her to marry, and at this point, her pride couldn't withstand another rejection.

Her gaze skittered from the king and assembled lairds to her dour-faced father who sat away from the assembled warriors, an unmanly, sullen pout twisting his features.

For a moment their stares locked and then his lip turned up into a snarl. She hadn't supported him in his bid to keep his position of laird. It was probably disloyal of her. She wasn't sure that Caelen McCabe would be a better laird, but surely he was a better man.

She became aware that all eyes were on her. She glanced nervously toward the priest and realized that she'd missed her cue to recite her vows. Even more embarrassing, she had no idea what the man had said.

"This is where you promise to obey me, cleave only

unto me, and remain faithful all your days," Caelen drawled.

His words stiffened her spine and she couldn't call back the glare as she speared him with her gaze.

"And what exactly are you promising me?"

His pale green eyes stroked coolly over her, assessing and then lifting as if he found nothing of import. She didn't like that look. He'd all but dismissed her.

"You'll gain my protection and the respect due a lady of your station."

"That's all?"

She whispered the words, and she'd have given anything not to have let them slip. It was no wonder she'd been left wanting, though. Ewan McCabe clearly adored his wife, Mairin, and Alaric had just defied king and country to be with the woman he loved—effectively casting Rionna aside in the process.

Not that she was angry. She dearly loved Keeley, and Keeley deserved happiness. That a man as strong and handsome as Alaric had publicly proclaimed his love for Keeley gladdened Rionna's heart.

But it also brought home how sterile her own marriage would be.

Caelen made a sound of exasperation. "Exactly what is it that you want, lass?"

She raised her chin and stared back at him every bit as cool. "Nothing. 'Tis enough. I'll have your respect and your regard. I won't be needing your protection, though."

His eyebrow rose. "Is that so?"

"Aye. I can see to my own protection."

Caelen chuckled and more laughter rose from the assembled men. "Say your vows, lass. We don't have all day. The men are hungry. They've been awaiting a feast for nearly a fortnight now."

Agreement rumbled through the room and her cheeks

burned. This was her wedding day and she wouldn't be rushed. Who cared about the food and the men's stomachs?

As if sensing that she was working herself into a righteous fury, Caelen reached over, snagged her hand, and pulled her up next to his side until his thigh burned into hers through the material of her dress.

"Father," Caelen said respectfully, "if you'll tell the lass what she needs to say again."

Rionna fumed the entire way through the recitation. Tears pricked her eyelids but she couldn't even say why. It wasn't as if she and Alaric had been a love match any more than she and Caelen were. The entire idea of wedding one of the McCabe brothers had been hatched by her father and embraced by the McCabes and the king himself.

She was but a pawn to be used and discarded.

She sighed and then shook her head. It was ridiculous to be this maudlin. There were worse things. She should be happy. She'd rediscovered the sister of her heart in Keeley, who was now happily married even if she faced a long recovery in the days ahead. And Rionna's father would no longer be laird of their clan.

She chanced another look only to see her father throw back yet another goblet of ale. She supposed she couldn't entirely blame him for being so deep into his cups. His entire way of life was gone in a moment's time. But she couldn't muster any regret.

Her clan could be great—*would* be great—under the right leadership. It had never been under her father. He'd weakened the McDonald name until they'd been reduced to begging for the aid and alliance of a stronger clan.

Her free hand curled into a tight fist at her side. It had been her dream to restore their glory. To shape the soldiers into a formidable fighting force. Now it would be

Caelen's task and she would be relegated to a position of observation rather than the participation she craved.

She gasped in surprise when Caelen suddenly leaned in and brushed his lips across hers. He was gone almost before she registered what he'd done and she stood there staring wide-eyed as she raised a trembling hand to her mouth.

The ceremony was done. Even now the serving women were flooding into the hall, bearing a veritable bounty of food, much of which came from her own stores after her father's foolish wager several months ago.

Caelen watched her a moment and then gestured for her to walk ahead of him toward the high table. Rionna was gratified to see Mairin join her husband. In a sea of gruff, indistinguishable faces, Mairin McCabe was a ray of sunshine. Tired sunshine, but warm nonetheless.

Mairin hurried forward with a bright smile. "Rionna, you look so beautiful. There isn't a woman here who can hold a candle to you today."

Rionna's cheeks warmed under Mairin's praise. She had been a little ashamed to be wearing the same dress she'd worn when she nearly married Alaric. She felt wrinkled, rumpled, and worn through. But the sincerity in Mairin's smile bolstered Rionna's flagging spirits.

Mairin gathered Rionna's hand in hers as if to offer further encouragement.

"Oh, your hands are like ice!" Mairin exclaimed. "I did so want to be present for your joining. I hope you'll accept my regrets."

"Of course," Rionna said with a genuine smile. "How is Keeley fairing this day?"

Some of the worry lifted from Mairin's gaze. "Come, sit so we may be served. And then I'll tell you of Keeley."

It irked Rionna that she first looked to her new husband only to catch his nod of permission. She gritted her teeth and moved to the table to sit beside Mairin. Already she was acting like a docile nitwit and she hadn't been married five minutes.

But in truth, Caelen frightened her. Alaric hadn't. Even Ewan didn't intimidate her. Caelen scared her witless.

Rionna slid into the chair beside Mairin, hoping for a brief reprieve before Caelen joined her. She wasn't so fortunate. Her husband pulled out the chair next to her and scooted to the table, his leg so close to her that it pressed to the whole of her thigh.

Deciding it would be rude—and obvious—were she to slide toward Mairin, she decided instead to ignore him. She couldn't forget that it was acceptable for him to be so familiar now. They were wed.

She sucked in her breath as realization hit her that he would of course exert his marital rights. Indeed, there was the whole wedding night, virginal deflowering. All the things women tittered about behind their hands when the men weren't around.

The problem was that Rionna was always with the men and she'd never tittered in her life. Keeley had been separated from her at a young age, long before Rionna had grown curious over such matters.

With a lecher for a father and Rionna's constant fear for Keeley, the mere thought of coupling nauseated her. Now she had a husband who'd expect . . . Well, he'd expect certain things, and God help her, she had no idea what.

Humiliation tightened her cheeks. She could ask Mairin. Or one of the McCabe women. They were all generous to a fault and they'd all been kind to Rionna. But the idea of having to admit to them all just how ignorant she was of such matters made her want to hide under the table.

She could wield a sword better than most men. She could fight. And she was fast. She could be ruthless when provoked. She didn't suffer a gentle constitution nor did she faint at the sight of blood.

But she didn't know the way of kissing.

"Are you going to eat?" Caelen asked.

She looked up to see that the places had been set and the food was on the table. Caelen had thoughtfully cut a choice piece of meat and placed it on her plate.

"Aye," she whispered.

'Twas the truth, she was fair to starving.

"Would you like water or ale?"

'Twas also true she never partook of spirits, but somehow today ale seemed to be the wise choice.

"Ale," she said, and waited as Caelen poured a goblet-full. She reached for it but to her surprise, he put it to his mouth and first sniffed and then drank a small portion of the ale.

" 'Tis not poisoned," he said as he slid it toward her place.

She gaped at him, not comprehending what he'd just done.

"But what if it *had* been poisoned?"

He touched her cheek. Just once. It was the only affectionate gesture he'd offered her and it might not even be construed as affectionate, but it was soft and a little comforting.

"Then you wouldn't have partaken of the poison, nor would you have died. We already nearly lost one McCabe to such cowardice. I'll not risk another."

Her mouth fell open. "That's ridiculous! Think you that *you* dying somehow makes it all better?"

"Rionna, I just took sacred vows to protect you. That means I'd lay down my life for you and for any future children we have. We've already a snake in our midst trying to poison Ewan. Now that you and I are wed, what better way to prevent the alliance between our clans than to kill you?"

"Or you," she felt compelled to point out.

"Aye, 'tis a possibility. But if McDonald's only heir is dead then his clan effectively crumbles, which makes it easy pickings for Duncan Cameron. You are the heart of this alliance, Rionna. Whether you wish to believe it or not. Much rides on your shoulders. I guarantee you it won't be easy for you."

"Nay, I never imagined differently."

"Smart lass."

He piddled with the goblet before sliding it toward her. Then he solicitously lifted it and held it to her mouth, just as a new husband would do for his bride during the wedding feast.

"Drink, Rionna. You look exhausted. You're on edge. You're so stiff that it can't be comfortable. Take a drink and try to relax. We've a long afternoon to endure."

He hadn't lied.

Rionna sat wearily at the table as toast after toast was given. There were toasts to the McCabes. Toasts to the new McCabe heir. Ewan and Mairin were the proud parents of a newborn lass, who also happened to be the heir to one of the largest and choicest holdings in all of Scotland.

Then there were toasts to Alaric and Keeley. To Keeley's health. Then the toasts to her marriage to Caelen began.

At one point they degenerated into lewd toasts to Caelen's prowess, and two lairds even began a wager as to how fast Rionna would find herself with child.

Rionna's eyes were glazing over and she wasn't entirely sure it was due to the lengthy accolades being tossed about. Her goblet had been refilled more times than she remembered but she drank on, ignoring the way it swirled around in her belly and made her head swim.

Laird McCabe had decreed that despite the many issues that bore discussion and the decisions that must be made, today would be spent in celebration of his brother's marriage.

Rionna suspected that Mairin had everything to do with that decree. She needn't have bothered, though. There was little cause for celebration in Rionna's mind.

She glanced sideways to see Caelen sitting back in his chair, lazily surveying the occupants of the table. He tossed back an insult when one was flung his way by one of the McCabe men. Something to do with his manhood. Rionna shuddered and purposely blanked her mind to the innuendo.

She gulped down another mouthful of the ale and put the goblet back down on the table with a bang that made her wince. No one seemed to notice, but then it *was* unbearably loud.

The food before her swam in her vision, and the idea of putting it to her mouth, despite Caelen having cut the meat into bite-sized morsels, turned her stomach.

"Rionna, is anything amiss?"

Mairin's soft inquiry jolted Rionna from her semi-daze. She glanced guiltily up at the other woman and then blinked when Mairin suddenly became two people.

"I should like to see Keeley," she blurted.

If the laird's wife thought it odd that Rionna would wish to visit with Keeley on Rionna's wedding day, she didn't react.

"I'll go up with you if you like."

Rionna sighed in relief then started to rise from her seat. Caelen's hand snapped around her wrist and he tugged her back down, a frown marring his features.

"I wish to see Keeley since she wasn't able to attend my wedding," Rionna said. "With your permission, of course."

She nearly choked on the words.

He studied her for a brief moment then relaxed his grip on her wrist. "You may go."

It sounded so imperious. So . . . husbandlike.

Her stomach heaved as she excused herself to the laird. Married. Jesus wept, but she was married. She was expected to submit to her husband. To obey him.

Her hands shook as she followed Mairin toward the stairs. They walked quietly up, one of Ewan's men tagging along behind, but then Mairin went nowhere without an escort.

Merciful heaven, would she be expected to be led about by the reins now that she was married to Caelen? The idea of being unable to go anywhere or do anything without someone breathing down her neck suffocated her.

At Keeley's door, Mairin knocked softly. Alaric answered, and Mairin spoke in low tones with her brother by marriage.

Alaric nodded and stepped out but then said, "Try not to be overlong. She tires easily."

Rionna glanced at the man who would have been her husband and couldn't help a silent comparison between him and his younger brother. The man she now found herself wed to.

There was no doubt both were fierce warriors, but she still couldn't help but feel she would have preferred marriage to Alaric. He didn't seem as . . . cold . . . as Caelen. Or indifferent. Or . . . something.

She couldn't quite put her finger on it, but there was something in Caelen's eyes that unsettled her, that made her wary, like prey poised to flee a predator. He made her feel tiny, defenseless. *Feminine.*

"Rionna," Alaric said with a nod. "Congratulations on your marriage."

There was still a hint of guilt in his eyes, and truly, she wasn't resentful. Not of why he hadn't married her. His falling in love with Keeley hadn't quite managed to banish her humiliation of being jilted, though. She was working on it.

"Thank you," she murmured.

She waited until Alaric passed her and then she entered Keeley's chamber.

Keeley lay propped on an abundance of pillows. She was pale and lines of fatigue etched grooves on her forehead. Still, she smiled weakly when her gaze met Rionna's.

"So sorry I missed your wedding," Keeley said.

Rionna smiled and went to her bed. She perched on the edge so she wouldn't cause Keeley pain and then gingerly reached for her hand.

" 'Twas not of import. I barely remember it myself."

Keeley snorted and a spasm of pain crossed her face.

"I had to see you," Rionna whispered. "There was something . . . I wanted to seek your counsel on something."

Keeley's eyes widened in surprise and then she glanced beyond Rionna to Mairin. "Of course. Is it all right if Mairin stays? She's completely trustworthy."

Rionna cast a hesitant glance in Mairin's direction.

"Perhaps I should go down and fetch us some ale," Mairin suggested. " 'Twill give you time to speak freely."

Rionna sighed. "Nay, I'll wait. 'Tis the truth I could use the counsel of more than one woman. Keeley is newly married after all."

A soft blush suffused Keeley's cheeks and Mairin chuckled. "I'll send for the ale then, and we'll talk. You have my word, naught will pass the doors of this chamber."

Rionna looked gratefully at Mairin, and then Mairin went to the door and conversed with Gannon, the warrior who'd accompanied them up the stairs.

"How easily is sound carried through the doors?" Rionna whispered to Keeley.

"I can assure you that nothing can be heard from the halls," Keeley said, a twinkle in her eyes. "Now what matter would you like to discuss?"

Rionna dutifully waited until Mairin returned to Keeley's bedside and then she licked her lips, feeling the worst sort of fool for exposing her ignorance.

" 'Tis about the marriage bed."

"Ah," Mairin said knowingly.

"Ah, indeed," Keeley said with a nod.

Rionna blew out her breath in frustration. "What am I to do? What am I supposed to do? I know nothing of kissing and coupling or . . . anything. 'Tis a sword and fighting I have knowledge of."

Mairin's expression softened and the amusement fled from her eyes. She covered Rionna's hand with her own and squeezed. " 'Tis the truth that not too long ago, I was in your same position. I sought out the counsel of some older ladies of the clan. 'Twas an eye opening experience to be sure."

"Aye, as did I," Keeley admitted. "It isn't as though we're born with such knowledge, and none of us had mothers to guide us through such things." She cast an apologetic look to Rionna. "At least I assume your mother never discussed such delicate issues with you."

Rionna snorted. "She despaired of me from the time I grew breasts."

Keeley's eyebrows rose. "You grew breasts?"

Rionna flushed and glanced down at her bosom. Her flat bosom. If Keely—or anyone—actually knew what lay beneath the wrappings . . . Her husband would know soon enough, unless Rionna figured out a way to consummate a marriage fully clothed.

Mairin smiled. " 'Tis not so difficult, Rionna. The men do most of the work, as they should in the beginning. Once you learn your way around, well, then you can certainly do all manner of things."

"Alaric is wonderful at loving," Keeley said with a sigh.

Mairin colored and cleared her throat. " 'Tis the truth

I didn't think Ewan overly skilled at first. Our wedding night was hastened by the fact that Duncan Cameron's army bore down on us. 'Twas an insult Ewan took exception to and made great effort to remedy. With very satisfying results, I might add."

Rionna's cheeks warmed as she glanced between the two women. Their eyes became all dreamy and soft as they spoke of their husbands. Rionna couldn't imagine ever having such a reaction to Caelen. He was simply too . . . forbidding. Aye, that was an apt description.

A knock at the door interrupted the discussion and the women went silent. Mairin issued a summons, and Gannon stepped inside, a disapproving look on his face.

"Thank you, Gannon," Mairin said, as he set the flagon and the goblets on the small table beside Keeley's bed. "You may go now."

He scowled but backed out of the room. Rionna glanced up at Mairin, curious as to why she accepted such insolence from her husband's man. Mairin simply smiled smugly as she poured the ale into the goblets.

"He knows we're up to mischief and it's killing him to say nothing."

She handed Rionna a goblet and then carefully placed one into Keeley's hand.

" 'Tis the truth it will dull the pain," Keeley said.

"I'm sorry, Keeley. Would you like me to go? I have no wish to cause you further distress," Rionna said.

Keeley sipped at the ale and then leaned back against her pillows with a sigh. "Nay. I'm about to go mad being sequestered in my chamber. I welcome the company. Besides, we must ease your fears about your wedding night."

Rionna gulped at her ale and then extended the goblet to Mairin for it to be refilled. She had a feeling she wasn't going to like this conversation.

" 'Tis no reason to fear," Mairin soothed. "I've no doubt Caelen will take care with you." Then she wrinkled her nose. "Give thanks you don't have an army bearing down on you. 'Tis the truth I had no liking for my wedding night."

Rionna felt the blood drain from her face.

"Hush, Mairin. You aren't helping," Keeley chided.

Mairin patted Rionna's hand. "All will be well. You'll see."

"But what do I *do*?"

"Exactly what is it that you know?" Keeley asked. "Let's start there."

Rionna closed her eyes in misery and then downed the entire contents of her goblet. "Nothing."

"Oh dear," Mairin said. " 'Tis the truth I was ignorant, but the nuns at the abbey did see fit to provide me cursory information."

"I think you should be honest with Caelen about your fears," Keeley suggested. "He'd be a brute to ignore a maiden's worry. If he has half of Alaric's skill, you'll not be left wanting."

Mairin giggled at the boast, and Rionna held out her goblet for another round of ale.

The very *last* thing she wanted was to talk to Caelen about her maidenly fears. The man would probably laugh at her. Or worse, give her that cool, indifferent gaze that made her feel so . . . insignificant.

"Will it hurt?" she strangled out.

Mairin's lips pursed in thought. Keeley's brow wrinkled a moment.

" 'Tis the truth it's not overly pleasant. At first. But the pain passes quickly and if the man is skilled, it's quite wonderful in the end."

Mairin snorted. "Again, as long as there isn't an army bearing down on you."

"Enough with the army," Keeley said in exasperation. "There is no army."

Then the two women looked at each other and laughed until Keeley groaned and went limp against her pillows.

Rionna just stared at them, never more certain that she had no desire to indulge in this marriage bed business. She yawned broadly and the room spun in curious little circles. Her head felt as though it weighed as much as a boulder, and it was harder and harder for her to hold it up.

She stood from her perch on the edge of Keeley's bed and started for the door, disgusted with her cowardice. She was acting . . . Well, she was acting just like a woman.

To her utter dismay, she ended up at the window and she blinked in confusion as a blast of cold air hit her in the face and the corner of the furs blew up.

"Careful, there," Mairin said in her ear.

She guided Rionna to a chair in the corner of the room and eased her down.

"Perhaps 'tis best if you sit here awhile. It wouldn't do for you to navigate those stairs, and we don't want the men to know what we've been about."

Rionna nodded. She did feel a bit peculiar. Aye, it would be best if she sat awhile until the room stopped spinning in such spectacular fashion.

Caelen looked toward the stairs for what seemed like the hundredth time, and Ewan looked impatient as well. Rionna and Mairin had been gone for some time. It was late into the night and Caelen was ready to have done with the entire wedding celebration.

Some celebration. His bride had been stiff and distant throughout the entire ceremony, and afterward she'd sat silent while the room celebrated around her.

If her demeanor was anything to go by, she was even less thrilled than he with the match. It mattered naught.

They were both bound by duty. And right now his duty was to consummate his marriage.

His loins tightened, and the surge of lust took him by surprise. It had been a long while since he'd had such a strong reaction to a woman. But it had been thus since the day he'd laid eyes on Rionna.

He'd been shamed by his reaction to his brother's betrothed. It was disloyal and disrespectful to feel such a keen burning in his gut.

But no matter that he damned himself, it didn't change the fact that she had only to walk in the room and his body leapt to life.

And now she was his.

He searched the entrance to the stairs one more time and then sent a pointed stare toward Ewan. It was time to collect his wife and take her to bed.

Ewan nodded then stood. It didn't seem to matter that the king was still heartily enjoying himself. Ewan merely announced that the festivities were at their end and that everyone should seek their beds.

Everyone would reconvene in the morning and talks would begin. Ewan had a legacy to claim on behalf of his daughter and there was a war to wage against Duncan Cameron.

Caelen followed Ewan up the stairs where they were met by Gannon.

"Lady McCabe took to her chamber an hour ago when the babe awoke for feeding," Gannon said to Ewan.

"And my wife?" Caelen drawled.

"Still within Keeley's chamber. Alaric is in Keeley's old chamber, but he's losing patience and fair itching to get back to Keeley."

"You may tell him Rionna will be gone within the minute," Caelen said as he strode toward the door.

He knocked, only because 'twas Keeley's chamber and he had no wish to alarm her by barging in. 'Twas an insult for Rionna to have spent so much time above stairs, missing most of their wedding celebration.

Upon hearing Keeley's soft summons, he opened the door and entered.

His expression eased when he saw Keeley propped haphazardly on her pillows. She looked as though she was about to slide off the bed, and he hurried to prop her up. Exhaustion ringed her eyes and she grunted as he positioned her better.

"Sorry," he muttered.

"'Tis all right," she said with a small smile.

"I've come for Rionna." He frowned when he realized she wasn't present.

Keeley nodded toward the far corner. "She's there."

Caelen turned and, to his surprise, saw her propped in a chair against the wall, sound asleep, her mouth open and head tilted back. Then as he took a closer look around the room, he saw the tankard of ale and the empty goblets.

With a suspicious frown, he peered into the tankard only to find it empty. He glanced back at Keeley, whose eyes looked precariously close to rolling back in her head, and then back to Rionna, who hadn't stirred a whit. He remembered all the ale she'd consumed at the table belowstairs and how little she'd eaten.

"You're soused!"

"Maybe," Keeley mumbled. "All right, probably."

Caelen shook his head. Foolheaded females.

He started toward Rionna when Keeley's soft entreaty stopped him.

"Be gentle with her, Caelen. She's afraid."

He stopped, stared down at the passed out woman in the chair, and then slowly turned to look back at Keeley. "Is that what this is about? She got herself soused because she's afraid of me?"

Keeley's brow wrinkled. "Not of you particularly.

Well, I suppose that could be part of it. But, Caelen, she's frightfully . . . ignorant of . . ."

She broke off and blushed to the roots of her hair.

"I understand your meaning," Caelen said gruffly. "No offense, Keeley, but 'tis a matter between me and my wife. I'll be taking her now. You should be resting, not consuming ridiculous amounts of ale."

"Has anyone ever told you that you're too rigid?" Keeley groused.

Caelen leaned down and slid his arms underneath Rionna's slight body and lifted her. She weighed next to nothing, and to his surprise, he liked the feel of her in his arms. It was . . . nice.

He strode toward the door, barked an order to Gannon, whom he knew to be standing on the other side, and the door quickly opened. In the hall Caelen met Alaric, who raised his eyebrow inquiringly.

"See to your own wife," Caelen said rudely. "She's probably unconscious by now."

"What?" Alaric demanded.

But Caelen ignored him and continued on to his chamber. He shouldered his way in and then gently laid Rionna down on his bed. With a sigh, he stepped back to stare down at her.

So the little warrior was frightened. And to escape him, she'd drank herself into oblivion. Hardly complimentary to Caelen, but then he supposed he couldn't blame her. He hadn't been . . . Well, he hadn't been a lot of things.

With a shake of his head, he began peeling away her clothing until she was down to her underclothes. His hands shook as he smoothed the thin linen garment over her body.

He could see nothing of her breasts. She was a slight woman and she didn't have much in the way of a bosom. Her body was lean and toned, unlike any other woman he'd ever encountered.

He ached to lift the hem of her underdress and pull it away from her body until she was naked to his gaze. It was his right. She was his wife.

But he couldn't bring himself to do it.

He could wake her now and assert his husbandly rights, but he had a sudden desire to see her eyes flame with the same want he felt. He wanted to hear her soft cries of pleasure. He didn't want her to be afraid.

He smiled and shook his head. When she woke in the morning, she'd likely have a raging headache, and she'd wonder what the hell happened the night before.

He might have a conscience about taking what was rightfully his until she was prepared to surrender herself body and soul, but that didn't mean she had to know it right away.

He slid into bed beside her and pulled the heavy fur over the both of them. The scent of her hair curled through his nose, and the warmth from her body beckoned to him.

With a muttered curse, he turned over until he faced away.

To his utter dismay, she murmured in her sleep and then snuggled up against his back, her warm, lush body molded so tightly to his that he hadn't a prayer of sleeping this night.